THE GARDEN
OF RAMA

Books by Arthur C. Clarke

NONFICTION

Ascent to Orbit: A Scientific
  Autobiography
Boy Beneath the Sea
The Challenge of the Sea
The Challenge of the Spaceship
The Coast of Coral
The Exploration of the Moon
The Exploration of Space
The First Five Fathoms
Going into Space
Indian Ocean Adventure
Indian Ocean Treasure
Interplanetary Flight
The Making of a Moon
Profiles of the Future
The Promise of Space
The Reefs of Taprobane
Report on Planet Three
The Treasure of the Great Reef
The View from Serendip
Voice across the Sea
Voices from the Sky
1984: Spring

WITH THE EDITORS OF *LIFE*
Man and Space

WITH THE ASTRONAUTS
First on the Moon

WITH ROBERT SILVERBERG
Into Space

WITH CHESLEY BONESTELL
Beyond Jupiter

WITH SIMON WELFARE AND
  JOHN FAIRLEY
Arthur C. Clarke's Mysterious World
Arthur C. Clarke's World of Strange
  Powers

FICTION

Across the Sea of Stars
Against the Fall of Night
Childhood's End
The City and the Stars
The Deep Range
Dolphin Island
Earthlight
Expedition to Earth
A Fall of Moondust
The Fountains of Paradise
From the Oceans, from the Stars
Glide Path
Imperial Earth
Islands in the Sky
The Lost Worlds of 2001
More Than One Universe
Prelude to Mars
Prelude to Space
Reach for Tomorrow
Rendezvous with Rama
The Sands of Mars
The Sentinel
Tales from the "White Hart"
2001: A Space Odyssey
2010: Odyssey Two
2061: Odyssey Three

WITH GENTRY LEE
Cradle
Rama II
The Garden of Rama

THE
GARDEN
OF RAMA

ARTHUR C. CLARKE
AND
GENTRY LEE

BANTAM BOOKS
NEW YORK • TORONTO • LONDON • SYDNEY • AUCKLAND

THE GARDEN OF RAMA
A Bantam Book / September 1991

Library of Congress Cataloging-in-Publication Data

Clarke, Arthur Charles, 1917–
    The Garden of Rama / by Arthur C. Clarke and Gentry Lee.
        p.   cm.
    ISBN 0-553-07261-7
    I. Lee, Gentry. II. Title.
PR6005.L36G37 1991
823'.914—dc20   91-2888
                                                          CIP

Published simultaneously in the United States and Canada

Bantam Books are published by Bantam Books, a division of Bantam
Doubleday Dell Publishing Group, Inc. Its trademark, consisting of the
words "Bantam Books" and the portrayal of a rooster, is Registered in
U.S. Patent and Trademark Office and in other countries. Marca Regis-
trada. Bantam Books, 666 Fifth Avenue, New York, New York 10103.

PRINTED IN THE UNITED STATES OF AMERICA

BVG   0 9 8 7 6 5 4 3 2 1

ACKNOWLEDGMENTS

Many people made valuable contributions to this novel. First among them, in terms of overall impact, was our editor, Lou Aronica. His early comments shaped the structure of the whole novel and his insightful final editing significantly strengthened the flow of the book.

Our good friend and polymath Gerry Snyder was again extremely helpful, generously tackling any technical problem, whether large or small. If the medical passages in the story are accurate and have verisimilitude, then credit should go to Dr. Jim Willerson. Any errors in the same passages are strictly the responsibility of the authors.

During the early writing, Jihei Akita went out of his way to help us find the proper locations for the Japanese scenes. He also was more than willing to discuss at length both the customs and history of his nation. In Thailand, Ms. Watcharee Monviboon was an excellent guide to the marvels of that country.

The novel deals in considerable detail with women, especially the way they feel and think. Both Bebe Barden and Stacey Lee were always available for conversations about the nature of the female. Ms. Barden was also especially helpful with the ideas for the life and poetry of Benita Garcia.

Stacey Kiddoo Lee made many direct contributions to *The Garden of Rama*, but it was her unselfish support of the entire effort that was absolutely critical. During the writing of the novel Stacey also gave birth to her fourth son, Travis Clarke Lee. For everything, Stacey, thank you very much.

NICOLE'S JOURNAL

1

Two nights ago, at 10:44 Greenwich time on the Earth, Simone Tiasso Wakefield greeted the universe. It was an incredible experience. I thought I had felt powerful emotions before, but nothing in my life—not the death of my mother, not the Olympic gold medal in Los Angeles, not my thirty-six hours with Prince Henry, and not even the birth of Genevieve under the watchful eyes of my father at the hospital in Tours—was as intense as my joy and relief when I finally heard Simone's first cry.

Michael had predicted that the baby would arrive on Christmas Day. In his usual lovable way, he told us that he believed God was going to "give us a sign" by having our spacechild born on Jesus' assumed birthday. Richard scoffed, as my husband always does when Michael's religious fervor gets carried away. But after I felt the first strong contractions on Christmas Eve, even Richard almost became a believer.

I slept fitfully the night before Christmas. Just before I awakened, I had a deep, vivid dream. I was walking beside our pond at Beauvois, playing with my pet duck Dunois and his wild mallard companions, when I heard a voice calling me. I could not identify the voice, but I definitely knew it was a woman speaking. She told me that the birth was going to be extremely difficult and that I would need every bit of my strength to bring my second child into the light.

On Christmas itself, after we exchanged the simple presents that each of us had clandestinely ordered from the Ramans, I began to train Michael and Richard for a range of possible emergencies. I think Simone would indeed have been born on Christmas Day if my conscious mind had not been so aware that neither of the two men was even remotely prepared to help me in case of a major problem. My will alone probably delayed the baby's birth those final two days.

One of the contingency procedures we discussed on Christmas was a breech baby. A couple of months ago, when my unborn baby girl still had some freedom of movement inside my womb, I was fairly certain that she was upside down. But I thought she had turned around during the last week before she dropped into the birth position. I was only partially correct. She did manage to come headfirst down the birth canal; however, her face was upward, toward my stomach, and after the first serious set of contractions, the top of her little head became awkwardly wedged against my pelvis.

In a hospital on Earth the physician would probably have performed a cesarean section. Certainly a doctor would have been on guard for fetal stress and at work early with all the robot instruments, striving to turn Simone's head around before she wedged into such an uncomfortable position.

Toward the end the pain was excruciating. In between the strong contractions driving her against my unyielding bones, I tried to yell out orders to Michael and Richard. Richard was almost useless. He could not deal with my pain (or "the mess," as he later called it), much less either assist with the episiotomy or use the makeshift forceps we had obtained from the Ramans. Michael, bless his heart, sweat pouring off his forehead despite the cool temperature in the room, struggled gallantly to follow my sometimes incoherent instructions. He used the scalpel from my kit to open me up wider and then, after only a moment's hesitation due to all the blood, he found Simone's head with the forceps. Somehow he managed, on his third attempt, both to force her backward in the birth canal and to turn her over so she could be born.

Both men screamed when she crowned. I kept concentrating on my breathing pattern, worried that I might not maintain consciousness. Despite the intense pain, I too bellowed when my next powerful contraction shot Simone forward into Michael's hands. As the father it was Richard's job to cut the umbilical cord. When Richard had finished, Michael lifted Simone up for me to see. "It's a girl," he said with tears in his eyes. He laid her softly on my stomach and I rose up slightly to look at her. My first impression was that she looked exactly like my mother.

I forced myself to stay alert until the placenta was removed and I had finished stitching, with Michael's assistance, the cuts he had made with the scalpel. Then I collapsed. I don't remember many details from the next twenty-four hours. I was so tired from the labor and delivery (my contractions were down to five minutes apart *eleven* hours before Simone was actually born) that I slept at every opportunity. My new daughter nursed readily, without any urging, and Michael insists that she even nursed once or twice while I was only partially awake. My milk now surges into my breasts immediately after Simone begins to suckle. She seems quite satisfied when she's finished. I'm delighted that my milk is adequate for her—I was worried that I might have the same problem that I had with Genevieve.

One of the two men is beside me every time I wake up. Richard's smiles always seem a little forced, but they are appreciated nevertheless. Michael is quick to place Simone in my arms or at my breasts when I am awake. He holds her comfortably, even when she is crying, and keeps mumbling, "She's beautiful."

At the moment Simone is sleeping beside me wrapped in the quasi-blanket manufactured by the Ramans (it is extremely difficult to define fabrics, particularly quality words like *soft*, in any of the quantitative terms that our hosts can understand). She does indeed look like my mother. Her skin is quite dark, maybe even darker than mine, and the thatch of hair on her head is jet black. Her eyes are a rich brown. With her head still coned and misshapen from the difficult birth, it is not easy to call Simone beautiful. But of course Michael is right. She is gorgeous. My eyes can readily see the beauty beyond the fragile, reddish creature breathing with such frantic rapidity. Welcome to the world, Simone Wakefield.

2

6 January 2201 I have been depressed now for two days. And tired, oh, so tired. Even though I am well aware that I have a typical case of postpartum syndrome, I have been unable to relieve my feelings of depression.

This morning was the worst. I woke before Richard and lay quietly on my portion of the mat. I looked over at Simone, who was sleeping peacefully in the Raman cradle against the wall. Despite my feelings of love for her, I could not manage any positive thoughts about her future. The glow of ecstasy that had surrounded her birth and lasted for seventy-two hours had completely vanished. An endless stream of hopeless observations and unanswerable questions kept running through my mind. What kind of life will you have, my little Simone? How can we, your parents, possibly provide for your happiness?

My darling daughter, you live with your parents and their good friend Michael O'Toole in an underground lair onboard a gargantuan spacecraft of extraterrestrial origin. The three adults in your life are all cosmonauts from the planet Earth, part of the crew of the Newton expedition sent to investigate a cylindrical worldlet called Rama almost a year ago. Your mother, father, and General O'Toole were the only human beings still onboard this alien craft when Rama abruptly changed its trajectory to avoid being annihilated by a nuclear phalanx launched from a paranoid Earth.

Above our lair is an island city of mysterious skyscrapers, which we call New York. It is surrounded by a frozen sea that completely circles this huge spacecraft and cuts it in half. At this moment, according to your father's calculations, we are just inside the orbit of Jupiter (although the great gasball itself is way over on the other side of the Sun), following a hyperbolic trajectory that will eventually leave the solar system altogether. We do not know where we are going. We do not know who built this spaceship or why they built it. We know there are other occupants onboard, but we have no idea where *they* came from and, in addition, have reason to suspect that at least some of them may be hostile.

Over and over my thoughts the last two days have continued in this same pattern. Each time I come to the same depressing conclusion: It is inexcusable that we, as supposedly mature adults, would bring such a helpless and innocent being into an environment about which we understand so little and over which we have absolutely no control.

Early this morning, as soon as I realized that today was my thirty-seventh birthday, I began to cry. At first the tears were soft and soundless, but as the memories of all my past birthdays flooded into my mind, deep sobs replaced the soft tears. I was feeling an acute, aching sorrow, not just for Simone, but also for myself. And as I remembered the magnificent blue planet of our origin and could not imagine it in Simone's future, I kept asking myself the same question. Why have I given birth to a child in the middle of this mess?

There's that word again. It's one of Richard's favorites. In his vocabulary, *mess* has virtually unlimited applications. Anything that is chaotic and/or out of control, whether it is a technical problem or a domestic crisis (like a wife sobbing in the grips of a fierce postpartum depression), is referred to as a mess.

The men were not much help earlier this morning. Their futile attempts to make me feel better only added to my gloom. A question: Why is it that almost every man, when confronted by an unhappy woman, immediately assumes that her unhappiness is somehow related to him? Actually I'm not being fair. Michael has had three children in his life and knows something about the feelings I'm experiencing. Mostly he just asked me what he could do to help. But Richard was absolutely devastated by my tears. He was frightened when he woke up and could hear my weeping. At first he thought that I was having some terrible physical pain. He was only minimally reassured when I explained to him that I was simply depressed.

After first establishing that he was not to blame for my mood, Richard listened silently while I expressed my concerns about Simone's future. I admit that I was slightly overwrought, but he didn't seem to grasp *anything* I was saying. He kept repeating the same phrase—that Simone's future was no more uncertain than our own—believing that since there was no logical reason for me to be so upset, my depression should immediately vanish. Eventually, after over an hour of miscommunication, Richard correctly concluded that he was not helping and decided to leave me alone.

(Six hours later.) I'm feeling better now. There are still three more hours before my birthday is over. We had a small party tonight. I just finished nursing Simone and she is again lying beside me. Michael left us about fifteen minutes ago to go to his room down the hall. Richard fell asleep within five minutes after his head was on the pillow. He had spent all day working on my request for some improved diapers.

Richard enjoys spending his time supervising and cataloging our interactions with the Ramans, or whoever it is that operates the computers we activate by using the keyboard in our room. We have never seen anyone or anything in the dark tunnel immediately behind the black screen. So we don't know for certain if there really are creatures back there responding to our requests and ordering their factories to manufacture our odd items, but it is convenient to refer to our hosts and benefactors as the Ramans.

Our communication process with them is both complicated and straightforward. It is complicated because we talk to them using pictures on the black screen and precise quantitative formulas in the language of mathematics, physics, and chemistry. It is straightforward because the actual sentences we input using the keyboard are amazingly simple in syntax. Our most often used sentence is "We would like" or "We want" (of course, we could not possibly know the exact translation of our requests and are just assuming that we are being polite—it could be the instructions we activate are in the form of rude commands beginning with "Give me"), followed by a detailed description of what we would like provided to us.

The hardest part is the chemistry. Simple everyday objects like soap, paper, and glass are very complex chemically and extremely difficult to specify exactly in terms of their number and kind of chemical compounds. Sometimes, as Richard discovered early in his work with the keyboard and black screen, we must also outline a manufacturing process, including thermal regimes, or what we receive does not bear any resemblance to what we ordered. The request process involves a lot of trial and error. In the beginning it was a very inefficient and frustrating interaction. All three of us kept wishing that we remembered more of our college chemistry. In fact, our inability to make satisfactory progress in equipping ourselves with everyday essentials was one of the catalysts for the Great Excursion, as Richard likes to call it, that occurred four months ago.

By then the ambient temperature, topside in New York as well as in the rest of Rama, was already five degrees below freezing and Richard had confirmed that the Cylindrical Sea was again solid ice. I was growing quite concerned that we were not going to be properly prepared for the baby's birth. It was taking us too long to accomplish everything. Procuring and installing a working toilet, for example, had turned out to be a month-long endeavor, and the result was still only marginally adequate. Most of the time our primary problem was that we kept providing incomplete specifications to our hosts. However, sometimes the difficulty was the Ramans themselves. Several times they informed us, using our mutual language of mathematical and chemical symbols, that they could not complete the manufacture of a specific item within our allocated time period.

Anyway, Richard announced one morning that he was going to leave our lair and try to reach the still-docked military ship from our Newton expedition. His expressed purpose was to retrieve the key components of the scientific data base stored on the ship's computers (this would help us immensely in formulating our requests to the Ramans), but he also acknowledged that he was terribly hungry for some decent food. We had been managing to stay healthy and alive with the chemical concoctions provided us by the Ramans. However, most of the food had been either tasteless or terrible.

In all fairness, our hosts had been responding correctly to our requests. Although we knew generally how to describe the essential chemical ingredients our bodies needed, none of us had ever studied in detail the complex biochemical process that takes place when we taste something. In those early days eating was a necessity, never a pleasure. Often the "goo" was difficult, if not impossible, to swallow. More than once nausea followed a meal.

The three of us spent most of a day debating the pros and cons of the Great Excursion. I was in the "heartburn" stage of my pregnancy and was feeling quite uncomfortable. Even though I did not relish the idea of remaining alone in our lair while the two men trekked across the ice, located the rover, drove across the Central Plain, and then rode or climbed the many kilometers to the Alpha relay station, I recognized that there were many ways in which they could help each other. I also agreed with them that a solo trip would be foolhardy.

Richard was quite certain the rover would still be operational but was less optimistic about the chairlift. We discussed at length the damage that might have been done to the Newton military ship, exposed as it was on the outside of Rama to the nuclear blasts that had occurred beyond the protective mesh shield. Richard conjectured that since there was no visible structural damage (using our access to the output of the Raman sensors, we had looked at images of the Newton military ship on the black screen several times during the intervening months), it was possible that Rama itself might have inadvertently protected the ship from all of the nuclear explosions and, as a result, there might not be any radiation damage inside either.

I was more sanguine about the prospects. I had worked with the environmental engineers on the designs for the spacecraft shielding and was aware of the radiation susceptibility of each of the subsystems of the Newton. Although I did think there was a high probability the scientific data base would be intact (both its processor and all its memories were made from radiation-hardened parts), I was virtually certain the food supply would be contaminated. We had always known that our packaged food was in a relatively unprotected location. Prior to launch, in fact, there had even been some concern that an unexpected solar flare might produce enough radiation to make the food unsafe to eat.

I was not afraid of staying alone for the few days or week that it might take for the men to make the round trip to the military ship. I was more worried about the possibility that one or both of them might not return. It wasn't just a question of the octospiders, or any other aliens that might be cohabiting this immense spaceship with us. There were environmental uncertainties to be considered as well. What if Rama suddenly started to maneuver? What if some other equally untoward event occurred and they couldn't make it back to New York?

Richard and Michael assured me that they would take no chances, that they would not do anything except go to the military ship and return. They departed just after dawn on a twenty-eight-hour Raman day. It was the first time I had been alone since my long, solitary sojourn in New York that started when I fell into the pit. Of course, I wasn't truly alone. I could feel Simone kicking inside me. It's an amazing feeling, carrying a baby. There's something indescribably wonderful about knowing there's another living soul inside you. Especially since the child is formed in significant part from your own genes. It's a shame that men are not able to experience being pregnant. If they could, maybe they would understand why we women are so concerned about the future.

By the third Earth day after the men left, I had developed a bad case of cabin fever. I decided to climb out of our lair and take a hike around New York. It was dark in Rama, but I was so restless I started to walk anyway. The air was quite cold. I zipped my heavy flight jacket around my bulging stomach. I had only been walking for a few minutes when I heard a sound in the distance. A chill ran down my spine and I stopped immediately. The adrenaline apparently surged into Simone as well, for she kicked vigorously while I listened for the noise. In about a minute I heard it again, the sound of brushes dragging across a metallic surface and accompanied by a high-frequency whine. The sound was unmistakable; an octospider was definitely wandering around in New York. I quickly went back to the lair and waited for dawn to come to Rama.

When it was light I returned to New York and wandered around. While I was in the vicinity of that curious barn where I fell into the pit, I began having my doubts about our conclusion that the octos only come out at night. Richard has insisted from the beginning that they are nocturnal creatures. During the first two months after we passed the Earth, before we built our protective grill that prevents unwelcome visitors from descending into our lair, Richard deployed a series of crude receivers (he had not yet perfected his ability to specify electronic parts to the Ramans) around the octospider lair covering and confirmed, at least to his satisfaction, that they only come topside at night. Eventually the octos discovered all his monitors and destroyed them, but not before Richard had what he believed to be conclusive data supporting his hypothesis.

Nevertheless, Richard's conclusion was no comfort to me when I suddenly heard a loud and totally unfamiliar sound coming from the direction of our lair. At the time I was standing inside the barn, staring into the pit where I had almost died nine months ago. My pulse immediately jumped up and my skin tingled. What disturbed me the most was that the noise was between me and my Raman home. I crept up on the intermittent sound cautiously, peering around buildings each time before committing myself. At length I discovered the source of the noise. Richard was cutting pieces of a lattice using a miniature chain saw that he had brought back from the Newton.

Actually he and Michael were having an argument when I discovered them. A relatively small lattice, about five hundred nodes altogether with square dimensions maybe three meters on a side, was affixed to one of those low, nondescript sheds about a hundred meters to the east of our lair opening. Michael was questioning the wisdom of attacking the lattice with a chain saw. At the moment they saw me, Richard was justifying his action by extolling the virtues of the elastic lattice material.

The three of us hugged and kissed for several minutes and then they reported on the Great Excursion. It had been an easy trip. The rover and the chairlift had worked without difficulty. Their instruments had shown that there was still quite a bit of radiation throughout the military ship, so they didn't stay long and didn't bring back any of the food. The scientific data base, however, had been in fine shape. Richard had used his data compression subroutines to strip much of the data base onto cubes compatible with our portable computers. They had also brought back a large backpack full of tools, like the chain saw, that they thought would be useful in finishing our living accommodations.

Richard and Michael worked incessantly from then until the birth of Simone. Using the extra chemical information contained in the data base, it became easier to order what we needed from the Ramans. I even experimented with sprinkling harmless esters and other simple organics on the food, resulting in some improvement in the taste. Michael completed his room down the corridor, Simone's cradle was constructed, and our bathrooms immeasurably improved. Considering all the constraints, our living conditions are now quite acceptable. Maybe soon . . . Hark. I hear a soft cry from beside me. It's time to feed my daughter.

Before the last thirty minutes of my birthday is history, I want to return to the vivid images of previous birthdays that catalyzed my depression this morning. For me, my birthday has always been the most significant event of the year. The Christmas–New Year time period is special, but in a different way, for it is a celebration shared by everyone. A birthday focuses more directly on the individual. I have always used my birthdays as a time for reflection and contemplation about the direction of my life.

If I tried, I could probably remember something about every single one of my birthdays since I was five years old. Some memories, of course, are more poignant than others. This morning many of the pictures from my past celebrations evoked powerful feelings of nostalgia and homesickness. In my depressed state I railed against my inability to provide order and security to Simone's life. But even at the bottom of my depression, confronted by the immense uncertainty surrounding our existence here, I would not have really wished that Simone were not here to experience life with me. No, we are voyagers tied together by the deepest bond, parent and child, sharing the miracle of consciousness that we call life.

I have shared a similar bond before, not only with my mother and father, but also with my first daughter Genevieve. Hmm. It's amazing that all the images of my mother still stand out so sharply in my mind. Even though she died twenty-seven years ago, when I was only ten years old, she left me with a cornucopia of wonderful memories. My last birthday with her was quite extraordinary. The three of us went into Paris on the train. Father was dressed in his new Italian suit and looked extremely handsome. Mother had chosen to wear one of her bright, multicolored native dresses. With her hair stacked in layers on her head, she looked like the Senoufo princess that she had been before she married Father.

We had dinner at a fancy restaurant just off the Champs-Élysées. Then we walked to a theater where we watched an all-black troupe perform a set of native dances from the western regions of Africa. After the show, we were allowed backstage, where Mother introduced me to one of the dancers, a tall, beautiful woman of exceptional blackness. She was one of Mother's distant cousins from the Ivory Coast.

I listened to their conversation in the Senoufo tribal language, remembering bits and pieces from my training before the Poro three years earlier, and marveled again at the way my mother's face always became more expressive when she was with her people. But fascinated as I was by the evening, I was only ten years old and would have preferred a normal birthday party with all my friends from school. Mother could tell I was disappointed while we were riding on the train back to our home in the suburb of Chilly-Mazarin. "Don't be sad, Nicole," she said, "next year you can have a party. Your father and I wanted to take this opportunity to remind you again of the other half of your heritage. You are a French citizen and have lived your whole life in France, but part of you is pure Senoufo with roots deep in the tribal customs of West Africa."

Earlier today, as I recalled the dances *ivoiriennes* performed by Mother's cousin and her associates, I imagined briefly, in my mind's eye, walking into a beautiful theater with my ten-year-old daughter Simone beside me—but then the fantasy vanished. There are no theaters beyond the orbit of Jupiter. In fact, the whole concept of a theater will probably never have any real meaning for my daughter. It is all so bewildering.

Some of my tears this morning were because Simone will never know her grandparents, and vice versa. They will be mythological characters in the fabric of her life and she will know them only from their photographs and videos. She will never have the joy of hearing my mother's amazing voice. And she will never see the soft and tender love in my father's eyes.

After Mother died, my father was very careful to make each of my birthdays very special. On my twelfth birthday, after we had just moved into the villa at Beauvois, Father and I walked together in the falling snow among the manicured gardens at the Chateau de Villandry. That day he promised me that he would always be beside me when I needed him. I tightened my grip on his hand as we walked along the hedges. I wept that day also, admitting to him (and to myself) how frightened I was that he too would abandon me. He cradled me against his chest and kissed my forehead. He never broke his promise.

Only last year, in what seems now to have been another life-time, my birthday began on a ski train just inside the French border. I was still awake at midnight, reliving my noon encounter with Henry at the chalet on the side of the Weissfluhjoch. I had not told him, when he indirectly inquired, that he was Genevieve's father. I would not give him that satisfaction.

But I remember thinking on the train, is it fair for me to keep from my daughter the fact that her father is the king of England? Are my self-respect and pride so important that I can justify pre-venting my daughter from knowing that she is a princess? I was mulling these questions over in my mind, staring blankly out at the night, when Genevieve, as if on cue, appeared in my sleeping berth. "Happy Birthday, Mother," she said with a grin. She gave me a hug. I almost told her then about her father. I would have, I am certain, if I had known what was going to happen to the Newton expedition. I miss you, Genevieve. I wish that I had been allowed a proper good-bye.

Memories are very peculiar. This morning, in my depression, the flood of images from previous birthdays heightened my feelings of isolation and loss. Now, when I'm in a stronger mood, I savor those same recollections. I'm no longer terribly sad at this moment that Simone will not be able to experience what I have known. Her birthdays will be completely different from mine and unique to *her* life. It is my privilege and duty to make them as memorable and loving as I can.

3

Five hours ago a series of extraordinary events began to occur
inside Rama. We were sitting together at that time, eating our evening meal of roast beef, potatoes, and salad (in an effort to persuade
ourselves that what we are eating is delicious, we have a code name
for each of the chemical combinations that we obtain from the
Ramans. The code names are roughly derived from the kind of nutri-
tion provided—thus our "roast beef" is rich in protein, "potatoes"
are primarily carbohydrates, etc.), when we heard a pure and distant
whistle. All of us stopped eating and the two men bundled up to
go topside. When the whistle persisted, I grabbed Simone and my
heavy clothes, wrapped the baby in numerous blankets, and followed
Michael and Richard up into the cold.

The whistle was much louder on the surface. We were fairly
certain that it was coming from the south, but since it was dark in
Rama we were leery about wandering away from our lair. After a
few minutes, however, we began to see splashes of light reflecting
off the mirrored surfaces of the surrounding skyscrapers, and our
curiosity could not be contained. We crept cautiously toward the
southern shore of the island, where no buildings would be between
us and the imposing horns of the southern bowl of Rama.

When we arrived at the shore of the Cylindrical Sea, a fascinating light show was already in progress. The arcs of multicolored light flying around and illuminating the gigantic spires of the southern bowl continued for over an hour. Even baby Simone was mesmerized by the long streamers of yellow, blue, and red bouncing between the spires and making rainbow patterns in the dark. When the show abruptly ceased, we switched on our flashlights and headed back toward our lair.

After a few minutes of walking, our animated conversation was interrupted by a distant long shriek, unmistakably the sound of one of the avian creatures that had helped Richard and me to escape from New York last year. We stopped abruptly and listened. Since we have neither seen nor heard any avians since we returned to New York to warn the Ramans of the incoming nuclear missiles, both Richard and I were very excited. Richard has been over to their lair a few times, but has never had any response to his shouts down the great vertical corridor. Just a month ago Richard said that he thought the avians had left New York altogether. The shriek tonight clearly indicates that at least one of our friends is still around.

Within seconds, before we had a chance to discuss whether or not one of us would go in the direction of the shriek, we heard another sound, also familiar, that was too loud for any of us to feel comfortable. Fortunately the dragging brushes were not between us and our lair. I put both of my arms around Simone and sprinted toward home, nearly running into buildings at least twice in my hurry in the dark. Michael was the last to arrive. By then I had finished opening both the cover and the grill. "There's several of them," Richard said breathlessly, as the sounds of the octospiders, growing louder, surrounded us. He cast his flashlight beam down the long lane leading east from our lair and we all saw two large, dark objects moving in our direction.

Normally we go to sleep within two or three hours after dinner, but tonight was an exception. The light show, the avian shriek, and the close encounter with the octospiders had energized all three of us. We talked and talked. Richard was convinced that something really major was about to happen. He reminded us that the Earth impact maneuver by Rama had also been preceded by a small light show in the southern bowl. At that time, he recalled, the consensus of the Newton cosmonauts had been that the entire demonstration was intended as an announcement or possibly as some kind of an alert. What, Richard wondered, was the significance of tonight's dazzling display?

For Michael, who was not inside Rama for any extended period of time before its close passage by the Earth and had never before had any direct contact with either the avians or the octospiders, tonight's events were of major proportions. The fleeting glance that he caught of the tentacled creatures coming toward us down the lane gave him some appreciation for the terror that Richard and I had felt when we were racing up those bizarre spikes and escaping from the octospider lair last year.

"Are the octospiders the Ramans?" Michael asked tonight. "If so," he continued, "then why should we run from them? Their technology has advanced so far beyond ours that they can basically do with us as they see fit."

"The octospiders are passengers on this vehicle," Richard responded quickly, "just as we are. So are the avians. The octos think we may be the Ramans, but they are not certain. The avians are a puzzle. Surely they cannot be a spacefaring species. How did they get onboard in the first place? Are they perhaps a part of the original Raman ecosystem?"

I instinctively clutched Simone against my body. So many questions. So few answers. A memory of poor Dr. Takagishi, stuffed like a huge fish or tiger and standing in the octospider museum, shot through my mind and gave me the shivers. "If we are passengers," I said quietly, "then where are we going?"

Richard sighed. "I've been doing some computations," he said. "And the results are not very encouraging. Even though we are traveling very fast with respect to the Sun, our speed is puny when the reference system is our local group of stars. If our trajectory does not change, we will exit the solar system in the general direction of Barnard's star. We will arrive in the Barnard system in several thousand years."

Simone began to cry. It was late and she was very tired. I excused myself and went down to Michael's room to feed her while the men surveyed all the sensor outputs on the black screen to see if they could determine what might be happening. Simone nursed fretfully at my breasts, even hurting me once. Her disquiet was extremely unusual. Ordinarily she is such a mellow baby. "You feel our fear, don't you?" I said to her. I've read that babies can sense the emotions of the adults around them. Maybe it's true.

I still could not rest, even after Simone was sleeping comfortably on her blanket on the floor. My premonitory senses were warning me that tonight's events signaled a transition into some new phase of our life onboard Rama. I had not been encouraged by Richard's calculation that Rama might sail through the interstellar void for several thousand years. I tried to imagine living in our current conditions for the rest of my life and my mind balked. It would certainly be a boring existence for Simone. I found myself formulating a prayer, to God, or the Ramans, or whoever had the power to alter the future. My prayer was very simple. I asked that the forthcoming changes would somehow enrich the future life of my baby daughter.

28 May 2201

Again tonight there was a long whistle followed by a spectacular light show in the southern bowl of Rama. I didn't go to see it. I stayed in the lair with Simone. Michael and Richard did not encounter any of the other occupants of New York. Richard said that the show was approximately the same length as the first one, but the individual displays were considerably different. Michael's impression was that the only major change in the show was in the colors. In his opinion the dominant color tonight was blue, whereas it had been yellow two days ago.

Richard is certain that the Ramans are in love with the number three and that, therefore, there will be another light show when night falls again. Since the days and nights on Rama are now approximately equal at twenty-three hours—a time period Richard calls the Raman equinox, correctly predicted by my brilliant husband in the almanac he issued to Michael and me four months ago—the third display will begin in another two Earth days. We all expect that something unusual will occur soon after this third demonstration. Unless Simone's safety is in doubt, I will definitely watch.

30 May 2201

Our massive cylindrical home is now undergoing a rapid acceleration that began over four hours ago. Richard is so excited that he can hardly contain himself. He is convinced that underneath the elevated Southern Hemicylinder is a propulsion system operating on physical principles beyond the wildest imaginings of human scientists and engineers. He stares at the external sensor data on the black screen, his beloved portable computer in his hand, and makes occasional entries based on what he sees on the monitor. From time to time he mumbles to himself or to us about what he thinks the maneuver is doing to our trajectory.

I was unconscious at the bottom of the pit at the time that Rama made the midcourse correction to achieve the Earth impact orbit, so I don't know how much the floor shook during that earlier maneuver. Richard says those vibrations were trivial compared to what we are experiencing now. Just walking around at present is difficult. The floor bounces up and down at a very high frequency, as if a jackhammer were operating only a few meters away. We have been holding Simone in our arms ever since the acceleration started. We cannot put her down on the floor or in her cradle, because the vibration frightens her. I am the only one who moves around with Simone, and I am exceptionally cautious. Losing my balance and falling is a real concern—Richard and Michael have each fallen twice already—and Simone could be seriously injured if I fell in the wrong position.

At this moment Richard is sitting against the wall, holding our sleeping daughter against his chest. Our meager furniture is hopping all over the room. One of the chairs actually bounced out into the corridor and headed for the stairs half an hour ago. At first we replaced the furniture in its proper position every ten minutes or so, but now we just ignore it—unless it heads out the entryway into the hall.

Altogether it has been an unbelievable time period, beginning with the third and final light show in the south. Richard went out first that night, by himself, just before dark. He rushed back excitedly a few minutes later and grabbed Michael. When the two of them returned, Michael looked as if he had seen a ghost. "Octospiders," Richard shouted. "Dozens of them are massed along the shoreline two kilometers to the east."

"Now, you don't really know how many there are," Michael said. "We only saw them for ten seconds at most before the lights went out."

"I watched them for longer when I was by myself," Richard continued. "I could see them very clearly with the binoculars. At first there were only a handful, but they suddenly started arriving in droves. I was just starting to count them when they organized themselves into some kind of an array. A giant octo with a red-and-blue-striped head appeared to be by itself at the front of their formation."

"I didn't see the red and blue giant, or any 'formation,' " Michael added as I stared at the two of them with disbelief. "But I definitely saw many of the creatures with the dark heads and the black and gold tentacles. In my opinion they were looking to the south, waiting for the light show to begin."

"We saw the avians too," Richard said to me. He turned to Michael. "How many would you say were airborne in that flock?"

"Twenty-five, maybe thirty," Michael replied.

"They soared high into the air over New York, shrieking as they rose, and then flew north, across the Cylindrical Sea." Richard paused for a moment. "I think those dumb birds have been through this before. I think they know what is going to happen."

I started wrapping Simone in her blankets. "What are you doing?" Richard asked. I explained that I wasn't about to miss the final light show. I also reminded Richard that he had sworn to me that the octospiders only ventured out at night. "This is a special occasion," he replied confidently just as the whistle began to sound.

Tonight's show seemed more spectacular to me. Maybe it was my sense of anticipation. Red was definitely the color of the night. At one point a fiery red arc inscribed a full and continuous hexagon connecting the tips of the six smaller horns. But as spectacular as the Raman lights were, they were not the highlight of the evening. About thirty minutes into the display, Michael suddenly shouted "Look!" and pointed down the shoreline in the direction where he and Richard had seen the octospiders earlier.

Several balls of light had ignited simultaneously in the sky above the frozen Cylindrical Sea. The "flares" were about fifty meters off the ground and illuminated an area of roughly one square kilometer on the ice below them. During the minute or so that we could see some detail, a large black mass moved south across the ice. Richard handed me his binoculars just as the light from the flares was fading away. I could see some individual creatures in the mass. A surprisingly large number of the octospiders had colored patterns on their heads, but most were dark charcoal gray, like the one that chased us in the lair. Both the black and gold tentacles and the shapes of their bodies confirmed that these creatures were the same species as the one we had seen climbing the spikes last year. And Richard was right. There were dozens of them.

When the maneuver began, we returned quickly to our lair. It was dangerous being outside in Rama during the extreme vibrations. Occasionally small parts of the surrounding skyscrapers would break free and crash to the ground. Simone began to cry as soon as the shaking started.

After a difficult descent into our lair, Richard began checking the external sensors, mostly looking at star and planet positions (Saturn is definitely identifiable in some of the Raman frames) and then making computations based on his observational data. Michael and I alternated holding Simone—eventually we sat in a corner of the room, where the two merging walls gave us some sense of stability—and talked about the amazing day.

Almost an hour later Richard announced the results of his preliminary orbit determination. He gave first the orbital elements, with respect to the Sun, of our hyperbolic trajectory *before* the maneuver started. Then he dramatically presented the new, osculating elements (as he called them) of our instantaneous trajectory. Somewhere in the recesses of my mind I must have stored the information that defines the term *osculating element*, but I luckily didn't need to fetch it. I was able, from the context, to understand that Richard was using a shorthand way of telling us how much our hyperbola had changed during the first three hours of the maneuver. However, the full implication of a change in hyperbolic eccentricity escaped me.

Michael remembered more of his celestial mechanics. "Are you certain?" he said almost immediately.

"The quantitative results have wide error bars," Richard replied. "But there can be no doubt about the qualitative nature of the trajectory change."

"Then our rate of escape from the solar system is *increasing*?" Michael asked.

Richard nodded. "That's right. Our acceleration is virtually all going into the direction that increases our speed with respect to the Sun. The maneuver has already added many kilometers per second to our Sun-based velocity."

"Whew," Michael replied. "That's staggering."

I understood the gist of what Richard was saying. If we had retained any hope that we might be on a circuitous voyage that would magically return us to the Earth, those hopes were now being shattered. Rama was going to leave the solar system much faster than any of us had expected. While Richard waxed lyrical about the kind of propulsion system that could impart such a velocity change to this "behemoth of a spacecraft," I nursed Simone and found myself again thinking about her future. *So we are definitely leaving the solar system*, I thought, *and going somewhere else. Will I ever see another world? Will Simone? Is it possible, my daughter, that Rama will be your home world for your entire lifetime?*

The floor continues to shake vigorously, but it comforts me. Richard says our escape velocity is still increasing rapidly. Good. As long as we are going someplace new, I want to travel there as fast as possible.

4

5 *June 2201*   I awakened in the middle of last
                                 night after hearing a persistent
knocking sound coming from the direction of the vertical corridor in
our lair. Even though the normal noise level from the constant shaking is substantial, Richard and I could both clearly hear the pounding
without any difficulty. After checking Simone—she was still comfortably sleeping in her cradle now mounted on Richard's makeshift
shock absorbers—we walked cautiously over to the vertical corridor.

The knocking grew louder as we climbed the stairs toward the
grill that protects us from unwanted visitors. At one landing Richard
leaned over and whispered to me that it "must be MacDuff knocking
at the gate" and that our "evil deed" would soon be discovered. I
was too tense to laugh. When we were still several meters below
the grill, we saw a large moving shadow projected on the wall in
front of us. We stopped to study it. Both Richard and I realized
immediately that our outside lair cover was open—there was daylight
topside in Rama at the time—and that the Raman creature or biot
responsible for the knocking was creating the bizarre shadow on the
wall.

I instinctively clutched Richard's hand. "What in the world is
it?" I wondered out loud.

"It must be something new," Richard said very softly.

I told him that the shadow resembled an old-fashioned oil pump going up and down in the middle of a producing field. He grinned nervously and agreed.

After waiting for what must have been five minutes and neither seeing nor hearing any change in the rhythmic knocking pattern of the visitor, Richard told me that he was going to climb to the grill, where he would be able to see something more definitive than a shadow. Of course that meant that whatever was outside beating on our door would also be able to see him, assuming that it had eyes or an approximate equivalent. For some reason I remembered Dr. Takagishi at that moment, and a wave of fear swept through me. I kissed Richard and told him not to take any chances.

When Richard reached the final landing, just above where I was waiting, his body was partially in the light and blocked the moving shadow. The knocking suddenly stopped abruptly. "It's a biot, all right," Richard shouted. "It looks like a praying mantis with an extra hand in the middle of its face. . . . And now it's *opening* the grill," he added a second later.

Richard jumped off the landing and was beside me in an instant. He grabbed my hand and we raced down several flights of stairs together. We didn't stop until we were back on our living level several landings below.

We could hear the sound of motion above us. "There was another mantis and at least one bulldozer biot behind the first mantis," Richard said breathlessly. "As soon as they saw me they started removing the grill. . . . Apparently they were just knocking to alert us to their presence."

"But what do they want?" I asked rhetorically. The noise above us continued to grow. "It sounds like an army," I remarked.

Within seconds we could hear them moving down the stairs. "We must be prepared to run for it," Richard said frantically. "You get Simone and I'll wake Michael."

We moved swiftly down the corridor toward our living area. Michael had been awakened already by all the noise, and Simone was stirring as well. We huddled together in our main room, sitting on the shaking floor opposite the black screen, and waited for the alien invaders. Richard had prepared a keyboard request for the Ramans that would, upon the input of two additional commands, cause the black screen to lift up just as it did when our unseen benefactors were about to supply us with some new product. "If we are attacked," Richard said, "we'll take our chances in the tunnels behind the screen."

Half an hour passed. From the hubbub in the direction of the stairs we could tell that the intruders were already on our level in the lair, but none of them had yet entered the passage toward our living area. After another fifteen minutes curiosity overpowered my husband. "I'll go check out the situation," Richard said, leaving Michael with me and Simone.

He returned in less than five minutes. "There are fifteen, maybe twenty of them," he told us with a puzzled frown. "Three mantises altogether, plus two different types of bulldozer biots. They seem to be building something on the opposite side of the lair."

Simone had fallen asleep again. I put her in the cradle and then followed the two men toward the noise. When we reached the circular area where the stairs climb toward the opening to New York, we encountered a maelstrom of activity. It was impossible to follow all the work being done on the opposite side of the room. The mantises appeared to be supervising the bulldozer biots as they were widening a horizontal corridor on the other side of the circular room.

"Does anybody have any idea what they are doing?" Michael asked in a whisper.

"Not a clue," Richard replied at the time.

It is almost twenty-four hours later now and it is still not clear exactly what the biots are building. Richard thinks that the corridor expansion has been made to accommodate some kind of a new facility. He has also suggested that all this activity almost certainly has something to do with us, for it is, after all, being done in our lair.

The biots work without stopping for rest, food, or sleep. The floor vibrations do not bother them at all. They seem to be following some master plan or procedure that has been thoroughly communicated, for none of them ever confer about anything. It is an awesome spectacle to watch their relentless activity. For their part, the biots have never once acknowledged that we are there watching them.

An hour ago Richard, Michael, and I talked briefly about the frustration we are all feeling because we do not know what is happening around us. At one point Richard smiled. "It's really not dramatically different from the situation on Earth," he said vaguely. When Michael and I pressed him to explain what he meant, Richard waved his hand in a sweeping gesture. "Even at home," he replied abstractedly, "our knowledge is severely limited. The search for truth is always a frustrating experience."

8 *June 2201*

It is inconceivable to me that the biots could have finished the facility so quickly. Two hours ago the last of them, the foreman mantis that had signaled to us (using the "hand" in the middle of its "face") to inspect the new room early this afternoon, finally trundled up the stairs and disappeared. Richard says that it had remained in our lair until it was satisfied that we understood everything.

The only object in the new room is a narrow rectangular tank that has obviously been designed for us. It has shiny metal sides and is about three meters high. At either end there is a ladder that goes from the floor to the lip of the tank. A sturdy walkway runs around the outside perimeter of the tank just centimeters below the lip.

Inside the rectangular structure are four webbed hammocks secured against the walls. Each of these fascinating creations has been individually crafted for a specific member of our family. The hammocks for Michael and Richard are at each end of the tank; Simone and I have webbed beds in the middle, with her tiny hammock being right beside mine.

Of course Richard has already examined the entire arrangement in detail. Because there is a cover to the tank and the hammocks are set down into the cavity between half a meter and a meter from the top, he has concluded that the tank closes and is then probably filled with a fluid. But why was it built? Are we going to undergo some set of experiments? Richard is certain that we are about to be tested in some way, but Michael says that our being used as guinea pigs is "inconsistent with the Raman personality" we have observed heretofore. I had to laugh at his comment. Michael has now spread his incurable religious optimism to encompass the Ramans as well. He always assumes, like Voltaire's Dr. Pangloss, that we are living in the best of all possible universes.

The foreman mantis hung around, mostly watching from the walkway of the tank, until each of the four of us had actually lain upon his or her hammock. Richard pointed out that although the hammocks had been positioned at varying depths along the walls, we each will "sink" to approximately the same level when occupying the webbed beds. The webbing is slightly elastic, reminiscent of the lattice material we have encountered before in Rama. While I was "testing" my hammock this afternoon, its bounce reminded me of both the fear and the exhilaration during my fantastic lattice harness ride across the Cylindrical Sea. When I closed my eyes it was easy to see myself again just above the water, suspended beneath the three great avians who were carrying me to freedom.

Along the lair wall, behind the tank from the point of view of our living area, there is a set of thick pipes that are connected directly to the tank. We suspect that their purpose is to carry some kind of fluid that fills up the volume of the tank. I guess we will find out soon enough.

So what do we do now? All three of us agree that we should just wait. Doubtless we will eventually be expected to spend some time in this tank. But we have to assume that we will be told when it is the proper time.

10 June 2201

Richard was right. He was certain that the intermittent, low-frequency whistle early yesterday was announcing another mission phase transition. He even suggested that maybe we should go over to the new tank and be prepared to take positions on our individual hammocks. Michael and I both argued with him, insisting that there was not "nearly enough information" to jump to such a conclusion.

We should have followed Richard's advice. Essentially we ignored the whistle and went on with our normal (if that term can ever be used for our existence inside this spacecraft of extraterrestrial origin) routine. About three hours later, the foreman mantis appeared suddenly in the doorway of our main room and scared me out of my wits. It pointed down the corridor with its peculiar fingers and made it clear that we were to move with some dispatch.

Simone was still asleep and not at all happy when I woke her up. She was also hungry, but the mantis biot would not let me take the time to feed her. So Simone was crying fitfully as we were herded across our lair to the tank.

A second mantis was waiting on the walkway that rings the lip of the tank. It was holding our transparent helmets in its strange hands. It must also have been the inspector, for this second mantis would not let us descend to our hammocks until it checked to ensure that the helmets were properly placed over our heads. The plastic or glass compound that forms the helmet front is remarkable; we can see perfectly through it. The bottoms of the helmets are also extraordinary. They are made of a sticky, rubberlike compound that adheres to the skin very tightly and creates an impermeable seal.

We had only been lying on our hammocks for thirty seconds when a powerful surge pressed us down against the webbed elements with such force that we sank halfway into the empty tank. An instant later tiny threads (they seemed to grow out of the hammock material) wrapped themselves around the trunks of our bodies, leaving only our arms and necks free. I glanced over at Simone to see if she was crying; she had a big smile on her face.

The tank had already begun to fill with a light green liquid. In less than a minute we were surrounded by the fluid. Its density was very close to our own, for we half floated on its surface. Soon thereafter the top of the tank closed. I became frightened as the liquid continued to fill the volume. Although I considered it unlikely that we were in any actual danger, I was relieved when the liquid stopped rising, leaving us a few centimeters of breathing space beneath the lid.

All this time the strong acceleration continued. Luckily it wasn't completely dark inside the tank. There were tiny lights scattered around the tank cover. I could see Simone next to me, her body bouncing like a buoy, and I could even see Richard in the distance.

We were inside the tank for slightly more than two hours. Richard was extremely excited when we were finished. He told Michael and me that he was certain we had just completed a "test" to see how we could withstand "excessive" forces.

"They are not satisfied with the paltry accelerations that we have been experiencing heretofore," he exuberantly informed us. "The Ramans want to *really* increase the velocity. To accomplish that, the spacecraft must be subjected to long duration, high gee forces. This tank has been designed to provide us with enough cushioning that our biological construction can accommodate the unusual environment."

Richard spent all day doing calculations and a few hours ago showed us his preliminary reconstruction of yesterday's "acceleration event." "Look at this," he shouted, barely able to contain himself. "We made an equivalent velocity change of *seventy* kilometers per second during that short two-hour period. That is absolutely monstrous for a spacecraft the size of Rama! We were accelerating at close to *ten* gees the entire time." He then grinned at us. "This ship has one hell of an overdrive mode."

When we finished the test in the tank, I inserted a new set of biometry probes in all of us, including Simone. I have not seen any unusual responses, at least nothing that has triggered a warning, but

I admit that I am still a little concerned about how our bodies will react to the stress. A few minutes ago Richard chided me. "The Ramans are certainly watching too," he said, indicating that he thought the biometry was unnecessary. "I bet they are taking their own data through those threads."

5

My vocabulary is inadequate to describe my experiences of the last several days. The word *amazing*, for example, falls far short of conveying the true sense of how extraordinary these long hours in the tank have been. The only remotely similar experiences in my life were both induced by the ingestion of catalytic chemicals, first during the Poro ceremony in the Ivory Coast when I was seven years old and then, more recently, after drinking Omeh's vial while I was at the bottom of the pit in Rama. But both those trips or visions or whatever were isolated incidents and comparatively short in duration. My recent episodes in the tank have lasted for hours.

Before throwing myself totally into a description of the world inside my mind, I should summarize first the "real" events of the past week so that the hallucinatory episodes can be placed in context. Our daily life has now evolved into a repeating pattern. The spacecraft continues to maneuver, but in two separate modes: "regular," when the floor shakes and everything moves but a quasi-normal life can be lived, and "overdrive," when Rama accelerates at a ferocious rate that Richard now estimates is in excess of eleven gees.

When the spacecraft is in overdrive, the four of us must be inside the tank. The overdrive periods last for just under eight hours out of each twenty-seven-hour, six-minute cycle in the repetitive pattern. We are clearly intended to sleep during the overdrive segments. The tiny lights above our heads in the closed tank are extinguished after the first twenty minutes of each segment and we lie there in the total darkness until five minutes before the end of the eight-hour period.

All this rapid velocity change, according to Richard, is speeding our escape from the Sun. If the current maneuver remains consistent in both magnitude and direction, and continues for as long as a month, we will then be traveling at half the speed of light with respect to our solar system.

"Where are we going?" Michael asked yesterday.

"It's still too early to tell," Richard responded. "All we know is that we're blasting away at a fantastic rate."

The temperature and density of the liquid inside the tank have been carefully adjusted each period until they are now exactly equal to ours. As a result, when I lie there in the dark, I can feel nothing at all except a barely perceptible downward force. My mind always tells me that I am inside an acceleration tank, surrounded by some kind of fluid cushioning my body against the powerful force, but the absence of sensation eventually causes me to lose my sense of body altogether. That's when the hallucinations begin. It's almost as if some normal sensory input to the brain is necessary to keep me properly functioning. If no sounds, no sights, no tastes, no smells, and no pain reach my brain, then its activity becomes unregulated.

I tried to discuss this phenomenon with Richard two days ago, but he just looked at me as if I were crazy. He has had no hallucinations. He spends his time in the "twilight zone" (his name for the period of no sensory input prior to deep sleep) doing mathematical calculations, conjuring up a wide variety of maps of the Earth, or even reliving his most outstanding sexual moments. He definitely *manages* his brain, even in the absence of sensory input. That is why we are so different. My mind wants to find a direction of its own when it is not being used for chores such as processing the billions of pieces of data coming from all the other cells in my body.

The hallucinations usually begin with a colored speck of red or green that appears in the total dark surrounding me. As the speck enlarges, it is joined by other colors, often yellow, blue, and purple. Each of the colors rapidly forms into its own irregular pattern and spreads across my vision screen. What I am seeing becomes a kaleidoscope of bright colors. The movement in the field accelerates until hundreds of strips and splotches fuse into one raging explosion.

In the middle of this riot of color a coherent image always forms.

At first I cannot tell exactly what it is, for the figure or figures are very small, as if they are far, far away. As the image moves closer, it changes colors several times, adding both to the surreal overtone of the vision and to my inner sense of dread. More than half the time the image that eventually resolves itself contains my mother, or some animal like a cheetah or a lioness that I intuitively recognize as my mother in disguise. As long as I just watch, and make no volitional attempt to interact with my mother, she remains a character in the changing image. However, if I try to contact Mother in any way, she, or the animal representing her, immediately disappears, leaving me with an overwhelming feeling of having been abandoned.

During one of my recent hallucinations the waves of color broke into geometric patterns and these in turn changed to human silhouettes marching single file across my field of view. Omeh was leading the procession in a bright green robe. The two figures at the rear of the group were both women, the heroines of my adolescence, Joan of Arc and Eleanor of Aquitaine. When I first heard their voices the procession dissolved and the scene instantly shifted. Suddenly I was in a small rowboat in the early morning fog on the small duck pond near our villa at Beauvois. I shivered with fear and began to weep uncontrollably. Joan and Eleanor appeared in the fog and mist to assure me that my father was *not* going to marry Helena, the English duchess with whom he had gone to Turkey on a vacation.

Another night the overture of color was followed by a bizarre theatrical performance somewhere in Japan. There were only two characters in the hallucinatory play, both of whom were wearing brilliant, expressive masks. The man who was dressed in the Western suit and tie recited poetry and had magnificently clear, open eyes that could be seen through his friendly mask. The other man looked like a seventeenth century samurai warrior. His mask was a perpetual scowl. He began to threaten both me and his more modern colleague. I screamed at the end of this hallucination because the two men met in the middle of the stage and merged into a single character.

Some of my most powerful hallucinatory images have only lasted for a few seconds. On the second or third night, a naked Prince Henry, engorged with desire, his body a vibrant purple in color, appeared for two or three seconds in the middle of another vision in which I was riding on a giant green octospider.

During yesterday's sleep period there were no colors for hours. Then, as I became aware of being incredibly hungry, a giant pink manna melon appeared in the darkness. When I attempted to eat the melon in my vision, it grew legs and scampered away, disappearing into unresolved colors.

Does any of this mean anything at all? Can I learn something about myself or my life from these apparently random outpourings of my undirected mind?

The debate about the significance of dreams has raged now for almost three centuries and is still unresolved. These hallucinations of mine, it seems to me, are even more removed from reality than normal dreams. In a sense they are distant cousins of the two psychedelic trips that I took earlier in my life, and any attempt to interpret them logically would be absurd. However, for some reason I still believe some fundamental truths are contained in these wild and seemingly unconnected rampagings of my mind. Maybe that's because I cannot accept that the human brain *ever* operates in a purely random manner.

22 July 2201

Yesterday the floor finally stopped shaking. Richard had predicted it. When we didn't go back into the tank two days ago at the customary time, Richard correctly conjectured that the maneuver was almost over.

So we enter still another phase of our incredible odyssey. My husband informs us that we are now traveling at a velocity of more than half the speed of light. That means we are covering the Earth-Moon distance approximately every two *seconds*. We are headed, more or less, in the direction of the star Sirius, the brightest true star in the night sky of our home planet. If there are no more maneuvers, we will arrive in the vicinity of Sirius in another twelve years.

I am relieved that our life may now return to some kind of local equilibrium. Simone seems to have weathered the long periods in the tank without any noticeable difficulties, but I can't believe that such an experience will leave an infant totally unscathed. It is important for her that we now reestablish a daily routine.

In my moments alone I still think often about those vivid hallucinations during the first ten days in the tank. I must admit that I was delighted when I finally endured several "twilight zones" of total sensory deprivation without the wild, colored patterns and disjointed images flooding my mind. By that time I was starting to worry about my sanity and, quite frankly, was already way past "overwhelm." Even though the hallucinations abruptly stopped, my recollection of the strength of those visions still made me wary each time the lights in the top of the tank were extinguished during the last several weeks.

I had only one additional vision after those first ten days—and it may actually just have been an extremely vivid dream during a normal period of sleep. Despite the fact that this particular image was not as sharp as the earlier ones, I have nevertheless retained all the details because of its similarity to one of the hallucinatory segments while I was at the bottom of the pit last year.

In my final dream or vision I was sitting with my father at an outdoor concert in an unknown place. An old Oriental gentleman with a long white beard was by himself on the stage, playing music on some kind of strange string instrument. Unlike my vision at the bottom of the pit, however, my father and I did not turn into little birds and fly away to Chinon in France. Instead, my father's body disappeared completely, leaving only his eyes. Within a few seconds there were five other pairs of eyes forming a hexagon in the air above me. I recognized Omeh's eyes immediately, and my mother's, but the other three were unknown. The eyes at the vertices of the hexagon all stared at me, unblinking, as if they were trying to communicate something. Just before the music stopped I heard a single distinct sound. Several voices simultaneously uttered the word "Danger."

What was the origin of my hallucinations and why was I the only one of the three of us to experience them? Richard and Michael also endured sensory deprivation, and they have each admitted seeing "bizarre colored patterns," but their images were never coherent. If, as we have conjectured, the Ramans initially injected us with a chemical or two, using the tiny threads that wound around our bodies, to help us sleep in the unfamiliar surroundings, why was I the only one to respond with such wild visions?

Richard and Michael both think the answer is simple, that I am a "drug labile individual with a hyperactive imagination." As far as they are concerned, that's the entire explanation. They don't pursue the subject any further and, although they are polite when I raise the many issues associated with my "trips," they don't even seem interested anymore. I might have expected that kind of a response from Richard, but certainly not from Michael.

Actually even our predictable General O'Toole has not been completely himself since we began our sessions in the tank. He has clearly been preoccupied with other matters. Only this morning did I obtain a small glimpse of what has been going on in his mind.

"I have always," Michael finally said slowly, after I had been pestering him with friendly questions for several minutes, "without consciously acknowledging it, redefined and relimited God with each new breakthrough in science. I had managed to integrate a concept of the Ramans into my Catholicism, but in so doing I had merely expanded my limited definition of Him. Now, when I find myself onboard a robot spacecraft traveling at relativistic speeds, I see that I must completely unfetter God. Only then can He be the supreme being of all the particles and processes in the universe."

The challenge of *my* life in the near future is at the other extreme. Richard and Michael are focused on profound ideas—Richard in the realm of science and engineering, Michael in the world of the soul. Although I thoroughly enjoy the stimulating ideas produced by each of them in his separate search for the truth, someone must pay attention to the everyday tasks of living. The three of us have the responsibility, after all, of preparing our only member of the next generation for her adult life. It looks as if the task of being the primary parent will always fall to me.

It is a responsibility I gladly embrace. When Simone smiles radiantly at me during a break from her nursing, I don't muse about my hallucinations, it really doesn't matter that much whether or not there is a God, and it is not of overwhelming significance that the Ramans have developed a method for using water as nuclear fuel. At that instant the only thing that is important is that I am Simone's mother.

31 July 2201

Spring has definitely come to Rama. The thaw began as soon as the maneuver was completed. By that time the temperature topside had reached a frigid twenty-five below zero, and we had begun to worry about how much lower the outside temperature could become before the system regulating the thermal conditions in our lair would be stretched to the limit. The temperature has been rising steadily almost a degree per day since then and, at that rate, will cross the freezing level within two more weeks.

We are now outside the solar system in the near-perfect vacuum that fills the immense voids between neighboring stars. Our sun is still the dominant object in the sky, but none of the planets is even visible. Two or three times a week Richard searches through the telescopic data for some sign of the comets in the Oort Cloud, but thus far he has seen nothing.

Where is the heat coming from that is warming the interior of our vehicle? Our master engineer, the handsome cosmonaut Richard Wakefield, had a quick explanation when Michael asked him that question yesterday. "The same nuclear system that was providing the huge velocity change is probably now generating the heat. Rama must have two different operating regimes. When it is in the neighborhood of a heat source, like a star, it turns off all its primary systems, including propulsion and thermal control."

Both Michael and I congratulated Richard for an eminently plausible explanation. "But," I asked him two days ago, "there are still many other questions. *Why*, for example, does it have the two separate engineering systems? And why does it turn off the primary one at all?"

"Here I can only speculate," Richard answered with his usual grin. "Maybe the primary systems need periodic repairs and these can only be accomplished when there is an external source of heat and power. You have seen how the various biots maintain the surface of Rama. Maybe there's another set of biots who perform all the maintenance on the primary systems."

"I have another idea," Michael said slowly. "Do you believe we are meant to be onboard this spacecraft?"

"What do you mean?" Richard asked, his brow furrowed.

"Do you think it is a random event that we are here? Or is it a likely event, given all the probabilities and the nature of our species, that some members of the human race would be inside Rama at this moment?"

I liked Michael's line of reasoning. He was hinting, although he didn't yet understand it completely himself, that perhaps the Ramans were not just geniuses in the hard sciences and engineering. Perhaps they knew something about universal psychology as well. Richard wasn't following.

"Are you suggesting," I asked, "that the Ramans *purposely* used their secondary systems in the neighborhood of the Earth, expecting thereby to lure us into a rendezvous?"

"That's preposterous," Richard said immediately.

"But Richard," Michael rejoined, "think about it. What would have been the probability of any contact if the Ramans had streaked into our system at a significant fraction of the speed of light, rounded the Sun, and then gone on their merry way? Absolutely zero. And, as you have indicated yourself, there may be other 'foreigners,' if we can call ourselves that, on this ship as well. I doubt if many species have the ability . . ."

The conversation continued for almost half an hour. When it was over I reminded the men that the Cylindrical Sea would soon melt from below, and that there would be hurricanes and tidal waves immediately afterward. We all later agreed that we should retrieve the backup sailboat from the Beta site.

It took the men slightly more than twelve hours to trek both ways across the ice. Night had already fallen by the time they returned. When Richard and Michael reached our lair, Simone, who is already completely aware of her surroundings, reached out her arms to Michael.

"I see someone is glad that I'm back," Michael said jokingly.

"As long as it's just Simone," Richard said. He seemed strangely tense and distant.

Last night his peculiar mood continued. "What's the matter, darling?" I asked him when we were alone together on our mat. He didn't reply immediately, so I kissed him on the cheek and waited.

"It's Michael," Richard said at length. "I just realized today, when we were carrying the sailboat across the ice, that he's in love with you. You should hear him. All he talks about is you. You're the perfect mother, the perfect wife, the perfect friend. He even admitted that he was envious of me."

I caressed Richard for a few seconds, trying to figure out how to respond. "I think you're making too much of some casual statements, darling," I said finally. "Michael was simply expressing his honest affection. I am very fond of him as well—"

"I know—that's what bothers me," Richard interrupted me abruptly. "He takes care of Simone most of the time when you're busy, the two of you talk for hours while I'm working on my projects—"

He stopped and stared at me with a strange, forlorn look in his eyes. His gaze was scary. This was not the same Richard Wakefield that I have known intimately for over a year. A chill rushed through my system before his eyes softened and he reached over to kiss me.

After we made love and he fell asleep, Simone stirred and I decided to feed her. While I was nursing I thought back over the entire period of time since Michael found us at the foot of the chairlift. There was nothing I could cite that should have caused Richard the slightest bit of jealousy. Even our lovemaking has remained regular and satisfying throughout, although I will admit it hasn't been too imaginative since Simone's birth.

The crazy look that I had seen in Richard's eyes continued to haunt me even after Simone was finished nursing. I promised myself I would find more time to be alone with Richard in the coming weeks.

6

20 June 2202   I verified today that I am indeed pregnant again. Michael was delighted, Richard surprisingly unresponsive. When I talked to Richard privately, he acknowledged that he had mixed feelings because Simone had finally reached the stage where she didn't need "constant attention" anymore. I reminded him that when we had talked two months ago about having another child, he had given his enthusiastic consent. Richard suggested to me that his eagerness to father a second child had been strongly influenced by my "obvious excitement" at the time.

The new baby should arrive in mid-March. By then we will have finished with the nursery and will have enough living space for the entire family. I am sorry that Richard is not thrilled about being a father again, but I am glad that Simone will now have a playmate.

15 March 2203

Catharine Colin Wakefield (we will call her Katie) was born on the thirteenth of March at 6:16 in the morning. It was an easy birth, only four hours from the first strong contraction to delivery. There was no significant pain at any time. I delivered squatting on my haunches and was in such good shape that I cut the umbilical myself.

Katie already cries a lot. Both Genevieve and Simone were sweet, mellow babies, but Katie is obviously going to be a noise-maker. Richard is pleased that I wanted to name her after his mother. I had hoped that he might be more interested in his role as father this time, but at present he is too busy working on his "perfect data base" (it will index and provide easy access to all our information) to pay much attention to Katie.

My third daughter weighed just under four kilograms at birth and was fifty-four centimeters long. Simone was almost certainly not as heavy when she was born, but we did not have an accurate scale at the time. Katie's skin color is quite fair, almost white in fact, and her hair is much lighter than the dark black tresses of her sister. Her eyes are surprisingly blue. I know that it's not unusual for babies to have blue eyes and that often they darken significantly in the first year. But I never expected a child of mine to have blue eyes for even a moment.

18 May 2203

It's hard for me to believe that Katie is already more than two months old. She is such a demanding baby! By now I should have been able to teach her not to pull on my nipples, but I cannot break her of the habit. She is especially difficult when anyone else is present while I am nursing. If I even turn my head to talk to Michael or Richard, or especially if I try to answer one of Simone's questions, then Katie jerks on my nipple with a vengeance.

Richard has been extremely moody lately. At times he is his usual brilliant, witty self, keeping Michael and me laughing with his erudite banter; however, his mood can shift in an instant. A single seemingly innocuous observation by either of us can plunge him into depression or even anger.

I suspect that Richard's real problem these days is boredom. He has finished his data base project and not yet started another major activity. The fabulous computer he built last year contains subroutines that make our interface with the black screen almost routine. Richard could add some variety to his days by playing a more active part in Simone's development and education, but I guess it's just not his style. He does not seem to be fascinated, as Michael and I are, with the complex patterns of growth that are emerging in Simone.

When I was first pregnant with Katie, I was quite concerned about Richard's apparent lack of interest in children. I decided to attack the problem directly by asking him to help me set up a mini-laboratory that would enable us to analyze part of Katie's genome from a sample of my amniotic fluid. The project involved complex chemistry, a level of interaction with the Ramans deeper than any we had ever tried before, and the creation and calibration of some sophisticated medical instruments.

Richard loved the task. I did too, for it reminded me of my days in medical school. We worked together for twelve, sometimes fourteen hours a day (leaving Michael to take care of Simone—those two are certainly fond of each other) until we were finished. Often we would talk about our work late into the night, even while we were making love.

When the day came, however, that we completed the analysis of our own future child's genome, I discovered, much to my amazement, that Richard was more excited about the fact that the equipment and analysis met all our specifications than he was about the characteristics of our second daughter. I was astonished. When I told him that the child was a girl, and didn't have Down's or Whittingham's syndrome, and none of her a priori cancer tendencies were outside the acceptable ranges, he reacted matter-of-factly. But when I praised the speed and accuracy with which the system had completed the test, Richard beamed with pride. What a different man my husband is! He is much more comfortable with the world of mathematics and engineering than he is with other people.

Michael has noticed Richard's recent restlessness as well. He has encouraged Richard to create more toys for Simone like the brilliant dolls he made when I was in the final months of my pregnancy with Katie. Those dolls are still Simone's favorite playthings. They walk around on their own and even respond to a dozen verbal commands. One night, when Richard was in one of his exuberant moods, he programmed TB to interact with the dolls. Simone was almost hysterical with laughter after The Bard (Michael insists on calling Richard's Shakespeare-spouting robot by its full name) chased all three of the dolls into a corner and then launched into a medley of love sonnets.

Not even TB has cheered Richard these last two weeks. He's not sleeping well, which is unusual for him, and he has shown no passion for anything. Our regular and varied sex life has even been suspended, so Richard must be really struggling with his internal demons. Three days ago he left early in the morning (it was also just after dawn in Rama—every now and then our Earth clock in the lair and the Raman clock outside are in synch) and stayed up in New York for over ten hours. When I asked him what he had been doing, he replied that he had sat on the wall and stared at the Cylindrical Sea. Then he changed the subject.

Michael and Richard are both convinced that we are now alone on our island. Richard has entered the avian lair twice recently, both times staying on the side of the vertical corridor away from the tank sentry. He even descended once to the second horizontal passageway, where I made my leap, but he saw no signs of life. The octospider lair now has a pair of complicated grills between the covering and the first landing. For the past four months, Richard has been electronically monitoring the region around the octo lair again; even though he admits there may be some ambiguities in his monitor data, Richard insists he can tell from visual inspection alone that the grills have not been opened for a long time.

The men assembled the sailboat a couple of months ago, and then spent two hours checking it out on the Cylindrical Sea. Simone and I waved to them from the shore. Fearful that the crab biots would define the boat as "garbage" (as they apparently did the other sailboat—we never did figure out what happened to it; a couple of days after we escaped from the phalanx of nuclear missiles we returned to where we had left the sailboat and it was gone), Richard and Michael disassembled it again and brought it into our lair for safekeeping.

Richard has said several times that he would like to sail across the sea, toward the south, and see if he can find any place where the five-hundred-meter cliff can be scaled. Our information about the Southern Hemicylinder of Rama is very limited. Except for the few days when we were on the biot hunt with the original Newton cosmonaut team, our knowledge of the region is limited to the crude mosaics assembled in realtime from the initial Newton drone images. It would certainly be fascinating and exciting to explore the south— maybe we could even find out where all those octospiders went. But we can't afford to take any risks at this juncture. Our family is critically dependent on each of the three adults—the loss of any one of us would be devastating.

I believe Michael O'Toole is content with the life we have made for ourselves on Rama, especially since the addition of Richard's large computer has made so much more information readily available to us. We now have access to all the encyclopedic data that was stored onboard the Newton military ship. Michael's current "study unit," as he calls his organized recreation, is art history. Last month his conversation was full of the Medici and the Catholic popes of the Renaissance, along with Michelangelo, Raphael, and the other great painters of the period. He is now involved with the nineteenth century, a time in art history that I find more interesting. We have had many recent discussions about the impressionist "revolution," but Michael does not accept my argument that impressionism was simply a natural by-product of the advent of the camera.

Michael spends hours with Simone. He is patient, tender, and caring. He has carefully monitored her development and has recorded her major milestones in his electronic notebook. At present Simone knows twenty-one of her twenty-six letters by sight (she confuses the pairs C and S, as well as Y and V, and for some reason cannot learn the K), and can count to twenty on a good day. Simone can also correctly identify drawings of an avian, an octospider, and the four most prevalent types of biots. She knows the names of the twelve disciples as well, a fact that does not make Richard happy. We have already had one "summit meeting" about the spiritual education of our daughters, and the result was polite disagreement.

That leaves me. I am happy most of the time, although I do have some days when Richard's restlessness or Katie's crying or just the absurdity of our strange life on this alien spaceship combine to overwhelm me. I am always busy. I plan most of the family activities, decide what we're eating and when, and organize the children's days, including their naps. I never stop asking the question, where are we going? But it no longer frustrates me that I do not know the answer.

My personal intellectual activity is more limited than I might choose if I were left to my own devices, but I tell myself that there are only so many hours in the day. Richard, Michael, and I engage often in lively conversation, so there is certainly no dearth of stimulation. But neither of them has much interest in some intellectual areas that have always been a part of my life. My skills in languages and linguistics, for example, have been a source of considerable pride for me since my earliest days in school. Several weeks ago I had a terrifying dream in which I had forgotten how to write or speak in anything but English. For two weeks thereafter I spent two hours by myself each day, not just reviewing my beloved French, but also studying Italian and Japanese as well.

One afternoon last month Richard projected on the black screen a Raman external telescope output that included our Sun and another thousand stars in the field of view. The sun was the brightest of the objects, but just barely. Richard reminded Michael and me that we are already more than twelve *trillion* kilometers away from our oceanic home planet in close orbit around that insignificant distant star.

Later the same evening we watched *Eleanor the Queen*, one of the thirty or so movies originally carried onboard the Newton to entertain the cosmonaut crew. The movie was loosely based on my father's successful novels about Eleanor of Aquitaine and was filmed in many of the locations that I had visited with my father when I was an adolescent. The final scenes of the movie, showing the years before Eleanor died, all took place in L'Abbaye de Fontevrault. I remember being fourteen years old and standing in the abbey beside my father opposite the carved effigy of Eleanor, my hands trembling with emotion as I clutched his. "You were a great woman," I once said to the spirit of the queen who had dominated twelfth century history in France and England, "and you have set an example for me to follow. I will not disappoint you."

That night, after Richard was asleep and while Katie was temporarily quiet, I thought about the day again and was filled with a deep sorrow, a sense of loss that I could not quite articulate. The juxtaposition of the retreating Sun and the image of myself as a teenager, making bold promises to a queen who had been dead for almost a thousand years, reminded me that everything I had ever known before Rama is now finished. My two new daughters will never see any of the places that meant so much to me and Genevieve. They will never know the smell of freshly mown grass in springtime, the radiant beauty of the flowers, the songs of the birds, or the glory of the full moon rising out of the ocean. They will not know the planet Earth at all, or any of its inhabitants, except for this small and motley crew they will call their family, a meager representation of the overflowing life on a blessed planet.

That night I wept quietly for several minutes, knowing even as I was weeping that by morning I would again be wearing my optimistic face. After all, it could be much worse. We have the essentials: food, water, shelter, clothing, good health, companionship, and, of course, love. Love is the most important ingredient for the happiness of any human life, either on Earth or on Rama. If Simone and Katie learn only of love from the world we've left behind, it will be enough.

7

Today was unusual in every respect. First, I announced as
soon as everyone was awake that we were going to dedicate the day
to the memory of Eleanor of Aquitaine, who died, if the historians
are correct and we have properly tracked the calendar, exactly one
thousand years ago today. To my delight, the entire family supported the idea and both Richard and Michael immediately volunteered to help with the festivities. Michael, whose art history unit
has now been replaced by one on cooking, suggested that he prepare
a special medieval brunch in honor of the queen. Richard dashed
off with TB, whispering to me that the little robot was going to
return as Henry Plantagenet.

I had developed a short history lesson for Simone, introducing
her to Eleanor and the twelfth century world. She was unusually
attentive. Even Katie, who never sits still for longer than five
minutes, was cooperative and didn't interrupt us. She played quietly
with her baby toys most of the morning. Simone asked me at the
end of the lesson why Queen Eleanor had died. When I responded
that the queen had died of old age, my three-year-old daughter then
asked if Queen Eleanor had "gone to heaven."

"Where did you get that idea?" I asked Simone.

"From Uncle Michael," she replied. "He told me that good
people go to heaven when they die and bad people go to hell."

"Some people believe there is a heaven," I said after a reflective pause. "Others believe in what's called reincarnation, where people come back and live again as a different person or even as a different kind of animal. Some other people believe that each special life is a unique miracle, awakening from conception to birth, and going to sleep forever at death." I smiled and tousled her hair.

"What do you believe, Mama?" my daughter then asked.

I felt something very close to panic. I temporized with a few comments while I tried to figure out what to say. An expression from my favorite T. S. Eliot poem, "to lead you to an overwhelming question," whisked in and out of my mind. Luckily I was rescued.

"Fare thee well, young lady." The little robot TB, dressed in what was supposed to pass for medieval riding garb, walked into the room and informed Simone that he was Henry Plantagenet, king of England, and husband of Queen Eleanor. Simone's smile brightened. Katie looked up and grinned.

"The queen and I built a grand empire," the robot said, making an expansive gesture with his little arms, "that eventually included all of England, Scotland, Ireland, Wales, and half of what is now France." TB recited a prepared lecture with gusto, amusing Simone and Katie with his winks and hand gestures. He then reached in his pocket and pulled out a miniature knife and fork, claiming that he had introduced the concept of eating utensils to the "barbaric English."

"But why did you put Queen Eleanor in prison?" Simone asked after the robot was finished. I smiled. She had indeed paid attention to her history lesson. The robot's head pivoted and looked in Richard's direction. Richard held up a finger, indicating a brief wait, and rushed out into the corridor. In no more than a minute TB, a.k.a. Henry II, returned. The robot walked over to Simone. "I fell in love with another woman," he said, "and Queen Eleanor was angry. To get even with me, she turned my sons against me. . . ."

A short time later Richard and I were involved in a mild argument about the *real* reasons why Henry imprisoned Eleanor (we have discovered many times that we each learned a different version of Anglo-French history) when we heard a distant but unmistakable shriek. Within moments all five of us were topside. The shriek repeated.

We looked up in the sky above us. A solitary avian was flying a wide pattern a few hundred meters above the tops of the skyscrapers. We hurried over to the ramparts, beside the Cylindrical Sea, so we could have a better look. Once, twice, three times the great creature flew around the perimeter of the island. At the end of each loop the avian emitted a single long shriek. Richard waved his arms and shouted throughout the flight, but there was no indication that he was noticed.

The children became restless after about an hour. We agreed that Michael would take them back to the lair and Richard and I would stay as long as there was any possibility of contact. The bird continued flying in the same pattern. "Do you think it's looking for something?" I asked Richard.

"I don't know," he said, shouting again and waving at the avian as it reached the point in its loop where it was closest to us. This time it changed course, inscribing long graceful arcs in its helical descent. As it grew closer, Richard and I could see both its gray velvet underbelly and the two bright, cherry-red rings around its neck.

"It's our friend," I whispered to Richard, remembering the avian leader who had agreed to transport us across the Cylindrical Sea four years earlier.

But this avian was not the healthy, robust creature that had flown in the center of the formation when we had escaped from New York. This bird was skinny and emaciated, its velvet dirty and unkempt. "It's sick," Richard said as the bird landed about twenty meters away from us.

The avian jabbered something softly and jerked its head around nervously, as if it were expecting more company. Richard took one step toward it and the creature waved its wings, flapped them once, and backed up a few meters. "What food do we have available," Richard said in a low voice, "that is chemically most like the manna melon?"

I shook my head. "We don't have any food at all except last night's chicken— Wait," I said, interrupting myself, "we do have that green punch the children like. It looks like the liquid in the center of the manna melon."

Richard was gone before I had finished my sentence. During the ten minutes until he returned, the avian and I stared silently at one another. I tried to focus my mind on friendly thoughts, hoping that somehow my good intentions would be communicated through my eyes. Once I did see the avian change its expression, but of course I had no idea what either expression meant.

Richard returned carrying one of our black bowls filled with the green punch. He set the bowl in front of us and pointed at it as we backed away six or eight meters. The avian approached it in small, halting steps, stopping eventually right in front of the bowl. The bird dropped its beak into the liquid, took a small sip, and then threw its head back to swallow. Apparently the punch was all right, for the liquid was drained in less than a minute. When the avian was finished, it backed up two steps, spread its wings to their full extent, and made a full circular turn.

"Now we should say you're welcome," I said, extending my hand to Richard. We executed our circular turn, as we had done when we had said good-bye and thank you four years earlier, and bowed slightly in the avian's direction when we were finished.

Both Richard and I thought that the creature smiled, but we readily admitted later that we might have imagined it. The gray velvet avian spread its wings, lifted off the ground, and soared over our heads into the air.

"Where do you think it's going?" I asked Richard.

"It's dying," he replied softly. "It's taking one last look around the world it has known."

6 January 2205

Today is my birthday. I am now forty-one years old. Last night I had another of my vivid dreams. I was very old. My hair was completely gray and my face was heavily wrinkled. I was living in a castle—somewhere near the Loire, not too far from Beauvois—with two grown daughters (neither of whom looked, in the dream, like Simone or Katie or Genevieve) and three grandsons. The boys were all teenagers, healthy physically, but there was something wrong with each of them. They were all dull, maybe even retarded. I remember in the dream trying to explain to them how the molecule of hemoglobin carries oxygen from the pulmonary system to the tissues. None of them could understand what I was saying.

I woke up from the dream in a depression. It was the middle of the night and everyone else in the family was asleep. As I often do, I walked down the corridor to the nursery to make certain that the girls were still covered by their light blankets. Simone hardly ever moves at night but Katie, as usual, had thrown her blanket off with her thrashing around. I put the cover back over Katie and then sat down in one of the chairs.

What is bothering me? I wondered. *Why have I been having so many dreams about children and grandchildren?* One day last week I made a joking reference to the possibility of having a third child and Richard, who is going through another of his extended gloomy periods, almost jumped out of his skin. I think he's still sorry I talked him into having Katie. I dropped the subject immediately, not wanting to provoke another of his nihilistic tirades.

Would I really want another baby at this juncture? Does it make any sense at all, given the situation in which we find ourselves? Putting aside for the moment any personal reasons I might have for giving birth to a third child, there is a powerful biological argument for continuing to reproduce. Our best guess at our destiny is that we will never have any future contact with other members of the human species. If we are the last in our line, it would be wise for us to pay heed to one of the fundamental tenets of evolution: Maximum genetic variation produces the highest probability of survival in an uncertain environment.

After I had thoroughly awakened from my dream last night, my mind carried the scenario even further. *Suppose,* I told myself, *that Rama is really not going anywhere, at least not soon, and that we will spend the rest of our lives in our current conditions. Then, in all likelihood, Simone and Katie will outlive the three of us adults. What will happen next?* I asked. *Unless we have somehow saved some semen from either Michael or Richard (and both the biological and sociological problems would be formidable), my daughters will not be able to reproduce. They themselves may arrive at paradise or nirvana or some other world, but they will eventually perish and the genes they carry will die with them.*

But suppose, I continued, *that I give birth to a son. Then the two girls will have a male companion their age and the problem of succeeding generations will be dramatically lessened.*

It was at this point in my thought pattern that a truly crazy idea jumped into my brain. One of my major areas of specialty during my medical training was genetics, especially hereditary defects. I remembered my case studies of the royal families of Europe between the fifteenth and eighteenth centuries and the many "inferior" individuals produced from the excessive inbreeding. A son produced by Richard and me would have the same genetic ingredients as Simone and Katie. That son's children with either of the girls, our grandchildren, would have a very high risk of defects. A son produced by *Michael* and me, on the other hand, would share only half his genes with the girls and, if my memory of the data serves me correctly, his offspring with Simone or Katie would have a drastically lower defect risk.

I immediately rejected this outrageous thought. It did not, however, go away. Later in the night, when I should have been sleeping, my mind returned to the same topic. *What if I become pregnant by Richard again*, I asked myself, *and I have a third girl? Then it will be necessary to repeat the entire process. I'm already forty-one. How many more years do I have before the onset of menopause, even if I delay it chemically?* On the basis of the two data points thus far, there is no evidence that Richard can produce a boy at all. We could establish a laboratory to permit male sperm selection from his semen, but it would take a monumental effort on our part and months of detailed interaction with the Ramans. And there would still remain the issues of sperm preservation and delivery to the ovaries.

I thought through the various proven techniques of altering the natural sex selection process (the man's diet, type and frequency of intercourse, timing with respect to ovulation, etc.) and concluded that Richard and I would probably have a good chance of producing a boy naturally, if we were very careful. But at the back of my mind the thought persisted that the odds would be still more favorable if Michael were the father. After all, he had two sons (out of three children) as a result of random behavior. However much I might be able to improve the probabilities with Richard, the same techniques with Michael would virtually guarantee a son.

Before I fell back asleep I considered briefly the impracticality of the entire idea. A foolproof method of artificial insemination (which I would be required to supervise, even though I was the subject) would have to be devised. Could we do that, in our current situation, and *guarantee* both the sex and the health of the embryo? Even hospitals on Earth, with all the resources at their command, are not always successful. The other alternative was to have sex with Michael. Although I did not find that thought unpleasant, the sociological ramifications seemed so great that I abandoned the idea altogether.

(Six hours later.) The men surprised me tonight with a special dinner. Michael is becoming quite a cook. The food tasted, as advertised, like beef Wellington, although it looked more like creamed spinach. Richard and Michael also served a red liquid that was labeled wine. It wasn't terrible, so I drank it, discovering much to my surprise that it contained some alcohol and I actually felt high.

All of us adults were, in fact, slightly tipsy by the end of the dinner. The girls, Simone especially, were puzzled by our behavior. During our dessert of coconut pie, Michael told me that 41 was a "very special number." He then explained to me that it was the largest prime that started a long quadratic sequence of other primes. When I asked him what a quadratic sequence was, he laughed and said he didn't know. He did, however, write out the forty-element sequence he was talking about: 41, 43, 47, 53, 61, 71, 83, 97, 113 . . . , concluding with the number 1,601. He assured me that every one of the forty numbers in the sequence was a prime. "Therefore," he said with a twinkle, "forty-one must be a magic number."

While I was laughing, our resident genius Richard looked at the numbers and then, after no more than a minute of playing with his computer, explained to Michael and me why the sequence was called "quadratic." "The second differences are constant," he said, showing us what he meant with an example. "Therefore the entire sequence can be generated by a simple quadratic expression. Take $f(N) = N^2 - N + 41$," he continued, "where N is any integer from 0 through 40. That function will generate your entire sequence.

"Better still," he said with a laugh, "consider $f(N) = N^2 - 81N + 1681$, where N is an integer running from 1 to 80. This quadratic formula starts at the tail end of your string of numbers, $f(1) = 1601$, and proceeds through the sequence in decreasing order first. It reverses itself at $f(40) = f(41) = 41$, and then generates your entire array of numbers again in increasing order."

Richard smiled. Michael and I just stared at him in awe.

13 March 2205

Katie had her second birthday today and everyone was in a good mood, Richard especially. He does like his little girl, even though she manipulates him outrageously. For her birthday he took her over to the octospider lair cover and they rattled the grills together. Both Michael and I expressed our disapproval, but Richard laughed and winked at Katie.

At dinner Simone played a short piano piece that Michael has been teaching her and Richard served a quite remarkable wine—a Raman chardonnay, he called it—with our poached salmon. In Rama poached salmon looks like scrambled eggs on Earth, which is a bit confusing, but we continue to adhere to our convention of labeling foods according to their tastes.

I'm feeling buoyantly happy, even though I must admit that I am slightly nervous about my coming discussion with Richard. He is very upbeat at the present time, mostly because he's busily working on not one, but two major projects. Not only is he making liquid concoctions whose taste and alcohol content rival the fine wines of the planet Earth, but also he is creating a new set of twenty-centimeter robots based on the characters from the plays of the twentieth century Nobel laureate Samuel Beckett. Michael and I have been urging Richard to reincarnate his Shakespeare troupe for several years, but the memory of his lost friends has always stopped him. But a new playwright—that's a different question. He has already finished the four characters in *Endgame*. Tonight the children laughed gleefully when the old folks "Nagg" and "Nell" rose out of their tiny garbage cans shouting, "My pap. Bring me my pap."

I am definitely going to present to Richard my idea of having a son with Michael as the father. He will, I am certain, appreciate the logic and the science of the suggestion, although I can hardly expect him to be terribly enthusiastic about it. Of course I have not mentioned my idea at all to Michael yet. He does know I have something serious on my mind, however, because I have asked him if he would look after the girls this afternoon while Richard and I go topside for a picnic and a talk.

My nervousness about this issue is probably unwarranted. It is doubtless based on a definition of proper behavior that simply has no application to our present situation. Richard is feeling good these days. His wit has been very sharp lately. He may throw a few sharp zingers at me during our discussion, but I bet he will be in favor of the idea at the end.

8

This has been the spring of our dis-
content. Oh, Lord, what fools
we mortals be. Richard, Richard, please come back.

Where to start? And how to begin? Do I dare to eat a peach? In
a minute there are visions and revisions that a minute . . . In the next
room Michael and Simone come and go, talking of Michelangelo.

My father always told me that everyone makes mistakes. Why
did mine have to be so colossal? The idea made good sense. My
left brain said it was logical. But deep down inside the human being,
reason does not always carry the day. Emotions are not rational.
Jealousy is not the output of a computer program.

There were plenty of warnings. That first afternoon, as we sat
beside the Cylindrical Sea and had our "picnic," I could tell from
Richard's eyes that there was a problem. *Uh-oh, back off, Nicole*, I
said to myself.

But later he seemed so reasonable. "Of course," Richard said
that same afternoon, "what you are suggesting is the genetically
correct thing to do. I will go with you to tell Michael. Let's get this
over as fast as we can, hoping one encounter will be all that is
necessary."

I felt elated at the time. It never occurred to me that Michael
might balk. "It would be a sin," he said in the evening, after the

girls were asleep, within seconds after he understood what we were proposing.

Richard took the offensive, arguing that the entire concept of sin was an anachronism even on Earth and that Michael was just being silly. "Do you really want me to do this?" Michael asked Richard directly at the end of the conversation.

"No," Richard answered after a brief hesitation, "but it's clearly in the best interests of our children." I should have paid more attention to the "no."

It never occurred to me that my plan might not work. I tracked my ovulation cycle very carefully. When the designated night finally arrived, I informed Richard and he stalked out of the lair for one of his long hikes in Rama. Michael was nervous and fighting his feelings of guilt, but even in my worst doomsday scenario I had not imagined that he might be unable to have intercourse with me.

When we took off our clothes (in the dark, so Michael would not feel uncomfortable) and lay beside each other on the mats, I discovered that his body was rigid and tense. I kissed him on the forehead and cheeks. Then I tried to loosen him up by rubbing his back and neck. After about thirty minutes of touching (but nothing that would be considered sexual foreplay), I snuggled my body against his in a suggestive way. It was obvious we had a problem. His penis was still completely flaccid.

I did not know what to do. My initial thought, which of course was completely irrational, was that Michael did not find me attractive. I felt terrible, as if someone had slapped me in the face. All my repressed feelings of inadequacy burst to the surface and I was surprisingly angry. Luckily I didn't say anything (neither of us talked during this entire period) and Michael couldn't see my face in the dark. But my body language must have signaled my disappointment.

"I'm sorry," he said softly.

"It's all right," I answered, trying to be nonchalant.

I propped myself up on an elbow and caressed his forehead with my other hand. I expanded my light massage, letting my fingers run gently around his face, neck, and shoulders. Michael was completely passive. He lay on his back without moving, his eyes closed most of the time. Although I am certain he was enjoying the rub, he neither said anything nor uttered any murmurs of pleasure. By this time I was becoming exceedingly anxious. I found myself wanting Michael to caress *me*, to tell *me* that I was all right.

At length I rolled over with part of my body across his. I let my breasts drop gently on his torso while my right hand played with the hair on his chest. I leaned up to kiss him on the lips, intending to arouse him elsewhere with my left hand, but he pulled away quickly and then sat up.

"I can't do this," Michael said, shaking his head.

"Why not?" I asked quietly, my body now in an awkward position beside him.

"It's wrong," he answered with great solemnity.

I tried several times in the next few minutes to start a conversation, but Michael did not want to talk. Eventually, because there was nothing else for me to do, I dressed silently in the dark. Michael barely managed a meager "Good night" when I left.

I did not return immediately to my room. Once I was out in the corridor I realized that I was not yet ready to confront Richard. I leaned against the wall and struggled with the powerful emotions engulfing me. Why had I assumed everything would be so simple? And what would I tell Richard now?

From the sound of Richard's breathing I knew that he was not asleep when I entered our room. If I had had more courage, I might have told him right then what had happened with Michael. But it was easier to ignore it for the moment. That was a serious mistake.

The next two days were strained. Nobody mentioned what Richard had once referred to as the "fertilization event." The men tried to act as if everything was normal. After dinner the second night I persuaded Richard to take a walk with me while Michael put the girls to bed.

Richard was explaining the chemistry of his new wine fermentation process as we stood on the ramparts overlooking the Cylindrical Sea. At one point I interrupted him and took his hand. "Richard," I said, my eyes searching for love and reassurance in his, "this is very difficult. . . ." My voice trailed off.

"What is it, Nikki?" he asked, forcing a smile.

"Well," I answered, "it's Michael. You see," I blurted out, "nothing really happened. . . . He couldn't . . ."

Richard stared at me for a long time. "You mean he's impotent?" he asked.

I nodded first and then completely confused him by shaking my head. "Probably not really," I stammered, "but he was the other night with me. I think he's just too tense or feels guilty or maybe it's been too long—" I stopped myself, realizing I was saying too much.

Richard gazed across the sea for what seemed like an eternity. "Do you want to try again?" he said eventually in a completely expressionless voice. He did not turn to look at me.

"I . . . I don't know," I answered. I squeezed his hand. I was going to say something else, to ask him if he could deal with the situation if I tried one more time, but Richard abruptly walked away from me. "Let me know when you make up your mind," he said tersely.

For a week or two I was certain that I was going to abandon the entire idea. Slowly, very slowly, a semblance of cheer returned to our little family. The night after my period was over Richard and I made love twice for the first time in a year. He seemed especially pleased and was very talkative as we cuddled after the second intercourse.

"I must say I was really worried there for a while," he said. "The thought of your having sex with Michael, even for supposedly logical reasons, was driving me crazy. I know it doesn't make rational sense, but I was terribly afraid that you might like it—do you understand?—and that somehow our relationship might be affected."

Richard was obviously assuming that I wasn't going to try again to become pregnant with Michael's child. I didn't argue with him that night because I too was momentarily content. A few days later, however, when I began reading about impotence in my medical books, I realized myself that I was still determined to proceed with my plan.

During the week before I ovulated again, Richard was busy brewing his wine (and maybe tasting it a bit more often than necessary—more than once he was a little drunk before dinner) and creating little robots out of Samuel Beckett's characters. My attention was focused on impotence. My curriculum at medical school had virtually ignored the subject. And since my own sexual experience has been comparatively limited, I had never personally been exposed to it before. I was surprised to learn that impotence is an extremely common malady, primarily psychological but very often with an exacerbating physical component as well, and that there are many well-defined treatment patterns, all of which focus on lessening the "performance anxiety" in the man.

Richard saw me preparing my urine for ovulation testing one morning. He didn't say anything, but I could tell from his face that he was hurt and disappointed. I wanted to reassure him, but the children were in the room and I was afraid there might be a scene.

I didn't tell Michael that we were going to make a second attempt. I thought that his anxiety would be reduced if he didn't have time to think about it. My plan almost worked. I went with Michael to his room, after we had put the children to bed, and explained to him what was happening while we undressed. He had the beginnings of an erection and, despite his mild protests, I moved quickly to sustain it. I am certain that we would have been successful if Katie had not started screaming "Mommy, Mommy" just when we were ready to begin intercourse.

Of course I left Michael and ran down the corridor to the nursery. Richard was already there. He was holding Katie in his arms. Simone was sitting up on her mat, rubbing her eyes. The three of them all stared at my naked body in the doorway. "I had a terrible dream," Katie said, holding tightly to Richard. "An octospider was eating me."

I walked into the room. "Are you feeling better now?" I asked, reaching out to take Katie. Richard continued to hold her and she made no effort to come to me. After an uncomfortable moment I went over to Simone and draped my arm across her shoulder.

"Where are your pajamas, Mother?" my four-year-old asked. Most of the time both Richard and I sleep in the Raman version of pajamas. The girls are quite accustomed to my naked body—the three of us shower together virtually every day—but at night, when I come into the nursery, I'm almost always wearing my pajamas.

I was going to give Simone a flippant answer when I noticed that Richard too was staring at me. His eyes were definitely hostile. "I can take care of things here," he said harshly. "Why don't you finish what you were doing?"

I returned to Michael to try one more time to achieve intercourse and conception. It was a bad decision. I made a futile attempt to arouse Michael for a couple of minutes and then he pushed my hand away. "It's useless," he said. "I'm almost sixty-three years old and I haven't had intercourse for five years. I never masturbate and I consciously try not to think about sex. My erection earlier was just a temporary stroke of luck." He was silent for almost a minute. "I'm sorry, Nicole," he then added, "but it's not going to work."

We lay silently side by side for several minutes. I was dressing and preparing to leave when I noticed that Michael had fallen into the rhythmic breathing pattern that precedes sleep. I suddenly remembered from my reading that men with psychological impotence often have erections during their sleep, and my mind dreamed up another crazy idea. I laid awake beside Michael for quite a while, waiting until I was certain he was in a deep sleep.

I stroked him very softly at first. I was delighted that he responded very quickly. After a while I slightly increased the vigor of my massage, but I was extremely careful not to wake him up. When he was definitely ready I prepared myself and moved over on top of him. I was only moments away from achieving intercourse when I jostled him too roughly and he awakened. I tried to continue, but in my haste I must have hurt him, for he uttered a yelp and looked at me with wild, startled eyes. Within seconds his erection had vanished.

I rolled over on my back and heaved a deep sigh. I was terribly disappointed. Michael was asking me questions, but I was too distraught to answer. Tears suffused my eyes. I dressed in a hurry, kissed Michael lightly on the forehead, and stumbled out into the corridor. I stood there for another five minutes before I had the strength to return to Richard.

My husband was still working. He was down on his knees beside Pozzo, from *Waiting for Godot*. The little robot was in the middle of one of his long, rambling speeches about the uselessness of everything. Richard ignored me at first. Then, after silencing Pozzo, he turned around. "Do you think you took long enough?" he asked sarcastically.

"It still didn't work," I answered dejectedly. "I guess—"

"Don't give me that shit," Richard suddenly shouted angrily. "I'm not *that* stupid. Do you expect me to believe that you spent *two hours* naked with him and nothing happened? I know about you women. You think that . . ."

I don't remember the rest of what he said. I do recall my terror as he advanced toward me, his eyes full of anger. I thought he was going to hit me and I braced myself. Tears burst from my eyes and rolled down my cheeks. Richard called me horrible names and even made a racist slur. He was insane. When he raised his arm in a fury I bolted from the room, rushing down the corridor toward the stairs to New York. I nearly ran over little Katie, who had been awakened by the shouting and was standing dumbfounded at the door of the nursery.

It was light in Rama. I walked around, crying intermittently, for most of an hour. I was furious with Richard, but I was also deeply unhappy with myself. In his rage Richard had said that I was "obsessed" with this idea of mine and that it was just a "clever excuse" to have intercourse with Michael so that I could be the "queen bee of the hive." I hadn't replied to any of his rantings. Was there even a smidgin of truth in his accusation? Was any part of my excitement about the project a desire on my part to have sex with Michael?

I convinced myself that my motivations had all been "proper," whatever that means, but that I had been incredibly stupid about this entire affair from the very beginning. I, of all people, should have known that what I was suggesting was impossible. Certainly after I saw Richard's initial response (and Michael's too, for that matter), I should have immediately forsaken the idea. Maybe Richard was right in some ways. Maybe I am stubborn, even obsessed with the idea of providing maximum genetic variation to our offspring. But I know for certain that I did not concoct the entire thing just so I could have sex with Michael.

It was dark in our room when I returned. I changed into my pajamas and plopped down, exhausted, on my mat. After a few seconds Richard rolled over, hugged me fiercely, and said, "My darling, Nicole, I'm so so sorry. Please forgive me."

I have not heard his voice since then. He has been gone now for six days. I slept soundly that night, unaware that Richard was packing his things and leaving me a note. At seven o'clock in the morning, an alarm sounded. There was a message filling the black screen. It said, "FOR NICOLE DES JARDINS ONLY—Push K when you want to read." The children were not yet awake, so I pushed the *K* button on the keyboard.

Dearest Nicole, this is the most difficult letter I have ever written in my life. I am temporarily leaving you and the family. I know that this will create considerable hardship for you, Michael, and the girls, but believe me, it is the only way. After last night it is apparent to me that there is no other solution.

My darling, I love you will all my heart and *know*, when my brain is in control of my emotions, that what you are trying to do is in the best interests of the family. I feel terrible about the accusations that I made last night. I feel even worse about all the names I called you, especially the racial epithets and my frequent use of the word "bitch." I hope that you can forgive me, even though I'm not certain I can forgive myself, and will remember my love for you instead of my insane, unbridled anger.

Jealousy is a terrible thing. "It doth mock the meat it feeds upon" is an understatement. Jealousy is completely consuming, totally irrational, and absolutely debilitating. The most wonderful people in the world are nothing but raging animals when trapped in the throes of jealousy.

Nicole, darling, I did not tell you the complete truth last year about the end of my marriage to Sarah. I suspected for months that she was seeing other men on those nights she was spending in London. There were plenty of telltale signs—her uneven interest in sex, new clothes that were never worn with me, sudden fascinations with new positions or different sexual practices, phone calls with nobody on the other end—

but I loved her so madly, and was so certain that our marriage would be over if I confronted her, that I didn't do anything until I was enraged by my jealousy.

Actually, as I would lie in my bed at Cambridge and picture Sarah having intercourse with another man, my jealousy would become so powerful that I could not fall asleep until I had imagined Sarah dead. When Mrs. Sinclair called me that night and I knew I could no longer pretend that Sarah was faithful, I went to London with the express intention of killing both my wife and her lover.

Luckily I had no gun and my rage upon seeing them together made me forget the knife I had placed in the pocket of my overcoat. But I definitely *would* have killed them if the melee had not aroused the neighbors and I had not been restrained.

You may be wondering what all this has to do with you. You see, my love, each of us develops definitive patterns of behavior in his life. My pattern of insane jealousy was already present before I met you. During the two times that you have gone to be intimate with Michael, I have been unable to stop the memories of Sarah from returning. I *know* you are not Sarah, and that you are *not* cheating on me, but nevertheless, my emotions return in that same lunatic pattern. In a very strange sense, because the idea of your betraying me is so impossible to conceive, I feel worse, *more* frightened, when you are with Michael than I did when Sarah was with Hugh Sinclair or any of her other actor friends.

I hope some of this makes sense. I am leaving because I cannot control my jealousy, even though I acknowledge it to be irrational. I do not want to become like my father, drinking away my misery and ruining the lives of everyone around me. I sense that you will achieve this conception, one way or another, and I would prefer to spare you my bad behavior during the process.

I expect that I will be back soon, unless I encounter unforeseen dangers in my explorations, but I do not know exactly when. I need a period of healing, so that I can again be a solid contributor to our family. Tell the girls that I am off on a journey. Be kind especially to Katie— she will miss me the most.

I love you, Nicole. I know that it will be difficult for you to understand why I am leaving, but please try.

Richard

13 May 2205

Today I spent five hours topside in New York searching for Richard. I went over to the pits, to both lattices, to all three plazas. I walked the perimeters of the island along the ramparts. I shook the grill on the octospider lair and descended briefly into the land of the avians. Everywhere I called his name. I remember that Richard found me five years ago because of the navigation beacon he had placed on his Shakespearean robot Prince Hal. I could have used a beacon today.

There were no signs of Richard anywhere. I believe that he has left the island. Richard is an excellent swimmer—he could easily have made it across to the Northern Hemicylinder—but what about the weird creatures inhabiting the Cylindrical Sea? Did they let him across?

Come back, Richard. I miss you. I love you.

He had obviously been thinking about leaving for several days. He had updated and arranged our catalog of interactions with the Ramans to make it as easy as possible for Michael and me. He took the largest of our packs and his best friend TB, but he left the Beckett robots behind.

Our family meals have been dreadful affairs since Richard left. Katie is nearly always angry. She wants to know when her daddy will be back and why he has been gone so long. Michael and Simone endure their sorrow in quiet. Their bond continues to deepen—they seem to be able to comfort one another quite well. For my part, I have tried to pay more attention to Katie, but I am no substitute for her beloved daddy.

The nights are terrible. I do not sleep. I go over and over all my interactions with Richard the last two months and relive all my mistakes. His letter before departing was very revealing. I never would have thought that his earlier difficulties with Sarah would have had the slightest impact on his marriage to me, but I recognize now what he was saying about patterns.

There are patterns in my emotional life as well. My mother's death when I was only ten taught me the terror of abandonment. Fear of losing a strong connection has made intimacy and trust difficult for me. Since my mother, I have lost Genevieve, my father, and now, at least temporarily, Richard. Each time the pattern recurs all the chimeras of the past are reactivated. When I cried myself to sleep two nights ago, I realized that I was missing not only Richard, but also Mother, Genevieve, and my marvelous father. I was feeling each of those losses all over again. So I can understand how my being with Michael could trigger Richard's painful memories of Sarah.

The process of learning never stops. Here I am, forty-one years old, and I am discovering another facet of the truth about human relationships. I have obviously wounded Richard deeply. It doesn't matter that there is no logical basis for Richard's concern that my sleeping with Michael might lead to an alienation of my affection for him. Logic has no application here. Perception and feeling are what count.

I had forgotten how devastating loneliness can be. Richard and I have been together for five years. He might not have had all the attributes of my prince charming, but he has been a wonderful companion and is, without a doubt, the smartest human being I have ever met. It would be an immeasurable tragedy if he were never to return. I grieve when I think, even for a moment, that I may have seen him for the last time.

At nights, when I am especially lonely, I often read poetry. Baudelaire and Eliot have been my favorites since my university days, but the last few evenings I have been finding comfort in the poems of Benita Garcia. During her days as a cadet at the Space Academy in Colorado, her wild passion for life caused her lots of pain. She threw herself into her cosmonaut studies and the arms of the men surrounding her with equal élan. When Benita was called before the cadet disciplinary committee for no transgression except her uninhibited sexuality, she realized how schizophrenic men were where sex was concerned.

Most of the literary critics prefer her first volume of poetry, *Dreams of a Mexican Girl*, which established her reputation when she was still a teenager, over the wiser, less lyrical book of poems she published during her final year at the academy. With Richard now gone and my mind still struggling to understand what has really occurred during these last months, it is Benita's poems of late adolescent angst and questioning that resonate with me. Her path to adulthood was extremely difficult. Although her work remained rich in images, Benita was no longer Pollyanna walking among the ruins at Uxmal. Tonight I read several times one of her university poems that I particularly like.

> My dresses brighten up my room,
> Like desert flowers after rain.
> You come tonight, my newest love,
> But which me do you want to see?

The pale pastels are best for books,
My blues and greens, an evening make,
As friend, or even wife to be.
But if it's sex that's in your mind,
Then red or black and darkened eyes,
Become the whore that I must be.

My childhood dreams were not like this,
My prince came only for a kiss,
Then carried me away from pain,
Can I not see him once again?
The masks offend me, college boy,
I wear my dress without much joy.
The price I pay to hold your hand,
Belittles me as you have planned.

9

14 December 2205 I guess I should celebrate, but I feel that I have won a Pyrrhic victory. I am finally pregnant with Michael's child. But what a cost. We still have heard nothing from Richard and I fear that I may have alienated Michael as well.

Michael and I each separately accepted the full responsibility for Richard's departure. I dealt with my culpability as well as I could, recognizing that I would have to put it behind me to be any kind of meaningful mother to the girls. Michael, on the other hand, responded to Richard's action and his own guilt by pouring himself into religious devotion. He is still reading his Bible at least twice every day. He prays before and after every meal, and often chooses not to take part in family activities so that he can "communicate" with God. The word *atonement* is currently very big in Michael's vocabulary.

He has swept Simone along in his reborn Christian zeal. My mild protests are essentially ignored. She loves the story of Jesus, even though she can't have more than the slightest notion of what it is really about. The miracles especially fascinate Simone. Like most children, she has no difficulty suspending her disbelief. Her mind never asks "how" when Jesus walks on the water or turns the water into wine.

My comments are not completely fair. I'm probably jealous of the rapport that exists between Michael and Simone. As her mother I should be delighted that they are so compatible. At least they have each other. Try as we might, poor Katie and I remain unable to make that deep connection.

Part of the problem is that Katie and I are both extremely stubborn. Although she is only two and a half years old, she already wants to control her own life. Take something simple, for example, like the planned set of activities for the day. I have been creating the schedules for everybody in the family since our first days in Rama. Nobody else has ever argued seriously with me, not even Richard. Michael and Simone always accept whatever I recommend—as long as there is ample unstructured time.

But Katie is a different story. If I schedule a walk topside in New York before an alphabet lesson, she wants to change the order. If I plan chicken for dinner, she wants pork or beef. We start virtually every morning with a fight about the activities for the day. When she doesn't like my decisions, Katie sulks, or pouts, or cries for her "daddy." It really hurts when she calls for Richard.

Michael says that I should acquiesce to her desires. He insists that it's just a phase of growing up. But when I point out to him that neither Genevieve nor Simone were ever like Katie, he smiles and shrugs.

Michael and I do not always agree on parenting techniques. We have had several interesting discussions about family life in our bizarre circumstances. Toward the end of one of the conversations, I was slightly miffed about Michael's assertion that I was "too strict" with the girls, so I decided to bring up the religion issue. I asked Michael why it was so important to him that Simone learn about the minutiae in Jesus' life.

"Someone has to carry on the tradition," he said vaguely.

"So you believe that there will be a tradition to carry on, that we are not going to drift forever in space and die one by one in terrifying loneliness."

"I believe that God has a plan for all human beings," he answered.

"But what is His plan for us?" I asked.

"We don't know," Michael replied. "Any more than those billions of people still back on Earth know what His plan is for them. The process of living is searching for His plan."

I shook my head and Michael continued. "You see, Nicole, it should be much easier for us. We have far fewer distractions. There is no excuse for our not remaining close to God. That's why my earlier preoccupations with food and art history are so difficult to forgive. In Rama, human beings have to make a major effort to fill up their time with something *other* than prayer and devotion."

I admit that his certitude annoys me at times. In our present circumstances, the life of Jesus seems to have no more relevance than the life of Attila the Hun or any other human being who has ever been alive on that distant planet two light-years away. We are no longer part of the human race. We are either doomed, or the beginning of what will essentially be a new species. Did Jesus die for all our sins as well, those of us who will never see the Earth again?

If Michael had not been a Catholic and programmed from birth in favor of procreation, I never would have convinced him to conceive a child. He had a hundred reasons why it was not the right thing to do. But in the end, maybe because I was disturbing his nightly devotions with my persistent attempts to persuade him, he finally consented. He warned me that it was highly likely that "it would never work" and that he "would not take any responsibility" for my frustration.

It took us three months to produce an embryo. During the first two ovulation cycles I was unable to arouse him. I tried laughter, body massage, music, food—everything mentioned in any of the articles about impotence. His guilt and tension were always stronger than my ardor. Fantasy finally provided the solution. When I suggested to Michael one night that he should imagine I was his wife Kathleen throughout the entire affair, he was finally able to sustain an erection. The mind is indeed a wonderful creation.

Even with fantasy, making love with Michael was not an easy task. In the first place, and this is probably an unkind thing for me to say, his preparations alone were enough to put any ordinary woman out of the mood. Just before he took off his clothes, Michael always offered a prayer to God. What did he pray for? It would be fascinating to know the answer.

Eleanor of Aquitaine's first husband, Louis VII of France, had been raised as a monk and only became king because of a historical accident. In my father's novel about Eleanor there is a long interior monologue in which she complains about making love "surrounded by solemnity and piety and the coarse cloth of the Cistercians." She longed for gaiety and laughter in the bedroom, for bawdy talk and wanton passion. I can understand why she divorced Louis and married Henry Plantagenet.

So I am now pregnant with the boy child (I hope) who will bring genetic variation to our progeny. It has been quite a struggle and almost certainly not worth it. Because of my desire to have Michael's child, Richard is gone and Michael is, at least temporarily, no longer the close friend and companion that he was during our first years on Rama. I have paid the price for my success. Now I must hope that this spacecraft does indeed have a destination.

1 March 2206

I repeated the partial genome test this morning to verify my initial results. There is no doubt about it. Our unborn baby boy definitely has Whittingham's syndrome. Fortunately there are no other identifiable defects, but Whittingham's is bad enough.

I showed the data to Michael when we had a few moments alone after breakfast. At first he didn't understand what I was telling him, but when I used the word *retarded*, he reacted immediately. I could tell that he was envisioning a child who would be completely unable to take care of himself. His concerns were only partially allayed when I explained that Whittingham's is nothing more than a learning disability, a simple failure of the electrochemical processes in the brain to operate properly.

When I performed the first partial genome test last week, I suspected Whittingham's, but since there was a possible ambiguity in the results, I didn't say anything to Michael. Before drawing a second amniotic sample, I wanted to review what was known about the condition. My abridged medical encyclopedia unfortunately did not contain enough information to satisfy me.

This afternoon, while Katie was napping, Michael and I asked Simone if she would read a book in the nursery for an hour or so. Our perfect angel readily complied. Michael was much calmer than he had been in the morning. He acknowledged that he had been devastated at first by the news about Benjy (Michael wants to name the child Benjamin Ryan O'Toole, after his grandfather). Apparently reading the book of Job had played a major role in helping him regain his perspective.

I explained to Michael that Benjy's mental development would be slow and tedious. He was comforted, however, when I informed him that many Whittingham's sufferers had eventually achieved twelve-year-old equivalency after twenty years of schooling. I assured Michael there would be no physical signs of the defect, as there are in Down's, and that since Whittingham's is a blocked recessive trait, there was little likelihood that any possible offspring would be affected before the third generation at the earliest.

"Is there any way of knowing which one of us has the syndrome in our genes?" Michael asked when we were near the end of our conversation.

"No," I replied. "It's a very difficult disorder to isolate because it apparently arises from several different defective genes. Only if the syndrome is active is the diagnosis straightforward. Even on Earth attempts to identify carriers have not been successful."

I started to tell him that since the disease was first diagnosed in 2068, there have been almost no cases in either Africa or Asia. It has been basically a Caucasian disorder, with the highest frequency of occurrence in Ireland. I decided Michael would learn this information soon enough (it is all in the main article in the medical encyclopedia—which he is reading now), and I didn't want him to feel any worse than he already did.

"Is there any cure?" he asked next.

"None for us," I said, shaking my head. "There was some indication in the last decade that genetic countermeasures could be effective, if used during the second trimester of pregnancy. However, the procedure is complicated, even on Earth, and can result in losing the fetus altogether."

That would have been a perfect time in the discussion for Michael to mention the word *abortion*. He didn't. His set of beliefs is so steadfast and unwavering that I'm certain he never even considered it. For him, abortion is an absolute wrong, on Rama as well as Earth. I found myself wondering if there were any conditions under which Michael would have considered an abortion. What if the baby had Down's syndrome and also was blind? Or had multiple congenital problems that guaranteed an early death?

If Richard had been here, we would have had a logical discussion about the advantages and disadvantages of an abortion. He would have created one of his famous Ben Franklin sheets, with pros and cons listed separately on the two sides of the large screen. I would have added a long list of emotional reasons (which Richard would have omitted in his original list) for not having an abortion, and in the end we almost certainly would have all agreed to bring Benjy into Rama. It would have been a rational, community decision.

I want to have this baby. But I also want Michael to reaffirm his commitment as Benjy's father. A discussion of the possibility of abortion would have elicited that renewed commitment. Blind acceptance of the rules of God or the church or any structured dogma can sometimes make it too easy for an individual to withhold his own support for a specific decision. I hope that Michael is not that kind of person.

10

30 August 2206   **B**enjy came early. Despite my re-peated assurances that he would look perfectly healthy, Michael seemed relieved when the boy was born three days ago with no physical abnormalities. It was another easy birth. Simone was surprisingly helpful during both the labor and delivery. For a girl who is not yet six years old, she is extremely mature.

Benjy also has blue eyes, but they're not as light as Katie's and I don't think they will stay blue. His skin is light brown, just a little darker than Katie's, but lighter than mine or Simone's. He weighed three and a half kilograms at birth and was fifty-two centimeters long.

Our world remains unchanged. We don't talk about it very much, but all of us except Katie have given up hope that Richard will ever return. We are headed for Raman winter again, with the long nights and the shorter days. Periodically either Michael or I goes topside and searches for some sign of Richard, but it's a mechanical ritual. We don't really expect to find anything. He has been gone now for sixteen months.

Michael and I now take turns computing our trajectory with the orbit determination program that Richard designed. In the beginning it took us several weeks to figure out how to use it, despite the fact that Richard had left explicit instructions with us. We reverify once a week that we are still headed in the direction of Sirius, with no other star system along our path.

Despite Benjy's presence, it seems that I have more time to myself than I have ever had before. I have been reading voraciously and have rekindled my fascination for the two heroines who dominated my adolescent mind and imagination. Why have Joan of Arc and Eleanor of Aquitaine always appealed so much to me? Because not only did they both display inner strength and self-sufficiency, but also each woman succeeded in a male-dominated world by ultimately relying on her own abilities.

I was a very lonely teenager. My physical surroundings at Beauvois were magnificent and my father's love was overflowing, but I spent virtually my entire adolescence by myself. In the back of my mind I was always terrified that death or marriage would take my precious father away from me. I wanted to make myself more self-contained to avoid the pain that would occur if I were ever separated from Father. Joan and Eleanor were perfect role models. Even today, I find reassurance in reading about their lives. Neither woman allowed the world around her to define what was really important in life.

Everyone's health continues to be good. This past spring, as much to keep myself busy as anything, I inserted a set of the leftover biometry probes in each of us and monitored the data for a few weeks. The monitoring process reminded me of the days of the Newton mission—can it really be more than six years since the twelve of us left the Earth to rendezvous with Rama?

Anyway, Katie was fascinated by the biometry. She would sit beside me while I was scanning Simone or Michael and ask dozens of questions about the data on the displays. In no time at all she understood how the system worked and what the warning files were all about. Michael has commented that she is extraordinarily bright. Like her father. Katie still misses Richard terribly.

Although Michael talks about feeling ancient, he is in excellent shape for a sixty-four-year-old man. He is very concerned about being physically active enough for the children and has been jogging twice a week since the beginning of my pregnancy. Twice a week. What a funny concept. We have held faithfully to our Earth calendar, even though it has absolutely no meaning here on Rama. The other night Simone asked about days, months, and years. As Michael was explaining the rotation of the Earth, the seasons of the year, and the orbit of the Earth around the Sun, I suddenly had a vision of a magnificent Utah sunset that I had shared with Genevieve on our trip to the American West. I wanted to tell Simone about it. But how can you explain a sunset to someone who has not seen the Sun?

The calendar reminds us of what we were. If we ever arrive at a new planet, with a real day and night instead of this artificial one in Rama, then we will most certainly abandon the Earth calendar. But for now, holidays, the passage of months, and most especially birthdays, all remind us of our roots on that beautiful planet we can no longer even find with the best Raman telescope.

Benjy is now ready to nurse. His mental capabilities may not be the best, but he certainly has no problem letting me know when he is hungry. Michael and I, by mutual consent, have not yet told Simone and Katie about their brother's condition. That he will take attention away from them while he is an infant will be difficult enough for them to handle. That his need for attention will continue, and even grow, when he becomes a toddler and a little boy is more than they can be expected to grasp at this point in their young lives.

13 March 2207

Katie is four years old today. When I asked her two weeks ago what she wanted for her birthday, she didn't hesitate a second. "I want my daddy back," she said.

She is a solitary, isolated little girl. Extremely quick to learn, she is also the moodiest child I have ever had. Richard was also extremely volatile. He would sometimes be so elated and exuberant that he couldn't contain himself, usually when he had just experienced something exciting for the first time. But his depressions were formidable. There were times when he would go a week or more without laughing or even smiling.

Katie has inherited his gift for mathematics. She can already add, subtract, multiply, and divide—at least with small numbers. Simone, who is certainly no slouch, appears more evenly talented. And more generally interested in a wide range of subjects. But Katie is certainly pressing her in math.

In the almost two years since Richard has been gone, I have tried without success to replace him in Katie's heart. The truth is that Katie and I clash. Our personalities are not compatible as mother and daughter. The individuality and wildness that I loved in Richard is threatening in Katie. Despite my best intentions, we always end up in a contest.

We could not, of course, produce Richard for Katie's birthday. But Michael and I did try very hard to have some interesting presents for her. Even though neither of us is particularly skilled at electronics, we did manage to create a small video game (it took many interactions with the Ramans to produce the right parts—and many nights working together to make something Richard probably could have finished in a day) called "Lost in Rama." We made it very simple, because Katie is only four years old. After playing with it for two hours she had exhausted all the options and had figured out how to get home to our lair from any starting point in Rama.

Our biggest surprise came tonight, when we asked her (this has become a tradition for us in Rama) what she would like to do on her birthday evening. "I want to go inside the avian lair," Katie said with a mischievous sparkle in her eyes.

We tried to talk her out of it by pointing out that the distance between the ledges was greater than her height. In response, Katie went over to the rope ladder of lattice material hanging at the side of the nursery and showed us that she could climb it. Michael smiled. "Some things she has inherited from her mother," he said.

"Please, Mom?" Katie then said in her precocious little voice. "Everything else is so boring. I want to look at the tank sentry myself, from only a few meters away."

Even though I had some misgivings, I walked over to the avian lair with Katie and told her to wait topside while I put the rope ladder in place. At the first landing, opposite the tank sentry, I stopped for a moment and looked across the chasm at that perpetual motion machine protecting the entry to the horizontal tunnel. *Are you always there?* I wondered. *And have you ever been replaced or repaired during all this time?*

"Are you ready, Mom?" I heard my daughter call from above. Before I could scramble up to meet her, Katie was already descending the ladder. I scolded her when I caught up with her at the second ledge, but she ignored me. She was terribly excited. "Did you see, Mom?" she said. "I did it by myself."

I congratulated her even though my mind was still reeling from a mental picture of Katie slipping off the ladder, banging into one of the ledges, and then careening into the bottomless depths of the vertical corridor. We continued down the ladder with my helping her from below until we reached the first landing and pair of horizontal tunnels. Across the chasm the tank sentry continued its repetitive motion. Katie was ecstatic.

"What's behind that tank thing?" she asked. "Who made it? What's it doing there? Did you really jump across this hole?"

In response to one of her questions, I turned and took several steps into the tunnel behind us, following my flashlight beam and assuming Katie was following me. Moments later, when I discovered that she was still standing back on the edge of the chasm, I froze with fear. I watched her pull a small object out of the pocket of her dress and throw it across the chasm at the tank sentry.

I yelled at Katie, but it was too late. The object hit the front of the tank. Immediately there was a loud pop like gunshots, and two metal projectiles smashed into the wall of the lair not more than a meter above her head.

"Yippee," Katie shouted as I jerked her back from the abyss. I was furious. My daughter began to cry. The noise in the lair was deafening.

She stopped crying abruptly several seconds later. "Did you hear it?" she asked.

"What?" I said, my heart still pounding wildly.

"Over there," she said. She pointed across the vertical corridor into the blackness behind the sentry. I shone the flashlight into the void, but we could see nothing.

We both stood absolutely still, holding hands. There *was* a sound coming from the tunnel behind the sentry. But it was at the very limit of my hearing, and I could not identify it.

"It's an avian," Katie said with conviction. "I can hear its wings flapping. *Yippee,*" she shouted again in her loudest voice.

The round ceased. Although we waited fifteen minutes before climbing out of the lair, we never heard anything else. Katie told Michael and Simone that we had heard an avian. I couldn't corroborate her story but chose not to argue with her. She was happy. It had been an eventful birthday.

8 March 2208

Patrick Erin O'Toole, a perfectly healthy baby in every respect, was born yesterday at 2:15 in the afternoon. The proud father is holding him at this very moment, smiling as my fingers dart across the keyboard on my electronic notebook.

It is late at night now. Simone put Benjy to sleep, as she does every night at nine o'clock, and then went to bed herself. She was very tired. She took care of Benjy without any help from anyone during my surprisingly long labor. Every time I would shout, Benjy would cry out in response and Simone would try to soothe him.

Katie has already claimed Patrick as her baby brother. She is very logical. If Benjy is Simone's, then Patrick must belong to Katie. At least she is showing some interest in another member of the family.

Patrick was not planned, but both Michael and I are delighted that he showed up to join our family. His conception was sometime late last spring, probably in the first month after Michael and I started sharing his bedroom at night. It was my idea that we should sleep together, although I'm certain that Michael had thought about it as well.

On the night that Richard had been gone for exactly two years, I was completely unable to sleep. I was feeling lonely, as usual. I tried to imagine sleeping all the rest of my nights by myself and I became very despondent. Just after midnight I walked down the corridor to Michael's room.

Michael and I have been relaxed and easy with each other from the beginning this time. I guess we were both ready. After Benjy's birth Michael was very busy helping me with all the children. During that period he eased up a little on his religious activities and made himself more accessible to all of us, including me. Eventually our natural compatibility reasserted itself. All that was left was for us both to acknowledge that Richard was never going to return.

Comfortable. That's the best way to describe my relationship with Michael. With Henry, it was ecstasy. With Richard, it was passion and excitement, a wild roller-coaster ride in life and bed. Michael comforts me. We sleep holding hands, the perfect symbol for our relationship. We make love rarely, but it is enough.

I have made some concessions. I even pray some, now and then, because it makes Michael happy. For his part, he has become more tolerant about exposing the children to ideas and value systems outside of his Catholicism. We have agreed that what we are seeking is harmony and consistency in our mutual parenting.

There are six of us now, a single family of human beings closer to several other stars than we are to the planet and star of our birth. We still do not know if this giant cylinder hurtling through space is really going anywhere. At times it does not seem to matter. We have created our own world here in Rama and, although it is limited, I believe that we are happy.

11

30 January 2209 — I had forgotten what it felt like to have adrenaline coursing through my system. In the last thirty hours our calm and placid life on Rama has been utterly destroyed.

It all began with two dreams. Yesterday morning, just before I woke up, I had a dream about Richard that was extraordinarily vivid. Richard wasn't actually in my dream—I mean, he didn't appear alongside Michael, Simone, Katie, and me. But Richard's face was inset in the upper left-hand corner of my dream screen while the four of us were engaged in some normal, everyday activity. He kept calling my name over and over. His call was so loud that I could still hear it when I awakened.

I had just begun to tell Michael about the dream when Katie appeared at the doorway in her pajamas. She was trembling and frightened. "What is it, darling?" I asked, beckoning to her with my open arms.

She came over and hugged me tightly. "It's Daddy," she said. "He was calling me last night in my dreams."

A chill ran down my spine and Michael sat up on his mat. I comforted Katie with my words, but I was unnerved by the coincidence. Had she heard my conversation with Michael? Impossible. We had seen her the moment she arrived at our room.

After Katie returned to the nursery to change her clothes, I told Michael that I could not possibly ignore the two dreams. He and I have often discussed my occasional psychic powers. Although he generally discounts the whole idea of extrasensory perception, Michael has always admitted that is is impossible to state categorically that my dreams and visions do not foreshadow the future.

"I must go topside and look for Richard," I told him after breakfast. Michael had expected me to make such an effort and was prepared to look after the children. But it was dark in Rama. We both agreed that it would be better if I waited until our evening, when it would again be light in the spacecraft world above our lair.

I took a long nap so that I would have plenty of energy for a thorough search. I slept fitfully, and kept dreaming that I was in danger. Before I left, I made certain that there was a reasonably accurate graphics drawing of Richard stored in my portable computer. I wanted to be able to show the object of my quest to any avians that I might encounter.

After kissing the children good night, I headed straight for the avian lair. I was not that surprised when I found that the tank sentry was gone. Years ago, when I was first invited into the lair by one of the avian residents, the tank sentry had also not been present. Could it be that I was somehow being invited again? And what did all this have to do with my dream? My heart was pounding like crazy as I passed the room with the cistern of water and headed deeper into the tunnel that the absent sentry had usually guarded.

I never heard a sound. I walked for almost a kilometer before I came to a tall doorway on my right. I cautiously peered around the corner. The room was dark, like everywhere in the avian lair except the vertical corridor. I switched on my flashlight. The room was not very deep, maybe fifteen meters at the most, but it was extremely tall. Against the wall opposite the door were rows and rows of oval storage bins. The beam from my light showed that the rows extended all the way to the high ceiling, which must have been just under one of the plazas in New York.

It did not take me long to figure out the purpose of the room. Each of the storage bins was the size and shape of a manna melon. *Of course*, I thought to myself. *This must have been where the food supply was kept. No wonder they didn't want anybody in here.*

After verifying that all the bins were indeed empty, I started to walk back toward the vertical corridor. Then, on a hunch, I reversed my direction, passed the storage room, and continued on down the tunnel. *It must go somewhere,* I reasoned, *or it would have ended at the melon room.*

After another half a kilometer the tunnel widened gradually until it entered a large circular chamber. In the center of the room, which had a high ceiling, was a broad domed structure. Around the walls were about twenty alcoves, cut into the walls at regular intervals. There was no light except my flashlight beam, so it took several minutes to integrate the room, with the domed building in the middle, into a composite picture.

I walked completely around the perimeter, examining the alcoves one after another. Most were empty. In one of them I found three identical tank sentries neatly arrayed against the back wall. My initial impulse was to be wary of the sentries, but it was not necessary. They were all dormant.

By far the most interesting of the alcoves, however, was the one at the center of the room, exactly one hundred and eighty degrees around the circle from the entrance tunnel. This special alcove was carefully organized and had thick shelves cut into its walls. There were fifteen shelves in all, five each on the two sides and five more on the wall opposite the doorway to the alcove. The shelves on the sides had objects arranged on them (everything was very orderly); the shelves against the far wall each had five round pits hollowed out along their lengths.

The contents of these pits, which were each further subdivided into sections, like portions of a pie, were fascinating. One of the sections in each of the pits contained a very fine material, like ash. A second section contained one, two, or three rings, either cherry red or gold, that I immediately recognized because of their similarity to the rings we had seen around the neck of our gray velvet avian friend. There did not seem to be any particular pattern to the rest of the articles in the pits—in fact, some of the pits were empty except for the ash and the rings.

Eventually I turned around and approached the domed structure. Its front door faced the special alcove. I examined the door with my flashlight. An intricate design was carved on its rectangular surface. There were four separate panels, or quadrants, in the design. An avian was in the top left quadrant, with a manna melon in the adjacent panel, on the right. The lower two quadrants contained unfamiliar pictures. On the left side was a carving of a jointed, striped creature running on six legs. The final panel, on the bottom right, featured a large box filled with very thin mesh or webbing.

After some hesitation I pushed open the door. I nearly jumped out of my skin when a loud alarm, like a Klaxon, pierced the silence. I stood inside the door without moving while the alarm sounded for almost a minute. When it was over, I still did not move. I was trying to hear if anyone (or anything) was responding to the alarm.

No sound disturbed the silence. After a few minutes I began examining the inside of the building. A transparent cube, roughly two and a half meters in each dimension, occupied the center of the single room. The walls of the cube were stained in spots, partially obscuring my vision, but I could still see that the bottom ten centimeters were covered by a fine, dark material. The room around the cube was decorated with geometric patterns on the walls, floors, and ceiling. One of the cube faces had a narrow entryway that permitted access to the cube interior.

I went inside. The fluffy black material appeared to be ash, but it was a slightly different consistency than the similar stuff I had found in the alcove pits. My eyes followed the beam of my flashlight as it moved in an orderly pattern around the cube. Near the center there was an object partially buried in the ash. I walked over, picked up the object, shook it off, and nearly fainted. It was Richard's robot TB.

TB was considerably altered. His exterior was blackened, his tiny control panel had melted off, and he no longer operated. But it was unmistakably him. I put the little robot to my lips and kissed him. In my mind's eye I could see him spouting one of Shakespeare's sonnets as Richard listened with rapt enjoyment.

It was obvious that TB had been in a fire. Had Richard also been trapped in an inferno inside the cube? I sifted through the ash carefully but found no bones. I did wonder, however, what it was that had burned and created all the ash. And what was TB doing inside the cube in the first place?

I was convinced that Richard was somewhere in the avian lair, so I spent another eight long hours scrambling up and down ledges and exploring tunnels. I visited all the places I had been before, during my short sojourn long ago, and even found some interesting new chambers of unknown purpose. But there were no signs of Richard. There were, in fact, no signs of life of any kind. Mindful that the short Raman day was almost over and that the four children would be waking up soon in our own lair, I finally returned, tired and dejected, to my Raman home.

Both the cover and the grill to our lair were open when I arrived. Although I was fairly certain that I had closed them both before leaving, I could not remember my exact actions at departure. Eventually I told myself that perhaps I had been too excited at the time and had forgotten to close everything. I had just started to descend when I heard Michael call "Nicole" from behind me.

I turned around. Michael was approaching from the lane to the east. He was moving quickly, which was unusual for him, and was carrying baby Patrick in his arms. "There you are," he said, panting as I walked up to him. "I was beginning to worry—"

He stopped abruptly, stared at me for an instant, and then looked around quickly. "But where's Katie?" he said anxiously.

"What do you mean, where's Katie?" I asked, the look on Michael's face causing me alarm.

"Isn't she with you?" he asked.

When I shook my head and said that I hadn't seen her, Michael suddenly erupted in tears. I rushed forward and comforted little Patrick, who was frightened by Michael's sobs and started crying himself.

"Oh, Nicole," Michael said. "I'm so, so sorry. Patrick was having a bad night, so I brought him into my room. Then Benjy had a stomachache and Simone and I had to nurse him for a couple of hours. We all fell asleep while Katie was alone in the nursery. About two hours ago, when we all woke up, she was gone."

I had never seen Michael so distraught before. I tried to comfort him, to tell him that Katie was probably just playing in the neighborhood somewhere (*And when we find her*, I was thinking, *I will give her a scolding she'll never forget*), but Michael argued with me.

"No, no," he said, "she's nowhere around. Patrick and I have been looking for over an hour."

Michael, Patrick, and I went downstairs to check on Simone and Benjy. Simone informed us that Katie had been extremely disappointed when I had decided to look for Richard alone. "She had hoped," Simone said serenely, "that you would take her with you."

"Why didn't you tell me this last night?" I asked my eight-year-old daughter.

"It didn't seem that important," Simone said. "Besides, it never occurred to me that Katie would try to find Daddy by herself."

Michael and I were both exhausted, but one of us had to look for Katie. I was the correct choice. I washed my face, ordered breakfast for everybody from the Ramans, and told a quick version of my descent into the avian lair. Simone and Michael turned the blackened TB over slowly in their hands. I could tell they too were wondering what had happened to Richard.

"Katie said that Daddy went to find the octospiders," Simone commented just before I left. "She said it was more exciting in their world."

I was filled with dread as I trudged over to the plaza near the octospider lair. While I was walking, the lights went out and it was night again in Rama. "Great," I muttered to myself. "Nothing like trying to find a missing child in the darkness."

Both the octospider covering and the pair of protective grills were open. I had never seen the grills open before. My heart skipped a beat. I knew instinctively that Katie had gone down into their lair and that, despite my fear, I was about to follow her. First I bent down on my knees and shouted "Katie" twice into the blackness beneath me. I heard her name echoing through the tunnels. I strained to listen for a response, but there were no sounds at all. *At least*, I told myself, *I also don't hear any dragging brushes accompanied by a high-frequency whine.*

I descended the ramp to the large cavern with the four tunnels that Richard and I had once labeled "Eenie, Meenie, Mynie, and Moe." It was difficult, but I forced myself to enter the tunnel that Richard and I had followed before. After a few steps, however, I stopped myself, backed up, and then went into the adjacent tunnel. This second corridor also led to the descending barrel corridor with the protruding spikes, but it passed the room that Richard and I called the octospider museum along the way. I remembered clearly the terror I had felt nine years earlier when I had found Dr. Takagishi, stuffed like a hunting trophy, hanging in that museum.

There was a reason I wanted to visit the octospider museum that was not necessarily related to my search for Katie. If Richard had been killed by the octospiders (as Takagishi apparently was— although I am still not convinced that he did not die from a heart attack), or if they had found his body somewhere else in Rama, then perhaps it too would be in the room. To say that I wasn't anxious to see an alien taxidermist's version of my husband would be an understatement; however, above all I wanted to know what *had* happened to Richard. Especially after my dream.

I took a deep breath when I arrived at the entrance to the museum. I turned slowly left through the doorway. The lights came on as soon as I crossed the threshold, but fortunately Dr. Takagishi was not staring directly in my face. He had been moved across the room. In fact, the whole museum had been rearranged in the intervening years. All the biot replicas, which had occupied most of the space in the room when Richard and I had visited it briefly before, had been removed. The two "exhibits," if one could call them that, were now the avians and the human beings.

The avian display was closer to the door. Three individuals were hanging from the ceiling, their wings outspread. One of them was the gray velvet avian with the two cherry red neck rings that Richard and I had seen just before its death. There were other fascinating objects and even photographs in the avian exhibit, but my eyes were drawn across the room, to the display surrounding Dr. Takagishi.

I sighed with relief when I realized that Richard was not in the room. Our sailboat was there, however, the one that Richard, Michael, and I had used to cross the Cylindrical Sea. It was on the floor right next to Dr. Takagishi. There was also an assortment of items that had been salvaged from our picnics and other activities in New York. But the center of the exhibit was a set of framed pictures on the back and side walls.

From across the room I could not tell much about the content of the pictures. I gasped, however, as I approached them. The images were photographs, set in rectangular frames, many of which showed life *inside* our lair. There were photos of all of us, including the children. They showed us eating, sleeping, even going to the bathroom. I was feeling numb as I scanned the display. "We are being watched," I commented to myself, "even in our own home." I felt a terrible chill.

On the side wall was a special collection of pictures that dismayed and embarrassed me. On Earth they would have been candidates for an erotic museum. The images showed me making love with Richard in several different positions. There was one picture of Michael and me as well, but it wasn't as sharp because it had been dark in our bedroom that night.

The line of pictures below the sex scenes were all photographs of the children's births. Each birth was shown, including Patrick's, confirming that the eavesdropping was still continuing. The juxtaposition of the sex and birth images made it clear that the octospiders (or the Ramans?) had definitely figured out our reproductive process.

I was totally consumed with the photographs for probably fifteen minutes. My concentration was finally broken when I heard a very loud sound of brushes dragging against metal coming from the direction of the museum door. I was absolutely terrified. I stood still, frozen in my spot, and looked around wildly. There was no other escape from the room.

Within seconds Katie came bouncing through the door. *"Mom,"* she shouted when she saw me. She raced across the museum, nearly toppling Dr. Takagishi, and jumped into my arms.

"Oh, Mom," she said, hugging and kissing me fiercely, "I knew you'd come."

I closed my eyes and held my lost child with all my strength. Tears cascaded down my cheeks. I swung Katie from side to side, comforting her by saying, "It's all right, darling, it's all right."

When I wiped my eyes and opened them, an octospider was standing in the museum doorway. It was momentarily not moving, almost as if it were watching the reunion between mother and daughter. I stood transfixed, swept by a wave of emotions ranging from joy to sheer terror.

Katie felt my fear. "Don't worry, Mother," she said, looking over her shoulder at the octospider. "He won't hurt you. He just wants to look. He's been close to me many times."

My adrenaline level was at an all-time high. The octospider continued to stand (or sit, or whatever octos do when they're not moving) in the door. Its large black head was almost spherical and sat on a body that spread, near the floor, into the eight black-and-gold-striped tentacles. In the center of its head were two parallel indentations, symmetric about an invisible axis, that ran from the top to the bottom. Precisely centered in between those two indentations, roughly a meter above the floor, was an amazing square lens structure, ten centimeters on a side, that was a gelatinous combination of grid lines plus flowing black and white material. While the octospider was staring at us, that lens was teeming with activity.

There were other organs embedded in the body between the two indentations, both above and below the lens, but I had no time to study them. The octospider moved toward us in the room and, despite Katie's assurances, my fear returned with full force. The brush sound was made by cilialike attachments to the bottom of the tentacles as they moved across the floor. The high-frequency whine was emanating from a small orifice in the lower right side of the head.

For several seconds fear immobilized my thought processes. As the creature drew closer, my natural flight responses took over. Unfortunately, they were useless in this situation. There was nowhere to run.

The octospider didn't stop until it was a scant five meters away. I had backed Katie against the wall and was standing between her and the octo. I held up my hand. Again there was a flurry of activity in its mysterious lens. Suddenly I had an idea. I reached into my flight suit and pulled out my computer. With my fingers trembling (the octospider had raised a pair of tentacles in front of its lens—in retrospect I wonder if it thought I was going to produce a weapon), I called the image of Richard up on the monitor and thrust it out toward the octospider.

When I made no additional movement the creature slowly returned its two protective tentacles to the floor. It stared at the monitor for almost a full minute and then, much to my astonishment, a wave of bright purple coloring ran completely around its head, starting at the edge of its indentation. This purple was followed a few seconds later by a rainbow pattern of red, blue, and green, each band a different thickness, that also came out of the same indentation and, after circling the head, retreated into the parallel indentation almost three hundred and sixty degrees away.

Katie and I both stared in awe. The octospider picked up one of its tentacles, pointed at the monitor, and repeated the wide purple wave. Moments later, as before, came the identical rainbow pattern.

"It's talking to us, Mommy," Katie said softly.

"I think you're right," I replied. "But I don't have any idea what it's saying."

After waiting for what seemed like forever, the octospider began to move backward toward the doorway, its extended tentacle beckoning us to follow. There were no more bands of color. Katie and I held hands and cautiously followed. She started looking around and noticed the photographs on the wall for the first time. "Look, Mommy," she said, "they have pictures of our family."

I shushed her and told her to please pay attention to the octospider. It backed into the tunnel and headed toward the spiked vertical corridor and the subways. That was the opening we needed. I picked Katie up, told her to hang on tight, and raced down the tunnel at top speed. My feet scarcely touched the floor until I was up on the ramp and back in New York.

Michael was ecstatic to see Katie safe, even though he was very concerned (as I still am) that there were cameras hidden in the walls and ceilings of our living quarters. I never did scold Katie properly for going off on her own—I was too relieved to find her at all. Katie told Simone that she had had a "fabulous adventure" and that the octospider was "nice." Such is the world of the child.

4 February 2209

Oh, joy of joys! We have found Richard! He is still *alive*! Just barely, for he is in a deep coma and has a high fever, but he is nevertheless alive.

Katie and Simone found him this morning, lying on the ground not fifty meters from the opening to our lair. The three of us had been planning to play some soccer in the plaza and were ready to leave the lair when Michael called me back for something. I told the girls to wait for me in the area around the lair entrance. When they both started screaming a few minutes later, I thought something terrible had happened. I rushed up the stairs and immediately saw Richard's comatose body in the distance.

At first I was afraid that Richard was dead. The doctor in me immediately went to work, checking his vital signs. The girls hung over me while I was examining him. Especially Katie. She kept saying, over and over, "Is Daddy alive? Oh, Mommy, make Daddy be all right."

Once I had confirmed that he was in a coma, Michael and Simone helped me carry Richard down the stairs. I injected a set of biometry probes into his system and have been monitoring the output ever since.

I took his clothes off and checked him from head to toe. He has some scratches and bruises that I have not seen before, but that's to be expected after all this time. His blood cell counts are peculiarly close to normal—I would have expected white cell abnormalities with his almost forty-degree temperature.

There was another big surprise when we examined Richard's clothing in detail. In his jacket pocket we found the Shakespearean robots Prince Hal and Falstaff, who had disappeared nine years ago in the strange world below the spiked corridor in what we thought was the octospider lair. Somehow Richard must have convinced the octos to return his playmates.

I have been sitting here beside Richard now for seven hours. Most of the time this morning other members of the family have also been here, but for the last hour Richard and I have been alone. My eyes have feasted on his face for minutes on end, my hands have roamed across his neck, his shoulders, and his back. My touching him has evoked a flood of memories and my eyes have often been filled with tears. I never thought I would see or touch him again. Oh, Richard, welcome home. Welcome home to your wife and family.

12

We have had an incredible day. Just after lunch, while I was sitting beside Richard and routinely checking all his biometry, Katie asked me if she could play with Prince Hal and Falstaff. "Of course," I told her without thinking. I was certain that the little robots were not functioning and, to tell the truth, I wanted her out of the room so that I could try another technique for bringing Richard out of his coma.

I have never seen a coma even remotely like Richard's. Most of the time his eyes are open, and occasionally they even seem to be following an object in his field of vision. But there are no other signs of life or consciousness. No muscles ever move. I have used a variety of stimuli, some mechanical, mostly chemical, to try to rouse him from his comatose state. None of them have worked. That's why I was so unprepared for what happened today.

After Katie had been gone for about ten minutes, I heard a very strange mix of sounds coming from the nursery. I left Richard's side and walked into the corridor. Before I reached the nursery the strange noise resolved itself into clipped speech with a very peculiar rhythm. "Hello," a voice that sounded as if it were in the bottom of a well said. "We are peaceful. Here is your man."

The voice was coming from Prince Hal, who was standing in

the middle of the room when I entered the nursery. The children were on the floor surrounding the robot, somewhat tentatively except for Katie. She was clearly excited.

"I was just playing with the buttons," Katie said to me in explanation when I gave her a questioning glance, "and suddenly he started talking."

No motions accompanied Prince Hal's speech. *How peculiar*, I thought, remembering that Richard took pride in the fact that his robots always moved and spoke in concert. *Richard did not do this*, a voice inside my head told me, but I initially dismissed the idea. I dropped down on the floor beside the children.

"Hello. We are peaceful. Here is your man," Prince Hal said again several seconds later. This time an eerie feeling swept through me. The girls were still laughing, but they quickly stopped when they noticed the strange expression on my face. Benjy crawled over beside me and grabbed my hand.

We were sitting on the floor with our backs to the door. I suddenly had a feeling there was someone behind me. I turned around and saw Richard standing in the doorway. I gasped and jumped up just as he fell and lost consciousness.

The children all screamed and began to cry. I tried to comfort them after quickly examining Richard. Since Michael was topside in New York having his afternoon walk, I cared for Richard on the floor outside the nursery for over an hour. During that time I watched him very closely. He was exactly as he had been when I left him in the bedroom earlier. There was no obvious sign that he had been awake for thirty or forty seconds in the interim.

When Michael returned he helped me carry Richard to the bedroom. We talked for over an hour about why Richard had awakened so abruptly. Later I read and reread every article about coma in my medical books. I am convinced that Richard's coma is caused by a mixture of physical and psychological problems. In my opinion the sound of that strange voice induced a trauma in him that temporarily overwhelmed the factors creating the coma.

But why did he then relapse so quickly? That's a more difficult issue. Perhaps he had exhausted his small energy base by walking down the hall. There's no way we can really know. In fact, we cannot answer most of the questions about what happened today, including the one that Katie keeps asking: *Who* is it that is peaceful?

1 May 2209

Let it be recorded that on this day Richard Colin Wakefield actually acknowledged his family and spoke his first words. For almost a week he has been working up to this moment, initially by giving signs of recognition with his face and eyes and then by moving his lips as if to make words. He smiled at me this morning and almost said my name, but his first actual word was "Katie," spoken this afternoon after his cherished daughter gave him one of her energetic hugs.

There is a feeling of euphoria in the family, especially among the girls. They are celebrating the return of their father. I have told Simone and Katie repeatedly that Richard's rehabilitation will almost certainly be long and painful, but I guess they are too young to comprehend what that means.

I am a very happy woman. It was impossible for me to restrain the tears when Richard distinctly whispered "Nicole" in my ear just before dinner. Even though I realize that my husband is not yet anywhere near normal, I am now certain that he will eventually recover and that fills my heart with joy.

18 August 2209

Slowly but surely Richard continues to improve. He only sleeps twelve hours a day now, can walk almost a mile before becoming fatigued, and is able to concentrate occasionally on a problem if it's especially interesting. He has not yet begun to interact with the Ramans through the keyboard and screen. He has, however, taken Prince Hal apart and tried unsuccessfully to determine what caused the strange voice in the nursery.

Richard is the first to admit that he is not himself. When he can talk about it, he says that he is "in a fog, like a dream but not quite as sharp." It has been over three months since he regained consciousness, but he still can't remember very much about what happened to him after he left us. He believes he was in the coma for the last year or so. His estimate is based more on vague feelings than on any particular fact.

Richard insists that he lived in the avian lair for some months and that he was present at a spectacular cremation. He can't supply any other details. Richard has also twice contended that he explored

the Southern Hemicylinder and found the main city of the octospiders near the southern bowl, but since what he *can* remember
changes from day to day, it is difficult to place much credence in
any specific recollection.

I have replaced Richard's biometry set twice already and have
very lengthy records of all his critical parameters. His charts are
normal except in two areas—his mental activity and his temperature.
His daily brain waves defy description. There is nothing in my medical encyclopedia that will allow me to interpret any pair of these
charts, much less the entire set. Sometimes the level of activity in
his brain is astronomically high; sometimes it seems to stop altogether. The electrochemical measurements are equally peculiar. His
hippocampus is virtually dormant—that could explain why Richard's
having such difficulty with his memory.

His temperature is also weird. It has been stable now, for two
months, at 37.8 degrees Celsius, eight tenths of a degree above
normal for an average human. I have checked all his preflight
records; Richard's "normal" temperature on Earth was a very steady
36.9. I cannot explain why this elevated temperature persists. It's
almost as if his body and some pathogen are in stable equilibrium,
neither able to subdue the other. But what pathogen could it be that
would elude all my attempts to identify it?

All the children have been especially disappointed in Richard's
lackadaisical behavior. During his absence we probably mythologized
him somewhat, but there's no doubt he was a very energetic man
before. This new Richard is only a shadow of his former self. Katie
swears she remembers wrestling and playing vigorously with her
daddy when she was only two (her memory has undoubtedly been
reinforced by the stories that Michael, Simone, and I told her while
Richard was gone), and is often quite angry that he spends so little
time with her now. I try to explain to her that "Daddy is still sick,"
but I don't think she is mollified by my explanation.

Michael moved all my things back to this room within twenty-
four hours after Richard's return. He is such a sweet man. He went
through another heavy religious phase for several weeks (I expect in
his mind he needed forgiveness for some fairly grievous sins) but
has since moderated because of the workload on me. He has been
marvelous with the children.

Simone acts as a backup mother. Benjy worships her and she
has incredible patience with him. Since she had commented several
times that Benjy was "a little slow," Michael and I have told Simone
about his Whittingham's syndrome. We still have not told Katie.

Right now Katie is having a difficult time. Not even Patrick, who follows her around like a pet dog, can cheer her up.

We all know, even the children, that we are being watched. We searched the walls in the nursery very carefully, almost as if it were a game, and found several minute irregularities in the surface finish that we declared to be cameras. We chipped them away with our tools, but we could not positively say that we had indeed found monitoring devices. They may be so small that we couldn't see them without a microscope. At least Richard remembered his favorite saying, about advanced alien technology being indistinguishable from magic.

Katie was the most disturbed about the prying cameras of the octospiders. She spoke openly and resentfully of their intrusion into her "private life." She probably has more secrets than any of us. When Simone told her younger sister that it was really not important, because "after all, God is also watching us all the time," we had our first sibling religious argument. Katie replied with "Bullshit," a rather unpleasant word for a six-year-old girl to use. Her expression reminded me to be more careful with my own language.

One day last month I took Richard over to the avian lair to see if perhaps being there would refresh his memory. He became very frightened as soon as we were in the tunnel off the vertical corridor. "Dark," I heard him mumble. "I cannot see in the dark. But *they* can see in the dark." He wouldn't walk any more after we passed the water and the cistern, so I brought him back to our lair.

Richard knows that both Benjy and Patrick are Michael's sons and probably suspects that Michael and I lived as husband and wife for part of the time he was gone, but he has never commented about it. Both Michael and I are prepared to ask for Richard's forgiveness and to stress to him that we were not lovers (except for Benjy's conception) until he had been gone for two years. At the moment, however, Richard doesn't seem much interested in the subject.

Richard and I have shared our old conjugal mat since soon after he awakened from his coma. We have touched a lot and been very friendly, but until two weeks ago there had never been any sex. In fact, I was starting to think that sex was another of the things that had been erased from his memory, so unresponsive had he been to my occasional provocative kisses.

Then came a night, however, when the old Richard was suddenly in bed with me. This is a pattern that has been occurring in other areas as well—every now and then his old wit, energy, and intelligence are all present for a short period of time. Anyway, the old Richard was ardent, funny, and imaginative. It was like heaven for me. I remembered levels of pleasure that I had long since buried.

His sexual interest continued for three consecutive nights. Then it departed as abruptly as it had arrived. At first I was disappointed (Isn't that human nature? Most of the time we want it to be better. When it's as good as it can be, we want it to last forever), but now I have accepted that this facet of his personality must also undergo a healing process.

Last night Richard computed our trajectory for the first time since he has been back with us. Both Michael and I were delighted. "We're still holding the same direction," he pronounced proudly. "We're now less than three light-years from Sirius."

6 January 2210

Forty-six years old. My hair is now mostly gray on the sides and in front. Back on Earth I would be debating whether or not to color my hair. Here on Rama it does not matter.

I am too old to be pregnant. I should tell that to the little girl growing inside my womb. I was quite astonished when I realized that I was indeed pregnant again. The onset of menopause had already begun, with its strange hot flashes, moments of daffiness, and totally unpredictable menstruations. But Richard's sperm has made one more baby, another addition to this homeless family adrift in space.

If we never encounter another human being (and Eleanor Joan Wakefield turns out to be a healthy baby, which seems likely at this point), then there will be a total of six possible combinations of parents for our grandchildren. Almost certainly all of those permutations will not occur, but it's fascinating to imagine. I used to think that Simone would mate with Benjy, and Katie with Patrick, but where will Ellie fit into the equation?

This is my tenth birthday onboard Rama. It seems utterly impossible that I have spent only twenty percent of my life in this giant cylinder. Did I have another life once, back on that oceanic planet trillions of kilometers away? Did I really know adult people other than Richard Wakefield and Michael O'Toole? Was my father actually Pierre des Jardins, the famous writer of historical fiction? Did I have a secret, dream affair with Henry, Prince of Wales, that produced my wonderful first daughter Genevieve?

None of it seems possible. At least not today, not on my forty-sixth birthday. It's funny. Richard and Michael have asked me, one time each, about Genevieve's father. I have still never told anyone. Isn't that ridiculous? What possible difference could it make here on Rama? None at all. But it has been my secret (shared only with my father) since the moment of Genevieve's conception. She was *my* daughter. I brought her into the world and I raised her. Her biological father, I always told myself, was of no importance.

That is, of course, poppycock. Hah. There's that word again. Dr. David Brown used it often. Goodness. I haven't thought about the other Newton cosmonauts for years. I wonder if Francesca and her friends made their millions off the Newton mission. I hope Janos got his share. Dear Mr. Tabori, an absolutely delightful man. Hmm. I also wonder how Rama's escape from the nuclear phalanx was explained to the citizens of Earth. Ah, yes, Nicole, this is a typical birthday. A long, unstructured voyage down memory lane.

Francesca was so beautiful. I was always jealous of how well she handled herself with people. Did she drug Borzov and Wilson? Probably. I don't think for a minute she meant to kill Valeriy. But she had a truly twisted morality. Most genuinely ambitious people do.

I am amused, now when I look back, at how obsessed I was as a young mother in my twenties. I had to succeed at everything. My ambition was quite different from Francesca's. I wanted to show the world that I could play by all the rules and still win, just as I had done with the triple jump in the Olympic games. What could be more impossible for an unmarried mother than to be selected as a cosmonaut? I was certainly full of myself during those years. Lucky for me, and for Genevieve, that Father was there.

I knew, of course, every time I looked at Genevieve that Henry's imprint was obvious. From the top of her lips to the bottom of her chin, Genevieve's face is exactly like his. And I did not really want to deny the genetics. It was just so important to me to make it on my own, to show at least myself that I was a superb mother and woman even if I was unsuitable to be the queen.

I was too black to be Queen Nicole of England, or even Joan of Arc in one of those French anniversary pageants. I wonder how many years it will be before skin color is no longer an issue among human beings on Earth. Five hundred years? A thousand? What was it that the American William Faulkner said—something about Sambo will be free only when all of his neighbors wake up in the morning and say, both to themselves and to their friends, that Sambo is free.

I think he is right. We have seen that racial prejudice cannot be eradicated by legislation. Or even by education. Each person's journey through life must have an epiphany, a moment of true awareness, when he or she realizes, once and for all, that Sambo and every other individual in the world who is in any way different from him or her *must* be free if we are to survive.

When I was down at the bottom of that pit ten years ago and certain that I was going to die, I asked myself what particular moments of my life I would live over if I were offered the opportunity. Those hours with Henry leapt into my mind, despite the fact that he later broke my heart. Even today I would gladly soar again with my prince. To have experienced total happiness, even if it's just for a few minutes or hours, is to have been alive. It is not that important, when you are faced with death, that your companion in your great moment subsequently disappointed or betrayed you. What *is* important is that sense of momentary joy so great you feel you have transcended the Earth.

It embarrassed me a little, in the pit, that my memories of Henry were on a level equal to my memories of my father, mother, and daughter. But I have since realized that I am not unique in cherishing my recollections of those hours with Henry. Each person has very special moments or events that are uniquely hers and are zealously protected by the heart.

My only close friend at the university, Gabrielle Moreau, spent a night with Genevieve and me at Beauvois the year before the Newton expedition was launched. We had not seen each other for seven years and spent most of the night talking, primarily about the major emotional events of our lives. Gabrielle was extremely happy. She had a handsome, sensitive, successful husband, three healthy, gorgeous children, and a beautiful manor house near Chinon. But Gabrielle's "most wonderful" moment, she confided to me after midnight with a girlish smile, had occurred before she met her husband. She had had a powerful schoolgirl crush on a famous movie star who one day happened to be on location in Tours. Gabrielle somehow managed to meet him in his hotel room and talk to him privately for almost an hour. She kissed him a single time on the lips before she left. That was her most precious memory.

Oh, my prince, it was ten years ago yesterday that I saw you for the last time. Are you happy? Are you a good king? Do you ever think of the black Olympic champion who gave herself to you, her first love, with such reckless abandon?

You asked me an indirect question, that day on the ski mountain, about the father of my daughter. I denied you the answer, not realizing that my denial meant I had still not forgiven you completely. If you were to ask me today, my prince, I would gladly tell you. Yes, Henry Rex, King of England, *you* are the father of Genevieve des Jardins. Go to her, know her, love her children. I cannot. I am more than fifty trillion kilometers away.

13

Everyone was too excited to sleep last night. Except for Benjy, bless his heart, who simply could not grasp what we were telling him. Simone has explained to him many times that our home is inside a giant cylindrical spacecraft—she has even shown him on the black screen the different views of Rama from the external sensors— but the concept continues to elude him.

When the whistle sounded yesterday Richard, Michael, and I stared at each other for several seconds. It had been so long since we last heard it. Then we all started talking at once. The children, including little Ellie, were full of questions and could feel our excitement. The eight of us went topside immediately. Richard and Katie ran over to the sea without waiting for the rest of the family. Simone walked with Benjy, Michael with Patrick. I carried Ellie because her little legs just wouldn't move fast enough.

Katie was bursting with enthusiasm when she ran back to greet us. "Come on, come on," she said, grabbing Simone by the hand. "You've got to see it. It's amazing. The colors are fantastic."

Indeed they were. The rainbow arcs of light crackled from horn to horn, filling the Raman night with an awesome display. Benjy stared southward with his mouth open. After many seconds he smiled and turned to Simone. "It's beau-ti-ful," he said slowly, proud of his use of the word.

"Yes, it is, Benjy," Simone replied. "Very beautiful."

"Ve-ry beau-ti-ful," Benjy repeated, turning back to look at the lights.

None of us said very much during the show itself. But after we returned to the lair the conversation was nonstop for hours. Of course, someone had to explain everything to the children. Simone was the only one born at the time of the last maneuver, and she was just an infant. Richard was the chief explainer. The whistle and light show really energized him—he seemed more like himself last night than he has at any time since he returned—and he was both entertaining and informative as he recounted everything we knew about whistles, light shows, and Raman maneuvers.

"Do you think the octospiders are going to return to New York?" Katie asked expectantly.

"I don't know," Richard said. "But that's definitely a possibility."

Katie spent the next fifteen minutes telling everyone, for the umpteenth time, about our encounter with the octospider four years ago. As usual, she embellished and exaggerated some of the details, especially from the solo part of the story before she saw me in the museum.

Patrick loves the tale. He wants Katie to tell it all the time. "There I was," Katie said last night, "lying on my stomach, my head peering over the edge of a gigantic round cylinder that dropped into the black gloom. Silver spikes were sticking out of the sides of the cylinder, and I could see them flashing in the dim light. 'Hey,' I shouted, 'anybody down there?'

"I heard a sound like dragging metal brushes together with a whine. Lights came on below me. At the bottom of the cylinder, beginning to climb the spikes, was a black *thing* with a round head and eight tentacles of black and gold. The tentacles wrapped around the spikes as it climbed swiftly in my direction. . . ."

"Oc-to-spi-der," Benjy said.

When Katie was finished with her story, Richard told the children that in four more days the floor was probably going to start shaking. He stressed that everything should be carefully anchored to the ground and that each of us should be prepared for another set of sessions in the deceleration tank. Michael pointed out that we needed at least one new toy box for the children, and several sturdy boxes for our stuff as well. We have accumulated so much junk over the years that it will be quite a task to secure everything in the next few days.

When Richard and I were lying alone on our mat, we held

hands and talked for over an hour. At one point I told him that I hoped this coming maneuver signaled the beginning of the end of our journey in Rama.

"Hope springs eternal in the human breast./ Man never is, but always to be blessed," he replied. He sat up for a moment and looked at me, his eyes twinkling in the near darkness. "Alexander Pope," he said. Then he laughed. "I bet he never thought he would be quoted sixty trillion kilometers away from Earth."

"You seem better, darling," I said, stroking his arm.

His brow furrowed. "Right now everything seems clear. But I don't know when the fog will descend again. It could be any minute. And I still cannot remember more than the barest outline of what happened during the three years that I was gone."

He lay back down. "What do you think will happen?" I asked.

"I'm guessing we'll have a maneuver," he replied. "And I hope it's a big one. We are approaching Sirius very quickly and will need to slow down considerably if our target is anywhere in the Sirius system." He reached over and took my hand. "For you," he said, "and especially for the children, I hope this is not a false alarm."

8 July 2213

The maneuver began four days ago, right on schedule, as soon as the third and final light show was finished. We didn't see or hear any avians or octospiders, as we haven't for four years now. Katie was very disappointed. She wanted to see the octospiders all return to New York.

Yesterday a pair of the mantis biots came into our lair and went straight to the deceleration tank. They were carrying a large container, in which were the five new webbed beds (Simone, of course, needs a different size now) and all the helmets. We watched them from a distance while they installed the beds and checked out the tank system. The children were fascinated. The short visit from the mantises confirmed that we will soon be undergoing a major change in velocity.

Richard was apparently correct with his hypothesis about the connection between the main propulsion system and the overall thermal control of Rama. The temperature has already started to drop topside. In anticipation of a long maneuver, we have been busy using the keyboard to order cold-weather clothing for all the children.

The constant shaking is again disrupting our lives. At first it was amusing for the children, but they are already complaining about it. For myself, I am hoping that we are now near our ultimate destination. Although Michael has been praying "God's will be done," my few prayers have definitely been more selfish and specific.

1 September 2213

Something new is definitely happening. For the last ten days, ever since we finished in the tank and the maneuver ended, we have been approaching a solitary light source situated about thirty astronomical units away from the star Sirius. Richard has ingeniously manipulated the sensor list and the black screen so that this source is dead center on our monitor at all times, regardless of which particular Raman telescope is observing it.

Two nights ago we began to see some definition in the object. We speculated that perhaps it was an inhabited planet and Richard rushed around computing the heat input from Sirius on a planet whose distance was roughly equal to Neptune's distance from our sun. Even though Sirius is much larger, brighter, and hotter than the Sun, Richard concluded that our paradise, if this was indeed our destination, was still going to be very cold.

Last night we could see our target more clearly. It is an elongated construction (Richard says it therefore cannot be a planet—anything "that size" that is decidedly nonspherical "must be artificial"), shaped like a cigar, with two rows of lights along the top and bottom. Because we don't know exactly how far away it is, we don't know its size for certain. However, Richard has been making some "guesstimates," based on our closing velocity, and he thinks the cigar is roughly a hundred and fifty kilometers long and fifty kilometers tall.

The entire family sits in our main room and stares at the monitor. This morning we had another surprise. Katie showed us that there were two other vehicles in the vicinity of our target. Richard had taught her last week how to change the Raman sensors providing input to the black screen and, while the rest of us were talking, she accessed the distant radar sensor that we had first used thirteen years ago to identify the nuclear missiles coming from Earth. The cigar-shaped object appeared at the edge of the radar field of view. Standing right in front of the cigar, almost indistinguishable from it in the wide field, were the two other blips. If the giant cigar is indeed our destination, then perhaps we are about to have company.

8 September 2213

There is no way I can adequately describe the astounding events of the last five days. The language does not have adjectives superlative enough to capture what we have seen and experienced. Michael has even commented that heaven may pale by comparison beside the wonders that we have witnessed.

At this moment our family is onboard a driverless small shuttle craft, no larger than a city bus on Earth, that is whizzing us from the way station to an unknown destination. The cigar-shaped way station is still visible, but just barely, out the domed window at the rear of the craft. To our left, our home for thirteen years, the cylindrical spaceship we call Rama, is headed in a slightly different direction than we are. It departed from the way station a few hours after we did, lit like a Christmas tree on the outside, and we are presently separated from it by about two hundred kilometers.

Four days and eleven hours ago our Rama spacecraft came to a stop relative to the way station. We were the third vehicle in an amazing queue. In front of us was a spinning starfish about one tenth the size of Rama and a giant wheel, with a hub and spokes, that entered the way station within hours after we stopped.

The way station itself turned out to be hollow. When the giant wheel moved into the center of the way station, gantries and other deployable elements rolled out to meet the wheel and fix it in place. A suite of special vehicles in three unusual shapes (one looked like a balloon, another like a blimp, and the third resembled a bathysphere on Earth) then entered the wheel from the way station. Although we couldn't see what was going on inside the wheel, we did see the special vehicles emerge, one by one, at odd intervals over the next two days. Each vehicle was met by a shuttle, like the one in which we are now flying but larger in size. These shuttles had all been parked in the dark in the right-hand side of the way station and had been moved into place thirty minutes or so before the rendezvous.

As soon as the shuttles were loaded, they always took off in a direction directly opposite our queue. About an hour after the final vehicle had emerged from the wheel and the last shuttle had departed, the many pieces of mechanical equipment attached to the wheel were retracted and the great circular spacecraft itself eased out of the way station.

The starfish in front of us had already entered the way station and was being handled by another set of gantries and attachments when a loud whistle summoned us topside in Rama. The whistle was followed by a light show in the southern bowl. However, this display was completely different from the ones that we had seen before. The Big Horn was the star of the new show. Circular rings of color formed near its tip and then sailed slowly north, centered along the spin axis of Rama. The rings were huge. Richard estimated they were at least a kilometer in diameter, with a ring thickness of forty meters.

The dark Raman night was illuminated by as many as eight of these rings at a time. The order remained the same—red, orange, yellow, green, blue, brown, pink, and purple—for three repetitions. As a ring would break up and disappear near the Alpha relay station at the northern bowl of Rama, a new ring of the same color would form back near the tip of the Big Horn.

We stood transfixed, our mouths agape, as this spectacle took place. As soon as the last ring disappeared from the third set, another astonishing event occurred. All the lights came on inside Rama! The Raman night had only begun three hours earlier—for thirteen years the sequence of night and day had been completely regular. Now, all of a sudden, it was changed. And it wasn't just the lights. There was music as well; at least I guess you could call it music. It sounded like millions of tiny bells and it seemed to be coming from everywhere.

None of us moved for many seconds. Then Richard, who had the best pair of binoculars, spied something flying toward us. "It's the avians," he shouted, jumping up and down and pointing at the sky. "I just remembered something. I visited them in their new home in the north while I was on my odyssey."

One at a time we each looked through his binoculars. At first it wasn't certain that Richard was correct in his identification, but as they came closer the fifty or sixty specks resolved themselves into the great birdlike creatures we know as the avians. They headed straight for New York. Half the avians hovered in the sky, maybe three hundred meters above their lair, as the other half dove down to the surface.

"Come on, Daddy," Katie yelled. "Let's go."

Before I could raise any objection, father and daughter were off at a sprint. I watched Katie run. She is already very fast. In my mind's eye I could see my mother's graceful stride across the grass in the park at Chilly-Mazarin—Katie has definitely inherited some characteristics from her mother's side of the family, even though she is first and foremost her father's daughter.

Simone and Benjy had already started toward our lair. Patrick was concerned about the avians. "Will they hurt Daddy and Katie?" he asked.

I smiled at my handsome five-year-old son. "No, darling," I answered, "not if they're careful." Michael, Patrick, Ellie, and I returned to the lair to watch the starfish being processed in the way station.

We couldn't see much because all the ports of entry to the starfish were on the opposite side, away from the Raman cameras. But we assumed some kind of unloading activity was occurring, because eventually five shuttles departed for some new location. The starfish was finished with its processing very quickly. It had already left the way station before Richard and Katie returned.

"Start packing," Richard said breathlessly as soon he arrived. "We're leaving. We're all leaving."

"You should have seen them," Katie said to Simone almost simultaneously. "They were huge. And ugly. They went down in their lair—"

"The avians returned to get some special things from their lair," Richard interrupted her. "Maybe they were mementos of some kind. Anyway, everything fits. We're getting out of here."

As I raced around trying to put our essentials into a few of the sturdy boxes, I criticized myself for not having figured everything out sooner. We had watched both the wheel and the starfish "unload" at the way station. But it had not occurred to us that *we* might be the cargo to be unloaded by Rama.

It was impossible to decide what to pack. We had been living in those six rooms (including the two we had fixed up for storage) for thirteen years. We had probably requested an average of five items a day using the keyboard. Granted, most of the objects had long since been thrown away, but still . . . We didn't know where we were going. How could we know what to take?

"Do you have any idea what's going to happen to us?" I asked Richard.

My husband was beside himself trying to figure out how to take his large computer. "Our history, our science—all that remains of our knowledge is there," he said, pointing at the computer in agitation. "What if it's irretrievably lost?"

It weighed only eighty kilograms altogether. I told him we could all help him carry the computer after we had packed clothing, personal items, and some food and water.

"Do you have any idea where we're going?" I repeated.

Richard shrugged his shoulders. "Not the slightest," he replied. "But wherever it is, I bet it will be amazing."

Katie came into our room. She was holding a small pouch and her eyes were alive with energy. "I'm packed and ready," she said. "Can I go topside and wait?"

Her father's affirmative nod was barely in motion when Katie bolted out the door. I shook my head, giving Richard a disapproving look, and went down the hall to help Simone with the other children. The process of packing for the boys was an ordeal. Benjy was cranky and confused. Even Patrick was irritable. Simone and I had just finished (the job was impossible until we forced the boys to take a nap) when Richard and Katie returned from topside.

"Our vehicle is here," Richard said calmly, suppressing his excitement.

"It's parked on the ice," Katie added, taking off her heavy jacket and gloves.

"How do you know it's ours?" Michael asked. He had entered the room only moments after Richard and Katie.

"It has eight seats and room for our bags," my ten-year-old daughter replied. "Who else could it be for?"

"Whom," I said mechanically, trying to integrate this latest new information. I felt as if I had been drinking from a fire hose for four consecutive days.

"Did you see any octospiders?" Patrick asked.

"Oc-to-spi-der," Benjy repeated carefully.

"No," answered Katie, "but we did see four mammoth planes, real flat, with wide wings. They flew over our heads, coming from the south. We think the flat planes were carrying the octos, don't we, Dad?"

Richard nodded.

I took a deep breath. "All right, then," I said. "Bundle up, everybody. Let's go. Carry the bags first. Richard, Michael, and I will make a second trip for the computer."

An hour later we were all in the vehicle. We had climbed the stairs of our lair for the last time. Richard pressed a flashing red button and our Raman helicopter (I call it that because it went straight up, not because it had any rotary blades) lifted off the ground.

Our flight path was slow and vertical for the first five minutes. Once we were close to the spin axis of Rama, where there was no gravity and very little atmosphere, the vehicle hovered in place for two or three minutes while it changed its external configuration.

It was an awesome final view of Rama. Many kilometers below us our island home was but a small patch of grayish brown in the middle of the frozen sea that circled the giant cylinder. I could see the horns in the south clearer than ever before. Those amazing long structures, supported by massive flying buttresses larger than small towns on the Earth, all pointed directly north.

I felt strangely emotional as our craft began to move again. After all, Rama had been my home for thirteen years. I had given birth to five children there. *I also have matured,* I remember telling myself, *and may finally be growing into the person I have always wanted to be.*

There was very little time to dwell on what had been. Once the external configuration change was complete, our vehicle zipped along the spin axis to the northern hub in a matter of a few minutes. Less than an hour later we were all safely in this shuttle. We had left Rama. I knew we would never return. I wiped the tears from my eyes as our shuttle pulled out of the way station.

AT THE NODE

1

Nicole was dancing. Her partner in the waltz was Henry. They were young and very much in love. The beautiful music filled the huge ballroom as the twenty or so couples moved in rhythm around the floor. Nicole looked stunning in her long white gown. Henry's eyes were fixed on hers. He held her firmly at the waist, but somehow she felt completely free.

Her father was one of the people standing around the edge of the dance floor. He was leaning against a massive column that rose almost twenty feet to the domed ceiling. He waved and smiled as Nicole danced by in the arms of her prince.

The waltz seemed to last forever. When it was finally over, Henry held her hands and told Nicole that he had something very important to ask her. At just that moment her father touched her on the back. "Nicole," he whispered, "we must go. It's very late."

Nicole curtsied to the prince. Henry was reluctant to let go of her hands. "Tomorrow," he said. "We'll talk tomorrow." He blew her a kiss as she left the dance floor.

When Nicole walked outside it was almost sunset. Her father's sedan was waiting. Moments later, as they raced down the highway beside the Loire, she was dressed in blouse and jeans. Nicole was younger now, maybe fourteen, and her father was driving much faster than usual. "We don't want to be late," he said. "The pageant starts at eight o'clock."

The Chateau d'Ussé loomed before them. With its many towers and spires, the castle had been the inspiration for the original story of Sleeping Beauty. It was only a few kilometers down the river from Beauvois and had always been one of her father's favorite places.

It was the evening of the annual pageant, when the story of Sleeping Beauty was replayed in front of a live audience. Pierre and Nicole attended every year. Each time Nicole longed desperately for Aurora to avoid the deadly spinning wheel that would throw her into a coma. And each year she wept adolescent tears when the kiss of the handsome prince awakened the beauty from her deathlike sleep.

The pageant was over, the audience gone. Nicole was climbing up the circular steps that led to the tower where the real Sleeping Beauty had supposedly lapsed into her coma. The teenager was racing up the steps, laughing, leaving her father far behind.

Aurora's room was on the other side of the long window. Nicole caught her breath and stared at all the sumptuous furnishings. The bed was canopied, the dressers richly decorated. Everything in the room was trimmed in white. It was magnificent. Nicole glanced back at the sleeping girl and gasped. It was she, Nicole, lying in the bed in a white gown!

Her heart pounded furiously as she heard the door open and the footsteps coming toward her in the room. Her eyes remained closed as the first aroma of his mint breath reached her nose. *This is it,* she thought excitedly to herself. He kissed her, gently, on the lips. Nicole felt as if she were flying on the softest of clouds. Music was all around her. She opened her eyes and saw Henry's smiling face only centimeters away. She reached her arms out to him and he kissed her again, this time with passion, as a man kisses a woman.

Nicole kissed him back, reserving nothing, allowing her kiss to tell him that she was his. But he pulled away. Her special prince was wearing a frown. He pointed at her face. Then he backed up slowly and left the room.

She had just started to cry when a distant sound intruded on her dream. A door was opening, light was coming into the room. Nicole blinked, then closed her eyes again to protect them against the light. The complicated set of ultrathin, plasticlike wires that were attached to her body automatically rewound themselves into their containers on either side of the canvas mat on which she was sleeping.

Nicole awakened very slowly. The dream had been extremely

vivid. Her feelings of unhappiness had not vanished as quickly as the dream. She tried to chase her despair by reminding herself that none of what she had dreamed was real.

"Are you going to just lie there forever?" Her daughter Katie, who had been asleep beside her on the left, was already up and bending over her.

Nicole smiled. "No," she said, "but I admit I am more than a little bit groggy. I was in the middle of a dream. . . . How long did we sleep this time?"

"A day short of five weeks," Simone answered from the other side. Her older daughter was sitting up, casually arranging her long hair that had become matted during the test.

Nicole glanced at her watch, verified that Simone was correct, and sat up herself. She yawned. "So how do you feel?" she said to the two girls.

"Full of energy," eleven-year-old Katie answered with a grin. "I want to run, jump, wrestle with Patrick. . . . I hope this was our last long sleep."

"The Eagle said it should be," Nicole replied. "They're hoping that they will have enough data now." She smiled. "The Eagle says we women are more difficult to understand—because of the wild monthly variations in our hormones."

Nicole stood up, stretched, and gave Katie a kiss. Then she eased over and hugged Simone. Although not quite fourteen, Simone was almost as tall as Nicole. She was a striking young woman with a dark brown face and soft, sensitive eyes. Simone always seemed calm and serene, in marked contrast to the restlessness and impatience of Katie.

"Why didn't Ellie come with us for this test?" Katie asked a little querulously. "She's a girl too, but it seems like she never has to do anything."

Nicole put her arm around Katie's shoulder as the three of them headed for the door and the light. "She's only four years old, Katie, and according to the Eagle, Ellie's too small to give them any of the critical data they still need."

In the small illuminated foyer, directly outside the room where they had been sleeping for five weeks, they put on their tight body suits, transparent helmets, and the slippers that anchored their feet on the floor. Nicole checked the two girls carefully before activating the outside door of the compartment. She needn't have worried. The door wouldn't have opened if any of them were unprepared for the environmental changes.

If Nicole and her daughters had not seen the large room outside their compartment several times before, they would have stopped in amazement and stared for several minutes. Stretching in front of them was a long chamber, a hundred or more meters in length and fifty meters wide. The ceiling above them, filled with banks of lights, was about five meters high. The room looked like a mixture of a hospital operating room and a semiconductor manufacturing plant on the Earth. There were no walls or cubicles dividing the room into partitions, yet its rectangular dimensions were clearly sub-allocated into different tasks. The room was busy—the robots were all either analyzing data from one set of tests or preparing for another set. Around the edges of the room were compartments, like the one in which Nicole, Simone, and Katie had slept for five weeks, in which the "experiments" were carried out.

Katie walked over to the closest compartment on the left. It was set back in the corner and was suspended from the wall and ceiling along two perpendicular axes. A display screen built next to the metallic door showed a wide array of what was presumably data in some bizarre cuneiformlike script.

"Weren't we in this one last time?" Katie asked, pointing at the compartment. "Wasn't this the place where we slept on that peculiar white foam and felt all the pressure?"

Her question was transmitted inside the helmets of her mother and sister. Nicole and Simone both nodded and then joined Katie in staring at the unintelligible screen.

"Your father thinks they are trying to find a way that we can sleep through an entire acceleration regime lasting for several months," Nicole said. "The Eagle will neither confirm nor deny this conjecture."

Although the three women had undergone four separate tests together in this laboratory, none of them had ever seen any forms of life or intelligence except for the dozen or so mechanical aliens that apparently were in charge. The humans called these beings "block robots" because, except for their cylindrical "feet" which allowed them to roll around the floor, the creatures were all made of rectangular solid chunks that looked like the blocks that human children played with on Earth.

"Why do you think we've never seen any of the Others?" Katie now asked. "I mean, in here. We see them for a second or two in the Tube and that's all. We know they're here—we aren't the only ones being tested."

"This room is scheduled very carefully," her mother replied. "It's obvious that we weren't *meant* to see the Others, except in passing."

"But *why?* The Eagle ought—" Katie persisted.

"Excuse me," Simone interrupted. "But I think Big Block is coming over to see us."

The largest of the block robots usually stayed in the square control area in the center of the room and monitored all the experiments that were under way. At that moment he was moving toward them down one of the lanes that formed a grid in the room.

Katie walked over to another compartment about twenty meters away. From the active monitor on its exterior wall, she could tell that an experiment was under way inside. Suddenly she pounded on the metal quite sharply with her gloved hand.

"Katie," Nicole shouted.

"Stop that," a sound came from Big Block almost simultaneously. He was about fifty meters away and approaching them very rapidly. "You must not do that," he said in perfect but clipped English.

"And what are you going to do about it?" Katie said defiantly as Big Block, all five square meters of him, ignored Nicole and Simone and headed for the young girl. Nicole ran over to protect her daughter.

"You must leave now," Big Block said, hovering over Nicole and Katie from only a couple of meters away. "Your test is over. The exit is over there where the lights are flashing."

Nicole tugged firmly on Katie's arm and the girl reluctantly accompanied her mother toward the exit. "But what *would* they do," Katie said stubbornly, "if we decided to stay here until another experiment was finished? Who knows? Maybe one of our octospiders is in there right now. Why are we never allowed to meet anyone else?"

"The Eagle has explained several times," Nicole replied, a trace of anger in her voice, "that during 'this phase' we will be permitted 'sightings' of other creatures but no additional contact. Your father has repeatedly asked why and the Eagle has always answered that we will find out in time. . . . And I wish you would try not to be so difficult, young lady."

"It's not much different from being in prison," Katie groused. "We have only limited freedom here. And we're never told the answers to the really important questions."

They had reached the long passageway that connected the transportation center to the laboratory. A small vehicle, sitting at the edge of a moving sidewalk, was waiting for them. When they sat down, the top of the car closed over them and interior lights were illuminated. "Before you ask," Nicole said to Katie, pulling off her helmet as they started to move, "we are not allowed to see out during this part of the transfer because we pass portions of the Engineering Module that are off limits to us. Your father and Uncle Michael asked this set of questions after their first sleep test."

"Do you agree with Daddy," Simone inquired after they had been riding in silence for several minutes, "that we have been having all these sleep tests in preparation for some kind of space voyage?"

"It seems likely," Nicole answered. "But of course we don't know for certain."

"And where are they going to send us?" asked Katie.

"I have no idea," Nicole replied. "The Eagle has been very evasive on all questions about our future."

The car was moving about twenty kilometers per hour. After a fifteen-minute ride it stopped. The "lid" of the vehicle rolled itself back as soon as all the helmets were properly in place again. The women exited into the main transportation center of the Engineering Module. It was laid out in a circle and was twenty meters tall. In addition to half a dozen moving sidewalks leading to locations interior to the module, the center contained two large, multilevel structures from which the sleek tubes departed. These tubes transported equipment, robots, and living creatures back and forth among the Habitation, Engineering, and Administration modules, the three huge spherical complexes that were the primary components of the Node.

As soon as they were inside the station, Nicole and her daughters heard a voice on their helmet receivers. "Your tube will be on the second level. Take the escalator on the right. You will be departing in four minutes."

Katie rolled her head from side to side, surveying the transportation center. She could see racks of equipment, cars waiting to take travelers to destinations inside the Engineering Module, lights, escalators, and station platforms. But there was nothing moving. No robots and no living creatures.

"What would happen," she said to her sister and mother, "if we refused to go up there?" She stopped in the middle of the station. "Then your schedule would be all fouled up," she shouted at the tall ceiling.

"Come on, Katie," Nicole said impatiently, "we just went through this in the laboratory."

Katie started walking again. "But I *do* want to see something different," she complained. "I know that this place is not always this empty. Why are we kept isolated? It's as if we're unclean or something."

"Your tube will depart in two minutes," the disembodied voice said. "Second level on the right."

"Isn't it amazing that the robots and controllers can communicate with each and every species in its own language?" Simone commented as they reached the escalator.

"I think it's freaky," Katie replied. "Just for once, I'd like to see whoever or whatever controls this place make a mistake. Everything is too slick. I'd like to hear them speak avian to us. Or for that matter, speak avian to the avians."

On the second level they shuffled along a platform for about forty meters until they reached a transparent vehicle, shaped like a bullet, the size of an extremely large automobile on Earth. It was parked, as always, on a track on the left side of the median. There were four parallel tracks on the platform altogether, two on either side of the median. All the others were currently empty.

Nicole turned and looked across the transportation center. Sixty degrees around the circle was an identical tube station. The tubes on that side went to the Administration Module. Simone was watching her mother. "Have you ever been over there?" she asked.

"No," replied Nicole. "But I bet it would be interesting. Your father says it looks wonderfully strange from up close."

Richard just had to explore, Nicole thought, remembering the night almost a year ago when her husband set out to "hitch" a ride to the Administration Module. Nicole shuddered. She had gone out into the atrium of their apartment with Richard and tried to dissuade him while he was putting on his space suit. He had figured out how to fool the door monitor (the next day a new, foolproof system was in place) and could hardly wait to take an "unsupervised" look around.

Nicole had barely slept that night. In the wee hours of the morning their light panel had signaled that someone or something was in the atrium. When she had looked on the monitor, there was a strange birdman standing there, holding her unconscious husband in his arms. That had been their first contact with the Eagle. . . .

The thrust of the tube momentarily pinned them against the backs of their seats and returned Nicole to the present. They zoomed away from the Engineering Module. In less than a minute they were hurtling at full speed down the long, extremely narrow cylinder that connected the two modules.

The median and four tube tracks were at the center of the long cylinder. Out to their right, in the far distance, the lights of the spherical Administration Module shone against a blue background of space. Katie had her tiny binoculars out. "I want to be ready," she said. "They always go by so fast."

Several minutes later she announced "It's coming" and the three women pressed against the right side of the vehicle. In the far distance another tube approached on the opposite side of the track. Within instants it was upon them and the humans had no more than a second to stare across at the occupants of the vehicle heading for the Engineering Module.

"Wow!" said Katie as the tube rushed past.

"There were two different types," said Simone.

"Eight or ten creatures altogether."

"One set was pink, the other gold. Both mostly spherical."

"And those long stringy tentacles, like gossamer. How big would you guess they were, Mother?"

"Five, maybe six meters in diameter," Nicole said. "Much bigger than we are."

"Wow!" said Katie again. "That was really something." There was excitement in her eyes. The girl loved the feeling of adrenaline rushing through her system.

I too have never stopped being amazed, Nicole thought. *Not once during these thirteen months. But is this all there is? Were we brought all the way here from Earth just to be tested? And titillated by the existence of creatures from other worlds? Or is there some other, deeper purpose?*

There was a momentary silence in the speeding vehicle. Nicole, who was sitting in the middle, drew her daughters closer to her. "You know I love you, don't you?" she said.

"Yes, Mother," Simone replied. "And we love you too."

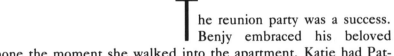

2

The reunion party was a success. Benjy embraced his beloved Simone the moment she walked into the apartment. Katie had Patrick pinned to the floor no more than a minute later.

"See," she said, "I can still beat you."

"But not by much," Patrick replied. "I'm getting stronger. You'd better watch out."

Nicole hugged both Richard and Michael before little Ellie ran over and leapt into her arms. It was evening, two hours after dinner on the twenty-four-hour clock used by the family, and Ellie had been almost ready for bed when her mother and sisters had arrived. The little girl walked down the hall to her room after proudly showing Nicole that she could now read *cat, dog,* and *boy*.

The adults let Patrick stay awake until he was exhausted. Michael carried him to bed and Nicole tucked him in. "I'm glad you're back, Mommy," he said. "I missed you very much."

"And I missed you too," Nicole answered. "I don't think I'll be going away for so long again."

"I hope not," the six-year-old said. "I like having you here."

Everyone but Nicole was asleep by one o'clock in the morning. Nicole was not tired. After all, she had just finished sleeping for five weeks. After lying restlessly beside Richard in bed for thirty minutes, she decided to take a walk.

Although their apartment itself had no windows, the small atrium just off the entrance hall had an exterior window that offered a breathtaking view of the other two vertices of the Node. Nicole walked into the atrium, put on her space suit, and stood in front of the outer door. It did not open. She smiled to herself. *Maybe Katie's right. Maybe we are just prisoners here.* It had been clear very early in their stay that the outside door was locked intermittently; the Eagle had explained that it was "necessary" to keep them from seeing things they "couldn't understand."

Nicole gazed out the window. At that moment a shuttle vehicle, similar in shape to the one that had brought them to the Node thirteen months before, was approaching the Habitation Module transportation center. *What kind of wonderful creatures do you contain?* Nicole thought. *And are they as astounded as we were when we first arrived?*

Nicole would never forget those first views of the Node. All of the family had thought, after they had left the way station, that they would reach their next destination within several hours. They had been wrong. Their separation from the illuminated Rama craft had grown slowly until after six hours they could no longer see Rama at all on their left. The lights of the Way Station behind them were becoming faint. They were all tired. Eventually the entire family had fallen asleep.

It had been Katie who had awakened them. "I see where we're going," she had shouted triumphantly, her excitement unrestrained. She had pointed out the front shuttle window, a little to the right, where one strong and growing light was dividing itself into three. For the next four hours the image of the Node grew and grew. From that distance it had been an awesome sight, an equilateral triangle with three glowing, transparent spheres at its vertices. And what a scale! Even their experience with Rama had not prepared them for the majesty of this incredible engineering creation. Each of the three sides, actually long transportation corridors connecting the three spherical modules, was over a hundred and fifty kilometers in length. The spheres at each vertex were twenty-five kilometers in diameter. Even from a great distance the humans could discern activity on many of the separate levels inside the modules.

"What is going to happen now?" Patrick had anxiously asked Nicole as the shuttle had altered its path and started heading toward one of the vertices of the triangle.

Nicole had picked Patrick up and held him in her arms. "I

don't know, darling," she had said softly to her son. "We have to wait and see."

Benjy had been completely awestruck. He had stared for hours at the great illuminated triangle in space. Simone had often stood beside him, holding his hand. While the shuttle was making its final approach to one of the spheres, she had felt his muscles tense. "Don't worry, Benjy," Simone had said reassuringly, "everything will be all right."

Their shuttle had entered a narrow corridor cut into the sphere and then docked in a berth at the edge of the transportation center. The family had cautiously left the craft, carrying with them their bags and Richard's computer. Then the shuttle had immediately departed, unnerving even the adults by its swift disappearance. Less than a minute later they heard the first disembodied voice.

"Welcome," it had said in an unmodulated tone. "You have arrived at the Habitation Module. Proceed straight ahead and stand in front of the gray wall."

"Where is that voice coming from?" Katie had asked. Her voice contained the fright they all were feeling.

"Everywhere," Richard had answered. "It's above us, around us, even below us." They all scanned the walls and ceiling.

"But how does it know English?" Simone had inquired. "Are there other people here?"

Richard laughed nervously. "Unlikely," he replied. "Probably this place has been in contact with Rama in some way and has a master language algorithm. I wonder—"

"Please move forward," the voice had interrupted. "You are in a transportation complex. The vehicle that will take you to your section of the module is waiting on a lower level."

It had taken them several minutes to reach the gray wall. The children had never been in unconfined weightlessness before. Katie and Patrick jumped off the platform and did flips and rolls in the air. Benjy, watching their fun, tried to copy their antics. Unfortunately, he was not able to figure out how to use the ceiling and walls to return to the platform. He was completely disoriented by the time Simone rescued him.

When the entire family and its baggage were properly positioned in front of the wall, a wide door opened and they entered a small room. Special tight-fitting suits, helmets, and slippers were neatly arranged on a bench. "The transportation center and most of the common areas here at the Node," the voice said in its absolute monotone, "do not have an atmosphere that is suitable for your species. You will need to wear this clothing unless you are inside your apartment."

When they were all dressed, a door on the opposite side of the room opened and they entered the main hall of the Habitation Module transportation center. The station was identical to the one they would later encounter at the Engineering Module. Nicole and her family descended two levels, as directed by the voice, and then proceeded around the circular periphery to where their "bus" was waiting. The closed vehicle was comfortable and well lit, but they were unable to see out during the hour and a half that it traveled through a maze of passageways. At length the bus halted and its top lifted off.

"Take the hall to your left," another, similar voice had directed as soon as all eight of them were standing on the metallic floor. "The hall splits into two pathways after four hundred meters. Take the path to your right and stop in front of the third square marker on the left. That is the door to your apartment."

Patrick had sprinted off down one of the halls. "That is the wrong hall," the voice had announced without inflection. "Return to the dock and take the next hall on your left."

There was nothing for them to see on the walk from the dock to their apartment. In the succeeding months, they would make the walk many times, either going to the exercise room or, occasionally, for tests over in the Engineering Module, and they would still never see anything except walls and ceilings and the square markers they would come to recognize as doors. The place was obviously carefully monitored. Nicole and Richard both felt certain, from the very beginning, that some, perhaps many, of the apartments in their area were occupied by someone or something, but they never ever saw any of the Others in the corridors.

After finding and entering the specified door to their apartment, Nicole and her family removed their special clothing in the atrium and stored it in the cabinets created for that purpose. The children took turns looking out the window at the other two spherical modules while they waited for the inner door to open. A few minutes later they saw the interior of their new home for the very first time.

They were all overwhelmed. Compared to the relatively primitive conditions in which they had been living in Rama, the family's apartment at the Node was paradise. Each of the children had his or her own room. Michael had a suite for himself at one end of the unit; Richard and Nicole's master bedroom, complete even with a king-sized bed, was at the opposite end of the apartment, just off the entrance hall. There were four bathrooms altogether, plus a kitchen, a dining room, and even a playroom for the children. The furniture in each room was surprisingly appropriate and tastefully designed. The apartment contained over four hundred square meters of living space.

Even the adults were stunned. "How in the world could they have done this?" Nicole had asked Richard that first night, out of earshot of the overjoyed children.

Richard had cast a bewildered glance around them. "I can only surmise," he had replied, "that somehow all our actions in Rama were monitored and telemetered here to the Node. They must also have had access to our data bases and extracted the way we live from that set of information." Richard grinned. "And of course, even way out here, if they have sensitive receivers, they could be picking up television signals from Earth. Isn't it embarrassing to think that we are represented by such—"

"Welcome," another identical voice had interrupted Richard's thought. Again the sound seemed to be coming from all directions. "We hope everything in your apartment is satisfactory. If it is not, please tell us. We cannot possibly respond to everything that all of you say at all times. Therefore, a simple communication regimen has been established. On your kitchen counter is a white button. We will assume that everything said by an individual after pushing the white button is directed at us. When you are finished with your communication, push the white button again. In that way—"

"I have one question first," Katie had then interrupted. She had run into the kitchen to push the button. "Just who are you, anyway?"

A tiny delay of maybe one second had preceded the answer. "We are the collective intelligence that governs the Node. We are here to assist you, to make you more comfortable, and to supply you with the essentials for living. We will also, from time to time, ask you to perform certain tasks that will help us to understand you better. . . ."

Nicole could no longer see the shuttle she had been watching out the window. Actually, she had been so deeply immersed in her memory of their arrival at the Node that she had temporarily forgotten the newcomers. Now, as she returned to the present, in her mind's eye she imagined an assemblage of strange creatures disembarking on a platform and being startled upon hearing a voice address them in their native language. *The experience of wonder must be universal*, she thought. *Belonging to all conscious chemicals.*

Her eyes lifted from the near field and focused on the Administration Module in the distance. *What goes on over there?* Nicole wondered. *We hapless creatures move back and forth between Habitation and Engineering. All our activities appear to be logically orchestrated. But by whom? And for what? Why has someone brought all these beings to this artificial world?*

Nicole had no answer to these infinite questions. As usual, they gave her a powerful sense of her own insignificance. Her immediate impulse was to go back inside and hug one of her children. She laughed at herself. *Both pictures are true indications of our position in the cosmos,* she thought. *We are both desperately important to our children and absolutely nothing in the grand scheme of things. It takes enormous wisdom to see that there is no inconsistency in those two points of view.*

3

Breakfast was a celebration. They ordered a feast from the exceptional cooks who prepared their food. The designers of their apartment had considerately provided them with a variety of ovens and a full refrigerator, in case they wanted to prepare their own meals from the raw materials. However, the alien (or robot) cooks were so good, and so quickly trained, that Nicole and her family almost never prepared the meals themselves—they just pushed the white button and ordered.

"I want pancakes this morning," Katie announced in the kitchen.

"Me too, me too," her sidekick Patrick added.

"What kind of pancakes?" the voice intoned. "We have four different types in our memory. There is buckwheat, buttermilk—"

"Buttermilk," interrupted Katie. "Three altogether." She glanced at her little brother. "Better make it four."

"With butter and maple syrup," Patrick shouted.

"Four pancakes with butter and maple syrup," said the voice. "Will that be all?"

"One apple juice and one orange juice as well," Katie said after a brief consultation with Patrick.

"Six minutes and eighteen seconds," the voice said.

When the food was ready, the family gathered at the round table in the kitchen. The youngest children explained to Nicole what they had been doing during her absence. Patrick was especially proud of his new personal record in the fifty-meter dash over in the exercise room. Benjy laboriously counted to ten and everyone applauded. They had just finished breakfast and were cleaning the dishes off the table when the doorbell rang.

The adults looked at each other and Richard walked over to the control console, where he turned on the video monitor. The Eagle was standing outside their door.

"I hope it's not another test," said Patrick spontaneously.

"No . . . no, I doubt it," Nicole replied, moving toward the entryway. "He's probably here to give us the results of the last experiments."

Nicole took a deep breath before she opened the door. No matter how many times she encountered the Eagle, her adrenaline level always increased in his presence. Why was that? Was it his awesome knowledge that frightened her? Or his power over them? Or just the bewildering fact of his existence?

The Eagle greeted her with what she had come to recognize as a smile. "May I come in?" he said pleasantly. "I would like to talk to you, your husband, and Mr. O'Toole."

Nicole stared at him (or *it*, her mind instantly flashed), as she always did. He was tall, maybe two and a quarter meters, and shaped like a human being from the neck down. His arms and torso, however, were covered with small, tightly woven charcoal gray feathers—except for the four fingers on each hand, which were creamy white and featherless. Below his waist, the surface of the Eagle's body was flesh-colored, but it was obvious from the sheen of his outer layer that no attempt had been made to duplicate real human skin. There was no hair below his waist and neither visible joints nor genitalia. His feet had no toes. When the Eagle walked, wrinkles developed around the knee area, but they disappeared when he was standing still.

The Eagle's face was mesmerizing. His head had two large, powder blue eyes on either side of a protruding grayish beak. When he talked the beak opened and his perfect English came from some kind of electronic voice box at the back of the throat. The feathers on the top of his head were white and contrasted sharply with the dark gray of his face, neck, and back. The feathering on his face was quite sparse and scattered.

"May I come in?" the Eagle repeated politely when Nicole did not move for several seconds.

"Of course . . . of course," she replied, moving away from the door. "I'm sorry . . . I just hadn't seen you for so long."

"Good morning, Mr. Wakefield, Mr. O'Toole. Hello, children," the Eagle said as he strode into the living room.

Patrick and Benjy both backed away from him. Of all the children, only Katie and little Ellie did not seem to be afraid.

"Good morning," Richard replied. "And what can we do for you today?" he inquired. The Eagle *never* made social calls. There was always some purpose for his visits.

"As I told your wife at the door," the Eagle replied, "I need to talk to all three of you adults. Can Simone take care of the other children while we chat for an hour or so?"

Nicole had already started herding the children back into the playroom when the Eagle stopped her. "That won't be necessary," he said. "They can use the whole apartment. The four of us are going to the conference room across the hall."

Uh-oh, Nicole thought immediately. *This is something big. We've never left the children alone in the apartment before.*

She was suddenly very concerned about their safety. "Excuse me, Mr. Eagle," she said. "Will the children be all right here? I mean, they're not going to have any special visitors or anything like that. . . ."

"No, Mrs. Wakefield," the Eagle responded matter-of-factly. "I give you my word that nothing will interfere with your children."

Out in the atrium, when the three humans started to put on their space suits, the Eagle stopped them. "That won't be necessary," he said. "Last night we reconfigured this portion of the sector. We have sealed off the hall just before the junction and transformed this whole area into an Earthlike habitat. You'll be able to use the conference room without putting on any special clothing."

The Eagle started talking as soon as they sat down in the large conference room across the hall. "Since our first encounter you have repeatedly asked me questions about what you are doing here and I have not given you direct answers. Now that your final set of sleep tests are completed—successfully, I might add—I have been empowered to inform you about the next phase of your mission.

"I have also been given permission to tell you something about myself. As all of you have suspected, I am not a living creature—at least not by your definition." The Eagle laughed. "I was created by the intelligence that governs the Node to interface with you on sensitive issues. Our early observations of your behavior indicated a reluctance on your part to interact with the disembodied voices. It had already been decided to create me, or something similar, as an emissary to your family when you, Mr. Wakefield, nearly caused serious chaos in this sector by trying to make an unscheduled and unapproved visit to the Administration Module. My appearance at that time was designed to preclude further untoward behavior.

"We have now entered," the Eagle continued after only a momentary hesitation, "the most important time period of your stay here. The spaceship you call Rama is over at the Hangar undergoing major refurbishment and engineering redesign. You human beings will now take part in that redesign process, for some of you will be returning with Rama to the solar system in which you originated."

Richard and Nicole both started to interrupt. "Let me finish first," the Eagle said. "We have very carefully prepared my remarks to cover your anticipated questions."

The alien birdman glanced at each of the three humans around the table before continuing at a slower pace. "Notice that I did not say that you will be going back to Earth. If the nominal plan succeeds, those of you who return will interact with other human beings in your solar system, but not on your home planet. Only if there is some required deviation from the baseline plan will you actually return to Earth.

"Notice also that only *some* of you will be returning. Mrs. Wakefield," the Eagle said directly to Nicole, "you will definitely be traveling again in Rama. This is one of the constraints that we are placing on the mission. We will let you and the rest of your family decide who will accompany you on the journey. You can go alone if you choose, leaving everyone else here at the Node, or you can take some of the others. However, you cannot *all* make the voyage on Rama. At least one reproductive pair must stay here at the Node—to ensure some data for our encyclopedia in the unlikely event that the mission is unsuccessful.

"The primary purpose of the Node is to catalogue life-forms in this part of the galaxy. Spacefaring life-forms have the highest priority and our specifications call for us to collect vast amounts of data about each and every spacefarer we encounter. To accomplish this task, we have worked out, over hundreds of thousands of years of your time, a method of gathering this data that minimizes the likelihood of a cataclysmic intrusion into the evolutionary pattern of those spacefarers while at the same time maximizing the probability of our obtaining the vital data.

"Our basic approach involves sending observing spacecraft on reconnaissance missions, hoping to lure spacefarers to us so they can be identified and phenotyped. Repeat spacecraft are later sent to the same target, first to expand the degree of interaction, and ultimately to capture a representative subset of the spacefaring species so that long-term and detailed observations can take place in an environment of our choice."

The Eagle paused. Nicole's mind and heart were both racing at a frantic pace. She had so many questions. Why had she been especially selected to return? Would she be able to see Genevieve? And what exactly did the Eagle mean by the word *capture*—did he understand that the word was usually interpreted in a hostile manner? Why did—

"I think I understood most of what you said," Richard spoke first, "but you have omitted some crucial information. Why are you gathering all this data about spacefaring species?"

The Eagle smiled. "In our information hierarchy there are three basic levels. Access to each level by an individual or a species is permitted or denied based on a set of established criteria. With my earlier statements we have given you, as representatives of your species, Level II information for the first time. It is a tribute to your intelligence that your initial question seeks an answer which is classified as Level III."

"Does all that gobbledygook mean you're not going to tell us?" Richard asked, laughing nervously.

The Eagle nodded.

"*Will* you tell us why I alone am required to make the return voyage?" Nicole now asked.

"There are many reasons," the Eagle answered. "First, we believe you are the best suited physically for the return voyage. Our data also indicates that your superior communication skills will be invaluable after the capture phase of the mission is completed. There are additional considerations as well, but those two are the most important."

"When will we be leaving?" Richard asked.

"That's not certain. Part of the schedule is dependent on you. We will let you know when a firm departure date is established. I will tell you, however, that it will almost certainly be in less than four of your months."

We're going to leave very soon, Nicole thought. *And at least two of us must stay here. But who?*

"*Any* reproductive pair can be left here at the Node?" Michael now inquired, following the same pattern of thought as Nicole.

"Almost, Mr. O'Toole," the Eagle replied. "The youngest girl Ellie would not be acceptable with you as a partner—we might not

be able to keep you alive and fertile until she reaches sexual maturity—but any other combination would be fine. We must have a high
probability of successfully producing healthy offspring."

"Why?" Nicole asked.

"There exists a very small probability that your mission will not
be successful and that the pair left at the Node will be the only
humans we are able to observe. As infant spacefarers, having reached
that stage without the usual assistance, you are especially interesting
to us."

The conversation could have lasted indefinitely. However, after
several more questions, the Eagle abruptly rose and announced that
his participation in the conference was over. He encouraged the
humans to deal quickly with the issue of "allocation," as he called
it, for he intended to begin work almost immediately with those
members of the family who would be returning in the direction of
Earth. It would be their job to help him design the "Earth module
inside Rama." Without any additional explanation, he left the room.

The three adults agreed not to tell the children the most important details of their meeting with the Eagle for at least a day, until
after they had had a chance to reflect and converse among themselves. That night, after the children had gone to bed, Nicole, Richard, and Michael talked quietly in the living room of their apartment.

Nicole opened the conversation by admitting that she was feeling angry and powerless. Despite the fact that the Eagle had been
very nice about it, she said, he had basically ordered them to participate in the return mission. And how could they refuse? The entire
family was absolutely dependent upon the Eagle—or at least the
intelligence that he represented—for its survival. No threats had
been made, but no threats were needed. They had no choice but
to comply with the Eagle's instructions.

But who among the family should stay at the Node? Nicole
wondered aloud. Michael said it was absolutely essential that at least
one adult remain at the Node. His argument was persuasive. Any
two of the children, even Simone and Patrick, would need the benefit of an adult's experience and wisdom to have any chance for happiness under the circumstances. Michael then volunteered to stay at
the Node, saying that it was unlikely he would survive a return trip
anyway.

All three of them agreed that it was clearly the Nodal intelligence's intention to have the humans sleep most of the way back
to the solar system. Otherwise, what was the purpose of all the sleep

tests? Nicole did not like the idea of the children missing out on the critical development periods of their lives. She suggested that she should return alone, leaving everyone else in the family at the Node. After all, she reasoned, it's not as if the children would have a "normal" life on Earth after they make the journey.

"If we are interpreting the Eagle correctly," she said, "anybody who returns will end up ultimately as a passenger on Rama heading to some other location in the Galaxy."

"We don't know that for certain," Richard argued. "On the other hand, whoever stays here is almost certainly doomed to never seeing any humans other than the family."

Richard added that he intended to make the return trip under any circumstances, not just to be a companion for Nicole, but also to experience the adventure.

The trio could not reach a final agreement about the deployment of the children during that first evening's discussion. But they did firmly resolve the issue of what the adults were going to do. Michael O'Toole would stay at the Node. Nicole and Richard would make the return journey to the solar system.

In bed after the meeting Nicole could not sleep. She kept running through all the options in her mind. She was certain that Simone would make a better mother than Katie. Besides, Simone and Uncle Michael were extremely compatible and Katie would not want to be separated from her father. But who should be left to mate with Simone? Should it be Benjy, who loved his sister madly, but would never be able to engage in an intelligent conversation?

Nicole tossed and turned for hours. In truth, she didn't like any of the choices. She understood well the source of her disquiet. However the issue was resolved, she would be forced once again to separate, probably permanently, from at least a few members of the family that she loved. As she lay in her bed in the middle of the night the ghosts and pain of past separations returned to haunt her. Nicole's heart ached as she imagined the parting that would come in a few months. Pictures of her mother, her father, and Genevieve tugged at her heartstrings. *Maybe that's all life is*, she thought in her temporary depression, *an endless sequence of painful partings*.

4

"Mother, Father, wake up. I want to talk to you."

Nicole had been dreaming. She had been walking in the woods behind her family villa at Beauvois. It had been springtime and the flowers had been magnificent. It took her a few seconds to realize that Simone was sitting on their bed.

Richard reached over and kissed his daughter on the forehead. "What is it, dear?" he asked.

"Uncle Michael and I were saying our matins together and I could tell that he was distressed." Simone's serene eyes moved slowly back and forth from one parent to the other. "He told me everything about your conversation yesterday with the Eagle."

Nicole sat up quickly as Simone continued. "I've had over an hour now to think carefully about everything. I know I'm only a thirteen-year-old girl, but I believe I have a solution to this, uh, allocation issue that will make everybody in the family happy."

"My dear Simone," Nicole replied, reaching out for her daughter, "it's not your responsibility to solve—"

"No, Mother," Simone gently interrupted. "Please hear me out. My solution involves something that none of you adults would ever even consider. It could only come from me. And it's obviously the best plan for everyone concerned."

Richard's brow was now furrowed. "What are you talking about?" he said.

Simone took a deep breath. "I want to stay at the Node with Uncle Michael. I will become his wife and we will be the Eagle's 'reproductive pair.' Nobody else needs to stay, but Michael and I would be happy to keep Benjy with us as well."

"*Whaat?*" Richard shouted. He was flabbergasted. "Uncle Michael is seventy-two years old! You're not even fourteen yet. It's preposterous, ridiculous—" He was suddenly silent.

The mature young woman who was his daughter smiled. "More preposterous than the Eagle?" she replied. "More ridiculous than the fact that we have traveled eight light-years from the Earth to rendezvous with a giant intelligent triangle that is now going to send some of us back in the opposite direction?"

Nicole regarded Simone with awe and admiration. She said nothing, but reached out and gave her daughter a strong hug. Tears swam in Nicole's eyes. "It's all right, Mother," Simone said after the embrace was ended. "After you recover from the initial shock, you'll realize that what I'm suggesting is by far the best solution. If you and Father make the return trip together—as I think you should—then either Katie or Ellie or I must stay here at the Node and mate with Patrick or Benjy or Uncle Michael. The only combination that is genetically sound is either Katie or I with Uncle Michael. I've thought through all the possibilities. Michael and I are very close. We have the same religion. If we stay and marry, then each of the other children is free to choose. They can either remain here with us or return to the solar system with you and Daddy."

Simone put her hand on her father's forearm. "Daddy, I know that in many ways this will be harder on you than it is on Mother. I have not yet mentioned my idea to Uncle Michael. He certainly did not suggest it. If you and Mother don't give me your support, then it can't work. This marriage will be difficult enough for Michael to accept even if you don't object."

Richard shook his head. "You are amazing, Simone." He embraced her. "Please let us think about it for a while. Promise me you won't say another word about this until your mother and I have had a chance to talk."

"I promise," Simone said. "Thank you both very much. I love you," she added at the door to their bedroom.

She turned and walked down the illuminated hall. Her long black hair reached almost to her waist. *You have become a woman,* Nicole thought, watching Simone's graceful walk. *And not just physi-*

cally. You are mature way beyond your years. Nicole imagined Michael and Simone as husband and wife and was surprised that she didn't find it at all objectionable. *Considering everything,* Nicole said to herself, realizing that after his protests Michael O'Toole would be very happy, *your idea may be the least unsatisfactory choice in our difficult situation.*

Simone did not waver from her intention even when Michael objected strenuously to what he called her "proposed martyrdom." She explained to him, patiently, that her marriage to him was the only one possible since Katie and he were, by everyone's assessment, incompatible personalities, and anyway Katie was still only a girl, a year or eighteen months away from sexual maturity. Would he prefer that she marry one of her half brothers and commit incest? No, no, he responded.

Michael assented when he saw that there were no other viable choices and that neither Richard nor Nicole raised any strong objections to the marriage. Richard, of course, tempered his approval with the phrase "in these unusual circumstances," but Michael could tell that Simone's father had at least partially accepted the idea of his thirteen-year-old daughter marrying a man old enough to be her grandfather.

Within a week it had been decided, with the children's involvement, that Katie, Patrick, and little Ellie would all make the return trip on Rama with Richard and Nicole. Patrick was reluctant to leave his father, but Michael O'Toole graciously agreed that his six-year-old son would probably have a "more interesting and fulfilling" life if he stayed with the rest of the family. That left only Benjy. The adorable boy, chronologically eight but mentally equivalent to an average three-year-old, was told that he would be welcome either in Rama or at the Node. He could barely comprehend what was going to happen to the family, and was certainly not prepared to make such a momentous choice. The decision frightened and confused him; he became quite distraught and lapsed into a deep depression. As a result, the family postponed discussions of Benjy's fate until an undefined time in the future.

"We will be gone a day and a half, maybe two," the Eagle said to Michael and the children. "Rama is being reconditioned at a facility about ten thousand kilometers from here."

"But I want to go too," Katie said petulantly. "I also have some good ideas for the Earth module."

"We'll involve you in later phases of the process," Richard assured Katie. "We'll have a design center right here beside us, in the conference room."

Eventually Richard and Nicole finished their good-byes and joined the Eagle in the hallway. They put on their special suits and crossed over into the common area of the sector. Nicole could tell that Richard was excited. "You do love adventure, don't you, darling?" she said.

He nodded. "I think it was Goethe who said that everything a human being wants can be divided into four components—love, adventure, power, and fame. Our personalities are shaped by how much of each component we seek. For me, adventure has always been numero uno."

Nicole was contemplative as they entered a waiting car along with the Eagle. The lid closed over them and again they could not see anything during their ride to the transportation center. *Adventure is very important to me also*, Nicole thought. *And as a young girl fame was my uppermost goal.* She smiled to herself. *But now it's definitely love. . . . We would be boring if we never changed.*

They traveled in a shuttle identical to the one that had brought them to the Node originally. The Eagle sat in front, Richard and Nicole in the rear. The view behind them of the spherical modules, the transportation corridors, and the entire lighted triangle was absolutely sensational.

The direction they were going was toward Sirius, the dominant feature in the space surrounding the Node. The large, young white star glowed in the distance, appearing roughly the same size as their native Sun would look from the asteroid belt.

"How did you happen to pick this location for the Node?" Richard asked the Eagle after they had been cruising for about an hour.

"What do you mean?" he replied.

"Why here, why in the Sirius system, instead of some other place?"

The Eagle laughed. "This location is only temporary," he said. "We'll be moving again as soon as Rama departs."

Richard was puzzled. "You mean the entire Node *moves*?" He turned around and glanced back at the triangle glowing faintly in the distance. "Where is the propulsion system?"

"There are small propulsion capabilities in each of the modules, but they are only used in case of an emergency. Transport between temporary holding sites is accomplished by what you would call tugs—they affix themselves to ports on the sides of the spheres and provide virtually all the trajectory change velocity."

Nicole thought about Michael and Simone and became worried. "Where will the Node go?" she asked.

"It's probably not specified exactly yet," the Eagle answered vaguely. "It's always a stochastic function anyway, depending on how the various activities are proceeding." He continued after a short silence. "When our work in a specific place is finished, the entire configuration—Node, Hangar, and Way Station—are moved to another region of interest."

Richard and Nicole stared silently at each other in the backseat. They were having difficulty grasping the magnitude of what the Eagle was telling them. The *entire* Node *moved*! It was too much to believe. Richard decided to change the subject.

"What is your definition of a spacefaring species?" he asked the Eagle.

"One that has ventured, either on its own or through its robot surrogates, outside the sensible atmosphere of its home planet. If its own planet has no atmosphere, or if the species has no home planet at all, then the definition is more complicated."

"You mean there are intelligent creatures that have evolved in a vacuum? How can that be possible?"

"You're an atmospheric chauvinist," the Eagle replied. "Like all creatures, you limit the ways that life might express itself to environments similar to your own."

"How many spacefaring species are there in our galaxy?" Richard asked a little later.

"That's one of the objectives of our project—to answer that question exactly. Remember, there are more than a hundred billion stars in the Milky Way. Slightly more than a quarter of them have planetary systems surrounding them. If only one out of every million stars with planets was home to a spacefaring species, then there would still be twenty-five thousand spacefarers in our galaxy alone."

The Eagle turned around and looked at Richard and Nicole. "The estimated number of spacefarers in the galaxy, as well as the spacefarer density in any specified zone, is Level III information. But I can tell you one thing. There are Life Dense Zones in the galaxy where the average number of spacefarers is greater than one per thousand stars."

Richard whistled. "This is staggering stuff," he said to Nicole excitedly. "It means that the local evolutionary miracle that pro- duced us is a common paradigm in the universe. We are unique, to be sure, for nowhere else would the process that produced us have been duplicated exactly. But the characteristic that is truly special about our species—namely our ability to model our world and understand both it and where we fit into its overall scheme—that capability must belong to thousands of creatures! For without that ability they could not have become spacefarers."

Nicole was overwhelmed. She recalled a similar moment, years before when she was with Richard in the photograph room of the octospider lair in Rama, when she had struggled to grasp the immensity of the universe in terms of total information content. Again now she realized that the entire set of knowledge in the human domain, everything that any member of the human species had ever learned or experienced, was no more than a single grain of sand on the great beach representing everything that had ever been known by all the sentient creatures of the universe.

5

Their shuttle stopped several hundred kilometers from the Hangar. The facility had a strange shape, completely flat on the bottom but with rounded sides and top. The three factories in the Hangar—one at each end and another in the middle—each looked from the outside like geodesic domes. They rose sixty or seventy kilometers above the bottom of the structure. Between these factories the roof was much lower, only eight or ten kilometers above the flat plane, so the overall appearance of the top of the Hangar was what might have been expected from the back of a three-humped camel, if such a creature had ever existed.

The Eagle, Nicole, and Richard had stopped to watch a starfish craft which, according to the Eagle, had been reconditioned and was now ready for its next voyage. The starfish had come out of the left hump. Although small compared to either the Hangar or Rama, the starfish was still almost ten kilometers from its center to the end of a ray. It had begun to spin as soon as it was free of the Hangar. As the shuttle remained "parked" some fifteen kilometers away, the starfish increased its spin rate to ten revolutions per minute. Once its spin rate was stabilized, the starfish zoomed away to the left.

"That leaves only Rama out of this set," the Eagle said. "The giant wheel, which was first in your queue at the Way Station, left four months ago. It required only minimal refurbishing."

Richard wanted to ask a question, but he restrained himself. He had already learned during the flight from the Node that the Eagle voluntarily gave them virtually all the information he was allowed to share. "Rama has been quite a challenge," the Eagle continued. "And we're still not certain exactly when we will finish."

The shuttle approached the right dome of the Hangar and lights began to shine at the five o'clock position on the dome's face. Upon closer inspection Richard and Nicole could see that some small doors had opened. "You'll need your suits," the Eagle said. "It would have been a major engineering feat to have designed this huge place with a variable environment."

Nicole and Richard dressed while the shuttle docked in a berth very similar to the one at their transportation center. "Can you hear me all right?" the Eagle said, testing the communication system.

"Roger," Richard replied from inside his helmet. He and Nicole glanced at each other and laughed as they remembered their days as Newton cosmonauts.

The Eagle led them down a long, wide corridor. At the end they turned right through a door and came out on a broad balcony ten kilometers above a factory floor larger than anyone could possibly imagine. Nicole felt her knees weaken as she stared into the giant abyss. Despite the weightlessness, waves of vertigo swept through both Richard and Nicole. They both turned away at the same moment. They focused their eyes on each other while they tried to comprehend what they had just seen.

"It's quite a sight," the Eagle commented.

What a colossal understatement, Nicole thought. She very slowly lowered her eyes again to the awesome spectacle. This time she held on to the rail with both hands to help her equilibrium.

The factory below them contained the entire Northern Hemicylinder of Rama, from the port end where they had docked the Newton and entered, down to the end of the Central Plain at the banks of the Cylindrical Sea. There was no sea, and no Raman city of New York, but there was almost as much real estate in this one enclosed factory as in the entire American state of Rhode Island.

The crater and bowl of the north end of Rama were still completely intact, including the outer shell. These segments of Rama were positioned to the right of Richard, Nicole, and the Eagle, almost behind them as they stood on the platform. Mounted in front of them on the railings were a dozen telescopes, each with a different resolution, through which the three of them could see the familiar ladders and stairways, resembling three ribs of an umbrella, that took thirty thousand steps to descend (or ascend) to the Central Plain of Rama.

The rest of the Northern Hemicylinder was split open and lying beneath them in parts, not directly connected to the bowl or to each other, but nevertheless lying with adjacent sectors in the proper alignment. Each part was roughly six to eight square kilometers and its edges rose, due to the curvature, substantially off the floor.

"It's easier to do the early work in this configuration," the Eagle explained. "Once we've closed the cylinder it's harder to get in and out with all the equipment."

Through the telescopes Richard and Nicole could see that two different areas of the Central Plain were teeming with activity. They could not begin to count the number of robots going to and fro on the floor of the factory below them. Nor could they determine exactly what was being done in many cases. It was engineering on a scale never dreamed of by humans.

"I brought you up here first to give you an overview," the Eagle said. "Later we will go down on the floor and you can see more of the details."

Richard and Nicole stared at him dumbfounded. The Eagle laughed and continued. "If you look carefully, and put the pieces together in your mind, you will see that two vast regions of the Central Plain, one near the Cylindrical Sea and another covering an area almost up to the end of the stairways, have been completely cleared. That's where all the new construction is going on. Between these two areas Rama looks exactly as it did when you left it. We have a general engineering guideline here—we only change those regions that are going to be used on the next mission."

Richard brightened. "Are you telling us that this spacecraft is used *over and over*? And that for each mission only *required* changes are made?"

The Eagle nodded.

"Then that conglomeration of skyscrapers we call New York might have been built for some much *earlier* mission, and simply *left* there because no changes were required?"

The Eagle did not say anything in response to Richard's rhetorical question. He was pointing at the northern area of the Central Plain. "That will be your habitat, over there. We have just finished the infrastructure, what you would call the 'utilities,' including water, power, sewer, and top-level environmental control. There is room for design flexibility in the rest of the process. That's why we have brought you over here."

"What is that tiny domed building south of the cleared area?" Richard asked. He was still staggered by the idea that New York might have been a leftover, a remnant from an earlier Raman voyage.

"That's the control center," the Eagle replied. "The equipment that manages your habitat will be stored there. Usually the control center is hidden beneath the living area, in the shell of Rama, but in your case the designers decided to put it on the Plain."

"What's that large region over there?" Nicole said, pointing at the cleared area immediately north of where the Cylindrical Sea would have been located if Rama had been completely reassembled.

"I'm not allowed to tell you what it's for," the Eagle replied. "In fact, I'm surprised that I have even been allowed to show you that it exists. Ordinarily our return voyagers are totally ignorant of the contents of their vehicle outside their own habitat. The nominal plan is, of course, for each species to stay within its own module."

"Look at that mound or tower in the center," Nicole said to Richard, directing his attention to the other region. "It must be almost two kilometers high."

"And it's shaped like a doughnut. I mean, the center is hollowed out."

They could see that the outside walls of what was possibly a second habitat were already quite advanced. None of its interior would be visible from the factory floor.

"Can you give us a hint as to who or what is going to live *there?*" Nicole asked.

"Come on," the Eagle said firmly, shaking his head. "It's time for us to descend."

Richard and Nicole disengaged themselves from the telescopes, took a quick look at the general layout of their own habitat (which was not nearly as far along in construction as the other one), and followed the Eagle back into the corridor. After five minutes of walking they reached what the Eagle told them was an elevator.

"You must buckle yourselves into these seats very carefully," their guide said. "This is quite a wild ride."

The acceleration in their bizarre oval capsule was powerful and swift. Less than two minutes later, the deceleration was equally abrupt. They had reached the factory floor. "This thing travels three hundred kilometers an hour?" Richard asked after doing some quick mental calculations.

"Unless it's in a hurry," the Eagle replied.

Richard and Nicole followed him out onto the factory floor. It was immense. In many ways it was more staggering than Rama itself, because almost half of the giant spacecraft was lying on the floor around them. They both remembered the overpowering feelings they had had riding in the chairlifts in Rama and looking out across the Cylindrical Sea at the mysterious horns in the southern bowl.

Those feelings of reverence and awe returned, and were even amplified, as Richard and Nicole stared at the activity going on around and above them in the factory.

The elevator had deposited them at the floor level just outside one of the portions of their habitat. The shell of Rama was in front of them. They checked its thickness as they walked across from the elevator exit. "About two hundred meters thick," Richard noted to Nicole, answering a question they had had since their first days in Rama.

"What will be beneath our habitat, in the shell?" Nicole asked.

The Eagle held up three of his four fingers, indicating that they were asking for Level III information. Both the humans laughed.

"Will you be going with us?" Nicole asked the Eagle a few moments later.

"Back to your solar system? No, I can't," he answered. "But I will admit that it would be interesting."

The Eagle led them over to an area of intense activity. Several dozen robots were working on a large, cylindrical structure about sixty meters tall. "This is the main fluid recycling plant," the Eagle said. "All the liquids that find their way into the drains or sewers in your habitat are eventually sent here. Purified water is piped back into the colony and the rest of the chemicals are retained for other possible uses. This plant will be sealed and impregnable. It uses technology far beyond your level of development."

The Eagle then led them up a ladder and into the habitat itself. He gave them an exhausting tour. In each sector the Eagle showed Richard and Nicole the main features of that particular area and then, without a break, commandeered a robot to transport them to the next adjacent sector.

"What exactly do you want us to do here?" Nicole inquired after several hours, as the Eagle prepared to take them to still another part of their future home.

"Nothing specific," the Eagle replied. "This will be your only visit to Rama itself. We wanted you to have a feel for the size of your habitat, in case you needed that to be more comfortable with the design process. We have a one-twentieth percent scale model back at the Habitation Module—all the rest of our work will be done there." He looked at Richard and Nicole. "We can leave whenever you want."

Nicole sat down on a gray metal box and gazed around her. The number and variety of the robots were enough to make her dizzy all by themselves. She had been overwhelmed since the moment she walked out on the balcony of the factory, and was now absolutely numb. She reached her hand out to Richard.

"I know I should be studying what I'm seeing, darling, but none of it makes sense anymore. I'm completely saturated."

"I am too," Richard confessed. "I never would have thought it possible that there was something more astonishing and awesome than Rama, but this factory certainly is."

"Have you wondered, since we've been here," Nicole said, "what the factory must look like that made this place? Better still, imagine the assembly line for the Node."

Richard laughed. "We can continue that comment into an infinite regression. If the Node is indeed a machine, as it appears to be, it assuredly is a higher order machine than Rama. Rama was probably designed here. It is controlled, I would guess, by the Node. But what created and controls the Node? Was it a creature like us, the result of biological evolution? And does it even still exist, in any sense that we can understand, or has it become some other kind of entity, content to let its influence be felt by the existence of these amazing machines that it created?"

Richard sat down beside his wife. "It's even too much for me. I guess I've had enough as well. . . . Let's go back to the children."

Nicole leaned over and kissed him. "You're a very smart man, Richard Wakefield," she said. "You know that's one of the reasons I love you."

A large robot resembling a forklift trundled close by them, carrying some rolled metal sheets. Richard again shook his head in wonder. "Thank you, darling," he said after a pause. "You know that I love you too.

They stood up together and signaled the Eagle that they were ready to leave.

The next night, back at their apartment in the Habitation Module, both Richard and Nicole were still alert thirty minutes after making love. "What is it, dear?" Nicole asked. "Is something wrong?"

"I had another foggy spell today," Richard said. "It lasted for almost three hours."

"Goodness," Nicole said. She sat up in bed. "Are you all right now? Should I get the scanner and see if I can tell anything from your biometry?"

"No," Richard answered, shaking his head. "My fogs have never registered on your machine. But this one really disturbed me.

I realized how incapacitated I am during them. I can barely function at all, much less help you or the children in any kind of crisis. They scare me."

"Do you remember what started this one?"

"Absolutely. Like always. I was thinking of our trip to the Hangar, especially about that other habitat. I inadvertently started remembering a few disconnected scenes from my odyssey and then suddenly there was the fog. It was total. I'm not certain I would have even recognized you during the first five minutes of its duration."

"I'm sorry, darling," Nicole said.

"It's almost as if something is monitoring my thoughts. And when I reach into a certain portion of my memory, then *bam*, I'm given some kind of warning."

Richard and Nicole were silent for almost a minute.

"When I close my eyes," Nicole said, "I still see all those robots scurrying around inside Rama."

"Me too."

"And yet, I still have great difficulty believing it was a real scene and not something I dreamed or saw in a movie." Nicole smiled. "We have lived an utterly unbelievable life these last fourteen years, haven't we?"

"Absolutely," Richard said, turning over on his side in his normal sleeping posture. "And who knows? The most interesting part may be still ahead of us."

6

The holographic model of New Eden was projected into the center of the large conference room at a 1/2,000 scale. Inside Rama the actual Earth habitat would occupy an area of one hundred and sixty square kilometers in the Central Plain, starting just opposite the bottom of the long northern stairway. Its enclosed volume would be twenty kilometers long in the direction around the cylinder, eight kilometers wide in the direction parallel to the cylindrical spin axis, and eight kilometers high from the colony floor to the towering ceiling.

The New Eden model at the Habitation Module, however, which the Eagle, Richard, and Nicole used for their design work, was a more manageable size. It easily fit into the single large room, and the holographic projections made it easy for the designers to walk through and among the various structures. Changes were made using the computer-aided design subroutines that acted upon the voice commands of the Eagle.

"We've changed our minds again," Nicole said, beginning their third marathon design discussion with the Eagle by encircling, with her black "flashlight," a concentration of buildings in the center of the colony. "We now think it's a bad idea to have everything in one place, with the people all on top of each other. Richard and I think it would make more sense if the living areas and small trade shops were in four separate villages at the corners of the rectangle. Only the buildings used by everyone in the colony would be in the central complex."

"Of course, our new concept will completely change the transportation flow you and I discussed yesterday," Richard added, "as well as the specific coordinate assignments for the parks, Sherwood Forest, Lake Shakespeare, and Mount Olympus. But all the original elements can still be accommodated in our current design for New Eden—here, take a look at this sketch and you can see where we have moved everything."

The Eagle seemed to grimace as he stared at his human helpers. After a second he looked at the map in Richard's electronic notebook. "I hope this will be the last major alteration," he commented. "We don't make much progress if every time we meet we essentially start the design all over."

"We're sorry," Nicole said. "But it has taken us a little while to grasp the magnitude of our task. We now understand that we're designing the long-term living situation for as many as two thousand human beings; if it takes several iterations to get it right, then we must spend the time."

"I see you've increased again the number of large structures in the central complex," the Eagle said. "What's the purpose of this building behind the library and auditorium?"

"It's a sports and recreation building," Nicole replied. "It will have a track, a baseball diamond, a soccer field, tennis courts, a gymnasium, and a swimming pool—plus enough seating in each area to handle almost all the citizens. Richard and I imagine that athletics will be very important in New Eden, especially since so many of the routine tasks will be handled by the biots."

"You've also expanded the sizes of the hospital and the schools—"

"We were too conservative in our original allocations of the space," Richard interrupted. "We didn't leave enough unassigned floor area for activities that we cannot yet define specifically."

The first two design meetings had lasted ten hours each. Both Richard and Nicole had marveled initially at how quickly the Eagle was able to integrate their comments into specific design recommendations. By the third meeting they were no longer amazed by the speed and accuracy of his synthesis. But the alien biot did surprise them regularly by showing a keen interest in some of the cultural details. For example, he queried them at length about the name the humans had given to their new colony. After Nicole had explained to him that it was essential that the habitat have some specific name, the Eagle asked about the meaning and significance of "New Eden."

"The whole family discussed the name of the habitat for most of one evening," Richard explained, "and there were many good suggestions, mostly derived from the history and literature of our species. Utopia was a leading candidate. Arcadia, Elysium, Paradise, Concordia, and Beauvois were all seriously considered. But in the end we thought New Eden was the best choice."

"You see," Nicole added, "the mythological Eden was a beginning, the start of what we might call our modern Western culture. It was a lush, verdant paradise, supposedly designed especially for humans by an all-powerful God who had also created everything else in the universe. That first Eden was rich in life-forms but devoid of technology.

"New Eden is also a beginning. But in almost every other way it is the opposite of the ancient garden. New Eden is a technological miracle without any life-forms, at least initially, except a few human beings."

Once the general layout of the colony was complete, there were still hundreds of details that had to be decided. Katie and Patrick were given the task of designing the neighborhood parks for each of the four villages. Even though neither of them had ever seen an actual blade of grass, a real flower, or a tall tree, they had watched plenty of movies and seen many, many photographs. They ended up with four different, tasteful designs for the five acres of open area, communal gardens, and peaceful walkways in each village.

"But where will we get the grass? And the flowers?" Katie asked the Eagle.

"They will be brought by the people from Earth," the Eagle replied.

"How will they know what to bring?"

"Someone will tell them."

It was also Katie who pointed out that the design of New Eden had omitted a key element, one that had played a major role in the bedtime stories her mother had told her when she was a little girl. "I've never seen a zoo," she said. "Can we have one in New Eden?"

The Eagle altered the master plan during the next design session to include a small zoo at the edge of Sherwood Forest.

Richard worked with the Eagle on most of the technological details for New Eden. Nicole's area of speciality was the living environment. The Eagle had originally suggested one kind of house with a standard set of furniture for all the homes in the colony. Nicole had laughed out loud. "You certainly haven't learned very much about us as a species," she said. "Human beings must have variety. Otherwise we become bored. If we make all the houses the same, people will start changing them immediately."

Because she had only limited time (the Eagle's requests for information were keeping Richard and Nicole working ten to twelve hours a day—luckily Michael and Simone were happy to look after the children), Nicole decided on eight basic house plans and four modular furniture arrangements. Altogether, then, there were thirty-two different living configurations. By varying the external design of the buildings in each of the four villages (details that Nicole worked out with Richard, after some useful input from art historian Michael O'Toole), Nicole finally achieved her goal of creating a design for everyday living that was neither uniform nor sterile.

Richard and the Eagle agreed on the New Eden transportation and communication systems, both external and internal, in just a few hours. They had more difficulty with the overall environmental control and biot designs. The Eagle's original concept, on which the infrastructure supporting New Eden was based, assumed twelve hours of light and twelve hours of darkness every day. Periods of sunlight, clouds, and rain were to be regular and predictable. There was to be virtually no variation in the temperature as a function of place and time.

When Richard requested seasonal changes in the length of the day and more variability in all the weather parameters, the Eagle stressed that allowing those "significant variations" in the enormous volume of air in the habitat would result in the use of much more "critical computational resource" than had originally been allocated during the infrastructure design. The Eagle also indicated that the major control algorithms would have to be restructured and retested, and that the departure date would be delayed as a result. Nicole supported Richard on the weather issue and the seasons, explaining to the Eagle that true human behavior ("which you and the Nodal Intelligence apparently want to observe") was definitely dependent on both these factors.

In the end a compromise was reached. The length of day and night throughout a year would match a location at thirty degrees latitude on the Earth. The weather in New Eden would be allowed to evolve naturally within specified limits, the master controller only acting when conditions reached the edge of the "design box." Thus the temperature, wind, and rainfall could freely fluctuate inside tolerances. The Eagle was adamant about two items, however. There could be no lightning and no ice. If either of those conditions (both of which introduced "new complexities" into his computational model) were imminent, even if the rest of the parameters were still within the design box, then the control system would take over automatically and regularize the weather.

It had been the Eagle's original intention to retain the same kind of biots that had been in the first two Rama craft. Richard and Nicole both, however, stressed to him that the Raman biots, especially the ones like the centipedes, mantises, crabs, and spiders, were not at all appropriate.

"The cosmonauts that have boarded the two Rama craft," Nicole explained, "would not be considered average humans. Far from it, in fact. We were especially trained to deal with sophisticated machines—and even some of *us* were frightened by a few of your biots. The more ordinary humans who will probably form the bulk of the New Eden inhabitants will not be at all comfortable with these bizarre mechanical contraptions scurrying all over their realm."

After several hours of discussion the Eagle agreed to redesign the biot maintenance staff. For example, garbage would be collected by robots that looked like typical garbage trucks on Earth—there just wouldn't be any drivers. Construction work, when required, would be done by robots whose shapes were the same as vehicles performing similar functions on Earth. Thus the strange machines would be familiar in appearance to the colonists, and their xenophobic fears should be mitigated.

"What about the performance of routine, everyday activities?" the Eagle asked at the end of one long meeting. "We had thought we would use human biots, voice responsive, deployed in large numbers, to free your colonists of all drudgery. We've spent considerable time since you arrived perfecting the design."

Richard liked the idea of having robot assistants, but Nicole was leery. "It is imperative," she said, "that these human biots be absolutely identifiable. There should be no chance that anyone, not even a small child, could mistake one for a real human being."

Richard chuckled. "You've read too much science fiction," he said.

"But this is a real worry," Nicole protested. "I can well imagine the quality of the human biots that would be made here at the Node. We're not talking about those vacant imitations we saw inside Rama. People would be terrified if they couldn't tell the difference between a human and a machine."

"So we'll limit the number of varieties," Richard responded.

"And they'll be easily classified by primary function. Does that satisfy your concern? It would be a shame not to take advantage of this incredible technology."

"That might work," Nicole said, "providing that one short briefing could easily familiarize everyone with the different types. We must absolutely ensure that there are no problems of misidentification."

After several weeks of intense effort, most of the critical design decisions had been made and the work load dropped for Richard and Nicole. They were able to resume a more or less normal life with the children and Michael. One evening the Eagle dropped by and informed the family that New Eden was in its final test period, primarily verifying the ability of the new algorithms to monitor and control the environment over the wide range of possible conditions.

"Incidentally," the Eagle continued, "we've inserted gas exchange devices, or GEDs, in all the places—Sherwood Forest, the parks, along the shores of the lake and the sides of the mountain— where plants coming from Earth will eventually be growing. The GEDs act like plants, absorbing carbon dioxide and producing oxygen, and are quantitatively equivalent as well. They prevent the buildup of atmospheric carbon dioxide, which over a long period of time would undermine the efficacy of the weather algorithms. Operating the GEDs requires some power, so we've slightly reduced the wattage available for human consumption during the early days of the colony. However, once the plants are flourishing the GEDs can be removed and there will be abundant power for any reasonable purpose."

"Okay, Mr. Eagle," Katie said when he was finished. "What we all want to know is when we are going to depart."

"I was going to tell you on Christmas," the Eagle replied, the small wrinkle that passed for a smile forming at the corner of his mouth, "and that's still two days away."

"Tell us now, oh, please, Mr. Eagle," Patrick said.

"Well . . . all right," their alien companion replied. "Our target date for finishing with Rama in the Hangar is January 11. We expect to load you in the shuttle and depart from the Node two days later, on the morning of January 13."

That's only three weeks, Nicole thought, her heart skipping a beat as the reality of their departure sunk in. *There is still so much to do.* She glanced across the room, where Michael and Simone were sitting beside each other on the couch. *Among other things, my beautiful daughter, I must prepare you for your wedding.*

"So we'll be married on your birthday, Mama," Simone said. "We've always said the ceremony would be one week before the rest of the family left."

Tears crept involuntarily into Nicole's eyes. She lowered her head so that the children would not see. *I am not ready to say good-bye,* Nicole thought. *I cannot bear to think that I will never see Simone again.*

Nicole had chosen to leave the family parlor game that was going on in the living room. She had given, as her excuse, that she had some final design data to develop for the Eagle, but in reality she desperately needed a few moments alone to organize the last three weeks of her life at the Node. All during dinner she had been thinking of all the things she needed to do. She had been close to panic. Nicole feared that there wasn't enough time, or that she would forget something critical altogether. Once she had made a thorough list of her remaining tasks, however, along with a timetable for accomplishing them, Nicole relaxed somewhat. It was not an impossible list.

One of the items that Nicole had entered in her electronic note-book, in all capital letters, was "BENJY??" As she sat on the side of her bed, thinking about her retarded eldest son and chastising herself for not having addressed the issue earlier, Nicole heard a loud knock on her open door. It was an astonishing coincidence.

"Mom-my," Benjy said very slowly with his wide, innocent smile, "can I talk to you?" He thought for a moment. "Now?" he added.

"Of course, darling," Nicole answered. "Come in and sit beside me on the bed."

Benjy came over next to his mother and gave her a big hug. He looked down at his lap and spoke haltingly. His emotional struggle was obvious. "You and Rich-ard and the other chil-dren are go-ing a-way soon for a ve-ry long time," he said.

"That's right," Nicole replied, trying to be cheerful.

"Dad-dy and Si-mone will stay here and be mar-ried?"

This was more of a question. Benjy had lifted his head and was waiting for Nicole to corroborate his statement. When she nodded, tears rushed instantly into his eyes and his face contorted. "What about Ben-jy?" he said. "What will hap-pen to Ben-jy?"

Nicole pulled his head to her shoulder and cried with her son. His entire body shook with his sobs. Nicole was now furious with herself for having procrastinated so long. *He's known all along,* she thought. *Ever since that first conversation. He's been waiting. He thinks nobody wants him.*

"You have a choice, darling," Nicole managed to say when she had collected her own emotions. "We would love to have you come with us. And your father and Simone would be delighted if you stayed here with them."

Benjy stared at his mother as if he did not believe her. Nicole repeated her statements very slowly. "You are tel-ling me the truth?" he asked.

Nicole nodded vigorously.

Benjy smiled for a second and then looked away. He was silent for a long time. "There will be no-bo-dy to play with here," he said at length, still staring at the wall. "And Simone will need to be with Dad-dy."

Nicole was astonished at how concisely Benjy had summarized his considerations. He seemed to be waiting. "Then come with us," Nicole said softly. "Your Uncle Richard and Katie and Patrick and Ellie and I all love you very much and want to have you with us."

Benjy turned to look at his mother. Fresh tears were running down his cheeks. "I will come with you, Mom-my," he said, and put his head on her shoulder.

He had already made up his mind, Nicole thought, holding Benjy against her body. *He's smarter than we think. He only came in here to make certain he was wanted.*

7

"And dear Lord, let me properly cherish this wonderful young girl that I am about to marry. Let us share Thy gift of love and let us grow together in our knowledge of Thee. . . . I ask these things in the name of Thy son, whom Thou sent to Earth to show Thy love and to redeem us for our sins. Amen."

Michael Ryan O'Toole, seventy-two years of age, unclasped his hands and opened his eyes. He was sitting at the desk in his bedroom. He checked his watch. *Only two more hours*, he thought, *until I will marry Simone*. Michael glanced briefly at the picture of Jesus and the small bust of St. Michael of Siena in front of him on his desk. *And then later tonight, after the meal that is both wedding feast for us and birthday dinner for Nicole, I will hold that angel in my arms.* He could not stop the next thought from coming. *Dear Lord, please do not let me disappoint her.*

Michael reached into his desk and pulled out a small Bible. It was the only real book he owned. All the rest of his reading material was in the form of small data cubes that he inserted into his electronic notebook. His Bible was very special, a memento of a life once lived on a planet far away.

During his childhood and adolescence that Bible had gone everywhere with him. As Michael turned the small black book over in his hands, he was flooded with memories. In his first recollection he was a small boy, six or seven years old. His father had come into his bedroom at home. Michael had been playing a baseball game on his personal computer and was somewhat embarrassed—he always felt ill at ease when his serious father found him engaging in play.

"Michael," his father had said, "I want to give you a present. Your very own Bible. It is a true book, one that you read by turning the pages. We've put your name on the cover."

His father had extended the book and little Michael had accepted it with a soft "Thank you." The cover was leather and felt good to his touch. "Inside that volume," his father had continued, "is some of the best teaching that human beings will ever know. Read it carefully. Read it often. And govern your life by its wisdom."

That night I put the Bible under my pillow, Michael recalled. *And it stayed there. All through my childhood. Even through high school.* He remembered his machinations when his high school baseball team had won the city championship and was going to Springfield for the state tournament. Michael had taken his Bible with him, but he didn't want his teammates to see it. A Bible wasn't "cool" for a high school athlete, and the young Michael O'Toole did not yet have enough self-esteem to overcome his fear of the laughter of his peers. So he designed a special compartment for his Bible in the side of his toiletry bag and stored the book there, enclosed in protective wrap. In his hotel room in Springfield he waited until his roommate took a bath. Then Michael removed the Bible from its hiding place and put it under his pillow.

I even took it on our honeymoon. Kathleen was so understanding. As she always was with everything. A brief memory of the bright sun and the white sand outside their suite in the Cayman Islands was quickly followed by a powerful feeling of loss. "How are you doing, Kathleen?" Michael said out loud. "Where has life taken you?" He could see her in his mind's eye, puttering around their brownstone condominium on Commonwealth Avenue in Boston. *Our grandson Matt must be a teenager by now*, he thought. *Are there others? How many altogether?*

The heartache deepened as he imagined his family—Kathleen, his daughter Colleen, his son Stephen, plus all the grandchildren—gathered around the long table for a Christmas feast without him. In his mental image a light snow was falling outside on the avenue. *I guess Stephen would give the family prayer now*, he thought. *He was always the most religious of the children.*

Michael shook his head, returning to the present, and opened the Bible to the first page. A beautiful script writing of the word *Milestones* appeared at the top of the sheet. The entries were sparse, a total of eight altogether, the chronicle of major events in his life.

7-13-67	Married Kathleen Murphy in Boston, Massachusetts
1-30-69	Birth of son, Thomas Murphy O'Toole, in Boston
4-13-70	Birth of daughter, Colleen Gavin O'Toole, in Boston
12-27-71	Birth of son, Stephen Molloy O'Toole, in Boston
2-14-92	Death of Thomas Murphy O'Toole in Pasadena, Calif.

Michael's eyes stopped there, at the death of his firstborn son, and they quickly filled with tears. He recalled vividly that terrible St. Valentine's Day many years before. He had taken Kathleen out to dinner at a lovely seafood restaurant on Boston Harbor. They had been almost finished with their meal when they first heard the news. "I'm sorry I'm late showing you the desserts," apologized the young man who was their waiter. "I've been watching the news in the bar. There has just been a devastating earthquake in Southern California."

Their fear had been immediate. Tommy, their pride and joy, had won a scholarship in physics at Cal Tech after graduating as the valedictorian at Holy Cross. The O'Tooles had abandoned what was left of their meal and rushed into the bar. There they had learned that the earthquake had struck at 5:45 in the evening, Pacific time. The giant San Andreas fault had ripped apart near Cajon Pass and the poor people, cars, and structures within a hundred miles of the epicenter had been tossed about on the surface of the Earth like hapless boats at sea during a hurricane.

Michael and Kathleen had listened to the news all night long, alternately hoping and fearing, as the full magnitude of the nation's worst disaster of the twenty-second century had become better understood. The quake had been a fearsome 8.2 on the Richter scale. Twenty million people had been left without water, electricity, transportation, and communications. Fifty-foot-deep cracks in the Earth had engulfed entire shopping centers. Virtually all the roads had become impassable. The damage was worse, and more widespread, than if the Los Angeles metropolitan area had been hit with several nuclear bombs.

Early in the morning, before dawn even, the Federal Emergency Administration had issued a telephone number to call for inquiries. Kathleen O'Toole gave the message machine all the information they knew—the address and phone number at Tommy's apartment, the name and address of the Mexican restaurant where he worked to earn spending money, and his girlfriend's address and phone number.

We waited all day and into the night, Michael remembered. *Then Cheryl called. She had managed somehow to drive to her parents' home in Poway.*

"The restaurant collapsed, Mr. O'Toole," Cheryl had said through her tears. "Then it caught fire. I talked to one of the other waiters, one who survived because he was out on the patio when the quake hit. Tommy had been working the closest station to the kitchen—"

Michael O'Toole took a deep breath. *This is wrong,* he said to himself, struggling to force the painful memories of his son's death out of his mind. *This is wrong,* he repeated. *This is a time for joy, not sorrow. For Simone's sake I must not think of Tommy now.*

He closed the Bible and wiped his eyes. He stood up at his desk and walked into the bathroom. First he shaved, slowly and deliberately, and then he stepped into the hot shower.

Fifteen minutes later, when he opened his Bible again, this time with pen in hand, Michael O'Toole had exorcised the demons of his son's death. With a flourish he wrote an additional entry on the Milestones page, pausing when he was finished to read the final four lines.

10-31-97	Birth of grandson, Matthew Arnold Rinaldi, in Toledo, Ohio
8-27-06	Birth of son, Benjamin Ryan O'Toole, in Rama
3-7-08	Birth of son, Patrick Erin O'Toole, in Rama
1-6-15	Marriage to Simone Tiasso Wakefield

You are an old man, O'Toole, he said to himself, looking at his thin gray hair in the mirror. He had closed his Bible several minutes earlier and returned to the bathroom to brush his hair one final time. *Too old to be getting married again.* He remembered his first wedding, forty-seven years earlier. *My hair was thick and blond then,* he recalled. *Kathleen was beautiful. The service was magnificent. I cried the moment I saw her at the end of the aisle.*

His picture of Kathleen in her wedding dress, holding on to her father's arm at the other end of the aisle in the cathedral, faded into another memory of her, this one also shrouded in tears. In this second image the tears belonged to his wife. She had been sitting beside him in the family room at Cape Kennedy when the time had come for him to check in for the flight to LEO-3 to join the rest of the Newton crew. "Be careful," she had said, in a surprisingly emotional farewell. They had hugged. "I'm so proud of you, darling," she had whispered in his ear. "And I love you very much."

"Because I love you very much," Simone had also said when Michael had asked her if she really, *really* wanted to marry him and, if so, why. A soft image of Simone came into his mind as his memory of his final good-bye with Kathleen gently faded away. *You are so innocent and trusting, Simone,* Michael mused, thinking of his young bride-to-be. *Back on Earth you wouldn't even be dating yet. You'd still be considered just a girl.*

The thirteen years in Rama flashed through his mind in an instant. Michael recalled first the struggle of Simone's birth, including the glorious moment when she had finally cried and he had laid her gently on her mother's stomach. His next image was of a very young Simone, a serious girl of six or so, earnestly studying her catechism under his tutelage. In another picture Simone was skipping rope with Katie and singing a joyous song. The final fleeting image was a scene of the family picnicking beside the Cylindrical Sea in Rama. There was Simone, standing proudly beside Benjy as if she were his guardian angel.

She was already a young woman when we arrived at the Node, General Michael O'Toole thought to himself, his mind moving to a more recent sequence of images. *Extremely devout. Patient and selfless with the younger children. And nobody has ever made Benjy smile like Simone.*

There was a common theme to all these pictures of Simone. In Michael's mind, they were bathed in the unusual love that he felt for his child bride. It was not the kind of love that a man normally feels for the woman he is going to marry—it was more like an adoration. But it was love, nevertheless, and that love had forged a powerful bond between the unlikely pair.

I am a very lucky man, Michael thought as he finished adjusting his clothing. *God has seen fit to show me His wonders in many ways.*

In the master suite at the other end of the apartment, Nicole was helping Simone with her dress. It was not a wedding dress in the classical sense, but it was white and full with small straps over the shoulders. It was certainly not the casual attire that all of the family were accustomed to wearing on an everyday basis.

Nicole carefully placed the combs in her daughter's long black hair and studied Simone in the mirror. "You look beautiful," Nicole said.

She glanced at her watch. They had ten more minutes. And

Simone was completely ready except for the shoes. *Good. Now we can talk*, Nicole thought fleetingly. "Darling," she started, her voice surprisingly catching in her throat.

"What is it, Mother?" Simone said pleasantly. She was sitting on the bed beside her mother, carefully putting the black shoes on her feet.

"When we had that talk last week about sex," Nicole began again, "there were several topics that we didn't discuss." Simone looked up at her mother. Her attention was so complete that Nicole momentarily forgot what she was going to say. "Did you read those books I gave you . . . ?" she eventually stammered.

Simone's wrinkled brow revealed her puzzlement. "Yes, of course," she replied. "We discussed that yesterday."

Nicole took her daughter's hands. "Michael is a wonderful man," she said. "Kind, considerate, loving—but he is older. And when men are older—"

"I'm not sure I'm following you, Mother," Simone gently interrupted. "I thought there was something you wanted to tell me about sex."

"What I'm trying to say," Nicole said after taking a deep breath, "is that you may need to be very patient and tender with Michael in bed. Everything might not work right away."

Simone stared at her mother for a long time. "I had suspected that," she said quietly, "both from your nervousness about the subject and some unspoken anxiety that I have read in Michael's face. Don't worry, Mother, I do not have unreasonable expectations. In the first place, we are not marrying because of a desire for sexual gratification. And since I have no experience of any kind, except for holding hands occasionally during this last week, whatever pleasure I feel will be new and therefore wonderful."

Nicole smiled at her amazingly mature fourteen-year-old daughter. "You are a jewel," she said, her eyes brimming with tears.

"Thank you," Simone replied, hugging her mother. "Remember," she added, "my marriage to Michael is blessed by God. Whatever problems we encounter, we will ask God to help us with. We will be fine."

A sudden heartache devastated Nicole. *One more week*, a voice inside her said, *and you will never see this beloved girl again.* She continued to embrace Simone until Richard knocked on the door and told them that everyone was ready for the ceremony.

8

"Good morning," Simone said with a soft smile. The rest of the family were all seated at the table having breakfast when she and Michael walked in, hand in hand.

"Good mor-ning," Benjy replied. His mouth was stuffed with buttered toast and jam. He rose from his seat, walked slowly around the table, and hugged his favorite sister.

Patrick was right behind him. "Are you going to help me with my math today?" he asked Simone. "Mother says that now that we're going back I have to be serious about my studies."

Michael and Simone sat down at the table after the boys had returned to their seats. Simone reached for the coffeepot. She was like her mother in one respect. She didn't function well in the morning until she had had her coffee.

"Well, is the honeymoon finally over?" Katie asked in her usual irreverent manner. "After all, it's been three nights and two days. You must have listened to every piece of classical music in the data base."

Michael laughed easily. "Yes, Katie," he said, smiling warmly at Simone. "We've taken the DO NOT DISTURB sign off the door. We want to do whatever we can to help everyone pack for the voyage."

"We're actually in pretty good shape," Nicole commented,

delighted to see Michael and her daughter so comfortable together after their long seclusion. *I needn't have worried,* she thought quickly. *In some ways Simone is more adult than I am.*

"I wish the Eagle would give us more specifics about our return trip," Richard complained. "He won't tell us how long the journey will take or whether or not we'll sleep all the way or anything definite."

"He says he doesn't know for certain," Nicole reminded her husband. "There are 'uncontrollable' variables that could result in many different scenarios."

"You always believe him," Richard countered. "You are the most trusting—"

The doorbell interrupted their conversation. Katie went to the door and returned a few moments later with the Eagle. "I hope I'm not disturbing your breakfast," the birdman apologized, "but we have much to accomplish today. I will need for Mrs. Wakefield to come with me."

Nicole took the final sip of her coffee and looked quizzically at the Eagle. "Alone?" she said. She was aware of a vague fear inside her. She had never left the apartment by herself with the Eagle during their sixteen-month stay at the Node.

"Yes," the Eagle replied. "You'll be coming with me alone. There is a special task that only you can perform."

"Do I have ten minutes to get ready?"

"Certainly," the Eagle replied.

While Nicole was out of the room, Richard peppered the Eagle with questions. "Okay," Richard said at one juncture, "I understand that as a result of all these tests, you are confident now that we can safely remain asleep throughout the acceleration and deceleration periods. But what about during normal cruise? Will we be awake or asleep?"

"Mostly asleep," the Eagle replied, "because that way we can both retard the aging process and ensure your good health. But there are many uncertainties in the schedule. It may be necessary to awaken you several times en route."

"Why have you not told us this before?"

"Because it wasn't yet decided. The scenario for your mission is quite complicated and the baseline plan has only recently been defined."

"I don't want my aging process to 'be retarded,' " Katie said. "I want to be a grown woman when we meet other people from the Earth."

"As I told your mother and father yesterday," the Eagle said to Katie, "it is important that we have the ability to slow the aging process while you and your family are asleep. We do not know exactly when you will return to your solar system. If you were to sleep for fifty years, for example—"

"Whaaat?" Richard interrupted in consternation. "Who said anything about fifty years? We reached here in twelve or thirteen. Why wouldn't—"

"I'll be older than Mama," Katie said, a frightened look on her face.

Nicole entered from the next room. "What's this I heard about fifty years? Why will it take so long? Are we going someplace else first?"

"Obviously," Richard said. He was angry. "Why were we not told all this before we made the 'allocation' decision? We might have done something differently. . . . My God, if it take fifty years, Nicole and I will be a hundred years old!"

"No, you won't," the Eagle replied without emotion. "We estimate that you and Mrs. Wakefield will only age one year in five or six while we have you 'suspended.' For the children, the ratio will be closer to one year in two, at least until their growth subsides. We are wary of tampering too much with the growth hormones. And besides, the fifty years is an upper bound, what a human engineer would call a three-sigma number."

"Now I'm completely confused," Katie said, walking over and directly confronting the Eagle. "How old will I be when I meet up with a human being who is not part of my family?"

"I can't answer that question exactly, because there are statistical uncertainties involved," their alien colleague replied. "But your body should be at the equivalent development level of your early to mid-twenties. At least that's a *most likely* answer." The Eagle motioned to Nicole. "Now that's all I'm going to say. I have business with your mother. We should return before dinner tonight."

"As usual," Richard grumbled, "we're told almost nothing. Sometimes I wish that we had not been so cooperative."

"You could have been more difficult," the Eagle remarked as he and Nicole were leaving the room, "and in fact our predictions, based on our observational data, were for less cooperation than we have had. In the end, though, there would have been no substantive difference in the outcome. This way it has been more pleasant for you."

"Good-bye," Nicole said.

"Good-bye," said Benjy, waving to his mother after the door was already closed.

It was a long document. Nicole calculated that it would take her at least ten, maybe fifteen minutes to read the entire text out loud.

"Are you almost finished with your study?" the Eagle inquired again. "We'd like to begin the shooting, as you call it, as soon as possible."

"Explain to me again what happens to this video after I make it," Nicole requested.

"We broadcast it toward the Earth several years before you arrive in your solar system. That gives your fellow human beings ample time to respond."

"How do you know if they have actually heard it?"

"We have requested a simple return signal acknowledging receipt."

"And what if you don't ever receive this return signal?"

"That's what contingency plans are for."

Nicole had serious misgivings about reading the message. She asked if she could have some time to discuss the document with Richard and Michael.

"What is it that you are worried about?" the Eagle asked.

"Everything," Nicole replied. "It just doesn't seem right. I feel as if I'm being used to further your purpose—and since I don't know exactly what your purpose is, I'm afraid that I'm being a traitor to the human species."

The Eagle brought Nicole a glass of water and sat down beside her in the alien studio. "Let's look at this logically," the Eagle said. "We have very clearly told you that our primary objective is to gather detailed information about spacefaring species in the galaxy. Right?"

Nicole nodded.

"We have also constructed a habitat inside Rama for two thousand Earthlings and are sending you and your family back to gather those humans for an observational voyage. All you're doing, with that video, is informing the Earth that we are on our way and that the two thousand members of your species, along with the supporting artifacts of your culture, should meet us in Mars orbit. What could be wrong with that?"

"The text of this document," Nicole protested, pointing at the electronic notebook the Eagle had given her, "is extremely vague. I never indicate, for example, what will be the eventual fate of all these humans—only that they will be 'cared for' and 'observed' during some kind of a journey. There is also no mention of *why* the humans are being studied, or anything at all about the Node and its controlling intelligence. In addition, the tone is definitely threatening. I am telling the people on Earth who receive this transmission that if a contingent of humans does not rendezvous with Rama in Mars orbit, then the spaceship will approach closer to the Earth and 'acquire its specimens in a less organized way.' That is clearly a hostile statement."

"You may edit the remarks, if you would like, just as long as the intent is not changed," the Eagle replied. "But I should tell you that we have a great deal of experience with this type of communication. With species similar to yours, we have always been more successful when the message has not been too specific."

"But why won't you let me take the document back to the apartment? I could discuss it with Richard and Michael and we could jointly edit it to soften the tone."

"Because the video must be prepared by you today," the Eagle said stubbornly. "We are open to discussing modifications to the content and will work with you as long as necessary. But the sequence must be completed before you return to your family."

The voice sounded friendly but the meaning was absolutely clear. *I have no choice*, Nicole thought. *I am being ordered to do the video.* She stared for several seconds at the strange creature sitting beside her. *This Eagle is just a machine*, Nicole said to herself, feeling her anger rise. *He is carrying out his programmed instructions. . . . My quarrel is not with him.*

"No," she said abruptly, astonishing even herself. She shook her head. "I won't do it."

The Eagle was not prepared for Nicole's response. There was a long silence. Despite her emotional agitation, Nicole was fascinated by her companion. *What's going on with him now?* she wondered. *Are complicated new logic loops being exercised in his equivalent of a brain? Or is he perhaps receiving signals from somewhere else?*

At length the Eagle stood up. "Well," he said, "this is quite a surprise. . . . We never expected you to refuse to do the video."

"Then you haven't been paying attention to what I've been saying. . . . I feel as if you, or whoever is commanding you, are using me . . . and purposely telling me as little as possible. If you want me to do something for you, then at least some of my questions should be answered."

"What is it *precisely* that you want to know?"

"I've told you already," Nicole replied, her frustration showing. "What the hell is really going on in this place? Who or what are you? Why do you want to observe us? And while you're at it, how about a good explanation of why you need for us to leave a 'reproductive pair' here? I've never liked the idea of breaking up my family—I should have protested more forcefully at the beginning. If your technology is so wonderful that it can create something like this incredible Node, why can't you simply take a human egg and some sperm—"

"Calm down, Mrs. Wakefield," the Eagle said. "I've never seen you so agitated before. I had you classified as the most stable individual in your group."

And most malleable too, I'll bet, Nicole thought. She waited for her anger to subside. *Somewhere in that bizarre brain is doubtless a quantitative assessment of the probability that I would meekly follow orders. . . . Well, I fooled you this time. . . .*

"Look, Mr. Eagle," Nicole said a few seconds later, "I'm not stupid. I know who is in control here. I just think we humans deserve to be treated with a little more respect. Our questions are quite legitimate."

"And if we answer them to your satisfaction?"

"You've been watching me carefully for over a year," Nicole said. She smiled. "Have I ever been completely unreasonable?"

"Where are we going?" Nicole asked.

"On a short tour," the Eagle replied. "That may be the best way to deal with your uncertainties."

The strange vehicle was small and spherical, just large enough for the Eagle and Nicole. The entire front hemisphere was transparent. Behind the window, on the side where the alien birdman was sitting, was a small control panel. During the flight the Eagle occasionally touched the panel, but most of the time the craft seemed to be operating on its own.

Within seconds after they were seated inside, the sphere zipped down a long corridor and through a large set of double doors into total blackness. Nicole gasped. She felt as if she were floating in space.

"Each of the three spherical modules of the Node," the Eagle said, as Nicole struggled vainly to see anything at all, "has a hollow center. We have now entered a passageway that leads to the core of the Habitation Module."

After almost a minute some distant lights appeared in front of their small craft. Soon thereafter the vehicle emerged from the black passageway and entered the immense hollow core. The sphere flipped and turned, disorienting Nicole as it headed toward the darkness, away from the many lights on what must have been the inside of the main body of the Habitation Module.

"We observe everything that occurs with all our guest species, both temporary and permanent," the Eagle said. "As you have suspected, we have hundreds of monitoring devices inside your apartment. But all your walls are also one-way mirrors—from this core region we can watch your activities from a wider perspective."

Nicole had grown accustomed to the wonders of the Node, but the new sights around her were still staggering. Dozens, maybe hundreds of tiny blinking lights moved about in the vast darkness of the core. They looked like a group of scattered fireflies on a dark summer night. Some of the lights were hovering near the walls; others were moving slowly across the void. Some were so far away that they seemed to be standing still.

"We have a major maintenance center here as well," the Eagle said, pointing in front of them at a dense collection of lights in the distance. "Every element of the module can be reached very quickly from this core, in case there are engineering or any other kind of problems."

"What's going on over there?" Nicole asked, tapping on the window. About twenty kilometers to the right a group of vehicles were stationed just away from a large, illuminated portion of the Habitation Module.

"That's a special observation session," the Eagle replied, "using our most advanced remote sensing monitors. Those particular apartments house an unusual species, one that has characteristics never before recorded in this sector of the Galaxy. Many of its individuals are dying and we do not understand why. We are trying to figure out how to save them."

"So everything doesn't always work the way you planned it?"

"No," replied the Eagle. In the reflected light the creature seemed to be smiling. "That's why we have so many contingency plans."

"What would you have done if no humans had ever come to find out about Rama in the first place?" Nicole suddenly asked.

"We have alternate methods of accomplishing the same goals," the Eagle answered vaguely.

The vehicle accelerated along its chordal path in the darkness. Soon a similar sphere, slightly larger than theirs, approached them from the left. "Would you like to meet a member of a species whose development level is approximately equal to yours?" the Eagle said. He touched the control panel and the interior of their craft was illuminated by soft lights.

Before Nicole could respond, the second vehicle was beside them. It also had a transparent forward hemisphere. This second sphere was filled with a colorless liquid, and two creatures were swimming about. They looked like large eels wearing capes, and they moved in undulations through the liquid. Nicole estimated that the creatures were about three meters long and twenty centimeters thick. The black cape, which spread out like a wing during movement, was about a meter wide when fully extended.

"The one on your right, without the colored markings," the Eagle said, "is an artificial intelligence system. It serves a role similar to mine, acting as a host for the aquatic species. The other being is a spacefarer from another world."

Nicole stared at the alien. It had folded its cape tightly around its slightly greenish body and was sitting nearly motionless in the liquid. The creature had arranged itself in a horseshoe configuration with both ends of its body facing her. A burst of bubbles came from one of its two ends.

"It says, 'Hello, and wow are you intriguing,' " the Eagle said.

"How do you know that?" Nicole replied, unable to take her eyes off the bizarre being. Its two ends, one bright red and the other gray, had now wrapped around each other. Both were pressed against the window of the craft.

"My colleague in the other vehicle is translating and then communicating to me. . . . Do you wish to respond?"

Nicole's mind was a blank. *What do I say?* she thought, her eyes focused on the unusual wrinkles and protuberances on the alien's extremities. There were half a dozen separate features on each end, including a pair of white slits on the red "face." None of the markings looked like anything that Nicole had ever seen on the Earth. She stared silently, remembering the many conversations that she and Richard and Michael had had about the questions they would ask if, and when, they were ever able to communicate directly with an intelligent extraterrestrial. *But we never imagined a situation like this*, Nicole thought.

More bubbles flooded the window opposite her. "Our home planet accreted five billion years ago," the Eagle said, translating. "Our binary stars reached stability a billion years later. Our system has fourteen major planets, on two of which some kind of life evolved. Our oceanic planet has three intelligent species, but we are the only spacefarers. We began our space exploration slightly more than two thousand years ago."

Nicole was now embarrassed by her silence. "Hello . . . hello," she said haltingly. "It is a pleasure to meet you. . . . Our species has only been spacefarers for three hundred years. We are the only highly intelligent organism on a planet that is two thirds covered by water. Our heat and light come from a solitary, stable, yellow star. Our evolution began in the water, three or four billion years ago, but now we live on the land—"

Nicole stopped. The other creature, its two ends still entwined, had now brought the rest of its body over against the window so that the details of its physical structure could be seen more clearly. Nicole understood. She stood up next to the window and turned around slowly. Then she held her hands out, wiggling her fingers. More bubbles followed.

"Do you have an alternate manifestation?" the Eagle translated a few seconds later.

"I don't understand," Nicole replied. The Nodal host in the other sphere communicated her message using both body motions and bubbles.

"We have two manifestations," the alien explained. "My off-spring will have appendages, not unlike yours, and will dwell mostly on ocean bottoms, building our homes and factories and spaceships. They in turn will produce another generation that looks like me."

"No, no," Nicole replied eventually. "We have only a single manifestation. Our children always resemble their parents."

The conversation lasted for five more minutes. The two space-farers talked mostly about biology. The alien was especially impressed by the wide thermal range in which humans could function successfully. It told Nicole that members of its species were unable to survive if the ambient temperature of the surrounding liquid was outside a narrow range.

Nicole was fascinated by the creature's description of a watery planet whose surface was almost totally covered by huge mats of photosynthetic organisms. The caped eels, or whatever they were, lived in the shallows just below these hundreds of different organisms and used the photosynthesizers for practically everything—food, building materials, even as reproductive aids.

At length the Eagle told Nicole that it was time to depart. She waved at the alien, which was still pressed against the window. It responded with a final flurry of bubbles and unwrapped its two ends.

Seconds later the distance between the two capsules was already hundreds of meters.

It was dark again inside the moving sphere. The Eagle was silent. Nicole was exhilarated. Her mind continued to race, still actively formulating questions for the alien creature with whom she had had the brief encounter. *Do you have families?* she thought. *And if so, how do dissimilar creatures live together? Can you communicate with the bottom-dwellers who are your children?*

Another genre of question intruded into Nicole's stream of consciousness and she suddenly felt slightly disappointed in herself. *I was much too clinical, too scientific,* she thought. *I should have asked about God, life after death, even ethics.*

"It would have been virtually impossible to have had what you would call a philosophical conversation," the Eagle said a few moments later after Nicole had expressed a lack of satisfaction in the topics that had been discussed. "There was absolutely no common ground for such an exchange. Until each of you knew a few basic facts about the other, there were no references for a discussion of values or other meaningful issues."

Still, Nicole reflected, *I could have tried. Who knows? That horsehoe-shaped alien might have had some answers. . . .*

Nicole was jolted out of her contemplation by the sound of human voices. As she looked questioningly at the Eagle, the sphere turned completely around and Nicole saw that they were hovering only a few meters away from her living quarters.

A light went on in the bedroom that Michael and Simone were sharing. "Is that Benjy?" Nicole heard her daughter whisper to her husband of a few days.

"I think so," Michael replied.

Nicole watched quietly as Simone rose from the bed, pulled her robe about her, and crossed into the hallway. When she switched on the light in the living room, Simone saw her retarded younger brother curled up on the sofa.

"What are you doing here, Benjy?" Simone asked kindly. "You should be in bed—it's very, very late." She stroked her brother's anxious brow.

"I could not sleep," Benjy replied with effort. "I was wor-ried a-bout Ma-ma."

"She'll be home soon," Simone said soothingly. "She'll be home soon."

Nicole felt a lump in her throat and a few tears eased into her eyes. She looked over at the Eagle, then at the illuminated apartment in front of her, and finally at the firefly vehicles in the distance above her head. She took a deep breath. "All right," Nicole said slowly, "I'm ready to do the video."

"I'm jealous," Richard said. "I really am. I would have been willing to trade both my arms for a conversation with that creature."

"It was amazing," Nicole said. "Even now, I'm still having difficulty believing that it actually happened. . . . It's also amazing that the Eagle somehow knew how I would respond to everything."

"He was just guessing. He really could not have expected to have solved his problem with you that easily. You didn't even make him answer your question about their need for a reproductive couple. . . ."

"Yes, I *did*," Nicole replied somewhat defensively. "He explained to me that human embryology was such an astonishingly complicated process that even *they* couldn't possibly know the exact role played by a human mother without ever having watched a fetus mature and develop."

"I'm sorry, darling," Richard said quickly. "I wasn't implying that you really had any choice—"

"I felt as if they were at least *trying* to satisfy my objections." Nicole sighed. "Maybe I'm kidding myself. After all, in the end I did make the video, exactly as they had planned."

Richard put his arms around Nicole. "As I said, you really had no choice, darling. Don't be too hard on yourself."

Nicole kissed Richard and sat up in bed. "But what if they *are* taking this data so that they can prepare an efficient invasion, or something like that?"

"We've discussed all this before," Richard replied. "Their technological capabilities are so advanced they could take over the Earth in minutes if that was their goal. The Eagle himself has pointed out that if invasion and subjugation was their objective, they could accomplish it with a far less elaborate procedure."

"Now who's the trusting one?" Nicole said, managing a smile.

"Not trusting. Just realistic. I'm certain that the overall welfare of the human species is not a significant factor in the priority queue of the Nodal Intelligence. But I do think you should stop worrying about being an accomplice in crime with your video. The Eagle is right. Most likely you have made the 'acquisition process' less difficult for the inhabitants of Earth as well."

They were silent for a few minutes. "Darling," Nicole said at length. "Why do you think we're not going directly to the Earth?"

"My guess is that we must stop somewhere else first. Presumably to pick up another species in the same phase of the project as we are."

"And they will live in that other module inside Rama?"

"That's what I would assume," Richard replied.

9

The day of departure was January 13, 2215, according to the calendar that had been fastidiously kept by Richard and/or Nicole ever since Rama had escaped from the nuclear phalanx. Of course this date didn't really mean anything—except to them. Their long trip to Sirius at slightly more than half the speed of light had slowed time inside Rama, at least relative to the Earth, so the date they were using was a complete artifice. Richard estimated that the actual date on the Earth, at the time of their departure from the Node, was three to four years later, in 2217 or 2218. It was impossible for him to compute the Earth date exactly, since he did not have an accurate velocity time history from the years that they had traveled inside Rama. Thus Richard could only approximate the relativistic corrections necessary to transform their own time basis into the one being experienced on the Earth.

"The date on Earth right now really has no significance to us anyway," Richard explained to Nicole soon after they had awakened for their final day at the Node. "Besides," he continued, "it's almost certain that we will be returning to our solar system at extremely high velocities, meaning there will be additional time dilation before we rendezvous in Mars orbit."

Nicole had never really understood relativity—it was totally inconsistent with her intuition—and she certainly wasn't going to spend any energy worrying about it on her last day before separating from Simone and Michael. She knew that the final partings would be extremely difficult, for everybody, and she wanted to concentrate all her resources on those last emotional moments.

"The Eagle said that he would come for us at eleven," Nicole said to Richard while they were dressing. "I was hoping that after breakfast we could all sit together in the living room. I want to encourage the children to express their feelings."

Breakfast was light, even cheerful, but when the eight members of the family gathered together in the living room, each mindful that there were less than two hours remaining before the Eagle arrived to take everyone but Michael and Simone away, the conversation was forced and strained.

The newlyweds sat together on the love seat, facing Richard, Nicole, and the other four children. Katie, as usual, was completely frenetic. She talked constantly. She jumped from subject to subject, steering safely away from any discussion of the imminent departure. Katie was in the middle of a long monologue about a wild dream she had had the night before when her story was interrupted by the sound of two voices coming from the entryway to the master suite.

"Dammit, Sir John," said the first variation in Richard's voice, "this is our last chance. I'm going out there to say good-bye whether you're coming or not."

"These good-byes, my prince, do wrench my very soul. I'm not yet in my cups enough to deaden the pain. You yourself said the lass was the very apparition of an angel. How can I possibly—"

"Well, then, I'm going out there without you," said Prince Hal. All the eyes in the family were on Richard's tiny robot prince as he came down the hall to the living room. Falstaff staggered after him, stopping every four or five steps to take a drink from his flask.

Hal walked over in front of Simone. "Dearest lady," he said, bending down on one knee, "I cannot find the words to express properly how much I will miss seeing your smiling face. Throughout my entire realm, there is not one member of the fairer sex who is your equal in beauty—"

"Zounds," Falstaff interrupted, throwing himself on both knees beside his prince. "Mayhap Sir John has made a mistake. Why am I going with this motley crew (he waved his arm at Richard, Nicole, and the other children—all of whom were smiling broadly) when I could remain here, in the presence of such magnificent grace, and only this one old man for competition? I remember Doll Tearsheet . . ."

While the pair of twenty-centimeter robots were entertaining the family, Benjy rose from his chair and approached Michael and Simone. "Si-mone," he said, fighting back his tears, "I am go-ing to miss you. I love you." Benjy paused for a moment, looking first at Simone and then at his father. "I hope that you and Dad-dy will be ve-ry hap-py."

Simone rose from her seat and put her arms around her trembling little brother. "Oh, Benjy, thank you," she said. "I will miss you too. And I will carry your spirit with me every day."

Her embrace was too much for the boy. Benjy's body was wracked by sobs and his soft, sorrowful moan brought tears to the eyes of everyone else. Within moments Patrick had crawled into his father's lap. He buried his swollen eyes in Michael's chest. "Daddy . . . Daddy," he kept saying over and over.

A choreographer could not have designed a more beautiful dance of good-bye. The radiant Simone, looking somehow still serene despite her tears, waltzed around the room, saying a meaningful farewell to each and every member of the family. Michael O'Toole remained sitting on the love seat, with Patrick on his lap and Benjy beside him. His eyes brimmed repeatedly as one by one the departing family members came to him for a final embrace.

I want to remember this moment forever. There is so much love here, Nicole said to herself as she glanced around the room. Michael was holding little Ellie in his arms; Simone was telling Katie how much she would miss their talks together. For once even Katie was in emotional knots—she was surprisingly silent when Simone walked back across the room to rejoin her husband.

Michael gently lifted Patrick off his lap and took Simone's extended hand. The two of them turned toward the others and dropped to their knees, their hands clasped in prayer. "Our heavenly Father," Michael said in a strong voice. He paused for several seconds while the rest of the family, even Richard, knelt beside the couple on the floor.

"We thank Thee for having allowed us the joyful love of this wonderful family. We thank Thee also for having shown us Thy miraculous handiwork throughout the universe. At this moment we beseech thee, if it be Thy will, to look after each of us as we go our separate ways. We know not if it is in Thy plan for us once again to share the camaraderie and love that has uplifted all of us. Stay with us all, wherever our paths take us in Thy amazing creation, and let us, O Lord, someday be joined together again—in this world or the next. Amen."

Seconds later the doorbell rang. The Eagle had arrived.

Nicole left the house, purposely designed as a smaller version of her family villa at Beauvois in France, and walked down the narrow lane in the direction of the station. She passed other houses, all dark and empty, and tried to imagine what it would be like when they were full of people. *My life has been like a dream*, she said to herself. *Surely no human has ever had a more varied experience.*

Some of the houses cast shadows on the lane as the simulated Sun completed its arc in the ceiling far above her head. *Another remarkable world*, Nicole mused, surveying the village in the southeast corner of New Eden. *The Eagle was correct when he said that the habitat would be indistinguishable from Earth.*

For a fleeting moment Nicole thought of that blue, oceanic world nine light-years away. In her mental picture she was standing beside Janos Tabori, thirteen years earlier, as the Newton spaceship had pulled away from LEO-3. "That's Budapest," Janos had said, circling with his fingers a specific feature on the lighted globe shimmering in the observation window.

Nicole had then located Beauvois, or at least the general region, by backtracking up the Loire River from where it emptied into the Atlantic. "My home is just about here," she had said to Janos. "Maybe my father and daughter are looking in this direction right now."

Genevieve, Nicole thought as the brief recollection faded, *my Genevieve. You would be a young woman now. Almost thirty.* She continued to walk slowly down the lane near her new house in the Earth habitat inside Rama. Thinking of her first daughter made Nicole remember a short conversation she had had with the Eagle during a break in the video recording at the Node.

"Will I be able to see my daughter Genevieve while we are close to the Earth?" Nicole had asked.

"We don't know," the Eagle had replied after a short hesitation. "It depends entirely on how your fellow humans respond to your message. You yourself will stay inside Rama, even if the contingency plans are invoked, but it is possible that your daughter will be one of the two thousand who come from Earth to live in New Eden. It has happened before, with other spacefarers."

"And what about Simone?" Nicole had asked when the Eagle was finished. "Will I ever see her again?"

"That is more difficult to answer," the Eagle had replied. "There are many, many factors involved." The alien creature had stared at his despondent human friend. "I'm sorry, Mrs. Wakefield," he had said.

One daughter left on earth. Another in an alien space world almost a hundred trillion kilometers away. And I will be somewhere else. Who knows where? Nicole was feeling extremely lonely. She stopped her walk and focused her eyes on the scene around her. She was standing beside a circular area in the village park. Inside the rock circumference was a slide, a sandbox, a jungle gym, and a merry-go-round— a perfect playground for Earth children. Underneath her feet, the network of GEDs was interleaved throughout the portions of the park that would eventually contain the grasses brought from Earth.

Nicole bent down to examine the individual gas exchange devices. They were compact round objects, only two centimeters in diameter. There were several thousand of them arrayed in rows and columns that crisscrossed the park. *Electronic plants*, Nicole thought. *Converting carbon dioxide to oxygen. Making it possible for us animals to survive.*

In her mind's eye Nicole could see the park with grass, trees, and lilies in the small pond, just as it had appeared in the holographic image in the conference room at the Node. But even though she knew that Rama was returning to the solar system to "acquire" human beings who would fill up this technological paradise, it was still difficult for her to imagine this park teeming with children. *I have not seen another human being, except for my family, in almost fourteen years.*

Nicole left the park and continued toward the station. The residential houses that had lined the narrow lanes were now replaced by row buildings containing what would eventually be small shops. Of course they were all empty, as was the large, rectangular structure, destined to be a supermarket, that was right opposite the station.

She walked through the gate and boarded the waiting train in the front, just behind the control cab that was manned by a Benita Garcia robot. "Almost dark," Nicole said out loud.

"Eighteen more minutes," the robot replied.

"How long to the somnarium?" Nicole asked.

"The ride to Grand Central Station takes ten minutes," Benita answered as the train left the southeast station. "Then you have a two-minute walk."

Nicole had known the answer to her question. She had just

wanted to hear another voice. This was her second day alone, and a conversation with a Garcia robot was better than talking to herself.

The train ride took her from the southeast corner of the colony to its geographic center. Along the way, Nicole could see Lake Shakespeare on the left-hand side of the train and the slopes of Mount Olympus (which were covered with more GEDs) on the right. Electronic message monitors inside the train displayed information about the sights that were being passed, the time of day, and the distance that had been traveled.

You and the Eagle did a good job on this train system, Nicole thought, thinking of her husband Richard, now asleep along with all the other members of her family. *Soon I will be joining you in the big round room.*

The somnarium was, in reality, just an extension of the main hospital that was located about two hundred meters from the central train station. After leaving the train and walking past the library, Nicole entered the hospital, walked through it, and then reached the somnarium through a long tunnel. The rest of her family were all asleep in a large, circular room on the second floor. Each was in a "berth" along the wall, a long, coffinlike contraption hermetically sealed against the outside environment. Only their faces were visible through the small windows near their heads. As she had been trained to do by the Eagle, Nicole examined the monitors containing the data about the physical condition of her husband, two daughters, and two sons. Everybody was fine. There were not even any hints of irregularities.

Nicole stopped and gazed longingly at each of her loved ones. This was to be her last inspection. According to the procedure, since everyone's critical parameters were well within tolerances, it was now time for Nicole to go to sleep herself. It could be many years before she saw any of her family again.

Dear, dear Benjy. Nicole sighed as she studied her retarded son in repose. *Of all of us, this break in life will be the hardest on you. Katie, Patrick, and Ellie will catch up quickly. Their minds are quick and agile. But you will miss the years that might have made you independent.*

The berths were held out from the circular wall by what looked like wrought-iron metalwork. The distance from the head of one berth to the foot of the next was only about a meter and a half. Nicole's empty berth was in the middle; Richard and then Katie were behind her head; Patrick, Benjy, and Ellie were at her feet.

She lingered for several minutes beside Richard's berth. He had been the last to go to sleep, two days before. As he had requested,

Prince Hal and Falstaff were lying on his chest inside the sealed container. *Those final three days were wonderful, my love*, Nicole said to herself as she stared at her husband's expressionless face through the window. *I could not have asked for more.*

They had swum and even water-skied in Lake Shakespeare, climbed Mount Olympus, and made love whenever either one of them had had the slightest inclination. They had clung to each other all through one night in the big bed in their new home. Richard and Nicole had checked on the sleeping children, once each day, but had mostly used the time for a thorough exploration of their new realm.

It had been an exciting, emotional time. Richard's last words, before Nicole activated the system that put him to sleep, were "You are a magnificent woman and I love you very much."

Now it was Nicole's turn. She could procrastinate no longer. She climbed into her berth, as she had practiced many times during their first week inside New Eden, and flipped all the switches except one. The foam around her was unbelievably comfortable. The top of the berth closed over her head. She had only to trip the final switch to bring the sleeping gas into her compartment.

She sighed deeply. As Nicole was lying on her back, she remembered the dream she had had about Sleeping Beauty during one of her final tests at the Node. Her mind then plunged backward to her childhood, to those wonderful weekends she had spent with her father watching the Sleeping Beauty pageants at the Chateau d'Ussé.

That's a nice way to go, she said to herself, feeling her drowsiness as the gas crept into her berth. *Thinking that it will be some Prince Charming who will awaken me.*

RENDEZVOUS
AT MARS

1

"Mrs. Wakefield."

The voice seemed far, far away. It intruded gently into her consciousness but did not quite awaken her from sleep.

"Mrs. Wakefield."

This time it was louder. Nicole tried to recall where she was before opening her eyes. She shifted her body and the foam reoriented itself to provide maximum comfort. Slowly her memory began to send signals to the remainder of her brain. *New Eden. Inside Rama. Back to the solar system,* she recalled. *Is this all just a dream?*

She finally opened her eyes. Nicole had difficulty focusing for several seconds. At length the figure bending over her resolved itself. It was her mother, dressed in a nurse's uniform!

"Mrs. Wakefield," the voice said. "It is now time to wake up and prepare for the rendezvous."

For a moment Nicole was in a state of shock. Where was she? What was her mother doing here? Then she remembered. *The robots,* she thought. *Mother is one of the five kinds of human robots. An Anawi Tiasso robot is a health and fitness specialist.*

The robot's helping arm steadied Nicole as she sat up in her berth. The room had not changed during the long time that she had been asleep. "Where are we?" Nicole asked as she prepared to climb out of the berth.

"We have completed the major deceleration profile and entered your solar system," the jet-black Anawi Tiasso replied. "Mars orbit insertion will be in six months."

Her muscles did not seem at all strange. Before Nicole had left the Node, the Eagle had informed her that each of the sleeping compartments included special electronic components that would not only regularly exercise the muscles and other biological systems to preclude any atrophy, but also monitor the health of all the vital organs. Nicole stepped down the ladder. When she reached the floor she stretched.

"How do you feel?" asked the robot. She was Anawi Tiasso #017. Her number was prominently displayed on the right shoulder of her uniform.

"Not bad," answered Nicole. "Not bad, 017," she repeated while examining the robot. It did look remarkably like her mother. Richard and she had seen all the prototypes before they had left the Node, but only the Benita Garcias had been operational during the two weeks before they went to sleep. All the rest of the New Eden robots had been built and tested during the long flight. *It really does look just like mother*, Nicole mused, admiring the handiwork of the unknown Raman artists. *They made all the changes to the prototype that I suggested.*

In the distance she heard footsteps coming toward them. Nicole turned around. Approaching them was a second Anawi Tiasso, also dressed in the white uniform of a nurse. "Number 009 has been assigned to help with the initialization procedure as well," the Tiasso robot beside her said.

"Assigned by whom?" Nicole asked, struggling to remember her discussions with the Eagle about the wake-up procedure.

"By the preprogrammed mission plan," #017 replied. "Once all you humans are alive and alert, we will take all our instructions from you."

Richard woke up more rapidly but was quite clumsy descending the short ladder. It was necessary for the two Tiassos to support him to prevent his falling. Richard was clearly delighted to see his wife. After a long hug and a kiss, he stared at Nicole for several seconds. "You look none the worse for wear," he said jokingly. "The gray in your hair has spread, but there are still healthy clutches of black in isolated spots."

Nicole smiled. It was great to be talking to Richard again.

"By the way," he asked a second later, "how long did we spend in those crazy coffins?"

Nicole shrugged her shoulders. "I don't know," she answered. "I haven't asked yet. The first thing I did was wake you up."

Richard turned to the two Tiassos. "Do you fine women know how long it has been since we left the Node?"

"You have slept for nineteen years of traveler's time," Tiasso #009 replied.

"What does she mean, traveler's time?" Nicole asked.

Richard smiled. "That's a relativistic expression, darling," he said. "Time doesn't mean anything unless you have a frame of reference. Inside Rama nineteen years have passed, but those years only pertain to—"

"Don't bother," Nicole interrupted. "I didn't sleep all this time to wake up to a relativity lesson. You can explain it to me later, over dinner. Meanwhile, we have a more important issue. In what order should we awaken the children?"

"I have a different suggestion," Richard replied after a moment's hesitation. "I know you're eager to see the children. So am I. However, why don't we let them sleep for several more hours? It certainly won't hurt them. . . . And you and I have a lot to discuss. We can begin our preparations for the rendezvous, outline what we are going to do about the children's education, maybe even take a moment or two to become reacquainted ourselves."

Nicole *was* anxious to talk to the children, but the logical part of her mind could see the merit in Richard's suggestion. The family had developed only a rudimentary plan for what would happen after they woke up, primarily because the Eagle had insisted that there were too many uncertainties to specify the conditions exactly. It would be much easier to do some planning before the children were awake.

"All right," Nicole said at length, "as long as I know for certain that everyone is all right." She glanced over at the first Tiasso.

"All the monitor data indicates that each of your children survived the sleep period without any significant irregularities," the biot said.

Nicole turned back to Richard and carefully studied his face. It had aged a little, but not as much as she had expected.

"Where's your beard?" she blurted out suddenly, realizing that his face was strangely clean-shaven.

"We shaved the men yesterday while they were sleeping," Tiasso #009 replied. "We also cut everybody's hair and gave everyone a bath—in accordance with the preprogrammed mission plan."

The men? Nicole thought. She was momentarily puzzled. *Of course,* she said to herself. *Benjy and Patrick are now men!*

She took Richard's hand and they walked quickly over to Patrick's berth. The face she saw through the window was astonishing.

Her little Patrick was no longer a boy. His features had lengthened considerably and the rounded contours of his face had disappeared. Nicole stared at her son silently for over a minute.

"His age equivalence is sixteen or seventeen," Tiasso #017 said in response to Nicole's questioning glance. "Mr. Benjamin O'Toole remains a year and a half older. Of course, these ages are only approximations. As the Eagle explained before your departure from the Node, we have been able to retard somewhat the key aging enzymes in each of you—but not all at the same rate. When we say that Mr. Patrick O'Toole is sixteen or seventeen now, we are referring only to his personal, internal biological clock. The age quoted is some kind of average across his growth, maturation, and subsystem aging processes."

Nicole and Richard stopped at each of the other berths and stared for several minutes through the windows at their sleeping children. Nicole repeatedly shook her head in bewilderment. "Where have my babies gone?" she said after seeing that even little Ellie had become a teenager during the long voyage.

"We knew this would happen," Richard commented without emotion, not helping the mother in Nicole cope with the sense of loss that she was feeling.

"*Knowing* it is one thing," said Nicole. "But *seeing* it and experiencing it is another. This is not a case of a typical mother who suddenly realizes her boys and girls have all grown up. What has happened to our children is truly staggering. Their mental and social development has been interrupted for the equivalent of ten to twelve years. We now have small children walking around in adult bodies. How can we prepare them to meet other humans in just six months?"

Nicole was overwhelmed. Had some part of her not believed the Eagle when he had described what was going to happen to her family? Perhaps. It was one more unbelievable event in a life that had long been beyond comprehension. *But as their mother*, Nicole thought to herself, *I have much to do and almost no time. Why didn't I plan for all this before we left the Node?*

While Nicole was struggling with her powerful emotional response to seeing her children suddenly grown, Richard chatted with the two Tiassos. They easily answered all his questions. He was extremely impressed with their capabilities, both physical and mental. "Do all of you have such a wealth of information stored in your memories?" he asked the robots in the middle of their conversation.

"Only we Tiassos have the detailed historical health data on your family," #009 replied. "But all the human biots can access a wide range of basic facts. However, a portion of that knowledge will be removed at the moment of first contact with other humans. At that time the memory devices of all biot types will be partially purged. Any event or piece of data pertaining to the Eagle, the Node, or any situations that transpired before you awakened will not remain in our data bases after we rendezvous with the other humans. Only your personal health information will be available from that earlier time period—and this data will be localized in the Tiassos."

Nicole had already been thinking about the Node before this last comment. "Are you still in contact with the Eagle?" she suddenly asked.

"No." It was Tiasso #017 who replied this time. "It is safe to assume that the Eagle, or at least some representative of the Nodal Intelligence, is periodically monitoring our mission, but there is never any interaction with Rama once it leaves the Hangar. You, we, Rama—we are on our own until the mission objectives are fulfilled."

Katie stood in front of the full-length mirror and studied her naked body. Even after a month it was still new to her. She loved to touch herself. She especially liked to run her fingers across her breasts and watch her nipples swell in response to the stimulation. Katie liked it even more at night when she was alone underneath the sheets. Then she could rub herself everywhere until waves of tingles rolled across her body and she wanted to cry out from pleasure.

Her mother had explained the phenomenon to her but had seemed a little uncomfortable when Katie had wanted to discuss it a second and a third time. "Masturbation is a very private affair, darling," Nicole had said in a low voice one night before dinner, "and generally only discussed, if at all, with one's closest friends."

Ellie was no help. Katie had never seen her sister examining herself, not even once. *She probably doesn't do it at all*, Katie thought. *And she certainly doesn't want to talk about it.*

"Are you through in the shower?" Katie heard Ellie call from the next room. Each of the girls had her own bedroom, but they shared the bath.

"Yes," Katie shouted in response.

Ellie came into the bathroom, modestly wrapped in a towel, and glanced briefly at her sister standing completely naked in front of the mirror. The younger girl started to say something, but apparently changed her mind, for she dropped the towel and stepped gingerly into the shower.

Katie watched Ellie through the transparent door. She looked first at Ellie's body, and then glanced in the mirror, comparing every possible anatomical feature. Katie preferred her own face and skin color—she was by far the lightest member of the family other than her father—but Ellie had a superior figure.

"Why do I have such a boyish shape?" Katie asked Nicole one evening two weeks later after Katie had finished reading through a data cube containing some very old fashion magazines.

"I can't explain exactly," Nicole replied, looking up from her own reading. "Genetics is a wonderfully complicated subject, far more complex than Gregor Mendel originally thought."

Nicole laughed at herself, realizing immediately that Katie could not possibly have understood what she had just said. "Katie," she continued in a less pedantic tone, "each child is a unique combination of the characteristics of her two parents. These identifying characteristics are stored in molecules called genes. There are literally billions of different ways the genes from one pair of parents can express themselves. That's why children from the same parents are not all identical."

Katie's brow furrowed. She had been expecting a different kind of answer. Nicole quickly understood. "Besides," she added in a comforting tone, "your figure is really not 'boyish' at all. 'Athletic' would be a more descriptive word."

"At any rate," Katie rejoined, pointing at her sister, who was studying hard over in the corner of the family room, "I certainly don't look like Ellie. Her body is really attractive—her breasts are even larger and rounder than yours."

Nicole laughed naturally. "Ellie does have an imposing figure," she said. "But yours is just as good—it's simply different." Nicole returned to her reading, thinking the conversation was over.

"They don't have many women with my kind of figure in these old magazines," Katie persisted after a short silence. She was holding up her electronic notebook, but Nicole was no longer paying attention. "You know, Mother," her daughter then said, "I think that the Eagle made some kind of mistake with the controls in my berth. I think I must have received some of the hormones that were meant for Patrick or Benjy."

"Katie, darling," Nicole replied, finally realizing that her daughter was obsessed with her figure, "it is virtually certain that you have become the person your genes were programmed to be at conception. You are a lovely, intelligent young woman. You would be happier if you spent your time thinking about your many excellent attributes, instead of finding an imperfection in yourself and wishing to be somebody different."

Since they had awakened, many of their mother-daughter conversations had had a similar pattern. To Katie, it seemed that her mother did not try to understand her and was too ready with a lecture and/or an epigram. "There's far more to life than just feeling good" was a regular refrain that resounded in Katie's ears. On the other hand, her mother's praise for Ellie seemed effusive to Katie. "Ellie is such a good student, even though she started so late," "Ellie is always helpful without our asking her," or "Why can't you be a little more patient with Benjy, like Ellie is?"

First Simone and now Ellie, Katie said to herself as she lay naked in bed late one night after she and her sister had quarreled and her mother had reprimanded only her. *I've never had a chance with Mother. We're just too different. I might as well stop trying.*

Her fingers roamed over her body, stimulating her desire, and Katie sighed in anticipation. *At least,* she thought, *there are some things that I don't need Mother for.*

"Richard," Nicole said one evening in bed when they were only six weeks away from Mars.

"Mmmmm," he responded slowly. He had been almost asleep.

"I'm concerned about Katie," she said. "I'm happy with the progress the other children are making—especially Benjy, bless his heart. But I have real worries about Katie."

"What exactly is it that's bothering you?" Richard said, propping himself up on one elbow.

"Her attitudes, mostly. Katie is incredibly self-centered. She also has a quick temper and is impatient with the other children, even Patrick, who absolutely adores her. She argues with me all the time, often when it's a nonsensical dispute. And I think she spends far too many hours alone in her room."

"She's just bored," Richard replied. "Remember, Nicole, physically she's a young woman in her early twenties. She should be dating, asserting her independence. There's really nobody here who is a peer. . . . And you must admit that sometimes we treat her like a twelve-year-old."

Nicole did not say anything. Richard leaned over and touched her arm. "We've always known that Katie was the most high-strung of the children. Unfortunately, she's a lot like me."

"But at least you channel your energy into worthwhile projects," Nicole said. "Katie is as likely to be destructive as constructive. . . . Really, Richard, I wish you would talk to her. Otherwise I'm afraid we're going to have big problems when we meet the other humans."

"What do you want me to say to her?" Richard replied after a short silence. "That life is not just one excitement after another? And why should I ask her not to retreat into her fantasy world in her own room? It's probably more interesting there. Unfortunately there's nothing very exciting for a young woman anywhere in New Eden at the present time."

"I had hoped you would be a little more understanding," Nicole replied, slightly miffed. "I need your help, Richard . . . and Katie responds better to you."

Again Richard was silent. "All right," he said finally in a frustrated tone. He lay back down in the bed. "I'll take Katie water-skiing tomorrow—she loves that—and at least ask her to be more considerate of the other members of the family."

"Very good. Excellent," Richard said, finishing his reading of the material in Patrick's notebook. He switched off the power and glanced over at his son, who was sitting somewhat nervously in the chair opposite Richard. "You have learned algebra quickly," Richard continued. "You are definitely gifted in mathematics. By the time we have other people in New Eden, you will be almost ready for university courses—at least in mathematics and science."

"But Mother says I'm still way behind in my English," Patrick replied. "She says that my compositions are those of a young child."

Nicole overheard the conversation and walked in from the kitchen. "Patrick, darling, Garcia #041 says that you do not take writing seriously. I know that you cannot learn everything overnight, but I don't want you to be embarrassed when we meet the other humans."

"But I like math and science better," Patrick protested. "Our Einstein robot says he could teach me calculus in three or four weeks—if I didn't have so many other subjects to study."

The front door suddenly opened and Katie and Ellie breezed in. Katie's face was bright and alive. "Sorry we're late," she said, "but we have had a *big* day." She turned to Patrick. "I drove the boat across Lake Shakespeare by *myself*. We left the Garcia on the shore."

Ellie was not nearly as ecstatic as her sister. In fact, she looked a little peaked. "Are you all right, dear?" Nicole said quietly to her younger daughter while Katie was regaling the rest of the family with her tales of their adventure on the lake.

Ellie nodded and didn't say anything.

"What was really exciting," Katie enthused, "was crossing over our own waves at high speeds. Bam-bam-bam, we bounced from wave to wave. Sometimes I felt as if we were flying."

"Those boats are not toys," Nicole commented a few moments later. She motioned for everyone to come to the dinner table. Benjy, who had been in the kitchen picking at the salad with his fingers, was the last to sit down.

"What would you have done if the boat had capsized?" Nicole asked Katie when everyone was seated.

"The Garcias would have rescued us," Katie answered flippantly. "There were three of them watching us from the shore. . . . After all, that's what they're for. Besides, we were wearing life vests and I can swim anyway."

"But your sister can't," Nicole replied quickly, a critical tone in her voice. "And you know she would have been terrified if she had been thrown into the lake."

Katie started to argue, but Richard interceded and changed the subject before the conflict escalated. In truth, the entire family was edgy. Rama had gone into orbit around Mars a month earlier and there was still no sign of the contingent from Earth that they were supposed to meet. Nicole had always assumed that their rendezvous with their fellow humans would take place immediately after Mars orbit insertion.

After dinner, the family went out into Richard's small backyard observatory to look at Mars. The observatory had access to all the external sensors on Rama (but none of the internal ones outside of New Eden—the Eagle had been very firm about this particular point during their design discussions) and could present a splendid telescopic view of the Red Planet for part of each Martian day.

Benjy especially liked the observing sessions with Richard. He proudly pointed out the volcanoes in the Tharsis region, the great canyon called Valles Marineris, and the Chryse area where the first Viking spacecraft had landed over two hundred years before. A dust storm was just forming south of Mutch Station, the hub of the large Martian colony that had been abandoned in the fitful days following the Great Chaos. Richard speculated that the dust might spread across the entire planet since it was the proper season for such global storms.

"What happens if the other Earthlings don't show up?" Katie

asked during a quiet point in their Martian observations. "And Mother, please give us a straight answer this time. After all, we're not children anymore."

Nicole ignored the challenging tone in Katie's comment. "If I remember correctly, the baseline plan is for us to wait here in Mars orbit for six months," she replied. "If there is no rendezvous during that time, Rama will head for Earth." She paused for several seconds. "Neither your father nor I know what the procedure will be from that point forward. The Eagle told us that if any of the contingency plans are invoked, we will be told at the time as much as we are required to know."

The room was quiet for almost a minute as images of Mars at different resolutions appeared on the giant screen on the wall. "Where is Earth?" Benjy then asked.

"It's the planet just inside Mars, the next one closer to the Sun," Richard answered. "Remember, I showed you the planetary lineup in the subroutine in my computer."

"That's not what I meant," Benjy answered very slowly. "I want to *see* Earth."

It was a simple enough request. It had never occurred to Richard, although he had brought the family out to the observatory several times before, that the children might be interested in that barely blue light in the Martian night sky. "Earth is not very impressive from this distance," Richard said, interrogating his data base to obtain the right sensor output. "In fact, it looks pretty much like any other bright object, such as Sirius, for example."

Richard had missed the point. Once he had identified the Earth in a specific celestial frame and then centered the image around that apparently insignificant reflection, the children all stared with rapt attention.

That is their home planet, Nicole thought, fascinated by the sudden change of mood in the room. *Even though they have never been there.* Pictures of the Earth from her memory flooded Nicole as she too stared at the tiny light in the center of the image. She became aware of a profound homesickness deep within her, a longing to return to that blessed, oceanic planet filled with so much beauty. Tears swelled into her eyes as she moved up closer to her children and put her arms around them.

"Wherever we go in this amazing universe," she said softly, "both now and in the future, that blue speck will always be our home."

2

Nai Buatong rose in the predawn dark. She slipped into a sleeveless cotton dress, stopped briefly to pay respects to her personal Buddha in the family's *hawng pra* adjacent to the living room, and then opened the front door without disturbing any of the other members of the family. The summer air was soft. In the breeze she could smell flowers mixed with Thai spices   someone was already cooking breakfast in the neighborhood.

Her sandals made no sound on the soft dirt lane. Nai walked slowly, her head turning from right to left, her eyes absorbing all the familiar shadows that would soon be only memories. *My last day,* she thought. *It has finally come.*

After a few minutes, she turned right onto the paved street that led to the small Lamphun business district. An occasional bicycle passed her, but the morning was mostly quiet. None of the shops were yet open.

As she approached a temple, Nai passed two Buddhist monks, one on either side of the road. Each of the monks was dressed in the customary saffron robe and was carrying a large metal urn. They were seeking their breakfasts, just as they did every morning throughout Thailand, and were counting on the generosity of the townspeople of Lamphun. A woman appeared in a shop doorway right in front of Nai and dropped some food in the monk's urn. No words were exchanged and the monk's expression did not visibly alter to acknowledge the donation.

They own nothing, Nai mused to herself, *not even the robes upon their backs. And yet they're happy.* She recited quickly the basic tenet, "The cause of suffering is desire," and recalled the incredible wealth of her new husband's family in the Higashiyama district on the edge of Kyoto, Japan. *Kenji says his mother has everything but peace. It eludes her because she cannot buy it.*

For a moment the recent memory of the grand house of the Watanabes filled her mind, pushing aside the image of the simple Thai road along which she was walking. Nai had been overwhelmed by the opulence of the Kyoto mansion. But it had not been a friendly place for her. It had been immediately obvious that Kenji's parents viewed her as an interloper, an inferior foreigner who had married their son without their support. They had not been unkind, just cold. They had dissected her with questions about her family and educational background that had been delivered with emotionless and logical precision. Kenji had later comforted Nai by pointing out that his family would not be with them on Mars.

She stopped in the street in Lamphun and looked across at the temple of Queen Chamatevi. It was Nai's favorite place in town, probably her favorite place in all of Thailand. Parts of the temple were fifteen hundred years old; its silent stone sentinels had seen a history so different from the present that it might as well have occurred on another planet.

Nai crossed the street and stood in the courtyard, just inside the temple walls. It was an unusually clear morning. Just above the uppermost *chedi* of the old Thai temple a strong light shone in the dark morning sky. Nai realized that the light was Mars, her next destination. The juxtaposition was perfect. For all twenty-six years of her life (except for the four years she had spent at the University of Chiang Mai) this town of Lamphun had been her home. Within six weeks she would be onboard a giant spaceship that would take her to her living quarters for the next five years, in a space colony on the red planet.

Nai sat down in the lotus position in a corner of the courtyard and stared fixedly at that light in the sky. *How fitting,* she thought, *that Mars is looking down on me this morning.* She began the rhythmic breathing that was the prelude for her morning meditation. But as she was preparing for the peace and calm that usually "centered" her for the day ahead, Nai recognized that there were many powerful and unresolved emotions inside her.

First I must reflect, Nai thought, deciding to forgo her meditation temporarily. *On this, my last day at home, I must make peace with the events that have changed my life completely.*

Eleven months earlier Nai Buatong had been sitting in the identical spot, her French and English lesson cubes neatly packed beside her in a carrying case. Nai had been planning to organize her material for the coming school term, determined that she was going to be more interesting and energetic as a high school language teacher.

Before she had started working on her lesson outlines on that fateful day the previous year, Nai had read the daily Chiang Mai newspaper. Slipping the cube into her reader, she had flipped quickly through the pages, scarcely reading more than the headlines. On the back page there had been a notice, written in English, that had caught her eye.

Doctor, Nurse, Teacher, Farmer

Are you adventurous, multilingual, healthy?

The International Space Agency (ISA) is mounting a major expedition to recolonize Mars. Outstanding individuals with the critical skills defined above are sought for a five-year assignment in the colony. Personal interviews will be held in Chiang Mai on Monday August 23, 2244. Pay and benefits are exceptional. Applications may be requested from Thai Telemail #462-62-4930.

When she had first submitted her application to the ISA, Nai had not thought that her chances were very high. She had been virtually certain that she would not pass the first screening and therefore would not even qualify for the personal interview. Nai was quite surprised, in fact, when six weeks later she received a notice in her electronic mailbox that she had been provisionally selected for the interviews. The notice also informed Nai that, according to the procedure, she should ask whatever personal questions she might have by mail first, before the interview. The ISA stressed that they only wanted to interview those candidates who intended to accept, if an assignment in the Martian colony were to be offered.

Nai responded by telemail with a single question. Could a significant portion of her earnings while she was living on Mars be directed to a bank on Earth? She added that this was an essential precondition for her acceptance.

Ten days later another electronic mail notice arrived. It was very succinct. Yes, the message said, a portion of her earnings could be regularly sent to a bank on Earth. However, it continued, Nai would have to be absolutely certain about her division of the monies—whatever split a colonist decided on could not be changed after he or she left the Earth.

Because the cost of living in Lamphun was low, the salary offered by the ISA for a language teacher in the Martian colony was almost double what Nai needed to handle all her family obligations. The young woman was heavily burdened with responsibility. She was the only wage earner in a family of five that included her invalid father, her mother, and her two younger sisters.

Her childhood had been difficult, but her family had managed to survive just above the poverty line. During Nai's final year at the university, however, disaster had struck. First her father had had a debilitating stroke. Then her mother, whose business sense was nonexistent, had ignored the recommendations of family and friends and had tried to manage the small family craft shop on her own. Within a year the family had lost everything and Nai was forced not only to use her personal savings to provide food and clothing for her family, but also to abandon her dream of doing literary translation work for one of the big publishing houses in Bangkok.

Nai taught school during the week and was a tourist guide on the weekend. On the Saturday before the ISA interview, Nai was conducting a tour in Chiang Mai, thirty kilometers from her home. In her group were several Japanese, one of whom was a handsome, articulate young man in his early thirties who spoke practically unaccented English. His name was Kenji Watanabe. He paid very close attention to everything Nai said, always asked intelligent questions, and was extremely polite.

Near the end of the tour of the Buddhist holy places in the Chiang Mai area, the group rode the cable car up the mountain Doi Suthep to visit the famous Buddhist temple on its summit. Most of the tourists were exhausted from the day's activities, but not Kenji Watanabe. First the man insisted on climbing the long dragon stairway, like a Buddhist pilgrim, rather than riding the funicular from the cable car exit to the top. Then he asked question after question while Nai was explaining the wonderful story of the founding of the temple. Finally, when they had descended and Nai was sitting by herself, having tea in the lovely restaurant at the foot of the mountain, Kenji left the other tourists in the souvenir shops and approached her table.

"*Kaw tode krap*," he said in excellent Thai, astonishing Miss Buatong. "May I sit down? I have a few more questions."

"Khun pode pasa thai dai mai ka?" Nai asked, still shocked.

"Pohm kao jai pasa thai dai nitnoy," he answered, indicating that he understood a little Thai. "How about you? *Anata wa nihon go hanashimasu ka?"*

Nai shook her head. *"Nihon go hanashimasen."* She smiled. "Only English, French, and Thai. Although I can sometimes understand simple Japanese if it is spoken very slowly."

"I was fascinated," Kenji said in English, after sitting down opposite Nai, "by the murals depicting the founding of the temple on Doi Suthep. It is a wonderful legend—a blend of history and mysticism—but as a historian, I'm curious about two things. First, couldn't this venerable monk from Sri Lanka have known, from some religious sources outside of the kingdom of Lan-na, that there was a relic of the Buddha in that nearby abandoned pagoda? It seems unlikely to me that he would have risked his reputation otherwise. Second, it seems too perfect, too much like life imitating art, for that white elephant carrying the relic to have climbed Doi Suthep by chance and then to have expired just when he reached the peak. Are there any non-Buddhist historical sources from the fifteenth century that corroborate the story?"

Nai stared at the eager Mr. Watanabe for several seconds before replying. "Sir," she said with a wan smile, "in my two years of conducting tours of the Buddhist sites of this region, I have never had anybody ask me either one of those questions. I certainly do not know the answers myself, but if you are interested, I can give you the name of a professor at Chiang Mai University who is extremely well versed in the Buddhist history of the kingdom of Lan-na. He is an expert on the entire time period, beginning with King Mengrai—"

Their conversation was interrupted by an announcement that the cable car was now ready to accommodate passengers for the trip back to the city. Nai rose from her seat and excused herself. Kenji rejoined the rest of the group. As Nai watched him from afar, she kept recalling the intensity in his eyes. *They were incredible,* she was thinking. *I have never seen eyes so clear and so full of curiosity.*

She saw those eyes again the following Monday afternoon, when she went to the Dusit Thani Hotel in Chiang Mai for her ISA interview. She was astonished to see Kenji sitting behind a desk with the official ISA emblem on his shirt. Nai was initially flustered. "I had not looked at your documents before Saturday," Kenji said as an apology. "I promise. If I had known you were one of the applicants, I would have taken a different tour."

The interview eventually went smoothly. Kenji was extremely

complimentary, both about Nai's outstanding academic record and her volunteer work with the orphanages in Lamphun and Chiang Mai. Nai was honest in admitting that she had not always had "an overpowering desire" to travel in space, but since she was basically "adventurous by nature" and this ISA position would also allow her to take care of her family obligations, she had applied for the assignment on Mars.

Toward the end of the interview there was a pause in the conversation. "Is that all?" Nai asked pleasantly, rising from her chair.

"One more thing, perhaps," Kenji Watanabe said, suddenly awkward. "That is, if you're any good at interpreting dreams."

Nai smiled and sat back down. "Go on," she said.

Kenji took a deep breath. "Saturday night I dreamed I was in the jungle, somewhere near the foot of Doi Suthep—I knew where I was because I could see the golden *chedi* at the top of my dream screen. I was rushing through the trees, trying to find my way, when I encountered a huge python sitting on a broad branch beside my head.

" 'Where are you going?' the python asked me.

" 'I'm looking for my girlfriend,' I answered.

" 'She's at the top of the mountain,' the python said.

"I broke free of the jungle, into the sunlight, and looked at the summit of Doi Suthep. My childhood sweetheart Keiko Murosawa was standing there waving down at me. I turned around and glanced back at the python.

" 'Look again,' it said.

"When I looked up the mountain the second time the woman's face had changed. It was no longer Keiko—it was you who was now waving to me from the top of Doi Suthep."

Kenji was silent for several seconds. "I have never had such an unusual or vivid dream. I thought perhaps—"

Nai had had goose bumps on her arm while Kenji was telling the story. She had known the ending—that she, Nai Buatong, would be the woman waving from the top of the mountain—before he had finished. Nai leaned forward in her chair. "Mr. Watanabe," she said slowly, "I hope that what I am going to say does not offend you in any way. . . ."

Nai was quiet for several seconds. "We have a famous Thai proverb," she said at length, her eyes avoiding his, "that says when a snake talks to you in a dream, you have found the man or woman that you will marry."

*   *   *

Six weeks later I received the notice, Nai remembered. She was still sitting in the courtyard beside Queen Chamatevi's temple in Lamphun. *The package of ISA materials came three days afterward. Along with the flowers from Kenji.*

Kenji himself had appeared in Lamphun the following weekend. "I'm sorry I didn't call or anything," he had apologized, "but it just didn't make sense to pursue the relationship unless you also were going to Mars."

He had proposed on Sunday afternoon and Nai had quickly accepted. They had been married in Kyoto three months later. The Watanabes had graciously paid for Nai's two sisters and three of her other Thai friends to travel to Japan for the wedding. Her mother could not come, unfortunately, for there was nobody else to look after Nai's father.

Nai took a deep breath. Her review of the recent changes in her life was now over. She was ready to begin her meditation. Thirty minutes later she was quite serene, happy and expectant about the unknown life in front of her. The sun had risen and there were other people on the temple grounds. She walked slowly around the perimeter, trying to savor her last moments in her home village.

Inside the main *viharn,* after an offering and the burning of incense at the altar, Nai carefully studied every panel of the paintings on the walls she had seen so many times before. The pictures told the life story of Queen Chamatevi, her one and only heroine ever since childhood. In the seventh century the many tribes in the Lamphun area had had different cultures and had often been at war with each other. All they had in common at that particular epoch was a legend, a myth that said a young queen would arrive from the south, "borne by huge elephants," and would unite all the diverse tribes into the Haripunchai kingdom.

Chamatevi had been only twenty-three when an old soothsayer identified her to some emissaries from the north as the future queen of the Haripunchai. She was a young and beautiful princess of the Mons, the Khmer people who would later construct Angkor Wat. Chamatevi was also extremely intelligent, a rare woman of the era, and very much favored by everyone at the royal court.

The Mons were therefore stunned when she announced that she was giving up her life of leisure and plenty and heading north on a harrowing six-month journey across seven hundred kilometers of mountains, jungles, and swamps. When Chamatevi and her retinue, "borne by huge elephants," reached the verdant valley in which Lamphun lay, her future subjects immediately put aside their factional quarrels and placed the beautiful young queen on the throne. She ruled for fifty years in wisdom and justice, lifting her kingdom from obscurity into an age of social progress and artistic accomplishment.

When she was seventy years old, Chamatevi abdicated her throne and divided her kingdom in half, each ruled by one of her twin sons. The queen then announced that she was dedicating the remainder of her life to God. She entered a Buddhist monastery and gave away all of her possessions. She lived a simple, pious life in the monastery, dying at the age of ninety-nine. By then the golden age of the Haripunchai was over.

On the final wall panel inside the temple an ascetic and wizened woman is carried away to nirvana in a magnificent chariot. A younger Queen Chamatevi, radiantly beautiful beside her Buddha, sits above the chariot in the splendor of the heavens. Nai Buatong Watanabe, Martian colonist-designate, sat on her knees in the temple in Lamphun, Thailand, and offered a silent prayer to the spirit of her heroine from the distant past.

Dear Chamatevi, she said. *You have watched over me for these twenty-six years. Now I am about to leave for an unknown place, much as you did when you came north to find the Haripunchai. Guide me with your wisdom and insight as I go to this new and wonderful world.*

3

Yukiko was wearing a black silk shirt, white pants, and a black and white beret. She crossed the living room to talk to her brother. "I wish you would come, Kenji," she said. "It's going to be the largest demonstration for peace that the world has ever seen."

Kenji smiled at his younger sister. "I would like to, Yuki," he replied. "But I only have two more days before I must leave and I want to spend the time with Mother and Father."

Their mother entered the room from the opposite side. She looked harried, as usual, and was carrying a large suitcase. "Everything is now packed properly," she said. "But I still wish you would change your mind. Hiroshima is going to be a madhouse. The Asahi Shimbun says they're expecting a *million* visitors, almost half of them from abroad."

"Thank you, Mother," Yukiko said, reaching for the suitcase. "As you know, Satoko and I will be at the Hiroshima Prince Hotel. Now, don't worry. We will call every morning, before the activities begin. And I'll be home Monday afternoon."

The young woman opened the suitcase and reached inside a special compartment, pulling out a diamond bracelet and a sapphire ring. She put them both on. "Don't you think you should leave those things at home?" her mother fussed. "Remember, there will be all those foreigners. Your jewelry may be too much temptation for them."

Yukiko laughed in the uninhibited way that Kenji adored. "Mother," she said, "you're such a worrywart. All your ever think about is what *bad* things might happen. . . . We're going to Hiroshima for the ceremonies commemorating the three hundredth anniversary of the dropping of the atomic bomb. Our prime minister will be there, as well as three of the members of the Central Council of the COG. Many of the world's most famous musicians will be performing in the evenings. This will be what Father calls an *enriching* experience—and all you can think about is who might steal my jewelry."

"When I was young it was unheard of for two girls, not yet finished at the university, to travel around Japan unchaperoned—"

"Mother, we've been through this before," Yuki interrupted. "I'm almost twenty-two years old. Next year, after I finish my degree, I'm going to live away from home, on my own, maybe even in another country. I'm no longer a child. And Satoko and I are perfectly capable of looking after one another."

Yukiko checked her watch. "I must go now," she said. "She is probably already waiting for me at the subway station."

She strode gracefully over to her mother and gave her a perfunctory kiss. Yuki shared a longer embrace with her brother.

"Be well, ani-san," she whispered in his ear. "Take care of yourself and your lovely wife on Mars. We're all very proud of you."

Kenji had never really known Yukiko very well. He was, after all, almost twelve years older than she. Yuki had been only four when Mr. Watanabe had been assigned to the position of president of the American division of International Robotics. The family had moved across the Pacific to a suburb of San Francisco. Kenji had not paid much attention to his younger sister in those days. In California he had been much more interested in his new life, especially after he started the university at UCLA.

The elder Watanabes and Yukiko had returned to Japan in 2232, leaving Kenji as a sophomore in history at the university. He had had very little contact with Yuki since then. During his annual visits to his home in Kyoto, Kenji always meant to spend some private hours with Yukiko, but it never seemed to happen. Either she was too deeply involved in her own life, or his parents had scheduled too many social functions, or Kenji himself had just not left enough time.

Kenji was vaguely sad as he stood at the door and watched Yukiko disappear in the distance. *I'm leaving this planet*, he thought, *and yet I've never taken the time to know my own sister.*

Mrs. Watanabe was talking in a monotone behind him, expressing her feeling that her life had been a failure because none of her children had any respect for her and they had all moved away. Now her only son, who had married a woman from Thailand just to embarrass them, was going off to live on Mars and she wouldn't see him for over five years. As for her middle daughter, she and her banker husband had at least given her two grandchildren, but they were as dull and boring as their parents—

"How is Fumiko?" Kenji interrupted his mother. "Will I have a chance to see her and my nieces before I leave?"

"They're coming over from Kobe for dinner tomorrow night," his mother replied. "Although I have no idea what I'm going to feed them. . . . Did you know that Tatsuo and Fumiko are not even teaching those girls how to use chopsticks? Can you imagine? A Japanese child who does not know how to use chopsticks? Is nothing sacred? We've given up our identity to become rich. I was telling your father . . ."

Kenji excused himself from his mother's querulous monologue and sought refuge in his father's study. Framed photographs lined the walls of the room, the archives of a successful man's personal and professional life. Two of the pictures held special memories for Kenji as well. In one of the photos, he and his father were each holding on to a large trophy given by the country club to the winners in the annual father-son golf tournament. In the other, the beaming Mr. Watanabe was presenting a large medal to his son after Kenji had won first prize in all Kyoto in the high school academic competition.

What Kenji had forgotten until seeing the photographs again was that Toshio Nakamura, the son of his father's closest friend and business associate, had been the runner-up in both contests. In both pictures the young Nakamura, almost a head taller than Kenji, was wearing an intense, angry frown on his face.

That was long before all his trouble, Kenji thought. He remembered the headline, OSAKA EXECUTIVE ARRESTED, which had proclaimed four years earlier the indictment of Toshio Nakamura. The article underneath the headline had explained that Mr. Nakamura, . who was at the time already a vice president in the Tomozawa Hotel Group, had been charged with very serious crimes, ranging from bribery to pandering to trafficking in human slavery. Within four months Nakamura had been convicted and sentenced to several years in detention. Kenji had been astonished. *What in the world happened to Nakamura?* he had wondered many times in the intervening four years.

While Kenji was remembering his boyhood rival, he felt very sorry for Keiko Murosawa, Nakamura's wife, for whom Kenji himself had had a special affection when he was a sixteen-year-old in Kyoto. Kenji and Nakamura had, in fact, vied for the love of Keiko for almost a year. When Keiko had finally made it clear that she preferred Kenji over Toshio, young Nakamura had been furious. He had even confronted Kenji one morning, near the Ryoanji Temple, and threatened him physically.

I might have married Keiko myself, Kenji thought, *if I had stayed in Japan.* He gazed out the window at the moss garden. It was raining outside. He suddenly had an especially poignant memory of a rainy day during his adolescence.

Kenji had walked over to her house as soon as his father had told him the news. A Chopin concerto had greeted his ears the moment he turned into the lane leading to her house. Mrs. Murosawa had answered the door and had addressed him sternly. "Keiko is practicing now," she had said to Kenji. "She won't be finished for over an hour."

"Please, Mrs. Murosawa," the sixteen-year-old boy had said, "it's very important."

Her mother was about to close the door when Keiko herself caught sight of Kenji through the window. She stopped playing and rushed over, her radiant smile sending a rush of joy through the young man. "Hi, Kenji," she said. "What's up?"

"Something *very* important," he replied mysteriously. "Can you come with me for a walk?"

Mrs. Murosawa had grumbled about the coming recital, but Keiko convinced her mother that she could afford to miss practice for one day. The girl grabbed an umbrella and joined Kenji in front of the house. As soon as they were out of view of her home, she slipped her arm through his, as she always did when they walked together.

"So, my friend," Keiko said as they followed their normal route toward the hills behind their section of Kyoto. "What's so *very* important?"

"I don't want to tell you now," Kenji answered. "Not here, anyway. I want to wait until we're in the right place."

Kenji and Keiko laughed and made small talk as they headed for Philosopher's Walk, a beautiful path that wound for several kilometers along the bottom of the eastern hills. The route had been made famous by the twentieth century philosopher Nishida Kitaro, who supposedly took the walk every morning. It led past some of Kyoto's most famous scenic spots, including Ginkaku-ji (the Silver Pavilion) and Kenji's personal favorite, the old Buddhist temple called the Honen-In.

Behind and to the side of the Honen-In was a small cemetery with about seventy or eighty graves and tombstones. Earlier that year Kenji and Keiko, while adventuring on their own, had discovered that the cemetery housed the remains of some of Kyoto's most prominent citizens of the twentieth century, including the celebrated novelist Junichiro Tanizaki and the doctor/poet Iwao Matsuo. After their discovery, Kenji and Keiko made the cemetery their regular meeting place. Once, after they had both read *The Makioka Sisters*, Tanizaki's masterpiece of Osaka life in the 1930s, they had laughingly argued for over an hour—while sitting beside the author's tombstone—about which of the Makioka sisters Keiko resembled the most.

On the day that Mr. Watanabe informed Kenji that the family was moving to America, it had already started to rain by the time Kenji and Keiko reached the Honen-In. There Kenji turned right onto a small lane and headed toward an old gate with a woven straw roof. As Keiko expected, they did not enter the temple, but instead climbed the steps leading to the cemetery. But Kenji did not stop at Tanizaki's tomb. He climbed up higher, to another grave site.

"This is where Dr. Iwao Matsuo is buried," Kenji said, pulling out his electronic notebook. "We are going to read a few of his poems."

Keiko sat close beside her friend, the two of them nestled under her umbrella in the light rain, while Kenji read three poems. "I have one final poem," Kenji then said, "a special haiku written by a friend of Dr. Matsuo's."

"One day in the month of June,
After a cooling dish of ice cream,
We bid each other farewell."

They were both silent for several seconds after Kenji recited the haiku from memory a second time. Keiko became alarmed and even a little frightened when Kenji's serious expression did not waver. "The poem talks of a parting," she said softly. "Are you telling me that—"

"Not by choice, Keiko," Kenji interrupted her. He hesitated for several seconds. "My father has been assigned to America," he continued at length. "We will move there next month."

Kenji had never seen such a forlorn look on Keiko's beautiful face. When she looked up at him with those terribly sad eyes, he thought his heart would tear apart. He held her tightly in the afternoon rain, both of them crying, and swore he would love only her forever.

4

The younger waitress, the one in the light blue kimono with the old-fashioned obi, pulled back the sliding screen and entered the room. She was carrying a tray with beer and sake.

"*Osake onegai shimasu,*" Kenji's father said politely, holding up his sake cup as the lady poured.

Kenji took a drink of his cold beer. The older waitress now returned, soundlessly, with a small plate of hors d'oeuvres. In the center was a shellfish of some kind, in a light sauce, but Kenji could not have identified either the mollusk or the sauce. He had not eaten more than a handful of these *kaiseki* meals in the seventeen years since he had left Kyoto.

"*Campai,*" Kenji said, clinking his beer glass against his father's sake cup. "Thank you, Father. I am honored to be having dinner here with you."

Kicho was the most famous restaurant in the Kansai region, perhaps in all of Japan. It was also frighteningly expensive, for it preserved the full traditions of personal service, private eating rooms, and seasonal dishes with only the highest quality ingredients. Every course was a delight to the eye as well as to the palate. When Mr. Watanabe had informed his son that they were going to dine alone, just the two of them, Kenji had never imagined that it would be at Kicho.

They had been talking about the expedition to Mars. "How many of the other colonists are Japanese?" Mr. Watanabe asked.

"Quite a few," Kenji replied. "Almost three hundred, if I remember correctly. There were many top-quality applications from Japan. Only America has a larger contingent."

"Do you know any of the others from Japan personally?"

"Two or three. Yasuko Horikawa was briefly in my class in Kyoto in junior high school. You may remember her. Very, very smart. Buck teeth. Thick glasses. She is, or *was*, I should say, a chemist with Dai-Nippon."

Mr. Watanabe smiled. "I think I do remember her," he said. "Did she come over to the house the night that Keiko played the piano?"

"Yes, I think so," Kenji said easily. He laughed. "But I have a hard time remembering anything other than Keiko from that night."

Mr. Watanabe emptied his sake cup. The younger attendant, who was sitting unobtrusively on her knees in a corner of the tatami mat room, came to the table to refill it. "Kenji, I'm concerned about the criminals," Mr. Watanabe said as the young lady departed.

"What are you talking about, Father?" Kenji said.

"I read a long story in a magazine that said the ISA had recruited several hundred convicts to be part of your Lowell Colony. The article stressed that all of the criminals had perfect records during their times of detention, as well as outstanding skills. But why was it necessary to accept convicts at all?"

Kenji took a swallow from his beer. "In truth, Father," he replied, "we have had some difficulty with the recruitment process. First, we had an unrealistic view of how many people would apply and we set up screening criteria that were far too tough. Second, the five-year minimum time requirement was a mistake. To young people in particular, a decision to do anything for that long a period is an overwhelming commitment. Most importantly, the press seriously undermined the entire staffing process. At the time we were soliciting applications, there were myriad articles in magazines and 'specials' on television about the demise of the Martian colonies a hundred years ago. People were frightened that history might repeat itself and they too could be left permanently abandoned on Mars."

Kenji paused briefly, but Mr. Watanabe said nothing. "In addition, as you are well aware, the project has had recurring financial crises. It was during a budget squeeze last year that we first began to consider skilled, model convicts as a way of solving some of our personnel and budgetary difficulties. Although they would be paid only modest salaries, there were still plenty of inducements to cause the convicts to apply. Selection meant granting of full pardons, and therefore freedom, when they returned to Earth after the five-year term. In addition, the ex-prisoners would be full citizens of Lowell Colony like everyone else, and would no longer have to tolerate the onerous monitoring of their every activity—"

Kenji stopped as two small pieces of broiled fish, delicate and beautiful and sitting on a bed of variegated leaves, were placed upon the table. Mr. Watanabe picked up a piece of fish with his chopsticks. *"Oishii desu,"* he commented, without glancing at his son.

Kenji reached for his piece of fish. The discussion of the convicts in Lowell Colony had apparently ended. Kenji looked behind his father, where he could see the lovely garden for which the restaurant was so famous. A tiny stream dropped down polished steps and ran beside a half dozen exquisite dwarf trees. The seat facing the garden was always the position of honor for a traditional Japanese meal. Mr. Watanabe had insisted that Kenji should have the garden view during this last dinner.

"You were not able to attract any Chinese colonists?" his father asked after they had finished the fish.

Kenji shook his head. "Only a few from Singapore and Malaysia. Both the Chinese and Brazilian governments forbade their citizens to apply. The Brazilian decision was expected—their South American empire is virtually at war with the COG—but we had hoped that the Chinese might soften their stand. I guess a hundred years of isolation doesn't die that easily."

"You can't really blame them," Mr. Watanabe commented. "Their nation suffered terribly during the Great Chaos. All the foreign capital disappeared overnight and their economy immediately collapsed."

"We did manage to recruit a few black Africans, maybe a hundred altogether, and a handful of Arabs. But most of the colonists are from the countries that contribute significantly to the ISA. That's probably to be expected."

Kenji became suddenly embarrassed. The entire conversation since they had entered the restaurant had been about him and his activities. During the next few courses Kenji asked his father questions about his work at International Robotics. Mr. Watanabe, who was now the chief operating officer of the corporation, always glowed with pride when he talked about "his" company. It was the world's largest manufacturer of robots for the factory and the office. The annual sales of IR, as it was always called, placed it among the top fifty manufacturers in the world.

"I'll be sixty-two next year," Mr. Watanabe said, the many cups of sake making him unusually talkative, "and I had thought that I might retire. But Nakamura says that would be a mistake. He says that the company still needs me. . . ."

Before the fruit arrived, Kenji and his father were again discussing the coming Martian expedition. Kenji explained that Nai and most of the other Asian colonists who were traveling on either the Pinta or the Niña were already at the Japanese training site in southern Kyushu. He would join his wife there as soon as he left Kyoto and, after ten more days of training, they and the rest of the passengers on the Pinta would be transported to a LEO (low Earth orbit) space station, where they would undergo a week of weightlessness training. The final leg of their near-Earth journey would be a ride aboard a space tug from LEO to the geosynchronous space station at GEO-4, where the Pinta was currently being assembled while undergoing its final checks and being outfitted for the long trip to Mars.

The younger waitress brought them two glasses of cognac. "That wife of yours is really a magnificent creature," Mr. Watanabe said, taking a small sip of the liqueur. "I have always thought that the Thai women were the most beautiful in the world."

"She's also beautiful inside," Kenji hastily added, suddenly missing his new bride. "And she is quite intelligent as well."

"Her English is excellent," Mr. Watanabe remarked. "But your mother says her Japanese is awful."

Kenji bristled. "Nai tried to speak Japanese—which, incidentally, she has never studied— because Mother refused to speak English. It was deliberately done to make Nai feel ill at ease—"

Kenji caught himself. His remarks defending Nai were not appropriate for the occasion.

"Gomen nasai," he said to his father.

Mr. Watanabe took a long drink from his cognac. "Well, Kenji," he said, "this is the last time we will be alone together for at least five years. I have very much enjoyed our dinner and our conversation." He paused. "There is, however, one more item that I want to discuss with you."

Kenji shifted his position (he was no longer used to sitting cross-legged on the floor for four hours at a time) and sat up straight, trying to clear his mind. He could tell from his father's tone that the "one more item" was a serious one.

"My interest in the criminals in your Lowell Colony is not just idle curiosity," Mr. Watanabe began. He paused to gather his thoughts before continuing. "Nakamura-san came into my office late last week, at the end of the business day, and told me that his son's second application for Lowell Colony had also been denied. He asked me if I would talk to you about looking into the matter."

The comment hit Kenji like a thunderbolt. He had never even been told that his boyhood rival had applied for Lowell Colony. Now here was his father—

"I have not been involved in the process of selecting the convict colonists," Kenji replied slowly. "That's an entirely different division in the project."

Mr. Watanabe did not say anything for several seconds. "Our connections tell us," he eventually continued, after finishing his cognac, "that the only real opposition to the application is coming from a psychiatrist, a Dr. Ridgemore from New Zealand, who has the opinion, despite Toshio's excellent record during his detention period, that Nakamura's son still does not recognize that he did anything wrong. . . . I believe that you were personally responsible for recruiting Dr. Ridgemore for the Lowell Colony team."

Kenji was staggered. This was no idle request his father was making. He had done extensive background research. *But why?* Kenji wondered. *Why is he so interested?*

"Nakamura-san is a brilliant engineer," Mr. Watanabe said. "He has personally been responsible for many of the products that have established us as leaders in our field. But his laboratory has not been very innovative lately. In fact, its productivity began to drop around the time of his son's arrest and conviction."

Mr. Watanabe leaned toward Kenji, resting his elbows on the table. "Nakamura-san has lost his self-confidence. He and his wife must visit Toshio in that detention apartment once a month. It is a constant reminder to Nakamura of how his family has been disgraced. If the son could go to Mars, then perhaps—"

Kenji understood too well what his father was asking. Emotions that had long been suppressed threatened to erupt. Kenji was angry and confused. He was going to tell his father that his request was "improper" when the elder Watanabe spoke again.

"It has been equally hard on Keiko and the little girl. Aiko is almost seven now. Every other weekend they dutifully ride the train to Ashiya. . . ."

Try as he might, Kenji could not prevent the tears from forming in the corners of his eyes. The picture of Keiko, broken and dejected, leading her daughter inside the restricted area for the biweekly visit with her father, was more than he could bear.

"I talked to Keiko myself last week," his father added, "at Nakamura-san's request. She was very despondent. But she seemed to perk up when I told her that I was going to ask you to intercede on her husband's behalf."

Kenji took a deep breath and gazed at his father's emotionless face. He knew what he was going to do. He knew also that it was indeed "improper"—not wrong, just improper. But it made no sense to agonize over a decision that was a foregone conclusion.

Kenji finished his cognac. "Tell Nakamura-san that I will call Dr. Ridgemore tomorrow," he said.

What if his intuition was wrong? *Then I will have wasted an hour, ninety minutes at the most,* Kenji thought as he excused himself from the family gathering with his sister Fumiko and her daughters and ran out into the street. He turned immediately toward the hills. It was about an hour before sunset. *She'll be there,* he said to himself. *This will be my only chance to say good-bye.*

Kenji went first to the small Anraku-Ji temple. He walked inside the hondo, expecting to find Keiko in her favorite spot, in front of the side wooden altar commemorating two twelfth century Buddhist nuns, formerly members of the court harem, who had committed suicide when Emperor Go-Toba had ordered them to repudiate the teachings of St. Honen. Keiko was not there. Nor was she outside where the two women were buried, just at the edge of the bamboo forest. Kenji began to think that he had been mistaken. *Keiko has not come,* he thought. *She feels that she has lost too much face.*

His only other hope was that Keiko was waiting for him in the cemetery beside the Honen-In, where seventeen years earlier he had informed her that he was moving away from Japan. Kenji's heart skipped a beat as he walked up the lane leading to the temple. Off in the distance to his right he could see a woman's figure. She was wearing a simple black dress and was standing beside the tomb of Junichiro Tanizaki.

Although her body was facing away from him and he could not see clearly in the fading twilight, Kenji was certain that the woman was Keiko. He raced up the steps and into the cemetery, finally stopping about five meters away from the woman in black.

"Keiko," he said, catching his breath. "I'm so glad—"

"Watanabe-san," the figure said formally, turning around with her head low and her eyes on the ground. She bowed very deeply, as if she were a servant. *"Domo arrigato gozaimasu,"* she repeated twice. Finally she rose, but she still did not look up at Kenji.

"Keiko," he said softly. "It's only Kenji. I'm alone. Please look at me."

"I cannot," she answered in a voice that was scarcely audible. "But I can thank you for what you have done for Aiko and me." Again she bowed. *"Domo arrigato gozaimasu,"* she said.

Kenji bent down impulsively and put his hand under Keiko's chin. He gently raised her head until he could see her face. Keiko was still beautiful. But Kenji was shocked to see such sadness permanently carved into those delicate features.

"Keiko," he murmured, her tears cutting into his heart like tiny knives.

"I must go," she said. "I wish you happiness." She pulled away from his touch and bowed again. Then she rose, without looking at him, and walked slowly down the path in the twilight shadows.

Kenji's eyes followed her until she disappeared in the distance. It was only then that he realized he had been leaning on Tanizaki's tombstones. He stared for several seconds at the two Kanji characters, Ku and Jaku, on the gray markers. One of them said EMPTINESS; the other SOLITUDE.

5

When the message from Rama was relayed to Earth from the tracking satellite system in 2241, it caused immediate consternation. Nicole's video was quickly classified top secret, of course, while the International Intelligence Agency (IIA), the security arm of the Council of Governments (COG), struggled to comprehend what it was all about. A dozen of the finest agents were soon assigned to the secure facility in Novosibirsk to analyze the signal that had been received from deep space and to develop a master plan for the COG response.

Once it was ascertained that neither the Chinese nor the Brazilians could have decoded the signal (their technological capabilities were not yet on a par with the COG), the requested acknowledgment was transmitted in the direction of Rama, thereby precluding any future replays of Nicole's video. Then the superagents focused on the detailed contents of the message itself.

They began by doing some historical research. It was widely accepted, despite some suggested (but discredited) evidence to the contrary, that the Rama II spacecraft had been destroyed by the barrage of nuclear missiles in April of 2200. Nicole des Jardins, the putative human being in the video, had been presumed dead before the Newton science ship had even left Rama. Certainly she, or what was left of her, must have been annihilated in the nuclear devastation. So the speaker could not actually be she.

But if the person or thing speaking in the television segment was a robot imitation or simulacrum of Madame des Jardins, it was vastly superior to any artificial intelligence designs on Earth. The preliminary conclusion, therefore, was that the Earth was again dealing with an advanced civilization of unbelievable capability, one that was consistent with the technological levels exhibited by the two Rama spacecraft.

There was no question about the implied threat in the message either, about that the superagents were unanimous. If there was indeed another Rama vehicle on its way to the solar system (although none had yet been detected by the pair of Excalibur stations), the Earth could certainly not ignore the message. Of course, there was some possibility that the entire thing was an elaborate hoax, concocted by the brilliant Chinese physicists (they were definitely the prime suspects), but until that was a confirmed fact, the COG needed to have a definitive plan.

Fortunately a multinational project had already been approved to establish a modest colony on Mars in the mid 2240s. During the two previous decades, a half dozen exploration missions to Mars had rekindled interest in the great idea of terra forming the red planet and making it habitable for the human species. Already there were unmanned scientific laboratories on Mars that were conducting experiments that were either too dangerous or too controversial to be performed on Earth. The easiest way to meet the intent of the Nicole des Jardins video—and not alarm the populace of the planet Earth—would be to announce and fund a considerably larger colony on Mars. If the entire affair turned out subsequently to be a hoax, then the size of the colony could be scaled back to the original proposed size.

One of the agents, an Indian named Ravi Srinivasan, carefully researched the massive ISA data archives from the year 2200 and became convinced that Rama II had *not* been destroyed by the nuclear phalanx. "It is possible," Mr. Srinivasan said, "that this video is legitimate and that the speaker is really the esteemed Madame des Jardins."

"But she would be seventy-seven years old today," another of the agents countered.

"There is nothing in the video that indicates when it was made," Mr. Srinivasan argued. "And if you compare the photographs of Madame des Jardins taken during the mission with the pictures of the woman in the transmission we received, they are decidedly different. Her face is older, maybe by as much as ten years. If the speaker in the video is a hoax or a simulacrum, then it is an amazingly clever one."

Mr. Srinivasan agreed, however, that the plan eventually developed by the IIA was the proper one even if the video was indeed presenting the truth. So it was not that important that he convince everyone that his point of view was correct. What was absolutely necessary, the superagents all agreed, was that a bare minimum of people know about the existence of the video.

The forty years since the beginning of the twenty-third century had seen some marked changes on the planet Earth. Following the Great Chaos, the Council of Governments (COG) had emerged as a monolithic organization controlling, or at least manipulating, the politics of the planet. Only China, which had retreated into isolation after its devastating experience during the Chaos, was outside the sphere of influence of the COG. But after 2200, there were signs that the unchallenged power of the COG was beginning to erode.

First came the Korean elections of 2209, when the people of that nation, disgusted with successive regimes of corrupt politicians who had grown rich at the expense of the populace, actually voted to federate with the Chinese. Of the major countries of the world, only China had a significantly different kind of government from the regulated capitalism practiced by the wealthy nations of North America, Asia, and Europe. The Chinese government was a kind of socialist democracy based on the humanist principles espoused by the canonized twenty-second century Italian Catholic, St. Michael of Siena.

The COG, and indeed the entire world, was dumbfounded by the stunning election results in Korea. By the time the IIA was able to foment a civil war (2211–2212), the new Korean government and their Chinese allies had already captured the hearts and minds of the people. The rebellion was easily quashed and Korea became a permanent part of the Chinese federation.

The Chinese openly acknowledged that they had no intention of exporting their form of government by military action, but the rest of the world did not accept their word. The COG military and intelligence budgets doubled between 2210 and 2220 as political tension returned to the world scene.

Meanwhile, in 2218, the three hundred and fifty million Brazilians elected a charismatic general, Joao Pereira, to head their nation. General Pereira believed that South America was mistreated and undervalued by the COG (he was not wrong) and he demanded changes in the COG character that would correct the problems. When the COG refused, Pereira galvanized South American regionalism by unilaterally abrogating the COG charter. Brazil seceded, in effect, from the Council of Governments, and over the next decade most of the rest of the South American nations, encouraged by the massive military strength in Brazil that successfully opposed the COG peacekeeping forces, followed suit. What emerged was a third player in the world geopolitical scene, a kind of Brazilian empire, energetically led by General Pereira.

At first the embargoes by the COG threatened to return Brazil and the rest of South America to the destitution that had ravaged the region in the wake of the Great Chaos. But Pereira fought back. Since the advanced nations of North America, Asia, and Europe would not buy his legal exports, he decided that he and his allies would export illegal products. Drugs became the primary trade of the Brazilian empire. It was an immensely successful policy. By 2240 there was a massive flow of all kinds and types of drugs from South America to the rest of the world.

It was in this political environment that Nicole's video was received on Earth. Although some cracks had appeared in the COG control of the planet, the organization still represented almost seventy percent of the population and ninety percent of the Earth's material wealth. It was natural that the COG and its implementing space agency, the ISA, should take the responsibility for managing the response. Carefully following the security criteria defined by the IIA, a fivefold increase in the number of people going to Mars as part of the Lowell Colony was announced in February 2242. Earth departure was scheduled for the late summer or early autumn of 2245.

The other four people in the room, all blond and blue-eyed and members of the same family from Malmo, Sweden, filed out the door, leaving Kenji and Nai Watanabe alone. She continued to gaze down at the Earth thirty-five thousand kilometers below her. Kenji joined her in front of the huge observation window.

"I never fully realized," Nai said to her husband, "just what it meant to be in geosynchronous orbit. The Earth doesn't move from here. It looks suspended in space."

Kenji laughed. "Actually we're both moving—and very fast. But since our orbital period and the Earth's rotation period are the same, the Earth always presents us with the same picture."

"It was different at that other space station," Nai said, shuffling away from the window in her slippers. "There the Earth was majestic, dynamic, much more impressive."

"But we were only three hundred kilometers from the surface. Of course it was—"

"*Shit*," they heard a voice shout from the other side of the observation lounge. A husky young man in a plaid shirt and blue jeans was flailing in the air, slightly more than a meter off the floor, and his frantic motion was causing him to tumble sideways. Kenji crossed over and helped the newcomer to stand upright on his feet.

"Thanks," the man said. "I forgot to keep one foot on the floor at all times. This weightlessness is fucking weird for a farmer."

He had a heavy southern accent. "Oops, I'm sorry about the language, ma'am. I've lived among cows and pigs too long." He extended his hand to Kenji. "I'm Max Puckett from De Queen, Arkansas."

Kenji introduced himself and his wife. Max Puckett had an open face and a quick grin. "You know," Max said, "when I signed up to go to Mars, I never realized we would be weightless for the whole goddamn trip. . . . What's going to happen to the poor hens? They'll probably never lay another egg."

Max walked over to the window. "It's almost noon at my home down there on that funny planet. My brother Clyde probably just opened a bottle of beer and his wife Winona is making him a sandwich." He paused for several seconds and then turned to the Watanabes. "What are you two going to do on Mars?"

"I'm the colony historian," Kenji replied. "Or at least one of them. My wife Nai is an English and French teacher."

"Shit," said Max Puckett. "I was hoping you were one of the farming couples from Vietnam or Laos. I want to learn something about rice."

"Did I hear you say something about hens?" Nai asked after a short silence. "Are we going to have chickens on the Pinta?"

"Ma'am," Max Puckett replied, "there are fifteen thousand of Puckett's finest packed in cages in a cargo tug parked at the other end of this station. The ISA paid enough for those chickens that Clyde and Winona could rest for a whole damn year if they wanted. . . . If those hens are not going with us, I'd like to know what the hell they're going to do with them."

"Passengers only occupy twenty percent of the space on the Pinta and the Santa Maria," Kenji reminded Nai. "Supplies and other cargo elements take up the rest of the space. We will only have a total of three hundred passengers on the Pinta, most of them ISA officials and other key personnel necessary to initialize the colony—"

"*E-nish-ul-eyes* the colony?" Max interrupted. "Shit, man, you talk like one of them robots." He grinned at Nai. "After two years with one of those talking cultivators, I threw the son of a bitch away and replaced him with one of those earlier silent versions."

Kenji laughed easily. "I guess I do use a lot of ISA jargon. I was one of the first civilians selected for New Lowell, and I managed the recruiting in the Orient."

Max had put a cigarette in his mouth. He glanced around in the observation lounge. "I don't see a smoking sign anywhere," he said. "So I guess if I light up I'll set off all the alarms." He put the cigarette behind his ear. "Winona hates it when me and Clyde smoke. She says only farmers and whores smoke anymore."

Max chuckled. Kenji and Nai laughed as well. He was a funny man. "Speaking of whores," Max said with a twinkle, "where's all those convict women I saw on television? Whoo-eee, some of them were mighty fine. Damn sight better looking than my chickens and pigs."

"All the colonists who had been held in detention on Earth are traveling on the Santa Maria," Kenji said. "We'll arrive about two months before them."

"You know an awful lot about this mission," Max said. "And you don't speak garbled English like the Japs I've met in Little Rock and Texarkana. Are you somebody special?"

"No," Kenji replied, unable to suppress another laugh. "As I told you, I'm just the lead colony historian."

Kenji was about to tell Max that he had lived in the United States for six years—which explained why his English was so good— when the door to the lounge opened and a dignified elderly gentleman in a gray suit and dark tie entered. "Pardon me," he said to Max, who had again placed the unlighted cigarette in his mouth, "have I mistakenly ended up in the smoking room?"

"No, Pops," Max answered. "This room is the observation lounge. It's much too nice to be the smoking area. Smoking is probably confined to a small room, without windows, near the bathrooms. My ISA interviewer told me—"

The elderly gentleman was staring at Max as if the man were a biologist and Max was a rare but unpleasant species. "My name, young man," he interrupted, "is not 'Pops.' It's Pyotr. Pyotr Mishkin, to be exact."

"Glad to know you, Peter," Max said, sticking out his hand. "I'm Max. This couple here's the Wabanyabes. They're from Japan."

"Kenji Watanabe," Kenji said in correction. "This is my wife Nai, who is a citizen of Thailand."

"Mr. Max," Pyotr Mishkin said formally, "my first name is Pyotr, not Peter. It is bad enough that I must speak English for five years. Surely I can ask that my name at least retain its original Russian sound."

"Okay, Pee-yot-ur," Max said, again grinning. "What do you do, anyway? No, let me guess . . . you're the colony undertaker."

For a fraction of a second Kenji was afraid that Mr. Mishkin was going to explode in anger. Instead, however, the smallest of smiles began to form upon his face. "It is apparent, Mr. Max," he said slowly, "that you have a certain comic gift. I can see where that might be a virtue on a long and boring space trip." He paused for a moment. "For your information, I am not the undertaker. I was trained in the law. Until two years ago, when I retired of my own volition to seek a 'new adventure,' I was a member of the Soviet Supreme Court."

"Holy shit," Max Puckett exclaimed. "Now I remember. I read about you in *Time* magazine. . . . Hey, Judge Mishkin, I'm sorry. I didn't recognize you—"

"Not at all," Judge Mishkin interrupted, an amused smile spreading across his face. "It was fascinating to be unknown for a moment and to be taken for an undertaker. Probably the practiced judge's mien is very close to the proper dour expression of the funeral attendant. By the way, Mr. . . ."

"Puckett, sir."

"By the way, Mr. Puckett," Judge Mishkin continued, "would you like to join me in the bar for a drink? A vodka would taste especially good right about now."

"So would some tequila," Max replied, walking toward the door with Judge Mishkin. "Incidentally, I don't suppose you know what happens when you feed tequila to pigs, do you? . . . I thought not. . . . Well, me and my brother Clyde . . ."

They disappeared out the door, leaving Kenji and Nai Watanabe alone again. The couple glanced at each other and laughed. "You don't think," Kenji said, "that those two are going to be friends, do you?"

"No chance," Nai replied with a smile. "What a pair of characters."

"Mishkin is considered to be one of the finest jurists of our century. His opinions are required reading in all the Soviet law schools. Puckett was president of the Southwest Arkansas Farmers Cooperative. He has incredible knowledge of farming techniques, and farm animals as well."

"Do you know the background of all the people in New Lowell?"

"No," Kenji replied. "But I have studied the files of everyone on the Pinta."

Nai put her arms around her husband. "Tell me about Nai Buatong Watanabe," she said.

"Thai schoolteacher, fluent in English and French, IE equals 2.48, SC of 91—"

Nai interrupted Kenji with a kiss. "You forgot the most important characteristic," she said.

"What's that?"

She kissed him again. "Adoring new bride of Kenji Watanabe, colony historian."

6

Most of the world was watching on television when the Pinta was formally dedicated several hours before it was scheduled to depart for Mars with its passenger and cargo. The second vice president of the COG, a Swiss real estate executive named Heinrich Jenzer, was present at GEO-4 for the dedication ceremonies. He gave a short address to commemorate both the completion of the three large spacecraft and the opening of a "new era of Martian colonization." When he was finished, Mr. Jenzer introduced Mr. Ian Macmillan, the Scottish commander of the Pinta. Macmillan, a boring speaker who appeared to be the quintessential ISA bureaucrat, read a six-minute speech reminding the world of the fundamental objectives of the project.

"These three vehicles," he said early in his speech, "will carry almost two thousand people on a hundred-million-kilometer voyage to another planet, Mars, where *this* time a permanent human presence will be established. Most of our future Martian colonists will be transported in the second ship, the Niña, which will depart from here at GEO-4 three weeks from today. Our ship, the Pinta, and the final spacecraft, the Santa Maria, will each carry about three hundred passengers as well as the thousands of kilograms of supplies and equipment that will be necessary to sustain the colony."

Carefully avoiding any mention of the demise of the first set of Martian outposts in the previous century, Commander Macmillan next tried to be poetic, comparing the forthcoming expedition to that of Christopher Columbus seven hundred and fifty years earlier. The language of the speech that had been written for him was excellent, but Macmillan's drab, monotonic delivery transformed words that would have been inspirational in the hands of an outstanding speaker into a dull and prosaic historical lecture.

He ended his speech by characterizing the colonists as a group, citing statistics about their ages, occupations, and countries of origin. "These men and women, then," Macmillan summarized, "are a representative cross section of the human species in almost every way. I say *almost* because there are at least two attributes common to this group that would not be found in a random collection of human beings of this size. First, the future residents of Lowell Colony are extremely intelligent—their average IE is slightly above 1.86. Second, and this goes without saying, they must be courageous or they would not have applied for and then accepted a long and difficult assignment in a new and unknown environment."

When he was finished, Commander Macmillan was handed a tiny bottle of champagne, which he broke across the 1/100 scale model of the Pinta that was displayed behind him and the other dignitaries on the dais. Moments later, as the colonists filed out of the auditorium and prepared to board the Pinta, Macmillan and Jenzer began the scheduled press conference.

"He's a jerk."

"He's a marginally competent bureaucrat."

"He's a fucking jerk."

Max Puckett and Judge Mishkin were discussing Commander Macmillan in between bites of lunch.

"He has no goddamn sense of humor."

"He is simply unable to appreciate things that are out of the ordinary."

Max was chafing. He had been censured by the Pinta command staff during an informal hearing earlier that morning. His friend Judge Mishkin had represented Max in the hearing and had prevented the proceedings from getting out of control.

"Those assholes have no right to pass judgment on my behavior."

"You are most certainly correct, my friend," Judge Mishkin replied, "in the general sense. But we have a set of unique conditions on this spacecraft. *They* are the authority here, at least until we arrive at Lowell Colony and establish our own government. . . . At any rate, there's no real harm done. You are not inconvenienced in any way by their declaration that your actions were "untenable." It could have been much worse."

Two nights earlier there had been a party celebrating the crossing of the halfway point in the Pinta's voyage from Earth to Mars. Max had flirted energetically for over an hour with lovely Angela Rendino, one of Macmillan's staff assistants. The bland Scotsman had then taken Max aside and strongly suggested that Max should leave Angela alone.

"Let her tell me that," Max had said sensibly.

"She's an inexperienced young woman," Macmillan had replied. "And she's too gracious to tell you how repulsive your animal humor is."

Max had been having a great time until then. "What's your angle here, Commander?" he had asked, after first quaffing another margarita. "Is she your private punch or something?"

Ian Macmillan had flushed crimson. "Mr. Puckett," the spacecraft officer had replied a few seconds later, "if your behavior does not improve, I will be forced to confine you to your living quarters."

The confrontation with Macmillan had ruined Max's evening. He had been incensed by the commander's use of his official authority in what was clearly a personal situation. Max had returned to his room, which he shared with another American, a pensive forester from the state of Oregon named Dave Denison, and quickly finished an entire bottle of tequila. In his drunken state Max had been both homesick and depressed. He had then decided to go to the communications center to phone his brother Clyde back in Arkansas.

By this time it was very late. To reach the communications complex, it was necessary for Max to cross the entire ship, passing first the common lounge where the party had just ended, and then the officers' quarters. In the central wing Max caught a fleeting glimpse of Ian Macmillan and Angela Rendino, arm in arm, going into the commander's private apartment.

"The son of a bitch," Max said to himself.

The drunken Max paced outside Macmillan's door in the hall, growing angrier and angrier. After five minutes he finally had an idea that he liked. Remembering his award-winning pig call from his days at the University of Arkansas, Max split the evening quiet with a horrendous noise.

"Sooo-eee, *pig, pig,*" Max hollered.

He repeated the call another time and then disappeared in a flash, just before every door in the officers' wing (including Macmillan's) opened to see what the disturbance had been. Commander Macmillan was not at all happy that his entire crew saw him, along with Miss Rendino, in a state of undress.

The cruise to Mars was a second honeymoon for Kenji and Nai. Neither of them had much work to do. The journey was relatively uneventful, at least from the point of view of a historian, and Nai's duties were minimal since most of her high school students were onboard the other two spaceships.

The Watanabes spent many evenings socializing with Judge Mishkin and Max Puckett. They played cards often (Max was as good at poker as he was terrible at bridge), talked about their hopes for Lowell Colony, and discussed the lives they had left behind on Earth.

When the Pinta was three weeks away from Mars, the staff announced a coming two-day communications outage and urged everyone to call home before the radio systems were temporarily out of commission. Since it was the year-end holiday period, it was the perfect time to phone.

Max hated the time delay and the long one-way conversations. After listening to a disjointed discussion of Christmas plans in Arkansas, Max informed Clyde and Winona that he wasn't going to call anymore because he disliked "waiting fifteen minutes to find out if anyone has laughed at my jokes."

It had snowed early in Kyoto. Kenji's mother and father had prepared a video showing Ginkaku-ji and the Honen-In under a soft blanket of snow; if Nai had not been with him Kenji would have been unbearably homesick. In a brief call to Thailand, Nai congratulated one of her sisters on having won a scholarship to the university.

Pyotr Mishkin didn't telephone anyone. The old Russian's wife was dead and he had no children. "I have wonderful memories," he told Max, "but there is nothing personal left for me on Earth."

On the first day of the planned communications blackout, it was announced that an important program, required viewing for everybody, would be shown at two o'clock in the afternoon. Kenji and Nai invited Max and Judge Mishkin to their small apartment to watch.

"I wonder what stupid lecture this is going to be," said Max, opposed, as always, to official pronouncements, which he considered a waste of his time.

When the video began, the president of the COG and the director of the ISA were shown sitting together at a large desk. The COG president underscored the importance of the message that they were about to receive from Werner Koch, the director of the ISA.

"Passengers on the Pinta," Dr. Koch began, "four years ago our satellite tracking systems decoded a coherent signal that had apparently originated in deep space in the general direction of the star Epsilon Eridani. When properly processed, the signal contained an amazing video, one that you will see in its entirety in about five minutes.

"As you will hear, the video announces the return to our system of a Rama spacecraft. In 2130 and 2200, giant cylinders, fifty kilometers long and twenty kilometers wide, created by an unknown alien intelligence for a purpose we still have not fathomed, visited our family of planets in orbit around the Sun. The second intruder, usually referred to as Rama II, made a velocity correction while inside the orbit of Venus that put it on an impact course with the Earth. A fleet of nuclear missiles was dispatched to encounter the alien cylinder and destroy it before Rama came close enough to our planet to do any harm.

"The following video claims that another of these Rama spacecraft has now come to our neighborhood with the sole purpose of 'acquiring' a representative sample of two thousand human beings for 'observation.' As bizarre as this claim may be, it is important to note that our radar has indeed confirmed that a Rama class vehicle did enter orbit around Mars less than a month ago.

"Unfortunately, we must take this fantastic message from deep space seriously. Therefore, you colonists on the Pinta have been assigned to rendezvous with the new object in Mars orbit. We realize that this news will come as a severe shock to most of you, but we did not have many viable options. If, as we suspect, some misguided genius has planned and orchestrated an elaborate hoax, then, after the brief detour, you will continue on with your colonization of Mars as originally conceived. If, however, the video you are about to see is actually telling the truth, then you and your associates onboard the Niña and the Santa Maria will become the contingent of human beings that the Raman intelligence will observe.

"You can well imagine that your mission now has uppermost priority among all COG activities. You can also understand the need for secrecy. From this moment forward, until this Rama issue is resolved one way or the other, all communication between your vehicle and the Earth will be strictly controlled. The IIA will monitor all the voice loops. Your friends and families will be told that you are safe, and eventually that you have landed on Mars, but that the Pinta communication systems have completely failed.

"You are being shown the following video now to give you three weeks to prepare for the encounter. A baseline plan and accompanying procedures for the rendezvous, worked out in great detail by the IIA in conjunction with ISA operations personnel, have already been transmitted to Commander Macmillan on the high-rate data stream. Each one of you will have a specific set of assignments. Each of you also has a personalized document packet that will provide you with the necessary background information for you to perform your duties.

"Of course we wish you well. Most likely this Rama affair will turn out to be nothing, in which case it will simply have delayed your initialization of Lowell Colony. If, however, this video is on the level, then you must move quickly to develop careful plans for accommodating the arrival of the Niña and the Santa Maria—none of the colonists on those other two spacecraft will have been told anything at all about Rama or the change in assignment."

There was a momentary silence in the Watanabe apartment as the video abruptly concluded and was replaced on the screen by a text message, *Next video in two minutes*. "Well, I'll be goddamned," was Max Puckett's only comment.

7

In the video Nicole was sitting on an ordinary brown chair with a featureless wall behind her. She was dressed in one of the ISA flight suits that had been her regular apparel during the Newton mission. Nicole read the message from an electronic notebook that she held in her hands.

"My fellow Earthlings," she began, "I am Newton cosmonaut Nicole des Jardins, speaking to you from billions of kilometers away. I am onboard a Rama spacecraft similar to the two great cylindrical spaceships that visited our solar system during the last two centuries. This third Rama vehicle is also heading toward our tiny region of the Galaxy. Approximately four years after your first receipt of this video, Rama III will go into orbit around the planet Mars.

"Since I left the Earth I have learned that the Rama class vehicles were constructed by an advanced extraterrestrial intelligence as elements in a vast information-gathering system whose ultimate objective is acquiring and cataloguing data about life in the universe. It is as part of this goal that this third Rama craft is returning to the vicinity of our home planet.

"Inside Rama III an Earthlike habitat has been designed to accommodate two thousand human beings, plus significant numbers of other animals and plants from our home planet. The exact biomass and other general specifications for these animals and plants are contained in the first appendix to this video; however, it should be stressed that the plants, especially those that are extremely efficient in the conversion of carbon dioxide to oxygen, are a key feature in the basic design of the Earth habitat onboard Rama. Without the plants, life for the humans inside Rama will be seriously compromised.

"What is expected, as a result of this transmission, is that the Earth will send a representative group of its inhabitants—together with the ancillary supplies detailed in the second appendix—to make a rendezvous with Rama III in Mars orbit. The voyagers will be taken inside Rama and carefully observed while they are living in a habitat that reproduces the environmental conditions on the Earth.

"Because of the hostile response to Rama II which, incidentally, resulted in only minor damage to the alien spacecraft, the nominal mission plan for this Rama vehicle involves no approach to Earth closer than Mars orbit. This nominal plan *assumes*, of course, that the authorities on Earth will indeed comply with the requests contained in this transmission. If no human beings are sent to rendezvous with Rama III in Mars orbit, I have no knowledge of how the spacecraft has been programmed to respond. I can say, however, based on my own observations, that it is easily within the capabilities of the extraterrestrial intelligence to acquire its desired observational data by other, less benign methods.

"With respect to the human beings to be transported to Mars, it goes without saying that the selected individuals should represent a broad cross section of humanity, including both sexes, all ages, and as many cultures as can be reasonably included. The large library of information about the Earth that is requested in the third video appendix will provide significant additional data that can be correlated with the observations taken inside Rama.

"I myself have no knowledge of how long the human beings will be inside Rama, or exactly where the spacecraft will take them, or even why the superior intelligence that created the Rama vehicles is gathering information about life in the universe. I can say, however, that the wonders I have witnessed since leaving our solar system have given me an entirely new sense of our place in the universe."

The total time for the video, more than half of which was allocated to the detailed appendices, was just over ten minutes. Throughout the transmission the basic scene did not change.

Nicole's delivery was measured and deliberate, punctuated by short pauses when her eyes moved from the camera to the notebook in her hands. Although there was some modulation in her tone, Nicole's earnest facial expression was virtually constant. Only when she implied that the Ramans might have "other, less benign methods" of obtaining their data did any strong emotion flash in her dark eyes.

Kenji Watanabe watched the first half of the video with intense concentration. During the appendices, however, his mind began to stray and to start asking questions. *Who are these extraterrestrials?* he wondered. *Where did they come from? Why do they want to observe us? And why have they picked Nicole des Jardines as their spokesperson?*

Kenji laughed to himself, realizing that there was an endless stream of such infinite questions. He decided to focus on more tractable issues.

If Nicole were still alive today, Kenji thought next, *then she would be eighty-one years old.* The woman on the television screen had some gray hair, and many more wrinkles than cosmonaut des Jardins had had when the Newton was launched from the Earth, but her age in the video was certainly nowhere near eighty. *Maybe fifty-two or fifty-three at the very most,* Kenji said to himself.

So did she make this video thirty years ago? he wondered. *Or has her aging process been somehow retarded?* It did not occur to him to question whether or not the speaker was really Nicole. Kenji had spent enough time in the Newton archives to recognize immediately Nicole's facial expressions and mannerisms. *She supposedly made the video about four years ago,* Kenji was thinking, *but if so . . .* He was still struggling with the entire situation when Nicole's transmission terminated and the director of the ISA appeared again on the monitor.

Dr. Koch explained quickly that the video would be replayed twice in its entirety on all channels and then would be available to each of the passengers and crew at his leisure.

"What the hell is *really* going on here?" Max Puckett demanded to know as soon as Nicole's face appeared on the monitor again. He directed his question at Kenji.

"If I have understood correctly," Kenji answered after watching for several seconds, "we have been purposely misled by the ISA about one of the primary purposes of our endeavor. Apparently, this message was first received about four years ago, back when the funding for the Lowell Colony was still somewhat uncertain, and it was decided then—*after* all efforts to prove the video to be a hoax were unsuccessful—that the investigation of Rama III would be a secret objective of our project."

"Shit," said Max Puckett, shaking his head vigorously. "Why the hell didn't they just tell us the truth?"

"My mind balks at the idea of supercreatures sending such awesome technology just to gather data about us," Judge Mishkin commented after a short silence. "On another level, however, at least now I understand some of the peculiarities in the personnel selection process. I was flabbergasted when that group of homeless American teenagers was added to the colony about eight months ago. Now I see that the selection criteria were based on satisfying the 'broad cross section' requested by Madame des Jardins; whether or not our particular mix of individuals and skills would produce a sociologically viable colony on Mars must have always been a secondary consideration."

"I *hate* lies and liars," Max now said. He had stood up from his chair and was pacing around the room. "All these politicians and government managers are the same—the bastards will lie without any conscience."

"But what could they have done, Max?" Judge Mishkin replied. "Almost certainly they didn't *really* take the video seriously. At least not until this new craft showed up in Mars orbit. And if they had told the truth from the beginning, there would have been worldwide panic."

"Look, Judge," Max said in a frustrated tone, "I thought I was hired to be a fucking farmer on a colony on Mars. I don't know anything about ETs and, quite frankly, I don't want to know anything. It's hard enough for me to deal with chickens, pigs, and people."

"Especially people," Judge Mishkin said quickly, smiling at his friend. Despite himself, Max chuckled.

A few minutes later Judge Mishkin and Max said good-bye and left Kenji and Nai alone. Soon after their guests were gone, the videophone rang in Kenji and Nai's apartment. "Watanabe?" they heard Ian Macmillan say.

"Yes, sir," Kenji replied.

"Sorry to disturb you, Watanabe," the commander said. "But you have the first assignment given to anyone other than my immediate staff. Your orders are to brief the entire Pinta crew on the Newton expedition, the Ramas, and Cosmonaut des Jardins at 1900 tonight. I thought you might want to begin your preparations."

*   *   *

". . . All the media reported in 2200 that Rama II was completely destroyed, vaporized by the multiple nuclear bombs that exploded in its vicinity. The missing cosmonauts des Jardins, O'Toole, Takagishi, and Wakefield were of course all considered to be dead. Actually, according to both the official documents of the Newton mission and the very successful books and television series distributed by Hagenest and Schmidt, Nicole des Jardins presumably died somewhere in New York, the island city in the middle of the Cylindrical Sea, *weeks* before the science ship of the Newton ever left Rama and returned to the Earth."

Kenji paused to look at his audience. Even though Commander Macmillan had explained to the Pinta passengers and crew that a videotape of Kenji's presentation would be immediately available, many of the listeners were taking notes. Kenji was enjoying his moment in the limelight. He glanced at Nai and smiled before continuing.

"Cosmonaut Francesca Sabatini, the most famous survivor of the ill-fated Newton expedition, postulated in her memoirs that Dr. des Jardins might have encountered a hostile biot, or had perhaps fallen, somewhere in one of the blackout regions of New York. Since the two women had been together for most of the day—they were searching for the Japanese scientist Shigeru Takagishi, who had mysteriously disappeared from the Beta campsite the night before— Signora Sabatini was well aware of the amount of food and water that Cosmonaut des Jardins was carrying. 'Even with her consummate knowledge of the human body,' Sabatini wrote, 'Nicole could not possibly have survived more than a week. And if, in a delirious state, she had tried to obtain water from the ice of the poisonous Cylindrical Sea, she would have died even sooner.'

"Of the half dozen Newton cosmonauts who did not return from the encounter with Rama II, it is Nicole des Jardins who has always attracted the most interest. Even before the brilliant statistician Roberto Lopez correctly conjectured seven years ago, on the basis of European genome information stored in The Hague, that the late King Henry XI of England was the father of Nicole's daughter Genevieve, Dr. des Jardins's reputation had become legendary. Recently the attendance at her memorial near her family villa in Beauvois, France, has increased markedly, especially among young females. People flock there, not only to pay Cosmonaut des Jardins homage and to view the many photographs and videos commemorating her outstanding life, but also to see the two superb bronze statues created by the Greek sculptor Theo Pappas. In one the youthful

Nicole is depicted in her track singlet and shorts with the Olympic gold medal around her neck; in the second she is shown as a mature woman, wearing an ISA flight suit similar to one you saw in the video."

Kenji pointed to the back of the room in the small Pinta auditorium and the lights were extinguished. Moments later a slide show began on one of the two screens behind him. "These are the few photographs of Nicole des Jardins that were stored in our Pinta files. The reference data base indicates that many more pictures, including historical film clips, are available in the reserve library stored out in the cargo bay, but those data are not accessible during cruise due to the limitations of the flight data network. The extra data are not needed, however, for it is clear from these photos that the individual who appeared in the transmission this afternoon is either Nicole des Jardins, *or an absolutely perfect copy of her.*"

A close-up still from the afternoon video was frozen on the left screen and juxtaposed to a head photo taken of Nicole the night of the New Year's Eve party at the Villa Adriani outside Rome. There was no question about it. The two pictures were definitely of the same woman. An appreciative murmur rose from the audience as Kenji paused in his presentation.

"Nicole des Jardins was born," Kenji continued in a slightly subdued tone, "on January 6, 2164. Therefore, if the video we watched this afternoon was actually filmed about four years ago, she should have been seventy-seven years old at the time. Now, we all know that Dr. des Jardins was in superb physical condition, and that she exercised regularly, but if the woman we saw this afternoon was seventy-seven, then the ETs who built Rama must also have discovered the fountain of youth."

Even though it was late at night and Kenji was very tired, he still could not sleep. The events of the day kept forcing themselves into his mind and exciting him again. Next to him in the small double bed Nai Buatong Watanabe was very much aware that her husband was awake.

"You're absolutely certain that we were seeing the real Nicole des Jardins, aren't you, dear?" Nai said softly after Kenji had turned over for the umpteenth time.

"Yes," said Kenji. "But Macmillan isn't. He demanded that I make that statement about the possibility of a perfect copy. He thinks everything in the video is a fake."

"After our discussion this afternoon," Nai said following a short pause, "I was able to recall all the brouhaha about Nicole and King Henry from seven years ago. It was in most of the personality magazines. But I've forgotten something. How was it established for certain that Henry was Genevieve's father? Wasn't the king already dead? And doesn't the royal family in England keep its genome information private and secret?"

"Lopez used the genomes belonging to the parents and siblings of people who had married into the royal family. Then, employing a data correlation technique that he himself had invented, Dr. Lopez showed that Henry, who was still the Prince of Wales during the 2184 Olympics, was more than three times as likely as any other person present in Los Angeles at the time to have been the father of Nicole's baby. After Darren Higgins admitted on his deathbed that Henry and Nicole had spent one night together during the Olympics, the royal family allowed a genetic specialist access to their genome data base. The expert concluded, beyond any reasonable doubt, that Henry was Genevieve's father."

"What an amazing woman," Nai said.

"She was indeed," Kenji replied. "But what prompted you to make that comment right now?"

"As a woman," Nai said, "I admire her protecting her secret and raising her princess herself as much or more than any of her other accomplishments."

8

Eponine located Kimberly in the corner of the smoky room and sat down beside her. She accepted the cigarette her friend offered, lit it, and inhaled deeply.

"Ah, what pleasure," Eponine said softly as she expelled the smoke in small circles and watched it rise slowly toward the ventilators.

"As much as you love tobacco and nicotine," Kimberly said in a whisper from beside her, "I know that you would absolutely adore kokomo." The American girl took a drag from her cigarette. "I know that you don't believe me, Eponine, but it's actually better than sex."

"Not for me, *mon amie*," Eponine replied in a warm, friendly tone. "I have enough vices. And I could never, never control something that was truly better than sex."

Kimberly Henderson laughed heartily, her long blond locks bouncing on her shoulders. She was twenty-four, a year younger than her French colleague. The two of them were sitting in the smoking lounge attached to the women's shower. It was a tiny square room, no more than four meters on a side, in which a dozen women were currently standing or sitting, all smoking cigarettes.

"This room reminds me of the back room at Willie's in Evergreen, just outside of Denver," Kimberly said. "While a hundred or more cowboys and rednecks would be dancing and drinking in the main bar, eight or ten of us would retreat into Willie's sacred 'office,' as he called it, and fuck ourselves completely up with kokomo."

Eponine stared through the haze at Kimberly. "At least in this lounge we aren't harassed by the men. They are absolutely impossible, even worse than the guys in the detention village at Bourges. These characters must think about nothing but sex all day long."

"That's understandable," Kimberly replied with another laugh. "They're not being closely watched for the first time in years. When Toshio's men sabotaged all the hidden monitors, everybody was suddenly free." She glanced over at Eponine. "But there's a grim side as well. There were two more rapes today, one right in the coed recreation area."

Kimberly finished one cigarette and immediately lit another. "You need someone to protect you," she continued, "and I know Walter would love the job. Because of Toshio, the cons have mostly stopped trying to hit on me. My main concern now is the ISA guards—they think they're hot shit. Only that gorgeous Italian hunk, Marcello something or other, interests me at all. He told me yesterday that he would make me 'moan with pleasure' if I would just join him in his room. I was sorely tempted until I saw one of Toshio's thugs watching the conversation."

Eponine also lit another cigarette. She knew it was ridiculous to smoke them one after another, but the passengers on the Santa Maria were only allowed three half-hour "breaks" each day and smoking was not permitted in the cramped living quarters. While Kimberly was momentarily sidetracked by a question from a burly woman in her early forties, Eponine thought about the first few days after they had left the Earth. *Our third day out,* she recalled, *Nakamura sent his go-between to see me. I must have been his first choice.*

The huge Japanese man, a sumo wrestler before he became a bill collector for a notorious gambling ring, had bowed formally when he had approached her in the coed lounge. "Miss Eponine," he had said in heavily accented English, "my friend Nakamura-san has asked me to tell you that he finds you very beautiful. He offers you complete protection in exchange for your companionship and an occasional favor of pleasure."

The offer was attractive in some ways, Eponine remembered, *and not unlike what most of the decent-looking women on the Santa Maria have eventually accepted. I knew at the time that Nakamura would be very powerful. But I didn't like his coldness. And I mistakenly thought that I could remain free.*

"Ready?" Kimberly repeated. Eponine snapped out of her reverie. She stubbed out her cigarette and walked with her friend into the dressing room. While they were taking off their clothes and preparing to shower, at least a dozen eyes feasted on their magnificent bodies.

"Doesn't it bother you," Eponine asked when they were standing side by side in the shower, "to have these dykes devouring you with their eyes?"

"Nope," Kimberly replied. "In a way I enjoy it. It's certainly flattering. There are not many women here who look like we do. It arouses me to have them stare so hungrily at me."

Eponine rinsed the soapy lather off her full, firm breasts and leaned over to Kimberly. "Then you have had sex with another woman?" she asked.

"Of course," Kimberly replied with another deep laugh. "Haven't you?"

Without waiting for a response, the American woman launched into one of her stories. "My first dealer in Denver was a dyke. I was only eighteen and absolutely perfect from head to toe. When Loretta first saw me naked, she thought she'd died and gone to heaven. I had just entered nursing school and couldn't afford much dope. So I made a deal with Loretta. She could fuck me, but only if she kept me supplied with cocaine. Our affair lasted almost six months. By then I was dealing on my own and, besides, I had fallen in love with the Magician."

"Poor Loretta," Kimberly continued as she and Eponine dried each other's backs in the lavatory that adjoined the shower. "She was brokenhearted. She offered me everything, including her client list. Eventually she became a nuisance, so I undercut her and had the Magician force her out of Denver."

Kimberly saw a fleeting look of disapproval on Eponine's face. "Jesus," she said, "there you go again, turning moral on me. You're the softest goddamn murderer I have ever met. Sometimes you remind me of all the goody two-shoes in my high school graduating class."

As they were about to leave the shower area, a tiny black girl with her hair in braids came up behind them. "You Kimberly Henderson?" she said.

"Yes." Kimberly nodded, turning around. "But why—"

"Is your man the king Jap Nakamura?" the girl interrupted.

Kimberly did not reply.

"If so, I need your help," the black girl continued.

"What do you want?" Kimberly asked in a noncommittal tone.

The girl suddenly broke into tears. "My man Reuben didn't mean nothing. He was drunk on that shit the guards sell. He didn't know he was talking to the king Jap."

Kimberly waited for the girl to dry her tears. "What have you got?" she whispered.

"Three knives and two joints of dynamite kokomo," the black girl replied in the same soft whisper.

"Bring them to me," Kimberly said with a smile. "And I'll arrange a time for your Reuben to apologize to Mr. Nakamura."

"You don't like Kimberly, do you?" Eponine said to Walter Brackeen. He was a huge American Negro with soft eyes and absolutely magical fingers on a keyboard. He was playing a light jazz medley and staring at his beautiful lady while his three roommates were out, by agreement, in the common areas.

"No, I don't," Walter replied slowly. "She's not like us. She can be very funny, but underneath I think she's truly bad."

"What do you mean?"

Walter changed to a soft ballad, with an easier melody, and played for almost a full minute before speaking. "I guess in the eyes of the law we're all equal, all murderers. But not in my eyes. I squashed the life out of a man who sodomized my baby brother. You killed a crazy bastard who was ruining your life." Walter paused for a moment and rolled his eyes. "But that friend of yours Kimberly, she and her boyfriend offed three people they didn't even know just for drugs and money."

"She was stoned at the time."

"No matter," Walter said. "Each of us is always responsible for his behavior If I put shit in me that makes me awful, that's my mistake. But I can't cop out of the responsibility for my actions."

"She had a perfect record in the detention center. Every one of the doctors who worked with her said she was an excellent nurse."

Walter stopped playing his keyboard and stared at Eponine for several seconds. "Let's not talk about Kimberly anymore," he said. "We have little enough time together. . . . Have you thought about my proposition?"

Eponine sighed. "Yes, I have, Walter. And although I like you, and enjoy making love with you, the arrangement you suggested sounds too much like a commitment. . . . Besides, I think this is mostly for your ego. Unless I miss my guess, you prefer Malcolm—"

"Malcolm has nothing to do with us," Walter interrupted. "He's been my close friend for years, since the very first days I entered the Georgia detention compound. We play music together. We share sex when we're both lonely. We're soul mates—"

"I know, I know. . . . Malcolm's not really the central issue. It's more the principle of the thing that bothers me. I *do* like you, Walter, you know that. But . . ." Her voice trailed off as Eponine struggled with her mixed feelings.

"We're three weeks away from Earth," Walter said, "and we have six more weeks before we reach Mars. I am the largest man on the Santa Maria. If I say that you're my girl, nobody will bother you for those six weeks."

Eponine recalled an unpleasant scene just that morning where two German inmates had discussed how easy it would be to commit rape in the convict quarters. They had known that she was within earshot but had made no effort to lower their voices.

At length she put herself in Walter's huge arms. "All right," she said softly. "But don't expect too much. . . . I'm sort of a difficult woman."

"I think Walter may have a heart problem," Eponine said in a whisper. It was the middle of the night and their other two roommates were asleep. Kimberly, in the bunk below Eponine, was still stoned on the kokomo she had smoked two hours earlier. Sleep would be impossible for her for several more hours.

"The rules on this ship are fucking stupid," Kimberly said. "Christ, even in the Pueblo Detention Complex there were fewer regulations. Why the hell can't we stay in the common areas after midnight? What harm are we doing?"

"He has occasional chest pains and, if we have vigorous sex, he often complains afterward of shortness of breath. . . . Do you think you could take a look at him?"

"And how about that Marcello? Huh! What a stupid ass! He tells me I can stay up all night if I want to come to his room. While I'm sitting there with Toshio. What does he think he's doing? I mean, not even the guards can mess with the king Jap. . . . What did you say, Eponine?"

Eponine raised herself on an elbow and leaned over the side of the bed. "Walter Brackeen, Kim," she said. "I'm talking about Walter Brackeen. Can you slow yourself down enough to pay attention to what I'm saying?"

"All right. All right. What about your Walter? What does he

want? Everybody wants something from the king Jap. I guess that makes me the queen, at least in a way—"

"I think Walter has a bad heart," the exasperated Eponine repeated in a loud voice. "I would like for you to look at him."

"Shh," Kimberly replied. "They'll come bust us, like they did that crazy Swedish girl. . . . Shit, Ep, I'm no doctor. I can tell when a heartbeat is irregular, but that's all. You ought to take Walter to that con doctor who's really a cardiologist, what's his name, the super quiet one who stays to himself when he's not examining somebody—"

"Dr. Robert Turner," Eponine interrupted.

"That's the one . . . very professional, aloof, distant, never speaks except in doctorese, hard to believe he blew the heads off two men in a courtroom with a shotgun, it just doesn't figure—"

"How do you know *that*?" Eponine said.

"Marcello told me. I was curious, we were laughing, he was teasing me, saying things like 'Does that Jap make you moan?' and 'How about that quiet heart doctor, can he make you moan?' "

"Christ, Kim," Eponine said, now alarmed, "have you been going to bed with Marcello too?"

Her roommate laughed. "Only twice. He talks better than he fucks. And what an ego. At least the king Jap is appreciative."

"Does Nakamura know?"

"Do you think I'm crazy?" Kimberly replied. "I don't want to die. But he may be suspicious. . . . I won't do it again, but if that Dr. Turner were to so much as whisper in my ear I would cream all over myself. . . ."

Kimberly continued her rambling chatter. Eponine thought briefly about Dr. Robert Turner. He had examined Eponine soon after launch when she had been having some peculiar spotting. *He never even noticed my body,* she remembered. *It was a thoroughly professional examination.*

Eponine tuned Kimberly out of her mind and focused on an image of the handsome doctor. She was surprised to discover that she was feeling a spark of romantic interest. There was something definitely mysterious about the doctor, for there was nothing in his manner or personality that was the least bit consistent with a double murder. *There must be an interesting story,* she thought.

Eponine was dreaming. It was the same nightmare that she had had a hundred times since the murder. Professor Moreau was lying with his eyes closed on the floor of his studio, blood streaming out of his chest. Eponine walked over to the basin, cleaned the large carving knife, and placed it back on the counter. As she stepped over the body those hated eyes opened. She saw the wild insanity in his eyes. He reached out for her with his arms—

"Nurse Henderson. Nurse Henderson." The knocking on the door was louder. Eponine awakened from her dream and rubbed her eyes. Kimberly and another of their roommates reached the door almost simultaneously.

Walter's friend Malcolm Peabody, a diminutive, effete white man in his early forties, was standing at the door. He was frantic. "Dr. Turner sent me for a nurse. Come quickly. Walter's had a heart attack."

As Kimberly began to dress, Eponine glided down from her bunk. "How is he, Malcolm?" she asked, pulling on her robe. "Is he dead?"

Malcolm was momentarily confused. "Oh, hi, Eponine," he said meekly. "I had forgotten that you and Nurse Henderson . . . When I left he was still breathing, but—"

Being careful to keep one foot on the floor at all times, Eponine hurried out the door, down the corridor, into the central common area, and then into the men's living quarters. Alarms sounded as the main monitors followed her progress. When she reached the entrance to Walter's wing, Eponine paused for a moment to catch her breath.

A crowd of people was standing in the corridor outside of Walter's room. His door was open wide and the bottom third of his body was lying outside, in the hallway. Eponine pushed her way through the crowd and into the room.

Dr. Robert Turner was kneeling beside his patient, holding electronic prods against Walter's naked chest. The big man's body recoiled with each jolt, and then rose slightly off the floor before the doctor pushed it down again against the surface.

Dr. Turner glanced up when Eponine arrived. "Are you the nurse?" he asked brusquely.

For a fleeting moment Eponine was speechless. And embarrassed. Here her friend was dying or dead and all she could think about was Dr. Turner's practically perfect blue eyes. "No," she said at length, definitely flustered. "I'm the girlfriend. . . . Nurse Henderson is my roommate. . . . She should be here any minute."

Kimberly and two ISA guard escorts arrived at that moment. "His heart stopped completely forty-five seconds ago," Dr. Turner said to Kimberly. "It's too late to move him to the infirmary. I'm going to open him up and try to use the Komori stimulator. Did you bring your gloves?"

While Kimberly pulled on her gloves, Dr. Turner ordered the crowd away from his patient. Eponine didn't move. When the guards grabbed her by the arms, the doctor mumbled something and the guards released her.

Dr. Turner handed Kimberly his set of surgical tools and then, working with both incredible speed and skill, cut a deep incision into Walter's chest. He laid back the folds of the skin, exposing the heart and rib cage. "Have you been through this procedure before, Nurse Henderson?" he asked.

"No," Kimberly replied.

"The Komori stimulator is an electrochemical device that attaches to the heart, forcing it to beat and continue to pump blood. If the pathology is temporary, like a blood clot or a spastic valve, then sometimes the problem can be fixed and the patient's heart will start functioning again."

Dr. Turner inserted the stamp-sized Komori stimulator behind the left ventricle of the heart and applied the power from the portable control system on the floor beside him. Walter's heart began to beat slowly three or four seconds later. "We have about eight minutes now to find the problem," the doctor said to himself.

He finished his analysis of the organ's primary subsystems in less than a minute. "No clots," he mumbled, "and no bad vessels or valves. . . . So why did it stop beating?"

Dr. Turner gingerly lifted up the throbbing heart and inspected the muscles underneath. The muscular tissue around the right auricle was discolored and soft. He touched it very lightly with the end of one of his pointed instruments and portions of the tissue flaked off.

"My God," the doctor said, "what in the world is this?" While Dr. Turner was holding the heart up, Walter Brackeen's heart contracted again and one of the long fiber structures in the middle of the discolored muscular tissue started to unravel. "What the—" Turner blinked twice and put his right hand on his cheek.

"Look at this, Nurse Henderson," he said quietly. "It's absolutely amazing. The muscles here have atrophied completely. I've never seen anything like it. We cannot help this man."

Eponine's eyes filled with tears as Dr. Turner withdrew the Komori stimulator and Walter's heart stopped beating again. Kimberly started to remove the clamps holding back the skin and tissue around the heart, but the doctor stopped her. "Not yet," he said.

"Let's take him over to the infirmary so I can perform a full autopsy. I want to learn whatever I can."

The guards and two of Walter's roommates eased the large man onto a gurney and the body was removed from the living quarters. Malcolm Peabody sobbed quietly on Walter's bunk. Eponine walked over to him. They shared a silent hug and then sat together, holding hands, for most of the rest of the night.

9

"You'll be in charge here while I'm inside," Commander Macmillan said to his deputy, a handsome young Russian engineer named Dmitri Ulanov. "Under all circumstances, your primary responsibility is the safety of the passengers and crew. If you hear or see anything threatening or even suspicious, blow the pyros and move the Pinta away from Rama."

It was the morning of the first reconnaissance mission from the Pinta into the interior of Rama. The spacecraft from Earth had docked the previous day on one of the circular ends of the huge cylindrical spacecraft. The Pinta had been parked right beside the external seal, in the same general location as the earlier Raman expeditions in 2130 and 2200.

As part of the preparations for the initial sortie, Kenji Watanabe had briefed the scouting party the night before on the geography of the first two Ramas. When he had finished with his comments, he had been approached by his friend Max Puckett.

"Do you think our Rama will look like all those pictures you showed us?" Max had asked.

"Not exactly," Kenji had replied. "I expect some changes. Remember that the video said that an Earth habitat had been constructed somewhere inside Rama. Nevertheless, since the exterior of this spacecraft is identical to the other two, I don't think everything inside will be changed."

Max had looked perplexed. "This is all *way* beyond me," he had said, shaking his head. "By the way," he had added a few seconds later, "you're *sure* you're not responsible for me being in the scouting party?"

"As I told you this afternoon," Kenji replied, "none of us onboard the Pinta had anything to do with the scouting selections. All sixteen members were chosen by the ISA and IIA back on Earth."

"But why have I been equipped with this goddamn arsenal? I have a state-of-the-art laser machine gun, self-guiding grenades, even a set of mass-sensitive mines. I have more firepower now than I had during the peacekeeping invasion of Belize."

Kenji had smiled. "Commander Macmillan, as well as many members of the military staff at COG Headquarters, still believes this whole affair is a trap of some kind. Your designator in this scouting operation is 'soldier.' My personal belief is that none of your weapons will be necessary."

Max was still grumbling the next morning when Macmillan left Dmitri Ulanov in charge of the Pinta and personally led the scouting party into Rama. Although he was weightless, the military equipment that Max was carrying on the outside of his space suit was unwieldy and severely restricted his freedom of movement. "This is ridiculous," he mumbled to himself. "I'm a farmer, not a goddamn commando."

The initial surprise came only minutes after the scouts from the Pinta had moved inside the external seal. Following a short walk down a broad corridor, the group came to a circular room from which three tunnels led deeper into the interior of the alien spaceship. Two of the tunnels were blocked with multiple metal gates. Commander Macmillan called Kenji in for consultation.

"This is a completely different design," Kenji said in response to the commander's questions. "We may as well throw out our maps."

"Then I presume we should proceed down the unblocked tunnel?" Macmillan asked.

"That's your call," Kenji replied, "but I don't see any other option, except to return to the Pinta."

The sixteen men trudged slowly down the open tunnel in their space suits. Every few minutes they would launch flares into the darkness ahead of them so that they could see where they were going. When they were about five hundred meters into Rama, two small figures suddenly appeared at the other end of the tunnel. Each of the four soldiers plus Commander Macmillan quickly pulled out his binoculars.

"They're coming toward us," said one of the soldier scouts excitedly.

"Well, I'll be damned," said Max Puckett, a shiver going down his spine, "it's Abraham Lincoln!"

"And a woman," said another, "in some kind of uniform."

"Prepare to fire," ordered Ian Macmillan.

The four soldier scouts scurried to the head of the party and knelt down, their guns pointed down the tunnel. "Halt," shouted Macmillan as the two strange figures drew within two hundred meters of the scouting party.

Abraham Lincoln and Benita Garcia stopped. "State your purpose," they heard the commander shout.

"We are here to welcome you," Abraham Lincoln said in a loud, deep voice.

"And to take you to New Eden," Benita Garcia added.

Commander Macmillan was thoroughly confused. He did not know what to do next. While he hesitated, the others in the scouting party talked among themselves.

"It's Abraham Lincoln, come back as a ghost," the American Terry Snyder said.

"The other one is Benita Garcia—I saw her statue in Mexico City once."

"Let's get the hell out of here. This place gives me the creeps," another scout said.

"What would ghosts be doing in orbit around Mars?"

"Excuse me, Commander," Kenji said at length to the befuddled Macmillan. "What do you intend to do now?"

The Scotsman turned to face his Japanese Rama expert. "It's difficult to decide on exactly the proper action pattern, of course," he said. "I mean, those two certainly look harmless enough, but remember the Trojan horse. Hah! Well, Watanabe, what do you suggest?"

"Why don't I go forward, perhaps alone, or maybe even with one of the soldiers, to talk to them? Then we'll know—"

"That's certainly brave of you, Watanabe, but unnecessary. No, I think we'll all go forward. Cautiously, of course. Leaving a couple of men at the rear to report in case we're zapped by a ray gun or something."

The commander turned on his radio. "Deputy Ulanov, Macmillan here. We've encountered two beings of some kind. They're either human or in human disguise. One looks like Abraham Lincoln and the other like that famous Mexican cosmonaut. . . . What's that, Dmitri? . . . Yes, you copy correctly. Lincoln and Garcia. We've encountered Lincoln and Garcia in a tunnel inside Rama. You may report that to the others. . . . Now, I'm leaving Snyder and Finzi here while the rest of us advance toward the strangers."

The two figures did not move as the fourteen explorers from the Pinta approached. The soldiers were spread out in front of the group, ready to fire at the fist sign of trouble.

"Welcome to Rama," Abraham Lincoln said when the first scout was only twenty meters away. "We are here to escort you to your new homes."

Commander Macmillan did not respond immediately. It was the irrepressible Max Puckett who broke the silence. "Are you a ghost?" he shouted. "I mean, are you *really* Abraham Lincoln?"

"Of course not," the Lincoln replied matter-of-factly. "Both Benita Garcia and I are human biots. You will find five categories of human biots in New Eden, each designed with specific capabilities to free humans from tedious, repetitive tasks. My areas of specialty are clerical and legal work, accounting, bookkeeping and housekeeping, home and office management, and other organizational tasks."

Max was dumbounded. Ignoring his commander's order to "stand back," Max walked up to within several centimeters of the Lincoln. "This is some fucking robot," he muttered to himself. Oblivious to any possible danger, Max next reached out and put his fingers on the Lincoln's face, first touching the skin around the nose and then feeling the whiskers in the long black beard. "Incredible," he said out loud. "Absolutely incredible."

"We have been manufactured with very careful attention to detail," the Lincoln now said. "Our skin is chemically similar to yours and our eyes operate on the same basic optical principles as yours, but we are not dynamic, constantly renewing creatures like you. Our subsystems must be maintained and sometimes even replaced by technicians."

Max's bold move had defused all the tension. By this time the entire scouting party, including Commander Macmillan, were poking and probing the two biots. Throughout the examination both the Lincoln and the Garcia answered questions about their design and implementation. At one point Kenji realized that Max Puckett had withdrawn from the rest of the scouting party and was sitting by himself against one of the walls of the tunnel.

Kenji walked over to his friend. "What's the matter, Max?" he asked.

Max shook his head. "What kind of genius could produce something like these two? It's positively scary." He was silent for several seconds. "Maybe I'm strange, but those two bi-ots frighten me much more than this huge cylinder."

The Lincoln and the Garcia walked with the scouting party to what appeared to be the end of the tunnel. Within seconds a door opened in the wall and the biots motioned for the humans to go inside. Under questioning from Macmillan, the biots explained that the humans were about to enter a "transportation device" that would carry them to the outskirts of the Earth habitat.

Macmillan communicated what the biots had said to Dmitri Ulanov on the Pinta and told his Russian deputy to "blast off" if he didn't hear anything from them within forty-eight hours.

The tube ride was astonishing. It reminded Max Puckett of the giant roller coaster at the state fair in Dallas, Texas. The bullet-shaped vehicle sped along an enclosed, helical track that dropped all the way from the bowl-shaped northern end of Rama to the Central Plain below. Outside the tube, which was encased in a heavy transparent plastic of some kind, Kenji and the others glimpsed the vast network of ladders and stairways that traversed the same territory as their ride. But they did not see the incomparable vistas reported by the previous Rama explorers—their view to the south was blocked by an extremely tall wall of metallic gray.

The ride took less than five minutes. It deposited them in an enclosed annulus that completely circumscribed the Earth habitat. When the Pinta scouts exited from the tube, the weightlessness in which they had been living since they had departed from Earth had vanished. The gravity was close to normal. "The atmosphere in this corridor, like the atmosphere in New Eden, is just like your home planet," the Lincoln biot said. "But that is not the case in the region on our right, outside the walls protecting your habitat."

The annulus surrounding New Eden was dimly lit, so the colonists were not prepared for the bright sunlight that greeted them when the huge door opened and they entered their new world. On the short walk to the nearby train station they carried their space helmets in their hands. The men passed empty buildings on both sides of the path—small structures that could be houses or shops, as well as a larger one ("That will be an elementary school," the Benita Garcia informed them) right opposite the station itself.

A train was waiting for them when they arrived. The sleek

subway car with soft, comfortable seats, and a constantly updating electronic status board, raced quickly toward the center of New Eden, where they were to have a "comprehensive briefing," according to the Lincoln biot. The train ran first along the side of a beautiful, crystalline lake ("Lake Shakespeare," the Benita Garcia said), and then turned to the left, heading away from the light gray walls that enclosed the colony. During the last part of the ride a large, barren mountain dominated the landscape on the right-hand side of the train.

Throughout the ride the entire contingent from the Pinta was very quiet. In truth they were all completely overwhelmed. Not even in the creative imagination of Kenji Watanabe had anything like what they were seeing ever been envisioned. It was all much too large, much more magnificent than they had pictured.

The central city, where all the major buildings had been located by the designers of New Eden, was the final stunner. The members of the party stood silently and gawked at the array of large and impressive structures that formed the heart of the colony. That the buildings were still empty only added to the mystical quality of the entire experience. Kenji Watanabe and Max Puckett were the last two men to enter the edifice where the briefing was to occur.

"What do you think?" Kenji asked Max as the two of them stood on the top of the stairs of the administration building and surveyed the astonishing complex around them.

"I cannot think," answered Max, the awe in his tone quite obvious. "This whole place defies thought. It is heaven, Alice's wonderland, and all the fairy tales of my boyhood wrapped up in one package. I keep pinching myself to make sure that I'm not dreaming."

"On the screen in front of you," the Lincoln biot said, "is an overview map of New Eden. Each of you will be given a full packet of maps, including all the roads and structures in the colony. We are *here*, in Central City, which was designed to be the administrative center of New Eden. Residences have been built, along with shops, small offices, and schools, in the four corners of the rectangle that is enclosed by the outside wall. Because the naming of these four towns will be left to the inhabitants, we will refer to them today as the Northeast, Northwest, Southeast, and Southwest villages. In doing this we are following the convention, adopted by earlier Raman explorers from the Earth, of referring to the end of Rama where your spacecraft docked as the north end.

"Each of the four sides of New Eden has an allocated geographic function. The freshwater lake along the south edge of the colony, as you have already been informed, is called Lake Shakespeare. Most of the fish and water life that you have brought with you will live there, although some of the specimens may be perfect for emplacement in the two rivers that empty into Lake Shakespeare from Mount Olympus, here on the east side of the colony, and Sherwood Forest on the west side.

"At present both the slopes of Mount Olympus and all the regions of Sherwood Forest, as well as the village parks and greenbelts throughout the colony, are covered with a fine lattice of gas exchange devices, or GEDs, as we call them. These tiny mechanisms serve but one function—they convert carbon dioxide into oxygen. In a very true sense they are mechanical plants. They are to be replaced by all the *real* plants that you have brought from the Earth.

"The north side of the colony, between the villages, is reserved for farming. Farm buildings have been constructed *here*, along the road that connects the two northern towns. You will grow most of your food in this area. Between the food supplies that you have brought with you and the synthetic food stored in the tall silos three hundred meters north of this building, you should be able to feed two thousand humans for at least a year, maybe eighteen months if waste is kept at a minimum. After that you are on your own. It goes without saying that farming, including the aquaculture that has been allocated to the eastern shores of Lake Shakespeare, will be an important component in your life in New Eden. . . ,"

To Kenji, the briefing experience was like drinking out of a fire hose. The Lincoln biot kept the information rate exceedingly high for ninety minutes, dismissing all questions either by saying "That's outside my knowledge base" or by referring to the page and paragraph numbers in the *Basic Guidebook* to New Eden that he had handed out. Finally there was a break in the briefing and everyone moved to an adjacent room, where a drink that tasted like Coca-Cola was served.

"Whew," said Terry Snyder as he wiped his brow, "am I the only one who is saturated?"

"Shit, Snyder," replied Max Puckett with an impish grin. "Are you saying you're inferior to that goddamn robot? He sure as hell ain't tired. I bet he could lecture all day."

"Maybe even all week," mused Kenji Watanabe. "I wonder how often these biots need to be serviced. My father's company makes robots, some of them exceedingly complex, but nothing like this. The information content in that Lincoln must be astronomical."

"The briefing will recommence in five minutes," the Lincoln announced. "Please be prompt."

In the second half of the briefing the various kinds of biots in New Eden were introduced and explained. Based on their recent studies of the previous Raman expeditions, the colonists were prepared for the bulldozer and other construction biots. The five categories of human biots, however, elicited a more emotional response.

"Our designers decided," the Lincoln told them, "to limit the physical appearances of the human biots so that there could be no question of someone mistaking one of us for one of you. I have already listed my basic functions—all the other Lincolns, three of whom are now joining us, have been identically programmed. At least originally. We are, however, capable of some low level of learning that will allow our data bases to be different as our specific uses evolve."

"How can we tell one Lincoln from another?" asked one bewildered member of the scouting party as the three new Lincolns circulated around the room.

"We each have an identification number, engraved both here, on the shoulder, and again here, on the left buttock. This same system is employed for the other categories of human biots. I, for example, am Lincoln 004. The three that just entered are 009, 024, and 071."

When the Lincoln biots left the briefing room, they were replaced by five Benita Garcias. One of the Garcias outlined the specialties of her category—police and fire protection, farming, sanitation, transportation, mail handling—and then answered a few questions before they all departed.

The Einstein biots were next. The scouts erupted with laughter when four of the Einsteins, each a wild, unkempt, white-haired replica of the twentieth century scientific genius, walked into the room together. The Einsteins explained that they were the engineers and scientists of the colony. Their primary function, a vital one encompassing many duties, was to "ensure the satisfactory working of the colony infrastructure," including of course the army of biots.

A group of tall, jet-black female biots introduced themselves as the Tiassos, specializing in health care. They would be the doctors, the nurses, the health officials, the ones who would provide child care when the parents were not available. Just as the Tiasso portion of the briefing was ending, a slight Oriental biot with intense eyes walked into the room. He was carrying a lyre and an electronic easel. He introduced himself as a Yasunari Kawabata before playing a beautiful, short piece on the lyre.

"We Kawabatas are creative artists," he said simply. "We are musicians, actors, painters, sculptors, writers, and sometimes photographers and cinematographers. We are few in number, but very important for the quality of life in New Eden."

When the official briefing was finally over, the scouting party was served an excellent dinner in the large hall. About twenty of the biots joined the humans at the gathering, although of course they did not eat anything. The simulated roast duck was staggeringly authentic, and even the wines could have passed the inspection of all but the most learned enologists on Earth.

Later in the evening, when the humans had grown more comfortable with their biot companions and were peppering them with questions, a solitary female figure appeared in the open doorway. At first she was unnoticed. But the room quieted quickly after Kenji Watanabe jumped up from his seat and approached the newcomer with an outstretched hand.

"Dr. des Jardins, I presume," he said with a smile.

10

Despite Nicole's assurances that everything in New Eden was completely consistent with her earlier remarks on the video, Commander Macmillan refused to allow the Pinta passengers and crew to enter Rama and occupy their new homes until he was certain there was no danger. After returning to the Pinta, he conferred at length with ISA personnel on Earth and then sent a small contingent headed by Dmitri Ulanov into Rama to obtain additional information. The chief medical officer of the Pinta, a dour Dutchman named Darl van Roos, was the most important member of Ulanov's team. Kenji Watanabe and two soldiers from the first scouting party also accompanied the Russian engineer.

The doctor's instructions were straightforward. He was to examine the Wakefields, all of them, and certify that they were indeed humans. His second assignment was to analyze the biots and categorize their nonbiological features. Everything was accomplished without incident, although Katie Wakefield was uncooperative and sarcastic during the examination. At Richard's suggestion, an Einstein biot took apart one of the Lincolns and demonstrated, at a functional level, how the most sophisticated subsystems worked. Deputy Ulanov was duly impressed.

Two days later the voyagers from the Pinta began moving their possessions into Rama. A large cadre of biots helped with the unloading of the spacecraft and the movement of all the supplies into New Eden. The process took almost three days to complete. But where would everyone settle? In a decision that would later have significant consequences for the colony, almost all of the three hundred travelers on the Pinta elected to live in the Southeast Village, where the Wakefields had made their home. Only Max Puckett and a handful of farmers, who moved directly into the farming region along the northern perimeter of New Eden, decided to live elsewhere in the colony.

The Watanabes moved into a small house just down the lane from Richard and Nicole. From the very beginning Kenji and Nicole had had a natural rapport and their initial friendship had grown with each subsequent interaction. On the first evening that Kenji and Nai spent in their new home, they were invited to share a family dinner with the Wakefields.

"Why don't we go into the living room? It's more comfortable there," Nicole said when the meal was completed. "The Lincoln will clear the table and take care of the dishes."

The Watanabes rose from their chairs and followed Richard through the entryway at the end of the dining room. The younger Wakefields politely waited for Kenji and Nai to go first, and then joined their parents and guests in the cozy living room at the front of the house.

It had been five days since the Pinta scouting party had entered Rama for the first time. *Five amazing days,* Kenji was thinking as he sat down in the Wakefield living room. His mind quickly scanned the kaleidoscope of jumbled impressions that were as yet unordered by his brain. *And in many ways this dinner was the most amazing of all. What this family has been through is incredible.*

"The stories you have told us," Nai said to Richard and Nicole when everyone was seated, "are absolutely astonishing. There are so many questions I want to ask, I don't know where to start. . . . I'm especially fascinated by this creature you call the Eagle. Was he one of the ETs who built the Node and Rama in the first place?"

"No," said Nicole. "The Eagle was a biot also. At least that's what he told us, and we have no reason not to believe him. He was created by the governing intelligence of the Node to give us a specific physical interface."

"But then who *did* build the Node?"

"That's definitely a Level III question," Richard said with a smile.

Kenji and Nai laughed. Nicole and Richard had explained the Eagle's informational hierarchy to them during the long stories at dinner. "I wonder if it is even possible," Kenji mused, "for us to conceive of beings so advanced that their machines can create other machines smarter than we are."

"I wonder if it is even possible," Katie now interrupted, "for us to discuss some more trivial issues. For example, where are all the young people my age? So far I don't think I have seen more than two colonists between twelve and twenty-five."

"Most of the younger set are onboard the Niña," Kenji responded. "It should arrive here in about three weeks with the bulk of the colony population. The passengers on the Pinta were hand-picked for the task of checking out the veracity of the video we received."

"What's *veracity*?" Katie asked.

"Truth and accuracy," Nicole said. "More or less. It was one of your grandfather's favorite words. . . . And speaking of your grandfather, he was also a great believer that young people should always be permitted to *listen* to adult conversation, but not to interrupt it. . . . We have many things to discuss tonight with the Watanabes. The four of you don't have to stay."

"I want to go out and see the lights," Benjy said. "Will you come with me, please, Ellie?"

Ellie Wakefield stood up and took Benjy by the hand. The two of them said good night politely and were followed out the door by Katie and Patrick. "We're going to see if we can find anything exciting to do," Katie said as they departed. "Good night, Mr. and Mrs. Watanabe. Mother, we'll be back in a couple of hours or so."

Nicole shook her head as the last of her children left the house. "Katie has been so frenetic since the Pinta arrived," she said in explanation, "she is barely even sleeping at night. She wants to meet and talk to *everybody*."

The Lincoln biot, who had now finished cleaning the kitchen, was standing unobtrusively by the door behind Benjy's chair. "Would you like something to drink?" Nicole asked Kenji and Nai, motioning in the direction of the biot. "We don't have anything as delicious as the fresh fruit drinks that you brought from Earth, but Linc can whip up some interesting synthetic concoctions."

"I'm fine," Kenji said, shaking his head. "But I just realized we have spent the entire evening talking about your incredible odyssey. Certainly you must have questions for us. After all, forty-five years have passed on Earth since the Newton was launched."

Forty-five years, Nicole suddenly thought. *Is that possible? Can Genevieve really be almost sixty years old?*

Nicole remembered clearly the last time she had seen her father and daughter on Earth. Pierre and Genevieve had accompanied her to the airport in Paris. Her daughter had hugged Nicole fiercely until the last call for boarding and then looked up at her mother with intense love and pride. The girl's eyes had been full of tears. Genevieve had been unable to say anything. *And during that forty-five years my father has died. Genevieve has become an older woman, a grandmother even, Kenji said. While I have been wandering in time and space. In a wonderland.*

The memories were too powerful for Nicole. She took a deep breath and steadied herself. There was still quiet in the Wakefield living room as she returned to the present.

"Is everything all right?" Kenji asked sensitively. Nicole nodded and stared at the soft, open eyes of her new friend. She imagined for a brief moment that she was talking to her fellow Newton cosmonaut Shigeru Takagishi. *This man is full of curiosity, as Shig was. I can trust him. And he has talked to Genevieve only a few years ago.*

"Most of the general Earth history has been explained to us, in bits and snippets, during our many conversations with other passengers from the Pinta," Nicole said after a protracted silence. "But we know absolutely nothing about our families except what you told us briefly that first night. Both Richard and I would like to know if you've remembered any additional details that might have been omitted in our first conversations."

"As a matter of fact," Kenji said, "I went back through my journals this afternoon and read again the entries I made when I was doing the preliminary research for my book on the Newton. The most important thing that I neglected to mention in our earlier discussion was how much your Genevieve looks like her father, at least from the chin down. King Henry's face was striking, as I'm certain you remember. As an adult Genevieve's face lengthened and began to resemble his quite markedly. . . . Here, look at these, I managed to find a couple of photographs from my three days at Beauvois stored in my data base."

Seeing the pictures of Genevieve overwhelmed Nicole. Tears rushed immediately into her eyes and overflowed onto her cheeks. Her hands trembled as she held the two photographs of Genevieve and her husband Louis Gaston. *Oh, Genevieve,* she cried to herself, *How I have missed you. How I would love to hold you in my arms for just a moment.*

Richard leaned over her shoulder to see the pictures. As he did so he caressed Nicole gently. "She does look something like the prince," he commented softly, "but I think she looks much more like her mother."

"Genevieve was also extremely courteous," Kenji added, "which surprised me considering how much she had suffered during all the media uproar in 2238. She answered my questions very patiently. I had intended to make her one of the centerpieces of the Newton book until my editor dissuaded me from the project altogether."

"How many of the Newton cosmonauts are still alive?" Richard asked, keeping the conversation going while Nicole continued to gaze at the two photographs.

"Only Sabatini, Tabori, and Yamanaka," Kenji replied. "Dr. David Brown had a massive stroke, and then died six months later under somewhat unusual circumstances. I believe that was in 2208. Admiral Heilmann died of cancer in 2214 or so. Irina Turgenyev suffered a complete mental breakdown, a victim of 'Return to Earth' syndrome identified among some of the twenty-first century cosmonauts, and eventually committed suicide in 2211."

Nicole was still struggling with her emotions. "Until three nights ago," she said to the Watanabes when the room was again silent, "I had never even told Richard or the children that Henry was Genevieve's father. While I was living on Earth, only my father knew the truth. Henry may have suspected, but he didn't know for certain. Then, when you told me about Genevieve, I realized that I should be the one to tell my family. I . . ."

Nicole's voice trailed off and more tears appeared in her eyes. She wiped her face with one of the tissues Nai handed her. "I'm sorry," Nicole said, "I'm never like this. It's just such a shock to see a picture and to recall so many things. . . ."

"When we were living in Rama II and then at the Node," Richard said, "Nicole was a model of stability. She was a rock. No matter what we encountered, no matter how bizarre, she was unflappable. The children and Michael O'Toole and I all depended on her. It's very rare to see her—"

"Enough," Nicole exclaimed after wiping her face. She put the photograph aside. "Let's go on to other subjects. Let's talk about the Newton cosmonauts, Francesca Sabatini in particular. Did she get what she wanted? Fame and riches beyond compare?"

"Pretty much," Kenji said. "I wasn't alive during her heyday in the first decade of the century, but even now she is still very famous. She was one of the people interviewed on television recently about the significance of recolonizing Mars."

Nicole leaned forward in her chair. "I didn't tell you this during dinner, but I'm certain Francesca and Brown drugged Borzov, causing his appendicitis symptoms. And she purposely left me at the bottom of that pit in New York. The woman was totally without scruples."

Kenji was silent for several seconds. "Back in 2208, just before Dr. Brown died, he had occasional lucid periods in his generally incoherent state. During one such period he gave a fantastic interview to a magazine reporter in which he confessed partial responsibility for Borzov's death and implicated Francesca in your disappearance. Signora Sabatini said the entire story was 'poppycock—the crazy outpourings of a diseased brain,' sued the magazine for a hundred million marks, and then settled comfortably out of court. The magazine fired the reporter and formally apologized to her."

"Francesca always wins in the end," Nicole remarked.

"I almost resurrected the whole story three years ago," Kenji continued, "when I was doing the research for my book. Since it had been more than twenty-five years, all the data from the Newton mission was in the public domain and therefore available to anyone who asked for it. I found the contents of your personal computer, including the data cube that must have come from Henry, scattered throughout the trickle telemetry. I became convinced that Dr. Brown's interview had indeed contained some truth."

"So what happened?"

"I went to interview Francesca at her palace in Sorrento. Soon thereafter I stopped working on the book—"

Kenji hesitated for an instant. *Should I say more?* he wondered. He glanced over at his loving wife. *No,* he said to himself, *this is not the time or the place.*

"I'm sorry, Richard."

He was almost asleep when he heard his wife's soft voice in the bedroom.

"Huh?" he said. "Did you say something, dear?"

"I'm sorry," Nicole repeated. She rolled over next to him and found his hand with hers underneath the covers. "I should have told you about Henry years ago. . . . Are you still angry?"

"I was never angry," Richard said. "Surprised, yes, maybe even flabbergasted. But not angry. You had your reasons for keeping it secret." He squeezed her hand. "Besides, it was back on Earth, in another life. If you had told me when we first met, it might have mattered. I might have been jealous, and almost certainly would have felt inadequate. But not now."

Nicole leaned over and gave him a kiss. "I love you, Richard Wakefield," she said.

"And I love you too," he responded.

Kenji and Nai made love for the first time since they had left the Pinta and she fell asleep immediately. Kenji was still surprisingly alert. He lay awake in bed, thinking about the evening with the Wakefields. For some reason an image of Francesca Sabatini came into his mind. *The most beautiful seventy-year-old woman I have ever seen,* was his first thought. *And what a fantastic life.*

Kenji remembered clearly the summer afternoon when his train had pulled into the station at Sorrento. The driver of the electric cab had recognized the address immediately. *"Capisco,"* he had said, waving his hands and then heading in the direction of *"il palazzo Sabatini."*

Francesca lived in a converted hotel overlooking the Bay of Naples. It was a twenty-room structure that had once belonged to a seventeenth century prince. From the office where Kenji waited for Signora Sabatini to appear, he could see a funicular carrying swimmers down a steep precipice to the dark blue bay below.

La signora was half an hour late and then quickly became impatient for the interview to be over. Twice Francesca informed Kenji that she had only agreed to talk to him at all because her publisher had told her he was an "outstanding young writer." "Frankly," she said in her excellent English, "at this stage I find all discussion of the Newton extremely boring."

Her interest in the conversation picked up considerably when Kenji told her about his "new data," the files from Nicole's personal computer that had been telemetered down to Earth in the "trickle mode" during the final few weeks of the mission. Francesca became quiet, even pensive, as Kenji compared the internal notes that Nicole had made with the "confession" given by Dr. David Brown to the magazine reporter in 2208.

"I underestimated you," Francesca said with a smile, when Kenji asked if she didn't think it was a "remarkable coincidence" that Nicole's Newton diary and David Brown's confession had so many points of agreement. She never answered his questions directly. Instead she stood up in the office, insisted that he stay for the evening, and told Kenji that she would talk to him later.

Near dusk a note came to Kenji's room in Francesca's palace telling him that dinner would be at eight-thirty and that he should wear a coat and a tie. A robot arrived at the appointed time and led him to a magnificent dining room with walls covered in murals and tapestries, glittering chandeliers hanging from the high ceilings, and delicate carvings on all the moldings. The table was set for ten. Francesca was already there, standing near a small robot server off to one side of the enormous room.

"Kon ban wa, Watanabe-san," Francesca said in Japanese as she offered him a glass of champagne. "I'm renovating the main sitting areas, so I'm afraid we're having our cocktails here. It's all very gauche, as the French would say, but it will have to do."

Francesca looked magnificent. Her blond hair was only slightly tinged by gray. It was stacked on top of her head, held by a large carved comb. A choker of diamonds was around her throat and an immense solitary sapphire dangled from an understated diamond necklace. Her strapless gown was white, with folds and pleats that accentuated the curves of her still youthful body. Kenji could not believe that she was seventy years old.

She took him by the hand, after explaining that she had quickly put together a dinner party in his honor, and led him over to the tapestries against the far wall. "Do you know Aubusson at all?" she asked. When he shook his head, Francesca launched into a discussion of the history of European tapestries.

Half an hour later, Francesca took her seat at the head of the table. A music professor from Naples and his wife (supposedly an actress), two handsome, swarthy professional soccer players, the curator of the Pompeii ruins (a man in his early fifties), a middle-aged Italian poetess, and two young women in their twenties, each stunningly attractive, occupied the other places. After some consultation with Francesca, one of the two young women sat opposite Kenji and the other beside him.

At first the armchair opposite Francesca, at the far end of the table, was empty. Francesca whispered something to her head-waiter, however, and five minutes later a very old man, halt and almost blind, was led into the room. Kenji recognized him immediately. It was Janos Tabori.

The meal was wonderful, the conversation lively. The food was all served by waiters, not by the robots used in all but the most fashionable restaurants, and each course was enhanced by a different Italian wine. And what a remarkable group! Everyone, even the soccer players, spoke passable English. They were also both interested in and knowledgeable of space history. The young woman opposite Kenji had even read his most popular book on the early exploration of Mars. As the evening wore on, Kenji, who was a bachelor of thirty at the time, became less inhibited. He was aroused by everything—the women, the wine, the discussions of history and poetry and music.

Only once during the two hours at the table was there any mention of the afternoon interview. During a lull in the conversation after dessert and before the cognac, Francesca nearly shouted at Janos. "This young Japanese man—he's very brilliant, you know—thinks he has found evidence from Nicole's personal computer that corroborates those awful lies David told before he died."

Janos did not comment. His facial expression did not change. But after the meal he handed Kenji a note and then disappeared. " 'You know nothing but the truth and have no tenderness,' " the note said. " 'Thus you judge unjustly.' Aglaya Yepanchin to Prince Myshkin. *The Idiot,* by Fyodor Dostoyevsky."

Kenji had only been in his room for five or ten minutes when there was a knock on his door. When he opened it he saw the young Italian woman who had been sitting opposite him at dinner. She was wearing a tiny bikini that revealed most of her exceptional body. She was also holding a man's bathing suit in her hand.

"Mr. Watanabe," she said with a sexy smile, "please join us for a swim. This suit ought to fit you."

Kenji felt an immediate and enormous surge of lust that did not quickly abate. Slightly embarrassed, he waited a minute or two after dressing before he joined the woman in the hall.

Three years later, even lying in his bed in New Eden next to the woman he loved, it was impossible for Kenji not to recall with sexual longing the night he spent in Francesca's palace. Six of them had taken the funicular down to the bay and swum in the moonlight. At the cabana next to the water, they had drunk and danced and laughed together. It had been a dream night.

Within an hour, Kenji remembered, *we were all happily naked. The game plan was clear. The two soccer players were for Francesca. The two Madonnas for me.*

Kenji squirmed in his bed recalling both the intensity of his pleasure and Francesca's free laughter when she found him entwined with the two young women at dawn in one of the oversized chaise lounges beside the bay.

When I reached New York four days later my editor told me that he thought I should abandon the Newton project. I didn't argue with him. I probably would have suggested it myself.

11

Ellie was fascinated by the porcelain figures. She picked one up, a little girl dressed in a light blue ballet gown, and turned it over in her hands. "Look at this, Benjy," she said to her brother. "Someone made this—all by himself."

"*That* one is actually a copy," the Spanish shopkeeper said, "but an artist did make the original from which the computer imprint was taken. The reproduction process is now so accurate that even the experts have a hard time telling which ones are the copies."

"And you collected all these back on Earth?" Ellie waved her hand at the hundred or so figures on the table and in the small glass cases.

"Yes," Mr. Murillo said proudly. "Although I was a civil servant in Seville—building permits and that sort of thing—my wife and I also owned a small shop. We fell in love with porcelain art about ten years ago and have been avid collectors ever since."

Mrs. Murillo, also in her late forties, came out of a back room where she was still unpacking merchandise. "We decided," she said, "long before we learned that we had actually been selected as colonists by the ISA, that no matter how restrictive our baggage requirements were for the voyage on the Niña, we would bring our entire collection of porcelain with us."

Benjy was holding the dancing girl only a few centimeters from his face. "Beau-ti-ful," he said with a broad smile.

"Thank you," Mr. Murillo said. "We had hoped to start a collectors' society in Lowell Colony," he added. "Three or four of the other passengers on the Niña brought several pieces as well."

"May we look at them?" Ellie asked. "We'll be very careful."

"Help yourself," Mrs. Murillo said. "Eventually, once everything settles down, we will sell or barter some of the objects—certainly the duplicates. Right now they're just on display to be appreciated."

While Ellie and Benjy were examining the porcelain creations, several other people entered the shop. The Murillos had opened for business only a few days before. They sold candles, fancy napkins, and other small household adornments.

"You certainly didn't waste any time, Carlos," a burly American said to Mr. Murillo several minutes later. From his initial greeting it was obvious that he had been a fellow passenger on the Niña.

"It was easier for us, Travis," Mr. Murillo said. "We had no family and needed only a small place to live."

"We haven't even settled into a house yet," Travis complained. "We're definitely going to live in this village, but Chelsea and the kids cannot find a house they all like. Chelsea is still spooked by the whole arrangement. She doesn't believe the ISA is telling us the truth even now."

"I admit that it is extremely difficult to accept that this space station was built by aliens just so they can observe us . . . and it would certainly be easier to believe the ISA story if there were pictures from that Node place. But why would they lie to us?"

"They have lied before. Nobody even mentioned this place until a day before the rendezvous. . . . Chelsea believes that we are part of an ISA space colony experiment. She says that we will stay here for a while, and then be transferred to the surface of Mars, so that the two types of colonies can be compared."

Mr. Murillo laughed. "I see Chelsea hasn't changed since we left the Niña." He became more serious. "You know, Juanita and I had our doubts too, especially after the first week passed and nobody had seen any sign of the aliens. We spent two full days wandering around, talking to other people—we essentially conducted our own investigation. We finally concluded that the ISA story must be true. First of all, it's just too preposterous to be a lie. Second, that Wakefield woman was very convincing. In her open meeting she answered questions for almost two hours and neither Juanita nor I detected a single inconsistency."

"It's hard for me to imagine anyone sleeping for twelve years," Travis said, shaking his head.

"Of course. It was for us too. But we actually inspected that somnarium where the Wakefield family supposedly slept. Everything was exactly as Nicole had described it in the meeting. The overall building, incidentally, is immense. There are enough berths and rooms to house everyone in the colony, if necessary. . . . It certainly doesn't make sense that the ISA would have built such a huge facility to support a lie."

"Maybe you're right."

"Anyway, we've decided to make the best of it. At least for the time being. And we certainly can't complain about our living conditions. All the housing is first rate. Juanita and I even have our own Lincoln robot to give us a hand both at home and around the store."

Ellie was following the discussion very closely. She remembered what her mother had told her the night before when she had asked if she and Benjy could go for a walk in the village. "I guess so, darling," Nicole had said, "but if anyone recognizes you as a Wakefield and starts to question you, don't talk to them. Be polite, and then come home as quickly as you can. Mr. Macmillan does not want us talking to any non-ISA personnel about our experiences just yet."

While Ellie was admiring the porcelain figures and listening intently to the conversation between Mr. Murillo and the man named Travis, Benjy wandered off on his own. When Ellie realized he was not beside her, she started to panic.

"What are you staring at, buddy?" Ellie heard a harsh male voice say on the other side of the shop.

"Her hair is ve-ry pret-ty," Benjy replied. He was blocking the aisle, preventing the man and his wife from moving forward. He smiled and reached out his hand toward the woman's magnificent long blond hair. "May I touch it?" he asked.

"Are you crazy? Of course not. Now get out of—"

"Jason, I think he's retarded," the woman said quietly, catching her husband's arm before he pushed Benjy.

At that moment Ellie walked up beside her brother. She realized that the man was angry, but she did not know what to do. She nudged Benjy gently on the shoulder. "Look, Ellie," he exclaimed, slurring his words in excitement, "look at her pret-ty yel-low hair."

"Is this goon a friend of yours?" the tall man asked Ellie.

"Benjy is my brother," Ellie answered with difficulty.

"Well, get him out of here. He's bothering my wife."

"Sir," Ellie said after summoning her courage, "my brother doesn't mean any harm. He's never seen long blond hair up close before."

The man's face wrinkled in anger and puzzlement. "Whaaat?" he said. He glanced at his wife. "What's with these two? One's a dummy and the other—"

"Aren't you two of the Wakefield children?" a pleasant female voice behind Ellie interrupted.

The distraught Ellie turned around. Mrs. Murillo stepped between the teenagers and the couple. She and her husband had crossed the shop as soon as they had heard the raised voices. "Yes, ma'am," Ellie said softly. "Yes, we are."

"You mean these are two of the children who came from outer space?" the man named Jason asked.

Ellie managed to pull Benjy quickly over to the door of the shop. "We're very sorry," Ellie said before she and Benjy departed. "We didn't mean to cause any trouble."

"Freaks!" Ellie heard somebody say as the door closed behind her.

It had been another exhausting day. Nicole was very tired. She stood in front of the mirror and finished washing her face. "Ellie and Benjy had some kind of unpleasant experience down in the village," Richard said from the bedroom. "They wouldn't tell me much about it."

Nicole had spent thirteen long hours that day helping to process the Niña passengers. No matter how hard she and Kenji Watanabe and the others had worked, it seemed as if nobody was ever satisfied and there were always more tasks that needed to be done. Many of the new colonists had been downright petulant when Nicole had tried to explain to them the procedures that the ISA had established for the allocation of food, living quarters, and working areas.

She had been too many days without enough sleep. Nicole looked at the bags under her eyes. *But we must finish with this group before the Santa Maria arrives,* she said to herself. *They will be far more difficult.*

Nicole wiped her face with a towel and crossed into the bedroom, where Richard was sitting up in his pajamas. "How was your day?" she asked.

"Not bad. . . . Fairly interesting, in fact. Slowly but surely the human engineers are becoming more comfortable with the Einsteins." He paused. "Did you hear what I said about Ellie and Benjy?"

Nicole sighed. From the tone in Richard's voice she understood his real message. Despite her fatigue, she exited from the bedroom and headed down the hall.

Ellie was already asleep, but Benjy was still awake in the room he shared with Patrick. Nicole sat down beside Benjy and took his hand. "Hel-lo, Ma-ma," the boy said.

"Uncle Richard mentioned that you and Ellie went into the village this afternoon," Nicole said to her eldest son.

An expression of pain creased the boy's face for a few seconds and then disappeared. "Yes, Ma-ma," he said.

"Ellie told me that they were recognized and that one of the new colonists called them some names," Patrick said from the opposite side of the room.

"Is that right, darling?" Nicole asked Benjy, still holding and stroking his hands.

The boy made a barely perceptible affirmative motion with his head and then stared silently at his mother. "What's a goon, Ma-ma?" he said suddenly, his eyes filling with tears.

Nicole put her arms around Benjy. "Did someone call you a goon today?" she asked softly.

Benjy nodded. "The word doesn't have a specific meaning," Nicole answered. "Anyone who is different, or perhaps objectionable, might be called a goon." She caressed Benjy again. "People use words like that when they aren't thinking. Whoever called you a goon was probably confused, or upset, by other events in his life, and he just lashed out at you because he didn't understand you. . . . Did you do anything to bother him?"

"No, Ma-ma. I just told him that I liked the wo-man's yel-low hair."

It took several minutes, but Nicole eventually learned the gist of what had occurred in the porcelain shop. When she thought that Benjy was all right, Nicole walked across the room to kiss Patrick good night. "And how about you?" she said. "Was your day all right?"

"Mostly," Patrick said. "I only had one disaster—down at the park." He tried to smile. "Some of the new boys were playing basketball and invited me to join them. . . . I was absolutely terrible. A couple of them laughed at me."

Nicole gave Patrick a long and tender hug. *Patrick is strong,* Nicole said to herself when she was out in the hall, headed back to her bedroom. *But even he needs support.* She took a deep breath. *Am I doing the right thing?* she asked herself for the umpteenth time since she had become deeply involved in all aspects of the planning for the colony. *I feel so responsible for everything here. I want New Eden to begin properly. . . . But my children still need more of my time. . . . Will I ever achieve the right balance?*

Richard was still awake when Nicole snuggled in beside him. She shared Benjy's story with her husband. "I'm sorry I wasn't able to help him," Richard said. "There are just some things that only a mother . . ."

Nicole was so exhausted that she was falling asleep before Richard even finished his sentence. He touched her firmly on the arm. "Nicole," he said, "there is something else we must talk about. Unfortunately it can't wait—we may not have any private time in the morning."

She rolled over and looked at Richard quizzically. "It's about Katie," he said. "I really need your help. . . . There's another of those youth get-acquainted dances tomorrow night—you remember we told Katie last week she could go, but only if Patrick went with her and she came home at a reasonable hour. Well, tonight I just happened to see her standing in front of her mirror in a new dress. It was short and very revealing. When I asked her about the dress, and then told her that it didn't seem like an appropriate outfit for a casual dance, she flew into a rage. She insisted that I was spying on her and then informed me that I was 'hopelessly ignorant' about fashion."

"What did you say?"

"I reprimanded her. She glared at me coldly and said nothing. Several minutes later she left the house without saying a word. The rest of the children and I ate dinner without her. . . . Katie came home only thirty minutes or so before you did. She smelled of tobacco and beer. When I tried to talk to her, she just said 'Don't bother me,' and then went to her room and slammed the door."

I have been afraid of this, Nicole thought as she lay next to Richard in silence. *All the signs have been there since she was a little girl. Katie is brilliant, but she is also selfish and impetuous.*

"I was going to tell Katie that she could not go to the dance tomorrow night," Richard was saying, "but then I realized that by any normal definition she is an adult. After all, her registry card at the administration office gives her age as twenty-four. We really can't treat her like a child."

But she's maybe fourteen emotionally, Nicole thought, squirming as Richard began reciting all the difficulties they had had with Katie since the first other humans had entered Rama. *Nothing matters to her but adventure and excitement.*

Nicole remembered the day she had spent with Katie at the hospital. It had been a week before the colonists from the Niña had arrived. Katie had been fascinated by all the sophisticated medical equipment and genuinely interested in how it worked; however, when Nicole had suggested that Katie might want to work at the hospital until the university opened, the young woman had laughed. "Are you kidding?" her daughter had said. "I can't imagine anything more boring. Especially when there will be hundreds of new people to meet."

There's not much either Richard or I can do, Nicole said to herself with a sigh. *We can ache for Katie, and offer her our love, but she has already decided that all our knowledge and experience is irrelevant.*

There was silence in the bedroom. Nicole reached over and kissed Richard. "I will talk to Katie tomorrow about the dress," she said, "but I doubt if it will do much good."

Patrick was sitting by himself in a folding chair against the wall of the school gymnasium. He took a sip from his soda and glanced at his watch as the slow music ended and a dozen couples dancing on the large floor slowed to a stop. Katie and Olaf Larsen, a tall Swede whose father was a member of Commander Macmillan's staff, shared a brief kiss before walking, arm in arm, in Patrick's direction.

"Olaf and I are going outside for a cigarette and another shot of whiskey," Katie said when the pair reached Patrick. "Why don't you come with us?"

"We're already late, Katie," Patrick replied. "We said we would be home by twelve-thirty."

The Swede gave Patrick a condescending pat on the back. "Come on, boy," he said. "Loosen up. Your sister and I are having a good time."

Olaf was already drunk. His fair face was flushed from the drinking and dancing. He pointed across the room. "You see that girl with the red hair, white dress, and big boobs? Her name is Beth and she's a hot number. She's been waiting all night for you to ask her to dance. Would you like for me to introduce you?"

Patrick shook his head. "Look, Katie," he said. "I want to go. I've been sitting here patiently—"

"Half an hour more, baby brother," Katie interrupted. "I'll go outside for a little while, then come back for a couple of dances. After that we'll leave. Okay?"

She kissed Patrick on the cheek and moved toward the door with Olaf. A fast dance began playing on the gymnasium sound system. Patrick watched in fascination as the young couples moved in tune with the heavy beat of the music.

"You don't dance?" a young man who was walking around the perimeter of the dance floor asked him.

"No," said Patrick. "I've never tried."

The young man gave Patrick a strange look. Then he stopped and smiled. "Of course," he said, "you're one of the Wakefields. . . . Hi, my name is Brian Walsh. I'm from Wisconsin, in the middle of the United States. My parents are the ones who are supposed to be organizing the university."

Patrick had not exchanged more than a couple of words with anyone except Katie since they had arrived at the dance several hours earlier. He gladly shook hands with Brian Walsh and the two of them chatted amiably for a few minutes. Brian, who had been half finished with his undergraduate degree in computer engineering when his family had been selected for Lowell Colony, was twenty and an only child. He was also extremely curious about his companion's experiences.

"Tell me," he said to Patrick when they had become more comfortable with each other, "does this place called the Node really exist? Or is it part of some cockamamy story dreamed up by the ISA?"

"No," said Patrick, forgetting that he was not supposed to discuss such things. "The Node is definitely there. My father says it's an extraterrestrial processing station."

Brian laughed easily. "So somewhere out near Sirius is a gigantic triangle built by an unknown superspecies? And its purpose is to help *them* study other creatures who travel in space? Wow. That's the most fantastic tale I have ever heard. In fact, almost everything your mother told us at that open meeting was unbelievable. I will, however, admit that both the existence of this space station and the technological level of the robots do make her story more plausible."

"Everything my mother said was true," Patrick said. "And some of the most incredible stories were purposely left out. For example, my mother had a conversation with a caped eel who talked in bubbles. Also—" Patrick stopped himself, remembering Nicole's admonitions.

Brian was fascinated. "A caped eel?" he said. "How did she know what it was saying?"

Patrick looked at his watch. "Excuse me, Brian," he said abruptly, "but I'm here with my sister and I'm supposed to meet her in a few minutes."

"Is she the one with the little red dress cut *really* low?"

Patrick nodded. Brian put his arm around his new friend's shoulder. "Let me give you some advice," he said. "Somebody needs to talk to your sister. The way she acts around all the guys makes people think she's an easy lay."

"That's just Katie," Patrick said defensively. "She's never been around anyone except the family."

"Sorry," Brian said with a shrug. "It's none of my business anyway. . . . Say, why don't you give me a call sometime? I've enjoyed our conversation very much."

Patrick said good-bye to Brian and started walking toward the door. Where was Katie? Why had she not come back inside the gymnasium?

He heard her loud laugh within seconds after he was outside. Katie was standing on the playground with three men, one of whom was Olaf Larsen. They were all smoking and laughing and drinking from a bottle that was being passed around.

"So what position do *you* like best?" a dark young man with a mustache asked.

"Oh, I prefer to be on top," Katie said with a laugh. She took a gulp from the bottle. "That way I'm in control."

"Sounds good to me," the man, whose name was Andrew, replied. He chuckled and placed his hand suggestively on her bottom. Katie pushed it away, still laughing. Seconds later she saw Patrick approaching.

"Come over here, baby brother," Katie shouted. "This shit we're drinking is dynamite."

The three men, who had been drawn in close around Katie, moved slightly away from her as Patrick walked toward them. Although he was still quite skinny and undeveloped, his height made him an imposing figure in the dim light.

"I'm going home now, Katie," Patrick said, refusing the bottle when he was beside her, "and I think you should go with me."

Andrew laughed. "Some party girl you have here, Larsen," he said sarcastically, "with a teenage brother as a chaperon."

Katie's eyes flared with anger. She took another swig from the bottle and handed it to Olaf. Then she grabbed Andrew and kissed him wildly on the lips, pressing her body tightly against his.

Patrick was embarrassed. Olaf and the third man cheered and whistled as Andrew returned Katie's kiss. After almost a minute Katie pulled away. "Let's go now, Patrick," she said with a smile, her eyes still fixed on the man she had kissed. "I think that's enough for one night."

12

Eponine stared out the second story window at the gently rolling slope. The GEDs covered the hillside, their fine gridwork pattern almost obscuring the brown soil underneath.

"So, Ep, what do you think?" Kimberly asked. "It's certainly nice enough. And once the forest is planted, we'll have trees and grass and maybe even a squirrel or two outside our window. That's definitely a plus."

"I don't know," a distracted Eponine replied after a few seconds. "It's a little smaller than the one I liked yesterday in Positano. And I have a few misgivings about living here, in Hakone. I haven't known that many Orientals. . . ."

"Look, roomie, we can't wait forever. I told you yesterday that we should have made backup choices. There were *seven* pairs that wanted the apartment in Positano—not surprising since there were only four units left in the whole village—and we just weren't lucky. All that's left now, except for those tiny flats over the shops on the main street in Beauvois—and I don't want to live there because there's absolutely no privacy—is either here or in San Miguel. And all the blacks and browns are living in San Miguel."

Eponine sat down in one of the chairs. They were in the living room of the small two-bedroom apartment. It was furnished modestly, but adequately, with two chairs and a large sofa that were the same brown color as the rectangular coffee table. Altogether the apartment, which had a single large bathroom and a small kitchen in addition to the living room and two bedrooms, was slightly more than one hundred square meters.

Kimberly Henderson paced around the room impatiently. "Kim," Eponine said slowly, "I'm sorry, but I'm having a hard time concentrating on selecting an apartment when so much is happening to us. What is this place? Where are we? Why are we here?" Her mind flashed back quickly to the incredible briefing three days earlier, when Commander Macmillan had informed them that they were inside a spaceship built and equipped by extraterrestrials "for the purpose of observing Earthlings."

Kimberly Henderson lit a cigarette and expelled the smoke forcefully into the air. She shrugged. "Shit, Eponine," she said, "I don't know the answers to any of those questions. But I do know that if we don't pick an apartment we'll be left with whatever nobody else has wanted."

Eponine looked at her friend for several seconds and then sighed. "I don't think this process has been very fair," she complained. "The passengers from the Pinta and the Niña were all able to pick their homes before we even arrived. We are being forced to choose among the rejects."

"What did you expect?" Kimberly replied quickly. "Our ship was carrying convicts—of course we got the dregs. But at least we're finally free."

"So I guess you want to live in this apartment?" Eponine said at length.

"Yes," replied Kimberly. "And I also want to put in a bid on the other two apartments we saw this morning, near the Hakone market, in case we are aced out of this one. If we don't have a definite home after the drawing tonight, I'm afraid we'll really be in bad shape."

This was a mistake, Eponine was thinking as she watched Kimberly walking around the room. *I never should have agreed to be her roommate. But what choices did I have? The living accommodations that are left for single people are abysmal.*

Eponine was not accustomed to rapid changes in her life. Unlike Kimberly Henderson, who had had an enormous variety of experiences before she was convicted of murder at the age of nineteen, Eponine had lived a relatively sheltered childhood and adolescence. She had grown up in an orphanage outside Limoges, France, and until Professor Moreau took her to Paris to see the great museums when Eponine was seventeen, she had never even been outside her native province. It had been a very difficult decision for her to sign up for the Lowell Colony in the first place. But Eponine was facing a lifetime of detention in Bourges, and she was offered a chance for freedom on Mars. After a long deliberation she had courageously decided to submit her application to the ISA.

Eponine had been selected as a colonist because she had an outstanding academic record, especially in all the arts, was fluent in English, and had been a perfect prisoner. Her dossier in the ISA files had identified her most likely placement in the Lowell Colony as "drama and/or art teacher in the secondary schools." Despite the difficulties associated with the cruise phase of the mission after leaving the Earth, Eponine had felt a palpable rush of adrenaline and excitement when Mars had first appeared in the observation window of the Santa Maria. It would be a new life on a new world.

Two days before the scheduled encounter, however, the ISA guards had announced that the spacecraft was not going to deploy its landing shuttles as planned. Instead, they had told the convict passengers, the Santa Maria was going to take a "temporary detour to rendezvous with a space station orbiting Mars." Eponine had been both confused and concerned by the announcement. Unlike most of her associates, she had read carefully all the ISA material for the colonists and she had never seen any mention of an orbiting space station around Mars.

It had not been until the Santa Maria was completely unloaded and all the people and supplies were inside New Eden that anyone had really told Eponine and the other convicts what was happening. And even after the Macmillan briefing, very few of the convicts believed they were being told the truth. "Come on, now," Willis Meeker had said, "does he really think we're that stupid? A bunch of ETs built this place and all those crazy robots? This whole thing is a setup. We're just testing some new kind of prison concept."

"But Willis," Malcolm Peabody had replied, "what about all the others, the ones who came on the Pinta and the Niña? I've talked to some of them. They're normal people—I mean, they aren't convicts. If your theory is right, what are *they* doing here?"

"How the hell should I know, fag? I'm no genius. I just know that Macmillan dude is not giving us the straight shit."

Eponine did not let her uncertainties about the Macmillan briefing deter her from going with Kimberly to Central City to submit requests for the three apartments in Hakone. They were fortunate in the drawing this time and were allocated their first choice. The two women spent a day moving into the apartment on the edge of Sherwood Forest and then reported to the employment office in the administrative complex for processing.

Because the other two spacecraft had arrived well before the Santa Maria, the procedures to integrate the convicts into the life in New Eden were quite carefully defined. It took virtually no time to assign Kimberly, who really did have an outstanding nursing record, to the central hospital.

Eponine interviewed with the school superintendent and four other teachers before accepting an assignment at Central High School. Her new job required a short commute by train, whereas she could have walked each day if she had decided to teach at Hakone Middle School. But Eponine thought it would be worth the trouble. She very much liked the principal and staff members who were teaching at the high school.

At first the other seven doctors working at the hospital were leery of the two convict physicians, especially Dr. Robert Turner, whose dossier cryptically mentioned his brutal murders without detailing any of the extenuating circumstances. But after a week or so, during which time his extraordinary skill, knowledge, and professionalism became apparent to everyone, the staff unanimously selected him to be the director of the hospital. Dr. Turner was quite astonished by his selection and pledged, in a brief acceptance speech, to dedicate himself completely to the welfare of the colony.

His first official act was to propose to the provisional government that a full physical examination be given to every citizen of New Eden so that all the personal medical files could be updated. When his proposal was accepted, Dr. Turner deployed the Tiassos throughout the colony as paramedics. The biots performed all the routine examinations and gathered data for the doctors to analyze. Simultaneously, remembering the excellent data network that had existed among all the hospitals in the Dallas metropolitan area, the indefatigable Dr. Turner began working with several of the Einsteins to design a fully computerized system for tracking the health of the colonists.

One evening during the third full week after the Santa Maria had docked with Rama, Eponine was home alone, as usual (Kimberly Henderson's daily pattern had already become established—she was almost never in the apartment. If she wasn't at work at the hospital, then she was out with Toshio Nakamura and his cronies), when her videophone sounded. It was Malcolm Peabody's face that appeared on the monitor. "Eponine," he said shyly, "I have a favor to ask."

"What is it, Malcolm?"

"I received a call from a Dr. Turner at the hospital about five minutes ago. He says there were some 'irregularities' in my health data taken by one of those robots last week. He wants me to come in for a more detailed examination."

Eponine waited patiently for several seconds. "I'm not following you," she said at length. "What's the favor?"

Malcolm took a deep breath. "It must be serious, Eponine. He wants to see me now. . . . Will you come with me?"

"*Now?*" said Eponine, glancing at her watch. "It's almost eleven o'clock at night." In a flash she remembered Kimberly Henderson complaining that Dr. Turner was a "workaholic, as bad as those black robot nurses." Eponine also recalled the amazing blue of his eyes.

"All right," she said to Malcolm. "I'll meet you at the station in ten minutes."

Eponine had not been out much at night. Since her teaching appointment, she had spent most of her evenings working on her lesson plans. On one Saturday night she had gone out with Kimberly, Toshio Nakamura, and several other people to a Japanese restaurant that had just opened. But the food was strange, the company mostly Oriental, and several of the men, after drinking too much, made pathetic passes at her. Kimberly chided her for being "picky and standoffish," but Eponine refused her roommate's later invitations to socialize.

Eponine reached the station before Malcolm. While she was waiting for him to arrive, she marveled at how completely the village had been transformed by the presence of humans. *Let's see,* she was thinking, *the Pinta arrived here four months ago, the Niña five weeks after that. Already there are shops everywhere, both around the station and in the village itself. The accoutrements of human existence. If we stay here a year or two this colony will be indistinguishable from Earth.*

Malcolm was quite nervous and talkative during the short train ride. "I know it's my heart, Eponine," he said. "I've been having sharp pains, here, ever since Walter died. At first I thought it was all in my mind."

"Don't worry," Eponine responded, comforting her friend. "I bet it's nothing really serious."

*   *   *

Eponine was having difficulty keeping her eyes open. It was after three o'clock in the morning. Malcolm was asleep on the bench beside her. *What's that doctor doing?* she wondered. *He said he wouldn't be long.*

Soon after their arrival, Dr. Turner had examined Malcolm with a computerized stethoscope and then, telling him he needed "more comprehensive tests," had taken him into a separate part of the hospital. Malcolm had returned to the waiting room an hour later. Eponine herself had seen the doctor only briefly, when he had admitted Malcolm to his office at the beginning of the examination.

"Are you Mr. Peabody's friend?" a voice suddenly said. Eponine must have been dozing. When her vision was in focus, the beautiful blue eyes were staring at her from only a meter away. The doctor looked tired and upset.

"Yes," Eponine said softly, trying not to disturb the man sleeping on her shoulder.

"He's going to die very soon," Dr. Turner said. "Possibly in the next two weeks."

Eponine felt her blood surge through her body. *Am I hearing correctly?* she thought. *Did he say Malcolm was going to die in the next two weeks?* Eponine was stunned.

"He will need a lot of support," the doctor was saying. He paused for a moment, staring at Eponine. Was he trying to remember where he had seen her before? "Will you be able to help him?" Dr. Turner asked.

"I . . . I hope so," Eponine answered.

Malcolm began to stir. "We must wake him up now," the doctor said.

There was no emotion detectable in Dr. Turner's eyes. He had delivered his diagnosis—no, his *assertion*—without a hint of feeling. *Kim is right*, Eponine thought. *He's as much an automaton as those Tiasso robots.*

At the doctor's suggestion, Eponine accompanied Malcolm down a corridor and into a room filled with medical instruments. "Someone intelligent," Dr. Turner said to Malcolm, "chose the equipment that was brought here from Earth. Although we are limited in staff, our diagnostic apparatus is first rate."

The three of them walked over to a transparent cube about one meter on a side. "This amazing device," Dr. Turner said, "is called an organ projector. It can reconstruct, with detailed fidelity, almost all the major organs of the human body. What we are seeing now, when we look inside, is a computer graphic representation of your heart, Mr. Peabody, just as it appeared ninety mintues ago when I injected the tracer material into your blood vessels."

Dr. Turner pointed at an adjacent room, where Malcolm had apparently undergone the tests. "While you were sitting on that table," he continued, "you were scanned a million times a second by the machine with the big lens. From the location of the tracer material and those billions of instantaneous scans, an extremely accurate, three-dimensional image of your heart was constructed. That is what you are seeing inside the cube."

Dr. Turner stopped a moment, looked away quickly, and then fixed his eyes on Malcolm. "I'm not trying to make it harder on you, Mr. Peabody," he said quietly, "but I wanted to explain how I am able to know what's wrong with you. So that you will understand there has been no mistake."

Malcolm's eyes were wild with fright. The doctor took him by the hand and led him to a specific position beside the cube. "Look right there, on the back of the heart, near the top. Do you see the strange webbing and striation in the tissues? Those are your heart muscles and they have undergone irreparable decay."

Malcolm stared inside the cube for what seemed like an eternity and then lowered his head. "Am I going to die, Doctor?" he asked meekly.

Robert Turner took his patient's other hand. "Yes, you are, Malcolm. On Earth, we could possibly wait for a heart transplant; here, however, it is out of the question since we have neither the right equipment nor a proper donor. . . . If you would like, I can open you up and take a firsthand look at your heart. But it's extremely unlikely that I would see anything that would change the prognosis."

Malcolm shook his head. Tears began to run down his cheeks. Eponine put her arms around the little man and began to weep as well. "I'm sorry it took me so long to complete my diagnosis," Dr. Turner said, "but in a case this serious I needed to be absolutely certain."

A few moments later Malcolm and Eponine walked toward the door. Malcolm turned around. "What do I do now?" he asked the doctor.

"Whatever you enjoy," Dr. Turner replied.

When they were gone Dr. Turner returned to his office, where hardcopy printout of Malcolm Peabody's charts and files lay strewn across his desk. The doctor was deeply worried. He was virtually certain—he could not know definitely until he had completed the autopsy—that Peabody's heart was suffering from the same kind of malady that had killed Walter Brackeen on the Santa Maria. The two of them had been close friends for several years, going all the way back to the beginning of their detention terms in Georgia. It was unlikely that they had both *coincidentally* contracted the same heart disease. But if it was not a coincidence, then the pathogen must be communicable.

Robert Turner shook his head. Any disease that struck the heart was alarming. But one that could be passed from one person to another? The specter was terrifying.

He was very tired. Before putting his head down on his desk Dr. Turner made a list of the references on heart viruses that he wanted to obtain from the data base. Then he fell quickly asleep.

Fifteen minutes later the phone aroused him suddenly. A Tiasso was on the other end, calling from the Emergency Room. "Two Garcias have found a human body out in Sherwood Forest," it said, "and are on the way here now. From the images they have transmitted, I can tell that this case will require your personal involvement."

Dr. Turner scrubbed his hands, put on his gown again, and reached the Emergency Room just before the two Garcias arrived with the body. As experienced as he was, Dr. Turner had to turn away from the horribly mutilated corpse. The head had been almost completely severed from the body—it was hanging by only a thin strand of muscle—and the face had been hacked and disfigured beyond recognition. In addition, in the genital area of the trousers there was a bloody, gaping hole.

A pair of Tiassos immediately went to work, cleaning up the blood and preparing the body for autopsy. Dr. Turner sat on a chair, away from the scene, and filled out the first death report in New Eden.

"What was his name?" he asked the biots.

One of the Tiassos rustled through what was left of the dead man's clothing and found his ISA identification card.

"Danni," the biot replied. "Marcello Danni."

EPITHALAMION

1

The train from Positano was full. It stopped at the small station on the shores of Lake Shakespeare, halfway to Beauvois, and disgorged its mixture of humans and biots. Many were carrying baskets of food and blankets and folding chairs. Some of the smaller children raced from the station out onto the thick, freshly mowed grass surrounding the lake. They laughed and tumbled down the gentle slope that covered the hundred and fifty meters between the station and the edge of the water.

For those who did not want to sit on the grass, wooden stands had been erected just opposite the narrow pier that extended fifty meters into the water before spreading out into a rectangular platform. A microphone, rostrum, and several chairs were set up on the platform; it was there that Governor Watanabe would deliver the Settlement Day address after the fireworks were finished.

Forty meters to the left of the stands the Wakefields and the Watanabes had placed a long table covered with a blue and white cloth. Finger foods were tastefully arranged on the table. Coolers underneath were filled with drinks. Their families and friends had gathered in the immediate area and were either eating, playing some kind of game, or engaged in animated conversation. Two Lincoln biots were moving around the group, offering drinks and canapés to those who were too far away from the table and the coolers.

It was a hot afternoon. Too hot, in fact, the third exceptionally warm day in a row. But as the artificial sun completed its mini-arc in the dome far above their heads and the light began to slowly dim, the expectant crowd on the banks of Lake Shakespeare forgot about the heat.

A final train arrived only minutes before the light disappeared completely. This one came from the Central City station to the north, bringing colonists who lived in Hakone or San Miguel. There were not many latecomers. Most of the people had arrived early to set up their picnics on the grass. Eponine was on the last train. She had originally planned not to attend the celebration at all, but had changed her mind at the last minute.

Eponine was confused when she stepped onto the grass from the station platform. There were so many people! *All of New Eden must be here*, she thought. For a moment she wished that she had not come. Everyone was with friends and family, and she was all alone.

Ellie Wakefield was playing horseshoes with Benjy when Eponine stepped off the train. She quickly recognized her teacher, even from the distance, because of her bright red armband. "It's Eponine, Mother," Ellie said, running over to Nicole. "May I ask her to join us?"

"Of course," Nicole replied.

A voice on the public address system interrupted the music being played by a small band to announce that the fireworks would begin in ten minutes. There was scattered applause.

"Eponine," Ellie shouted. "Over here." Ellie waved her arms.

Eponine heard her name being called but could not see very clearly in the dim light. After several seconds she started in Ellie's direction. Along the way she inadvertently bumped into a toddler who was roaming by himself in the grass. "Kevin," a mother shrieked, "stay away from her!"

In an instant a burly blond man grabbed the little boy and held him away from Eponine. "You shouldn't be here," the man said. "Not with decent people."

A little shaken, Eponine continued toward Ellie, who was walking in her direction across the grass. "Go home, Forty-one!" a woman who had watched the earlier incident shouted. A fat ten-year-old boy with a bulbous nose pointed his finger at Eponine and made an inaudible comment to his younger sister.

"I'm so glad to see you," Ellie said when she reached her teacher. "Will you come have something to eat?"

Eponine nodded. "I'm sorry for all these people," Ellie said in a voice loud enough for everyone around her to hear. "It's a shame they are so ignorant."

Ellie led Eponine back to the big table and made a general introduction. "Hey, everybody, for those of you who don't know her, this is my teacher and friend Eponine. She has no last name, so don't ask her what it is."

Eponine and Nicole had met several times before. They exchanged pleasantries now while Lincoln offered Eponine some vegetable sticks and a soda. Nai Watanabe pointedly brought her twin sons, Kepler and Galileo, who had just had their second birthday the week before, over to meet the new arrival. A large nearby group of colonists from Positano was staring as Eponine lifted Kepler in her arms. "Pretty," the little boy said, pointing at Eponine's face.

"It must be very difficult," Nicole said in French, her head nodding in the direction of the gawking bystanders.

"*Oui*," Eponine replied. *Difficult?* she thought. *That's the understatement of the year. How about absolutely impossible? It's not bad enough that I have some horrible disease that will probably kill me. No. I must also wear an armband so that others can avoid me if they choose.*

Max Puckett glanced up from the chessboard and noticed Eponine. "Hello, hello," he said. "You must be the teacher I've heard so much about."

"That's Max," Ellie said, bringing Eponine over in his direction. "He's a flirt, but he's harmless. And the older man who's ignoring us is Judge Pyotr Mishkin. . . . Did I say it correctly, Judge?"

"Yes, of course, young lady," Judge Mishkin replied, his eyes not leaving the chessboard. "Dammit, Puckett, what in the world are you trying to do with that knight? As usual, your play is either stupid or brilliant and I can't decide which."

The judge eventually looked up, saw Eponine's red armband, and scrambled to his feet. "I'm sorry, miss, truly sorry," he said. "You are forced to endure enough without having to bear slights from this selfish old codger."

A minute or two before the fireworks began, a large yacht could be seen approaching the picnic area from the western side of the lake. Brightly colored lights and pretty girls decorated its long deck. The name *Nakamura* was emblazoned on the side of the boat. Above the main deck, Eponine recognized Kimberly Henderson standing beside Toshio Nakamura at the helm.

The party on the yacht waved at the people on the shore. Patrick Wakefield ran excitedly over to the table. "Look, Mother," he said, "there's Katie on the boat."

Nicole put on her glasses for a better look. It was indeed her daughter in a bikini bathing suit, waving from the deck of the yacht. "That's just what we need," Nicole mumbled to herself, as the first of the fireworks exploded above them, filling the dark sky with color and light.

"Three years ago today," Kenji Watanabe began his speech, "a scouting party from the Pinta first set foot in this new world. None of us knew what to expect. All of us wondered, especially during the two long months that we spent eight hours each day in the somnarium, if anything resembling a normal life would ever be possible here in New Eden.

"Our early fears have not materialized. Our alien hosts, whoever they might be, have never once interfered with our lives. It may be true, as Nicole Wakefield and others have suggested, that they are continually observing us, but we do not feel their presence in any way. Outside our colony the Rama spacecraft is rushing toward the star we call Tau Ceti at an unbelievable speed. Inside, our daily activities are barely influenced by these remarkable external conditions of our existence.

"Before the days in the somnarium, while we were still voyagers inside the planetary system that revolves around our home star the Sun, many of us thought our 'observation period' would be short. We believed that after a few months or so we would be returned to Earth, or maybe even our original destination Mars, and that this third Rama spacecraft would disappear in the distant reaches of space like its two predecessors. As I stand before you today, however, our navigators tell me that we are still moving away from our sun, as we have been for more than two and a half years, at approximately half the speed of light. If, indeed, it will be our good fortune someday to return to our own solar system, that day will be at least several years in the future.

"These factors dictate the primary theme of this, my last Settlement Day address. The theme is simple: Fellow colonists, *we* must take full responsibility for our own destiny. We cannot expect the awesome powers that created our worldlet in the beginning to save us from our mistakes. We must manage New Eden as if we and our children will be here forever. It is up to us to ensure the quality of life here, both now and for our future generations.

"At present there are a number of challenges facing the colony.

Notice that I call them challenges, not problems. If we work together we can meet these challenges. If we carefully weigh the long-term consequences of our actions, we will make the right decisions. But if we are unable to understand the concepts of 'delayed gratification' and 'for the good of all,' then the future of New Eden will be bleak.

"Let me take an example to illustrate my point. Richard Wakefield has explained, both on television and in public fora, how the master scheme that controls our weather is based on certain assumptions about the atmospheric conditions inside our habitat. Specifically, our weather control algorithm assumes that both the carbon dioxide levels and the concentration of smoke particles are less than a given magnitude. Without understanding exactly how the mathematics works, you can appreciate that the computations governing the external inputs to our habitat will not be correct if the underlying assumptions are not accurate.

"It is not my intent today to give a scientific lecture about a very complex subject. What I really want to talk about is policy. Since most of our scientists believe that our unusual weather the last four months is a result of unduly high levels of carbon dioxide and smoke particles in the atmosphere, my government has made specific proposals to deal with these issues. All of our recommendations have been rejected by the Senate.

"And why? Our proposal to impose a gradual ban on fireplaces—which are totally unnecessary in New Eden in the first place—was called a 'restriction on personal freedom.' Our carefully detailed recommendation to reconstitute part of the GED network, so that the loss of plant cover resulting from the development of portions of Sherwood Forest and the northern grasslands could be offset, was voted down as well. The reason? The opposition argued that the colony cannot afford the task and, in addition, that the power consumed by the new segments of the GED network would result in painfully stringent electricity conservation measures.

"Ladies and gentlemen, it is ridiculous for us to bury our heads in the sand and hope that these environmental problems will go away. Each time that we postpone taking positive action means greater hardships for the colony in the future. I cannot believe that so many of you accept the opposition's wishful thinking, that somehow we will be able to figure out how the alien weather algorithms actually work and tune them to perform properly under conditions with higher levels of carbon dioxide and smoke particles. What colossal hubris! . . ."

Nicole and Nai were both watching the reaction to Kenji's speech very carefully. Several of his supporters had urged Kenji to give a light, optimistic talk, without any discussion of the crucial issues. The governor, however, had been firm in his determination to make a meaningful speech.

"He's lost them," Nai leaned over to whisper to Nicole. "He's being too pedantic."

There was definitely a restiveness in the stands, where approximately half the audience was now sitting. The Nakamura yacht, which had been anchored just offshore during the fireworks, had pointedly departed soon after Governor Watanabe began to speak.

Kenji switched topics from the environment to the retrovirus RV-41. Since this was an issue that aroused strong passions in the colony, the audience's attention increased markedly. The governor explained how the New Eden medical staff, under the leadership of Dr. Robert Turner, had made heroic strides in understanding the disease but still needed to perform more extensive research to determine how to treat it. He then decried the hysteria that had forced the passage of a bill, even over his veto, requiring all those colonists with RV-41 antibodies in their system to wear red armbands at all times.

"Boo," shouted a large group of mostly Oriental picnickers on the other side of the stands from Nicole and Nai.

". . . These poor, unfortunate people face enough anguish. . . ." Kenji was saying.

"They're whores and fags," a man cried from behind the Wakefield-Watanabe party. The people around him laughed and applauded.

". . . Dr. Turner has repeatedly affirmed that this disease, like most retroviruses, cannot be transmitted except by blood and semen. . . ."

The crowd was becoming unruly. Nicole hoped that Kenji was paying attention and would cut his comments short. He had intended to discuss also the wisdom (or lack thereof) of expanding the exploration of Rama outside of New Eden, but he could tell that he had lost his audience.

Governor Watanabe paused a second and then issued an ear-splitting whistle into the microphone. That temporarily quieted all the listeners. "I have only a few more remarks," he said, "and they should not offend anyone. . . .

"As you know, my wife Nai and I have twin sons. We feel that we are richly blessed. On this Settlement Day I ask each of you to think about *your* children and envision another Settlement Day, a hundred or maybe even a thousand years into the future. Imagine that you are face-to-face with those whom you have begotten, your children's children's children. As you talk to them, and hold them in your arms, will you be able to say that you did everything reasonably possible to leave them a world in which they had a good chance of finding happiness?"

Patrick was excited again. Just as the picnic was ending, Max had invited him to spend the night and the next day at the Puckett farm. "The new term at the university doesn't start until Wednesday," the young man told his mother. "May I go? Please?"

Nicole was still disturbed by the crowd's reaction to Kenji's speech and did not understand at first what her son was asking. After asking him to repeat his request she glanced at Max. "You'll take good care of my son?"

Max Puckett grinned and nodded his head. Max and Patrick waited until the biots had finished cleaning up all the trash from the picnic and then headed for the train station together. Half an hour later they were in the Central City station waiting for the infrequent train that served the farming region directly. Across the platform from them, a group of Patrick's college classmates were entering the train to Hakone. "You should come," one of the young men yelled to Patrick. "Free drinks for everybody all night long."

Max watched Patrick's eyes follow his friends onto the train. "Have you ever been to Vegas?" Max asked.

"No, sir," he answered. "My mother and father—"

"Would you like to go?"

Patrick's hesitation was all Max needed. A few seconds later they boarded the train to Hakone with all the merrymakers. "I'm not terribly fond of the place myself," Max commented as they were riding. "It seems too false, too superficial. . . . But it's certainly worth seeing and it's not a bad place to go for amusement when you're all alone."

Slightly more than two and a half years earlier, very soon after the daily accelerations ended, Toshio Nakamura had correctly calculated that the colonists were likely to stay in New Eden and Rama for a long time. Before even the first meeting of the constitutional committee and its selection of Nicole des Jardins Wakefield as provisional governor, Nakamura had decided that he was going to be the richest and most powerful person in the colony. Building on the convict support base he had established during the cruise from Earth to Mars on the Santa Maria, he expanded his personal contacts and was able, as soon as banks and currency had been created in the colony, to begin building his empire.

Nakamura was convinced that the best products to sell in New Eden were those that provided pleasure and excitement. His first venture, a small gambling casino, was an immediate success. Next he bought some of the farmland on the east side of Hakone and built the colony's initial hotel, along with a second, larger casino just off the lobby. He added a small, intimate club, with female hostesses trained in the Japanese manner, and then a more raucous girlie club. Everything he did was successful. Parlaying his investments shrewdly, Nakamura was in a position, soon after Kenji Watanabe was elected governor, to offer to buy one fifth of Sherwood Forest from the government. His offer allowed the Senate to forestall higher taxes that would otherwise have been required to pay for the initial RV-41 research.

Part of the burgeoning forest was cleared and replaced with Nakamura's personal palace as well as a new, glittering hotel/casino, an entertainment arena, a restaurant complex, and several clubs. Consolidating his monopoly, Nakamura lobbied intensely (and successfully) for legislation that would limit gambling to the region around Hakone. His thugs then convinced all prospective entrepreneurs that nobody really wanted to enter the gambling business in competition with the "king Jap."

When his power was beyond attack, Nakamura permitted his associates to branch out into prostitution and drugs, neither of which were illegal in the New Eden society. Toward the end of the Watanabe term, when government policies began to conflict increasingly with his personal agenda, Nakamura decided he should control the government also. But he didn't want to be saddled with the boring job himself. He needed a dupe. So he recruited Ian Macmillan, the hapless ex-commander of the Pinta who had been an also-ran in the first gubernatorial election won by Kenji Watanabe. Nakamura offered Macmillan the governorship in exchange for the Scotsman's fealty.

There was nothing even remotely like Vegas anywhere else in the colony. The basic New Eden architecture designed by the Wakefields and the Eagle had all been spare, functional in the extreme, with simple geometries and plain facades. Vegas was overdone, garish, inconsistent—a mishmash of architectural styles. But it *was* interesting, and young Patrick O'Toole was visibly impressed when he and Max Puckett entered the outside gates of the compound.

"Wow," he said, staring at the huge blinking sign above the portal.

"I don't want to diminish your appreciation any, my boy," Max said, lighting a cigarette, "but the power required to operate that one sign would drive almost a square kilometer of GEDs."

"You sound like my mother and father," Patrick replied.

Before entering the casino or any of the clubs, each person had to sign the master register. Nakamura missed no bets. He had a complete file on what every Vegas visitor had done every time he had come inside. That way Nakamura knew which portions of his business should be expanded *and,* more importantly, the special and favored vice (or vices) of each of his customers.

Max and Patrick went into the casino. While they were standing by one of the two craps tables, Max tried to explain to the young man how the game worked. Patrick, however, could not keep his eyes off the cocktail waitresses in their scanty outfits.

"Ever been laid, boy?" Max asked.

"Excuse me, sir?" Patrick replied.

"Have you ever had sex—you know, intercourse with a woman?"

"No, sir," the young man answered.

A voice inside Max's head told him that it was not *his* responsibility to usher the young man into the world of pleasure. The same voice also reminded Max that this was New Eden, and not Arkansas, or otherwise he would have taken Patrick over to the Xanadu and treated him to his first sex.

There were more than a hundred people in the casino, a huge crowd considering the size of the colony, and everyone seemed to be having fun. The waitresses were indeed dispensing free drinks just as fast as they could—Max grabbed a margarita and handed one to Patrick.

"I don't see any biots," Patrick commented.

"There aren't any in the casino," Max replied. "Not even working the tables, where they would be more efficient than humans. The king Jap believes their presence inhibits the gambling instinct. But he uses them exclusively in all the restaurants."

"Max Puckett. Well, I do declare."

Max and Patrick turned around. A beautiful young woman in a soft, pink dress was approaching them. "I haven't seen you in months," she said.

"Hello, Samantha," Max said after being uncharacteristically tongue-tied for several seconds.

"And who is this handsome young man?" Samantha said, batting her long eyelashes at Patrick.

"This is Patrick O'Toole," Max answered. "He is—"

"Oh, my goodness," Samantha exclaimed. "I've never met one of the o-*rig*-inal colonists before." She studied Patrick for a few seconds before continuing. "Tell me, Mr. O'Toole," she said, "is it really true that you went to sleep for *years?*"

Patrick nodded shyly.

"My friend Goldie says that the whole story is bullshit, that you and your family are really all agents for the IIA. She doesn't even believe we have ever left Mars orbit. Goldie says all that dreary time in the tanks was also part of the hoax."

"I assure you, ma'am," Patrick politely responded, "that my family did indeed sleep for years. I was only six years old when my parents put me in a berth. I looked almost like I do now the next time I woke up."

"Well, I find it *fas*-cinatin', even if I don't know what to make of it all. . . . So, Max, what are you up to? And by the way, are you going to officially introduce *me?*"

"I'm sorry. Patrick, this is Miss Samantha Porter from the great state of Mississippi. She works at the Xanadu—"

"I'm a prostitute, Mr. O'Toole. One of the very best. . . . Have you ever met a prostitute before?"

Patrick blushed. "No, ma'am," he said.

Samantha put a finger under his chin. "He's cute," she said to Max. "Bring him over. If he's a virgin, I might do him for free." She gave Patrick a small kiss on the lips and then turned around and departed.

Max couldn't think of anything appropriate to say after Samantha left. He thought about apologizing but decided it wasn't necessary. Max put his arm around Patrick and the two of them walked toward the back of the casino, where the higher stakes tables were cordoned off.

"All right, now, *yo*," cried a young woman with her back toward them. "Five and six makes a *yo.*"

Patrick glanced over at Max with surprise. "That's Katie," he said, hastening his step in her direction.

Katie was completely absorbed in the game. She took a quick drag from a cigarette, belted down the drink she was handed by the swarthy man on her right, and then held the dice high above her head. "All the numbers," she said, handing chips to the croupier. "Here's twenty-six—plus five marks on the hard eight. . . . Now, be there, forty-four," she said, flinging the dice against the opposite end of the table with a flick of her wrist.

"Forty-four," the crowd around the table shouted in unison.

Katie jumped up and down in her place, gave her date a hug, quaffed another drink, and took a long, languorous pull from her cigarette.

"Katie," Patrick said just as she was about to throw the dice again.

She stopped in midthrow and turned around with a quizzical look on her face. "Well, I'll be damned," she said. "It's my baby brother."

Katie stumbled over to greet him as the croupiers and other players at the table yelled for her to continue the game.

"You're drunk, Katie," Patrick said quietly while he was holding her in his arms.

"No, Patrick," Katie replied, jerking herself backward toward the table. "I am *flying*. I am on my own personal shuttle to the stars."

She turned back to the craps table and raised her right arm high. "All right, now, *yo*. Are you in there, *yo*?" she shouted.

2

Again the dreams came in the early morning hours. Nicole woke up and tried to remember what she had been dreaming, but all she could recall was an isolated image here and there. Omeh's disembodied face had been in one of her dreams. Her Senoufo great-grandfather had been warning her about something, but Nicole had not been able to understand what he was saying. In another dream Nicole had watched Richard walk into a quiet ocean just before a devastating wave came rushing toward the shore.

Nicole rubbed her eyes and glanced at the clock. It was just before four o'clock. *Almost the same time every morning this week,* she thought. *What do they mean?* She stood up and crossed into the bathroom.

Moments later she was in the kitchen dressed in her exercise clothes. She drank a glass of water. An Abraham Lincoln biot, who had been resting immobile against the wall at the end of the kitchen counter, activated and approached Nicole.

"Would you like some coffee, Mrs. Wakefield?" he asked, taking the empty water glass from her.

"No, Linc," she answered. "I'm going out now. If anyone wakes up tell them I'll be back before six."

Nicole walked down the hallway toward the door. Before leaving the house she passed the study on the right-hand side of the corridor. Papers were strewn all over Richard's desk, both beside and on top of the new computer he had designed and constructed himself. Richard was extremely proud of his new computer, which Nicole had urged him to build, even though it was unlikely that it would ever completely replace his favorite electronic toy, the standard ISA pocket computer. Richard had religiously carried the little portable since before the launch of the Newton.

Nicole recognized Richard's writing on some of the paper sheets but could not read any of his symbolic computer language. *He has spent many long hours in here recently*, Nicole thought, feeling a pang of guilt. *Even though he believes that what he's doing is wrong.*

At first Richard had refused to participate in the effort to decode the algorithm that governed the weather in New Eden. Nicole recalled their discussions clearly. "We have agreed to participate in this democracy," she had argued. "If you and I choose to ignore its laws, then we set a dangerous example for the others—"

"This is *not* a law," Richard had interrupted her. "It's only a resolution. And you know as well as I do that it's an incredibly dumb idea. You and Kenji both fought against it. And besides, aren't you the one who told me once that we have a *duty* to protest majority stupidity?"

"Please, Richard," Nicole had replied. "You may of course explain to everyone why you think the resolution is wrong. But this algorithm effort has now become a campaign issue. All the colonists know that we are close to the Watanabes. If you ignore the resolution it will look as if Kenji is purposely trying to undermine . . ."

While Nicole was remembering her earlier conversation with her husband, her eyes roamed idly around the study. She was somewhat surprised, when her mind again focused on the present, to find that she was staring at three little figures on an open shelf above Richard's desk. *Prince Hal, Falstaff, TB*, she thought. *How long has it been since Richard entertained us with you?*

Nicole thought back to the long and monotonous weeks after her family had awakened from their years of sleep. While they were waiting for the arrival of the other colonists, Richard's robots had been their primary source of amusement. In her memory Nicole could still hear the children's mirthful laughter and see her husband smiling with delight. *Those were simpler, easier times*, she said to herself. She closed the door to the study and continued down the hall. *Before life became too complicated for play. Now your little friends just sit silently on the shelf.*

Out in the lane, underneath the streetlight, Nicole stopped for a moment beside the bicycle rack. She hesitated, looking at her bicycle, and then turned around and headed for the backyard. A minute later she had crossed the grassy area behind the house and was on the path that wound up Mount Olympus.

Nicole walked briskly. She was very deep in thought. For a long time she paid no attention to her surroundings. Her mind jumped around from subject to subject, from the problems besetting New Eden, to her strange dream patterns, to her anxieties about her children, especially Katie.

She arrived at a fork in the path. A small, tasteful sign explained that the path to the left led to the cable car station, eighty meters away, where one could ride to the top of Mount Olympus. Nicole's presence at the fork was electronically detected and prompted a Garcia biot to approach from the direction of the cable car.

"Don't bother," Nicole shouted. "I'm going to walk."

The view became more and more spectacular as the switchbacks wound up the side of the mountain that faced the rest of the colony. Nicole paused at one of the viewpoints, five hundred meters in altitude and just under three kilometers walking distance from the Wakefield home, and looked out across New Eden. It had been a clear night, with little or no moisture in the air.

No rain today, Nicole thought, noting that the mornings were always damp with water vapor on the days that showers fell. Just below her was the village of Beauvois—the lights from the new furniture factory allowed her to identify most of the familiar buildings of her region, even from this distance. To the north the village of San Miguel was hidden behind the bulky mountain. But out across the colony, far on the other side of a darkened Central City, Nicole could discern the splashes of light that marked Nakamura's Vegas.

She was instantly plunged into a bad mood. *That damn place stays open all night long,* she grumbled silently, *using critical power resources and offering unsavory amusements.*

It was impossible for Nicole not to think of Katie when she looked at Vegas. *Such natural talent,* Nicole remarked to herself, a dull heartache accompanying the image of her daughter. She could not help wondering if Katie was still awake in the glittering fantasy life on the other side of the colony. *And such a colossal waste,* Nicole thought, shaking her head.

Richard and she had discussed Katie often. There were only two subjects about which they fought—Katie and New Eden politics. And it wasn't entirely accurate to say they fought about politics. Richard basically felt that all politicians, except Nicole and *maybe* Kenji Watanabe, were essentially without principles. His method of discussion was to make sweeping pronouncements about the insipid goings-on in the Senate, or even in Nicole's own courtroom, and then to refuse to consider the subject anymore.

Katie was another issue. Richard always argued that Nicole was much too hard on Katie. *He also blames me,* Nicole thought as she gazed at the faraway lights, *for not spending enough time with her. He contends my jumping into colony politics left the children with only a part-time mother at the most critical period of their lives.*

Katie was almost never at home anymore. She still had a room in the Wakefield house, but she spent most of her nights in one of the fancy apartments that Nakamura had built inside the Vegas compound.

"How do you pay the rent?" Nicole had asked her daughter one night, just before the usual unpleasantness.

"How do you think, Mother?" Katie had answered belligerently. "I work. I have plenty of time. I'm only taking three courses at the university."

"What kind of work do you do?" Nicole had asked.

"I'm a hostess, an entertainer . . . you know, whatever is needed," Katie had answered vaguely.

Nicole turned away from the lights of Vegas. *Of course,* she said to herself, *it is entirely understandable that Katie is confused. She never had any adolescence. But still, she doesn't seem to be getting any better. . . .* Nicole started walking briskly up the mountain again, trying to dispel her mounting gloom.

Between five hundred and a thousand meters in altitude, the mountain was covered with thick trees that were already five meters high. Here the path to the summit ran between the mountain and the outside wall of the colony in an extremely dark stretch that lasted for more than a kilometer. There was one break in the blackness, near the end, at a lookout point facing north.

Nicole had reached the highest point in her ascent. She stopped at the lookout and stared across at San Miguel. *There is the proof,* she thought, shaking her head, *that we have failed here in New Eden. Despite everything, there is poverty and despair in paradise.*

She had seen the problem coming, had even accurately predicted it toward the end of her one-year term as provisional governor. Ironically, the process that had produced San Miguel, where the standard of living was only half what it was in the other three New

Eden villages, had begun soon after the arrival of the Pinta. That first group of colonists had mostly settled in the Southeast Village, which would later become Beauvois, setting a precedent that was accentuated after the Niña reached Rama. As the free settlement plan was implemented, almost all the Orientals decided to live together in Hakone; the Europeans, white Americans, and middle Asians chose either Positano or what was left of Beauvois. The Mexicans, other Hispanics, black Americans, and Africans all gravitated toward San Miguel.

As governor, Nicole had tried to resolve the de facto segregation in the colony with a utopian resettlement plan that would have allocated to each of the four villages racial percentages that mirrored the colony as a whole. Her proposal might have been accepted very early in the colony's history, especially right after the days in the somnarium, when most of the other citizens viewed Nicole as a goddess. But it was too late after more than a year. Free enterprise had already created gaps in both personal wealth and real estate values. Even Nicole's most loyal followers realized the impracticality of her resettlement concept at that point.

After Nicole's term as governor was completed, the Senate had resoundingly approved Kenji's appointment of Nicole as one of New Eden's five permanent judges. Nevertheless, her image in the colony suffered considerably when the remarks she had made in defense of the aborted resettlement plan became widely circulated. Nicole had argued that it was essential for the colonists to live in small, integrated neighborhoods to develop any real appreciation of racial and cultural differences. Her critics had thought that her views were "hopelessly naive."

Nicole stared at the twinkling lights of San Miguel for several more minutes as she warmed down from her strenuous climb up the mountain. Just before she turned around and headed back toward her home in Beauvois, she suddenly recalled another set of twinkling lights, from the town of Davos, in Switzerland, back on the planet Earth. During Nicole's last ski vacation, she and her daughter Genevieve had had dinner on the mountain above Davos and, after eating, had held hands in the bracing cold out on the restaurant balcony. The lights of Davos had shone like tiny jewels many kilometers below them. Tears came into Nicole's eyes as she thought of the grace and humor of her first daughter, whom she had not seen for so many years. *Thank you again, Kenji*, she mumbled as she began to walk, recalling the photographs her new friend had brought from Earth, *for sharing with me your visit with Genevieve.*

It was again black all around her as Nicole wound back down the side of the mountain. The outer wall of the colony was now on her left. She continued to think about life in New Eden. *We need special courage now*, she said to herself. *Courage, and values, and vision.* But in her heart she feared the worst was still ahead for the colonists. *Unfortunately,* she reflected gloomily, *Richard and I and even the children have remained outsiders, despite everything we have tried to do. It is unlikely that we will be able to change anything very much.*

Richard checked to ensure that the three Einstein biots had all properly copied the procedures and data that had been on the several monitors in his study. As the four of them were leaving the house, Nicole gave him a kiss.

"You are a wonderful man, Richard Wakefield," she said.

"You're the only one who thinks so," he replied, forcing a smile.

"I'm also the only one who knows," Nicole said. She paused for a moment. "Seriously, darling," she continued, "I appreciate what you're doing. I know—"

"I won't be very late," he interrupted. "The three Als and I have only two basic ideas left to try. . . . If we aren't successful today, we're giving up."

With the three Einsteins following close behind him, Richard hurried down to the Beauvois station and caught the train for Positano. The train stopped momentarily by the big park on Lake Shakespeare where the Settlement Day picnic had been two months earlier. Richard and his supporting biot cast disembarked several minutes later at Positano and walked through the village to the southwest corner of the colony. There, after having their identification checked by one human and two Garcias, they were allowed to pass through the colony exit into the annulus that circumscribed New Eden. There was one more brief electronic inspection before they reached the only door that had been cut in the thick external wall surrounding the habitat. It swung open and Richard led the biots into Rama itself.

Richard had had misgivings when, eighteen months earlier, the Senate had voted to develop and deploy a penetrating probe to test the environmental conditions in Rama just outside their module. Richard had served on the committee that had reviewed the engineering design of the probe; he had been afraid that the external environment might be overwhelmingly hostile and that the design of the probe might not properly protect the integrity of their habitat.

Much time and money had been spent guaranteeing that the boundaries of New Eden were hermetically sealed during the entire procedure, even while the probe was inching its way through the wall.

Richard had lost credibility in the colony when the environment in Rama had turned out to be not significantly different from that in New Eden. Outside there was permanent darkness, and some small, periodic variations in both atmospheric pressure and constituents, but the ambient Raman environment was so similar to the one in the colony that the human explorers did not even need their space suits. Within two weeks after the first probe revealed the benign atmosphere in Rama, the colonists had completed the mapping of the area of the Central Plain that was now accessible to them.

New Eden and a second, almost identical rectangular construct to the south, which Richard and Nicole both believed to be a habitat for a second life-form, were enclosed together in a larger, also rectangular region whose extremely tall, metallic gray barriers separated it from the rest of Rama. The barriers on the north and south sides of this larger region were extensions of the walls of the habitats themselves. On both the east and west side of the two enclosed habitats, however, there were about two kilometers of open space.

At the four corners of this outer rectangle were massive cylindrical structures. Richard and the other technological personnel in the colony were convinced that the impenetrable corner cylinders contained the fluids and pumping mechanisms whereby the environmental conditions inside the habitats were maintained.

The new outer region, which had no ceiling except for the opposite side of Rama itself, covered most of the Northern Hemicylinder of the spacecraft. A large metal hut, shaped like an igloo, was the only building in the Central Plain between the two habitats. This hut was the control center for New Eden and was located approximately two kilometers south of the colony wall.

When they exited from New Eden, Richard and the three Einsteins were headed for the control center, where they had been working together for almost two weeks in an attempt to break into the master control logic governing the weather inside New Eden. Despite Kenji Watanabe's objection, the Senate had earlier appropriated funds for an "all-out effort" by the colony's "best engineers" to alter the alien weather algorithm. They had promulgated this legislation after hearing testimony from a group of Japanese scientists, who had suggested that stable weather conditions *could* indeed be maintained inside New Eden, even with the higher levels of carbon dioxide and smoke in the atmosphere.

It was an appealing conclusion for the politicians. If, perhaps, neither barring wood-burning nor deploying a reconstituted GED network were truly *required,* and it was only necessary to adjust a few parameters in the alien algorithm that had, after all, been initially designed with some assumptions that were no longer valid, well, then . . .

Richard hated that kind of thinking. Avoid the issue as long as possible, he called it. Nevertheless, both because of Nicole's pleas and the total failure of the other colony engineers to understand any facet of the weather control process, Richard had agreed to tackle the task. He had insisted, however, that he work essentially alone, with only the Einsteins helping him.

On the day that Richard planned to make his last attempt to decode the New Eden weather algorithm, he and his biots stopped first near a site one kilometer away from the colony exit. Under the large lights Richard could see a group of architects and engineers working at a very long table.

"The canal will not be difficult to build—the soil is very soft."

"But what about sewage? Should we dig cesspools, or haul the waste material back to New Eden for processing?"

"The power requirements for this settlement will be substantial. Not only the lighting, because of the ambient darkness, but also all the appliances. In addition, we're far enough away from New Eden that we must account for nontrivial losses on the lines. . . . Our best superconducting materials are too critical for this usage."

Richard felt a mixture of disgust and anger as he listened to the conversations. The architects and engineers were conducting a feasibility study for an external village that could house the RV-41 carriers. The project, whose name was Avalon, was the result of a delicate political compromise between Governor Watanabe and his opposition. Kenji had permitted the study to be funded to show that he was "open-minded" on the issue of how to deal with the RV-41 problem.

Richard and the three Einsteins continued down the path in a southerly direction. Just north of the control center they caught up with a group of humans and biots headed toward the second habitat probe site with some impressive equipment.

"Hi, Richard," said Marilyn Blackstone, the fellow Brit whom Richard had recommended to head the probe effort. Marilyn was from Taunton, in Somerset. She had received her engineering degree from Cambridge in 2232 and was extremely competent.

"How's the work coming?" Richard asked.

"If you have a minute, come take a look," Marilyn suggested.

Richard left the three Einsteins at the control center and accompanied Marilyn and her team across the Central Plain to the second habitat. As he was walking, he remembered his conversation with Kenji Watanabe and Dmitri Ulanov in the governor's office one afternoon before the probe project was officially approved.

"I want it understood," Richard had said, "that I am categorically against any and all efforts to intrude upon the sanctity of that other habitat. Nicole and I are virtually positive that it harbors another kind of life. There is no argument for penetration that is compelling."

"Suppose it's empty," Dmitri had replied. "Suppose the habitat has been placed there for us, assuming we are clever enough to figure out how to use it."

"Dmitri," Richard had almost shouted, "have you listened to anything that Nicole and I have been telling you all these months? You are still clinging to an absurd homocentric notion about our place in the universe. Because we are the dominant species on the planet Earth, you *assume* we are superior beings. We are *not*. There must be hundreds—"

"Richard," Kenji had interrupted him in a soft voice, "we know your opinion on this subject. But the colonists of New Eden do not agree with you. They have never seen the Eagle, the octospiders, or any of the other wonderful creatures that you talk about. They want to know if we have room to expand. . . ."

Kenji was already afraid then, Richard was thinking as he and the exploration team neared the second habitat. *He's still terrified that Macmillan will beat Ulanov in the election and turn the colony over to Nakamura.*

Two Einstein biots began working as soon as the team arrived at the probe site. They carefully installed the compact laser drill in the spot where a hole in the wall had already been created. Within five minutes the drill was slowly expanding the hole in the metal.

"How far have you penetrated?" Richard asked.

"Only about thirty-five centimeters so far," Marilyn replied. "We're taking it very slowly. If the wall has the same thickness as ours, it will be another three or four weeks before we are all the way through. . . . Incidentally, the spectrographic analysis of the wall parts indicates it's the same material as our wall."

"And once you've penetrated into the interior?"

Marilyn laughed. "Don't worry, Richard. We're following all the procedures you recommended. We will have a minimum of two weeks of passive observation before we continue to the next phase. We'll give *them* a chance to respond—if *they* are indeed inside."

The skepticism in her voice was obvious. "Not you too, Marilyn," Richard said. "What's the matter with everybody? Do you think Nicole and the children and I just made up all those stories?"

"Extraordinary claims require extraordinary evidence," she replied.

Richard shook his head. He started to argue with Marilyn, but he realized he had more important things to do. After a few minutes of polite engineering conversation, he walked back toward the control center where his Einsteins were waiting.

The great thing about working with the Einstein biots was that Richard could try many ideas at once. Whenever he had a particular approach in mind, he could outline it to one of the biots and have complete confidence that it would be implemented properly. The Einsteins never suggested a new method themselves; however, they were perfect memory devices and often reminded Richard when one of his ideas was similar to an earlier technique that had failed.

All the other colony engineers attempting to modify the weather algorithm had tried first to understand the inner workings of the alien supercomputer that was located in the middle of the control center. That had been their fundamental mistake. Richard, knowing a priori that the supercomputer's internal operation would be indistinguishable from magic to him, concentrated on isolating and identifying the output signals that emanated from the huge processor. After all, he reasoned, the basic structure of the process must be straightforward. Some set of measurements defines the conditions inside New Eden at any given time. The alien algorithms must use this measurement data to compute commands that are somehow passed to the huge cylindrical structures, where the actual physical activity takes place that leads to modifications in the atmosphere inside the habitat.

It did not take Richard long to draw a functional block diagram of the process. Because there were no direct electrical contacts between the control center and the cylindrical structures, it was obvious that there was some kind of electromagnetic communication between the two entities. But what kind? When Richard scanned the spectrum to see at what wavelengths the communication was taking place, he found many potential signals.

Analyzing and interpreting those signals was a little like looking for a needle in a haystack. With the Einstein biots helping him, Richard eventually determined that the most frequent transmissions were in the microwave bandwidth. For a week he and the Einsteins catalogued the microwave exchanges, reviewing the weather conditions in New Eden both before and after, and trying to zero in on the specific parameter set modulating the strength of the response on the cylinder side of the interface. During that week Richard also tested and validated a portable microwave transmitter that he and the biots had constructed together. His goal was to create a command signal that would look as if it had come from the control center.

His first serious attempt on the final day was a complete failure. Guessing that the accuracy of the timing of his transmission might be the problem, he and the Einsteins next developed a sequencing control routine that would enable them to issue a signal with femto-second precision, so that the cylinders would receive the command within an extremely tiny time slice.

An instant after Richard had sent what he thought was a new set of parameters to the cylinders, a loud alarm sounded in the control center. Within seconds a wraithlike image of the Eagle appeared in the air above Richard and the biots.

"Human beings," the holographic Eagle said, "be very careful. Great care and knowledge were used to design the delicate balance of your habitat. Do not change these critical algorithms unless there is a genuine emergency."

Even though he was shocked, Richard acted immediately, ordering the Einsteins to record what they were seeing. The Eagle repeated his warning a second time and then vanished, but the entire scene was stored in the videorecording subsystems of the biots.

3

"Are you going to be depressed forever?" Nicole asked, looking across the breakfast table at her husband. "Besides, thus far nothing terrible has happened. The weather has been fine."

"I think it's better than before, Uncle Richard," Patrick offered. "You're a hero at the university—even if some of the kids do think you're part alien."

Richard managed a smile. "The government is not following my recommendations," he said quietly, "and is paying no heed whatsoever to the Eagle's warning. There are even some people in the engineering office who are saying I created the hologram of the Eagle myself. Can you imagine that?"

"Kenji believes what you told him, darling."

"Then why is he letting those weather people continually increase the strength of the commanded response? They can't possibly predict the long-term effects."

"What is it you're worried about, Father?" Ellie asked a moment later.

"Managing such a large volume of gas is a very complicated process, Ellie, and I have great respect for the ETs who designed the New Eden infrastructure in the first place. *They* were the ones who insisted the carbon dioxide and particulate concentrations must be maintained below specified levels. They must have known *some*thing."

Patrick and Ellie finished their breakfasts and excused themselves. Several minutes later, after the children had left the house, Nicole walked around the table and put her hands on Richard's shoulders. "Do you remember the night we discussed Albert Einstein with Patrick and Ellie?"

Richard looked at Nicole with a furrowed brow.

"Later on that night, when we were in bed, I commented that Einstein's discovery of the relationship between matter and energy was 'horrible,' because it led to the existence of nuclear weapons. . . . Do you remember your response?"

Richard shook his head.

"You told me that Einstein was a scientist, whose life work was searching for knowledge and truth. 'There is no knowledge that is horrible,' you said. 'Only what other human beings *do* with that knowledge can be called horrible.' "

Richard smiled. "Are you trying to absolve me of responsibility on this weather issue?"

"Maybe," Nicole replied. She reached down and kissed him on the lips. "I know that you are one of the smartest, most creative human beings who ever lived and I don't like to see you carrying all the burdens of the colony on your shoulders."

Richard kissed her back with considerable vigor. "Do you think we can finish before Benjy wakes up?" he whispered. "He doesn't have school today and he stayed up very late last night."

"Maybe," Nicole answered with a coquettish grin. "We can at least try. My first case is not until ten o'clock."

Eponine's senior class at Central High School, called simply "Art and Literature," encompassed many aspects of the culture that the colonists had at least temporarily left behind. In her basic curriculum, Eponine covered a multicultural, eclectic set of sources, encouraging the students to pursue independent study in any specific areas they found stimulating. Although she always used lesson plans and a syllabus in her teaching, Eponine was the kind of instructor who tailored each of her classes to the interests of the students.

Eponine herself thought *Les Misérables* by Victor Hugo was the greatest novel ever written, and the nineteenth century impressionist painter Pierre-Auguste Renoir, from her home city of Limoges, the finest painter who had ever lived. She included the works of both of her countrymen in the class, but carefully structured the rest of the source material to give fair representation to other nations and cultures.

Since the Kawabata biots helped her each year with the class play, it was natural to use the real Kawabata's novels *A Thousand Cranes* and *Snow Country* as examples of Japanese literature. The three weeks on poetry ranged from Frost to Rilke to Omar Khayyám. However, the principal poetic focus was Benita Garcia, not only because of the presence of the Garcia biots all over New Eden, but also because Benita's poetry and life were both fascinating to young people.

There were only eleven students in Eponine's senior class the year she was required to wear the red armband for having tested positive for RV-41 antibodies. The results of her test had presented the school administration with a difficult dilemma. Although the superintendent had courageously resisted the efforts of a strident group of parents, mostly from Hakone, who had demanded that Eponine be "dismissed" from the high school, he and his staff had nevertheless bowed somewhat to the hysteria in the colony by making Eponine's senior course optional. As a result her class was much smaller than it had been in the previous two years.

Ellie Wakefield was Eponine's favorite student. Despite the great gaps in the young woman's knowledge due to her years asleep on the trip back to the solar system from the Node, her natural intelligence and hunger for learning made her a joy in the classroom. Eponine often asked Ellie to perform special tasks. On the morning that the class began its study of Benita Garcia, which was, incidentally, the same morning that Richard Wakefield had discussed with his daughter his worries about the weather control activities in the colony, Ellie had been asked to memorize one of the poems from Benita Garcia's first book, *Dreams of a Mexican Girl,* written when the Mexican woman was still a teenager. Before Ellie's recitation, however, Eponine tried to fire the imaginations of the young people with a short lecture on Benita's life.

"The *real* Benita Garcia was one of the most amazing women who ever lived," Eponine said, nodding at the expressionless Garcia biot in the corner who helped her with all the routine chores of teaching. "Poet, cosmonaut, political leader, mystic—her life was both a reflection of the history of her time and an inspiration for everyone.

"Her father was a large landowner in the Mexican state of Yucatán, far from the artistic and political heart of the nation. Benita was an only child, the daughter of a Mayan mother and a much older father. She spent most of her childhood alone on the family plantation that touched the marvelous Puuc Mayan ruins at Uxmal. As a small girl Benita often played among the pyramids and buildings of that thousand-year-old ceremonial center.

"She was a gifted student from the beginning, but it was her imagination and élan that truly separated her from the others in her class. Benita wrote her first poem when she was nine, and by the age of fifteen, at which time she was in a Catholic boarding school in the Yucatecan capital of Mérida, two of her poems had been published in the prestigious *Diario de Mexico*.

"After finishing secondary school, Benita surprised her teachers and her family by announcing that she wanted to be a cosmonaut. In 2129 she was the first Mexican woman ever admitted to the Space Academy in Colorado. When she graduated four years later, the deep cutbacks in space had already begun. Following the crash of 2134 the world plunged into the depression known as the Great Chaos and virtually all space exploration was stopped. Benita was laid off by the ISA in 2137 and thought that her space career was over.

"In 2144 one of the last interplanetary transport cruisers, the James Martin, limped home from Mars to Earth carrying mostly women and children from the Martian colonies. The spacecraft was barely able to make it into Earth orbit and it appeared as if all the passengers would die. Benita Garcia and three of her friends from the cosmonaut corps jerryrigged a rescue vehicle and managed to save twenty-four of the voyagers in the most spectacular space mission of all times. . . ."

Ellie's mind floated free from Eponine's narrative and imagined how exhilarating it must have been on Benita's rescue mission. Benita had flown her space vehicle manually, without a lifeline to mission operations on the Earth, and risked her life to save others. Could there be any greater commitment to one's fellow members of the species?

As she thought about Benita Garcia's selflessness, an image of her mother came into Ellie's mind. A montage of pictures of Nicole rapidly followed. First, Ellie saw her mother in her judge's robes speaking articulately before the Senate. Next Nicole was rubbing Ellie's father's neck in the study late at night, patiently teaching Benjy to read day after day, riding off beside Patrick on a bicycle for a game of tennis in the park, or telling Linc what to prepare for dinner. In the last image Nicole was sitting on Ellie's bed late at night, answering questions about life and love. *My mother is my hero*, Ellie suddenly realized. *She is as unselfish as Benita Garcia.*

". . . Imagine, if you will, a young Mexican girl of sixteen, home from boarding school for vacation, climbing slowly up the steep steps of the Pyramid of the Magician in Uxmal. Below her, in the already warm spring morning, iguanas play among the rocks and the ruins."

Eponine nodded at Ellie. It was time for her poem. She stood at her seat and recited.

"You have seen it all, old lizard
Seen our joys, our tears,
Our hearts full of dreams
and terrible desires.
And does it never change?
Did my Indian mother's mother
Sit here on these steps
One thousand years ago
And tell to you the passions
she would not, could not share?
At night I look unto the stars
And dare to see myself among them.
My heart soars above these pyramids,
flying free into the everything-can-be.
Yes, Benita, the iguanas tell me,
Yes to you and your mother's mother,
whose yearning dreams years ago
will now become fulfilled in you."

When Ellie had finished her cheeks were glistening from the silent tears that had fallen. Her teacher and the other students probably thought that she had been deeply moved by the poem and by the lecture on Benita Garcia. They couldn't have understood that Ellie had just experienced an emotional epiphany, that she had just discovered the true depth of her love and respect for her mother.

It was the last week of rehearsals for the school play. Eponine had picked an old work, *Waiting for Godot,* by the twentieth century Nobel laureate Samuel Beckett, because its theme was so germane to life in New Eden. The two main characters, both dressed in rags throughout, were played by Ellie Wakefield and Pedro Martinez, a handsome nineteen-year-old who had been one of the "troubled" teenagers added to the colony contingent during the last months before launch.

Eponine could not have produced the play without the Kawabatas. The biots designed and created the sets and the costumes, controlled the lights, and even conducted rehearsals when she could not be present. The school had four Kawabatas altogether, and three of them were under Eponine's jurisdiction during the six weeks immediately preceding the play.

"Good work," Eponine called out, approaching her students on the stage. "Let's call it quits for today."

"Miss Wakefield," Kawabata #052 said, "there were three places where your words were not exactly correct. In your speech beginning—"

"Tell her tomorrow," Eponine interrupted, gently waving the biot away. "It will mean more to her then." She turned to face the small cast. "Are there any questions?"

"I know we've been through this before, Miss Eponine," Pedro Martinez said hesitantly, "but it would help me if we could discuss it again. . . . You told us that Godot was not a person, that he or it was actually a concept, or a fantasy . . . that we were all waiting for something. . . . I'm sorry, but it's difficult for me to understand exactly what . . ."

"The whole play is basically a commentary on the absurdity of life," Eponine replied after a few seconds. "We laugh because we see ourselves in those bums on the stage, we hear our words when they speak. What Beckett has captured is the essential longing of the human spirit. Whoever he is, Godot will make everything all right. He will somehow transform our lives and make us happy."

"Couldn't Godot be God?" Pedro asked.

"Absolutely," Eponine said. "Or even the superadvanced extraterrestrials who built the Rama spacecraft and oversaw the Node where Ellie and her family stayed. Any power or force or being that is a panacea for the woes of the world could be Godot. That's why the play is universal."

"Pedro," a demanding voice shouted from the back of the small auditorium, "are you almost finished?"

"Just a minute, Mariko," the young man answered. "We're having an interesting discussion. Why don't you come join us?"

The Japanese girl remained in the doorway. "No," she said rudely. "I don't want to—let's go now."

Eponine dismissed the cast and Pedro jumped down from the stage. Ellie came over beside her teacher as the young man hurried toward the door.

"Why does he let her act that way?" Ellie mused out loud.

"Don't ask me," Eponine replied with a shrug. "I'm certainly no expert when it comes to relationships."

That Kobayashi girl is trouble, Eponine thought, remembering how Mariko had treated both Ellie and her as if they were insects one night after rehearsal. *Men are so stupid sometimes.*

"Eponine," Ellie asked, "do you have any objections if my parents come to the dress rehearsal? Beckett is one of my father's favorite playwrights and—"

"That would be fine," Eponine replied. "Your parents are welcome anytime. Besides, I want to thank them—"

"*Miss Eponine,*" a young male voice shouted from across the room. It was Derek Brewer, one of Eponine's students who had a schoolboy crush on her. Derek ran a few steps toward her and then shouted again. "Have you heard the news?"

Eponine shook her head. Derek was obviously very excited. "Judge Mishkin has ruled the armbands unconstitutional!"

It took a few seconds for Eponine to absorb the information. By then Derek was at her side, delighted to be the one giving her the news. "Are . . . are you certain?" Eponine asked.

"We just heard it on the radio in the office."

Eponine reached for her arm and the hated red band. She glanced at Derek and Ellie and with one swift movement pulled the band off her arm and tossed it into the air. As she watched it arc toward the floor her eyes filled with tears.

"Thank you, Derek," she said.

Within moments Eponine felt four young arms embracing her. "Congratulations," Ellie said softly.

4

The hamburger stand in Central City was completely run by biots. Two Lincolns managed the busy restaurant and four Garcias filled the customer orders. The food preparation was done by a pair of Einsteins and the entire eating area was kept spotless by a single Tiasso. The stand generated an enormous profit for its owner, because there were no costs except the initial building conversion and the raw materials.

Ellie always ate there on Thursday nights, when she worked at the hospital as a volunteer. On the day of what became known as the Mishkin Proclamation, Ellie was joined at the hamburger stand by her now bandless teacher Eponine.

"I wonder why I've never seen you at the hospital," Eponine said as she took a bite of a French fried potato. "What do you do there anyway?"

"Mostly I talk to the sick children," Ellie replied. "There are four or five with serious illnesses, one little boy even with RV-41, and they appreciate visits from humans. The Tiasso biots are very efficient at operating the hospital and performing all the procedures, but they are not that sympathetic."

"If you don't mind my asking," Eponine said after chewing and swallowing a bite of her hamburger, "why do you do it? You are young, beautiful, healthy. There must be a thousand things you'd rather do."

"Not really," Ellie answered. "My mother has a very strong sense of community, as you know, and I feel worthwhile after I talk to the kids." She hesitated a moment. "Besides, I'm socially awkward. . . . I'm physically nineteen or twenty, which is old for high school, but I have almost no social experience." Ellie blushed. "One of my girl friends in school told me that the boys are convinced I'm an extraterrestrial."

Eponine smiled at her protégée. *Even being an alien would be better than having RV-41*, she thought. *But the young men are really missing something if they're passing you by.*

The two women finished their dinner and left the small restaurant. They walked out into the Central City square. In the middle of the square was a monument, appropriately cylindrical in shape, that had been dedicated in the ceremonies associated with the first Settlement Day celebration. The monument was two and a half meters tall altogether. Suspended in the cylinder at eye level was a transparent sphere with a diameter of fifty centimeters. The small light at the center of the sphere represented the Sun, the plane parallel to the ground was the ecliptic plane that contained the Earth and the other planets of the solar system, and the lights scattered throughout the sphere showed the correct relative positions of all the stars within a twenty-light-year radius of the Sun.

A line of illumination connected the Sun and Sirius, indicating the path that the Wakefields had taken on their odyssey to and from the Node. Another tiny line of light extended from the solar system along the trajectory that had been followed by Rama III since it had acquired the human colonists in Mars orbit. The host spacecraft, which was represented by a large, blinking red light, was currently in a position about one third of the way between the Sun and the star Tau Ceti.

"I understand the idea for this monument originally came from your father," Eponine said as the two women stood beside the celestial sphere.

"Yes," said Ellie. "Father is really extremely creative where science and electronics are concerned."

Eponine stared at the blinking red light. "Does it bother him at all that we are going in a different direction, not toward Sirius or the Node at all?"

Ellie shrugged. "I don't think so," she said. "We don't talk about it very much. . . . He told me one time that none of us was capable of understanding what the extraterrestrials were doing anyway."

Eponine glanced around her in the square. "Look at all the people, hurrying here and there. Most of them never even stop to see where we are. . . . I check our location at least once a week." She was suddenly very serious. "Ever since I was diagnosed with RV-41 I have had a compulsive need to know exactly where I am in the universe. . . . I wonder if that's part of my fear of dying."

After a long silence Eponine put her arm on Ellie's shoulder. "Did you ever ask the Eagle about death?" she said.

"No," Ellie replied softly. "But I was only four years old when I left the Node. I certainly had no concept of death."

"When I was a child, I thought like a child," Eponine said to herself. She laughed. "What *did* you talk to the Eagle about?"

"I don't recall exactly," Ellie said. "Patrick told me that the Eagle especially liked to watch us play with our toys."

"Really?" Eponine said. "That's a surprise. From your mother's description I would have imagined the Eagle was much too serious to be interested in play."

"I can still see him clearly in my mind's eye," Ellie said, "even though I was so young. But I can't remember what he sounded like."

"Have you ever dreamed about him?" Eponine asked a few seconds later.

"Oh, yes. Many times. Once he was standing on top of a huge tree, looking down at me from the clouds."

Eponine laughed again. Then she quickly checked her watch. "Oh, my," she said. "I'm late for my appointment. What time are you due at the hospital?"

"Seven o'clock," Ellie said.

"Then we'd better be on our way."

When Eponine reported to Dr. Turner's office for her biweekly checkup, the Tiasso in charge took her to the laboratory, obtained blood and urine specimens, and then asked her to take a seat. The biot informed Eponine that the doctor was "running behind."

A dark black man with sharp eyes and a friendly smile was also sitting in the waiting room. "Hello," he said when their eyes met, "my name is Amadou Diaba. I'm a pharmacist."

Eponine introduced herself, thinking that she had seen the man before.

"Great day, huh?" the man asked after a brief silence. "What a relief to take off that cursed armband."

Eponine now remembered Amadou. She had seen him once or twice in group meetings for the RV-41 sufferers. Someone had told Eponine that Amadou had contracted the retrovirus through a blood transfusion in the early days of the colony. *How many of us are there altogether?* Eponine thought. *Ninety-three. Or is it ninety-four? Five of whom caught the disease through a transfusion. . . .*

"It seems that big news always happens in pairs," Amadou was saying. "The Mishkin Proclamation was announced only hours before the leggie things were seen for the first time."

Eponine looked at him quizzically. "What are you talking about?" she asked.

"You haven't heard about the leggies yet?" Amadou said, laughing slightly. "Where in the world have you been?"

Amadou waited a few seconds before launching into an explanation. "The exploration team over at the other habitat has been in the process of widening their penetration site for the last few days. Today they were suddenly confronted by six strange creatures who crawled out of the hole that had been made in the wall. These leggies, as the television reporter called them, apparently live in the other habitat. They look like hairy golf balls attached to six giant, jointed legs, and they move very, very quickly. . . . They crawled all over the men, the biots, and the equipment for about an hour. Then they disappeared back into the penetration site."

Eponine was about to ask some questions about the leggies when Dr. Turner came out of his office. "Mr. Diaba and Miss Eponine," he said. "I have a detailed report for each of you. Who wants to be first?"

The doctor still had the most magnificent blue eyes. "Mr. Diaba was here before me," Eponine replied. "So—"

"Ladies always go first," Amadou interrupted. "Even in New Eden."

Eponine went into Dr. Turner's inner office. "So far, so good," the doctor told her when they were alone. "You definitely have the virus in your system, but there's no sign of any heart muscle deterioration. I don't know why for certain, but the disease definitely progresses more rapidly in some than others."

How can it be, my handsome doctor, Eponine thought, *that you follow all my health data so closely but never once have noticed the looks I've been giving you all this time?*

"We'll keep you on the regular immune system medication. It has no serious side effects, and it may be partially responsible for our not seeing any evidence of the virus's destructive activities. . . . Are you feeling all right otherwise?"

They walked back out to the waiting room together. Dr. Turner reviewed for Eponine the symptoms that would indicate the virus had moved to another stage in its development. While they were talking, the door opened and Ellie Wakefield came into the room. At first Dr. Turner ignored her presence, but moments later he did an obvious double take.

"May I help you, young lady?" he said to Ellie.

"I've come to ask Eponine a question," Ellie replied deferentially. "If I'm disturbing you, I can wait outside."

Dr. Turner shook his head and then was surprisingly disorganized in his final comments to Eponine. At first she did not understand what had happened. But when Eponine started to leave with Ellie, she saw the doctor staring at her student. *For three years,* Eponine thought, *I have yearned to see a look like that in his eyes. I didn't think he was capable of it. And Ellie, bless her heart, missed it altogether.*

It had been a long day. Eponine was extremely tired by the time she walked from the station to her apartment in Hakone. The emotional release she had felt after removing her armband had passed. She was now a little depressed. Eponine was also fighting feelings of jealousy toward Ellie Wakefield.

She stopped in front of her apartment. The broad red stripe on her door reminded everyone that an RV-41 carrier lived inside. Thanking Judge Mishkin again, Eponine carefully pulled off the stripe. It left an outline on the door. *I'll paint it tomorrow,* Eponine thought.

Once in her apartment, she plopped down in her soft chair and reached for a cigarette. Eponine felt the surge of anticipatory pleasure as she put the cigarette in her mouth. *I never smoke at school in front of my students,* she rationalized. *I do not set a bad example for them. I smoke only here. At home. When I'm lonely.*

Eponine hardly ever went out at night. The villagers in Hakone had made it very clear to her that they didn't want her in their midst—two separate delegations had asked her to leave the village and there had been several nasty notes on her apartment door. But Eponine had stubbornly refused to move. Since Kimberly Henderson was never there, Eponine had much more living space than she would have been able to afford under normal circumstances. She also knew that an RV-41 carrier would not be welcomed in any neighborhood in the colony.

Eponine had fallen asleep in her chair and was dreaming of

fields of yellow flowers. She almost didn't hear the knock, even though it was very loud. She glanced at her watch—it was eleven o'clock. When Eponine opened the door, Kimberly Henderson entered the apartment.

"Oh, Ep," she said, "I'm so glad you're here. I need to talk to someone desperately. Someone I can trust."

Kimberly lit a cigarette with a jerky motion and immediately burst into a rambling monologue. "Yes, yes, I know," Kimberly said, seeing the disapproval in Eponine's eyes. "You're right, I'm stoned. . . . But I needed it. . . . Good old kokomo. . . . Artificial feelings of self-confidence are at least better than thinking of yourself as a piece of shit."

She took a frantic drag and exhaled the smoke in short, choppy bursts. "The asshole has really done it this time, Ep . . . he's pushed me over the brink. . . . Cocky son of a bitch—thinks he can do whatever he wants. . . . I tolerated his affairs and even let some of the younger girls join me sometimes—the threesomes relieved the boredom . . . but I was always *ichiban, numero uno*, or at least I thought I was—"

Kimberly stubbed out her cigarette and began to wring her hands. She was close to tears. "So tonight he tells me I'm moving. . . . 'What,' I say, 'What do you mean?' . . . 'You're moving,' he says. . . . No smile, no discussion. . . . 'Pack your things,' he says, 'there's an apartment for you over behind Xanadu.'

" 'That's where the whores live,' I answer. . . . He smiles a little and says nothing. . . . 'That's it, I'm dismissed,' I say. . . . I flew into a rage. . . . 'You can't do this,' I said. . . . I tried to hit him but he grabbed my hand and smacked me hard on the face. . . . 'You'll do as I order,' he says. . . . 'I will *not*, you motherfucker.' . . . I picked up a vase and threw it. It smashed into a table and shattered. In seconds two men had pinned my arms behind me. . . . 'Take her away,' the king Jap said.

"They took me to my new apartment. It was very nice. In the dressing room was a large box of rolled kokomo. . . . I smoked an entire number and was flying. . . . *Hey*, I said to myself, *this is not so bad. At least I don't have to cater to Toshio's bizarre sexual desires.* . . . I went over to the casino and was having fun, higher than a kite, until I saw them . . . out in public in front of everybody else. . . . I went wild—hollering, screaming, cursing—I even attacked her. . . . Somebody hit me in the head. . . . I was down on the casino floor with Toshio bending over me. . . . 'If you ever do anything like that again,' he hissed, 'you'll be buried beside Marcello Danni.' "

Kimberly put her face in her hands and started to sob. "Oh, Ep," she said seconds later, "I feel so helpless. I have nowhere to turn. What can I do?"

Before Eponine could say anything, Kimberly was talking again. "I know, I know," she said. "I could go back to work at the hospital. They still need nurses, real ones—by the way, where is your Lincoln?"

Eponine smiled and pointed to the closet. "Good for you." Kimberly laughed. "Keep the robot in the dark. Bring him out to clean the bathroom, wash the dishes, cook the meals. Then, whoosh, back in the closet. . . ." She chuckled. "Their dicks don't work, you know. I mean, they have one, or sort of, anatomically perfect after all, but they don't get hard. One night when I was stoned and alone I had one mount me but he didn't know what I meant when I said 'thrust.' . . . As bad as some men I've known."

Kimberly jumped up and paced around the room. "I'm not really sure why I came," she said, lighting another cigarette. "I thought maybe you and I . . . I mean, we were friends for a while. . . ." Her voice trailed off. "I'm coming down now, starting to feel depressed. It's awful, terrible. I can't stand it. I don't know what I expected, but you have your own life. . . . I'd better be going."

Kimberly crossed the room and gave Eponine a perfunctory hug. "Take care, now, okay?" Kimberly said. "Don't worry about me, I'll be all right."

It was only after the door closed and Kimberly left that Eponine realized she had not uttered one word while her ex-friend was in the room. Eponine was certain that she would never see Kimberly again.

5

It was an open meeting of the Senate and anyone in the colony could attend. The gallery had only three hundred seats and they were all filled. Another hundred people were standing along the walls and sitting in the aisles. On the main floor the twenty-four members of the New Eden legislative body were called to attention by their presiding officer, Governor Kenji Watanabe.

"Our budget hearings continue today," Kenji said after striking the gavel several times to quiet the onlookers, "with a presentation by the director of the New Eden Hospital, Dr. Robert Turner. He will summarize what was accomplished with the health budget last year and present his requests for the coming year."

Dr. Turner walked to the rostrum and motioned to the two Tiassos who had been sitting beside him. The biots quickly set up a projector and a suspended cube screen for the visual material that would support Dr. Turner's talk.

"We have made great strides in the last year," Dr. Turner began, "both in building a solid medical environment for the colony and in understanding our nemesis, the RV-41 retrovirus that continues to plague our populace. During the last twelve months not only have we completely determined the life cycle of this complex organism, but also we have developed screening tests that allow us to identify accurately any and all persons who carry the disease.

"Everyone in New Eden was tested during a three-week period that ended seven months ago. Ninety-six individuals in the colony were identified as being infected with the retrovirus at that time. Since the completion of the testing, only one new carrier has been found. There have been three deaths from RV-41 during the interim, so our current infected population is ninety-four.

"RV-41 is a deadly retrovirus that attacks the muscles of the heart, causing them to atrophy irreversibly. Ultimately the human carrier dies. There is no known cure. We are experimenting with a variety of techniques for remitting the progression of the disease and have recently had some sporadic but inconclusive success. At this moment, until we score a significant breakthrough in our work, we must reluctantly assume that all individuals afflicted by the retrovirus will eventually succumb to its virulence.

"The chart I'm placing on the projection cube shows the various stages of the disease. The retrovirus is passed between individuals during a sharing of bodily fluids involving any combination of semen and blood. There is no indication that there is any other method of transfer. I repeat," Dr. Turner said, now shouting to be heard above the hubbub of the gallery, "we have verified passage *only* where semen or blood is involved. We cannot categorically declare that other bodily fluids, such as sweat, mucus, tears, saliva, and urine, cannot be agents in the transfer, but our data thus far strongly suggests that RV-41 cannot be passed in these fluids."

The talking in the gallery was now widespread. Governor Watanabe struck his gavel several times to quiet the room. Robert Turner cleared his throat and then continued. "This particular retrovirus is very clever, if I can use that word, and especially well adapted to its human host. As you can see from the diagram on the cube, it is relatively benign in its first two stages, when it essentially just resides, without harm, inside the blood and semen cells. It may be that during this time it has already begun its attack on the immune system. We cannot say for certain, because during this stage all diagnostic data shows that the immune system is healthy.

"We do not know what triggers the decline of the immune system. Some inexplicable process in our complex bodies—and here is an area where we need to do more intensive research—suddenly signals to the RV-41 virus that the immune system is vulnerable and a mighty attack begins. The virus density in the blood and semen suddenly rises by several orders of magnitude. This is when the disease is the most contagious, and also when the immune system is overwhelmed."

Dr. Turner paused. He shuffled the papers from which he was reading before continuing. "It is curious that the immune system *never* survives this attack. Somehow RV-41 knows when it can win, and never multiplies until that particular condition of vulnerability has been reached. Once the immune system is destroyed, the atrophy of the heart muscles begins and a predictable death follows.

"In the later stages of the disease, the RV-41 retrovirus disappears completely from the semen and the blood. As you can well imagine, this vanishing wreaks havoc with the diagnostic process. Where does it go? Does it 'hide' in some way, become something else we have not yet identified? Is it supervising the gradual destruction of the heart muscles, or is the atrophy simply a side effect of the earlier attack on the immune system? All these questions we cannot answer at the present time."

The doctor stopped momentarily for a drink of water. "Part of our charter last year," he then said, "was to investigate the origin of this disease. There have been rumors that RV-41 was somehow indigenous to New Eden, perhaps placed here as some kind of diabolical extraterrestrial experiment. That kind of talk is complete nonsense. We definitely brought this retrovirus here from the Earth. Two passengers on the Santa Maria died from RV-41 within three months of each other, the first during the cruise from Earth to Mars. We can be certain, although this is hardly encouraging, that our friends and colleagues back on Earth are struggling with this devil as well.

"As for the origin of RV-41, here I can only speculate. If the medical data base that we had brought along from Earth had been an order of magnitude larger, then perhaps I would be able to identify its origin without any guessing. . . . Nevertheless, I will point out that the genome of this RV-41 retrovirus is astonishingly similar to a pathogen genetically engineered, by humans, as part of the vaccine envelope testing performed in the early years of the twenty-second century.

"Let me explain in more detail. After the successful development of preventive vaccines for the AIDS retrovirus, which was a horrible scourge during the last two decades of the twentieth century, medical technology took advantage of biological engineering to expand the range of all the available vaccines. Specifically, the biologists and the doctors purposely *engineered* new and more deadly retroviruses and bacteria to prove that a given vaccine class had a broad range of successful application. All this work was done, of course, under careful controls and at no risk to the populace.

"When the Great Chaos occurred, however, research monies were severely cut and many of the medical laboratories had to be abandoned. The dangerous pathogens stored in isolated spots around the world were presumably all destroyed. Unless . . . and here is where my speculation enters into the explanation.

"The retrovirus that is afflicting us here in New Eden is amazingly similar to the AQT19 retrovirus engineered in 2107 at the Laffont Medical Laboratory in Senegal. It is possible, I will admit, that a naturally occurring agent could have a genome similar to AQT19, and therefore my speculation could be wrong. However, it is my belief that all the AQT19 in that abandoned lab in Senegal was *not* destroyed. I am convinced that this particular retrovirus somehow survived *and* mutated slightly in the subsequent century—perhaps by living in simian hosts—and eventually found its way into human beings. In that case, *we* are the ultimate creators of the disease that is killing us."

There was an uproar in the gallery. Governor Watanabe again gaveled the audience to quiet, privately wishing that Dr. Turner had kept his conjectures to himself. At this point the hospital director began his discussion of all the projects for which funding was needed in the coming year. Dr. Turner was requesting an appropriation *double* what his department had had in the past year. There was an audible groan on the Senate floor.

The several speakers who immediately followed Robert Turner were really just window dressing. Everyone knew that the only other important speech of the day would be given by Ian Macmillan, the opposition candidate for governor in the elections three months hence. It was understood that both the current governor, Kenji Watanabe, and the choice of his political party, Dmitri Ulanov, favored a significant increase in the medical budget even if new taxes were required to finance it. Macmillan was reportedly opposed to any increase in Dr. Turner's funds.

Ian Macmillan had been soundly defeated by Kenji Watanabe in the first general election held in the colony. Since that time, Mr. Macmillan had moved his residence from Beauvois to Hakone, had been elected to the Senate from the Vegas district, and had taken a lucrative position in Toshio Nakamura's expanding business empire. It was the perfect marriage. Nakamura needed someone "acceptable" to run the colony for him, and Macmillan, who was an ambitious man without any clearly defined values or principles, wanted to be governor.

"It is too easy," Ian Macmillan began reading his speech, "to listen to Dr. Turner and then to open our hearts and purses, allocating funds for all his requests. That's what is wrong with these budget hearings. Each department head can make a strong case for his proposals. But by listening to each item separately, we lose sight of the larger picture. I do not mean to suggest that Dr. Turner's program is anything but worthy. However, I do think that a discussion of priorities is warranted at this time."

Macmillan's speaking style had improved considerably since he had moved to Hakone. He had obviously been carefully coached. However, he was not a natural orator, so at times his practiced gestures seemed almost comical. His primary point was that the RV-41 carriers made up less than five percent of the population of New Eden and the cost of helping them was incredibly expensive.

"Why should the rest of the citizens of the colony be forced to suffer deprivation for the benefit of such a small group?" he said. "Besides," he added, "there are other, more compelling issues that require added monies, issues that touch each and every colonist and will likely impact our very survival."

When Ian Macmillan presented his version of the story about the leggies that had "rushed out" of the adjoining module in Rama and "frightened" the colony exploration team, he made it sound as if their "attack" had been the first foray in a planned interspecies war. Macmillan raised the specter of the leggies being followed by "more fearsome creatures" that would terrify the colonists, especially the women and children. "Money for defense," he said, "is money spent for all of us."

Candidate Macmillan also suggested that environmental research was another activity "far more important for the general welfare of the colony" than the medical program outlined by Dr. Turner. He praised the work being done to control the environment, and envisioned a future where the colonists would have complete knowledge of the coming weather.

His speech was interrupted by applause from the gallery many times. When he did finally discuss the individuals suffering from RV-41, Mr. Macmillan outlined a "more cost-effective" plan to deal with "their terrible tragedy." "We will create a new village for them," he intoned, "outside of New Eden, where they can live out their final days in peace."

"In my opinion," he said, "the RV-41 medical effort in the future should be restricted to isolating and identifying all the mechanisms by which this scourge is passed from individual to individual.

Until this research is completed, it is in the best interests of everyone in the colony, including the unfortunate people who carry the disease, to quarantine the carriers so that there can be no more accidental contamination."

Nicole and her family were all in the gallery. They had badgered Richard into coming, even though he disliked political gatherings. Richard was disgusted by Macmillan's speech. For her part, Nicole was frightened. What the man was saying had a certain appeal. *I wonder who is writing his material,* she thought at the conclusion of his speech. She chastised herself for having underestimated Nakamura.

Toward the end of Macmillan's oration, Ellie Wakefield quietly left her place in the gallery. Her parents were astonished, a few moments later, to see her down on the Senate floor approaching the rostrum. So were the other members of the gallery, who had thought that Ian Macmillan was the last speaker of the day. Everyone was preparing to depart. Most of them sat down again when Kenji Watanabe introduced Ellie.

"In our civics class in high school," she started, her nervousness apparent in her voice, "we have been studying the colony constitution and the Senate procedures. It's a little-known fact that *any* citizen of New Eden may address one of these open hearings. . . ."

Ellie took a deep breath before continuing. In the gallery, both her mother and her teacher Eponine leaned forward and grabbed the rail in front of them. "I wanted to speak today," Ellie said more forcefully, "because I believe I have a unique point of view on this issue of the RV-41 sufferers. First, I am young, and second, until a little over three years ago I had never had the privilege of interacting with a human being other than my family.

"For both those reasons I treasure human life. My word was picked carefully. A treasure is something you value greatly. This man, this incredible doctor who works all day and sometimes all night to keep us healthy, obviously treasures human life as well.

"When he spoke earlier, Dr. Turner didn't tell you *why* we should fund his program, only *what* the disease was and *how* he would try to combat it. He assumed you all understood *why*. After listening to Mr. Macmillan," Ellie said, glancing at the previous speaker, "I have some doubts.

"We must continue to study this horrible disease, until we can contain and control it, because a human life is a precious commodity. Each individual person is a unique miracle, an amazing combination of complex chemicals with special talents, dreams, and experiences.

Nothing can be more important to the overall colony than an activity aimed at the preservation of human life.

"I understand from the discussion today that Dr. Turner's program is expensive. If taxes must be raised to pay for it, then perhaps each of us will have to do without some special item that we wanted. It is a small enough price to pay for the treasure of another human's company.

"My family and friends tell me sometimes that I am hopelessly naive. That may be true. But perhaps my innocence allows me to see things more clearly than other people can. In this case I believe there is only one question that needs to be asked. If you, or some member of your family, had been diagnosed with RV-41, would *you* support Dr. Turner's program? . . . Thank you very much."

There was an eerie silence as Ellie stepped away from the rostrum. Then thunderous applause erupted. Tears flowed in both Nicole's and Eponine's eyes. On the Senate floor Dr. Robert Turner reached both his hands out to Ellie.

6

When Nicole opened her eyes Richard was sitting beside her on the bed. He was holding a cup of coffee. "You told us to wake you at seven," he said.

She sat up and took the coffee from him. "Thank you, darling," Nicole said. "But why didn't you let Linc—"

"I decided to bring your coffee myself. . . . There is news from the Central Plain again. I wanted to discuss it with you, even though I know how you dislike being jabbered at first thing in the morning."

Nicole took a long, slow sip from her cup. She smiled at her husband. "What's the news?" she said.

"There were two more leggie incidents last night. That makes almost a dozen this week. Our defense forces reportedly destroyed three leggies who were 'harassing' the engineering crew."

"Did the leggies make any attempts to fight back?"

"No, they didn't. At the first sound of gunfire they raced for the hole in the other habitat. . . . Most of them escaped, as they did the day before yesterday."

"And you still think they're remote observers, like the spider biots in Ramas I and II?"

Richard nodded. "And you can just imagine what kind of a picture the Others are developing of us. We fire on unarmed creatures without provocation . . . we react in a hostile manner to what is certainly an attempt at contact. . . ."

"I don't like it either," Nicole said softly. "But what can we do? The Senate explicitly authorized the exploration teams to defend themselves."

Richard was about to reply when he noticed Benjy standing in the doorway. The young man was smiling broadly. "May I come in, Mother?" he asked.

"Of course, dear," Nicole replied. She opened her arms wide. "Come give me a big birthday hug."

"Happy birthday, Benjy," Richard said as the boy, who was larger than most men, crawled onto the bed and embraced his mother.

"Thank you, Uncle Richard."

"Are we still having a picnic in Sherwood Forest today?" Benjy asked slowly.

"Yes, indeed," his mother answered. "And then tonight we're having a big party."

"Hooray," Benjy said.

It was a Saturday. Patrick and Ellie were both sleeping late because they did not have classes. Linc served breakfast to Richard, Nicole, and Benjy while the adults watched the morning news on television. There was a short film of the most recent "leggie confrontation" near the second habitat as well as comments from both of the gubernatorial candidates.

"As I have been saying for weeks now," Ian Macmillan remarked to the television reporter, "we must dramatically expand our defense preparations. We have finally started to upgrade the weapons available to our forces, but we need to move more boldly in this arena."

An interview with the weather director concluded the morning news. The woman explained that the unusually dry and windy recent weather had been caused by a "modeling error" in their computer simulation. "All week long," she said, "we have been trying unsuccessfully to create rain. Now, of course, since it's the weekend, we have programmed sunshine. . . . But we promise it will rain next week."

"They don't have the slightest idea what they're doing," Richard grumbled, switching off the television. "They're overcommanding the system and generating chaos."

"What's k-oss, Uncle Richard?" Benjy asked.

Richard hesitated for a moment. "I guess the simplest definition is the absence of order. But in mathematics, the word has a more precise meaning. It is used to describe unbounded responses to small perturbations." Richard laughed. "I'm sorry, Benjy. Sometimes I talk in scientific gobbledygook."

Benjy smiled. "I like it when you talk to me as if I'm nor-mal," he said carefully. "And some-times I do un-der-stand a lit-tle."

Nicole seemed preoccupied while Linc was clearing the breakfast dishes off the table. When Benjy left the room to brush his teeth, she leaned toward her husband. "Have you talked to Katie?" she asked. "She didn't answer her phone yesterday afternoon or last night."

Richard shook his head.

"Benjy will be crushed if she doesn't show up for his party. I'm going to send Patrick off to find her this morning."

Richard stood up from his chair and walked around the table. He reached down and took Nicole's hand. "And what about you, Mrs. Wakefield? Have you scheduled some rest and relaxation anywhere in your busy program? After all, it is the weekend."

"I'm going by the hospital this morning to help train the two new paramedics. Then Ellie and I will leave here with Benjy at ten. On the way back I'll stop by the courtroom—I haven't even read the submitted briefs for the cases on Monday. I have a quick meeting with Kenji at two-thirty and my pathology lecture at three. . . . I should be home by four-thirty."

"Which will give you just enough time to organize Benjy's party. Really, darling, you need to slow down. After all, you're not a biot."

Nicole kissed her husband. "You should talk. Aren't you the one who works twenty or thirty straight hours when you're involved in an exciting project?" She stopped a moment and became serious. "All this is very important, darling. . . . I feel we're at a cusp in the affairs of the colony and that I really am making a difference here."

"No question, Nicole. You are definitely having an impact. But you never have any time for yourself."

"That's a luxury item," Nicole said, opening the door to Patrick's room. "To be savored in my later years."

As they emerged from the trees into the wide meadow, rabbits and squirrels scurried out of their way. On the opposite side of the meadow, quietly eating in the middle of a patch of tall purple flowers, was a young stag. He turned his head of new antlers toward Nicole, Ellie, and Benjy as they approached him, and then bounded away into the forest.

Nicole consulted her map. "There should be some picnic tables here somewhere, right beside the meadow."

Benjy was kneeling down over a group of yellow flowers that were full of bees. "Ho-ney," he said with a smile. "Bees make honey in their hives."

After several mintues they located the tables and spread out a cloth on top of one of them. Linc had packed sandwiches—Benjy liked peanut butter and jelly best—plus fresh oranges and grapefruit from the orchards near San Miguel. While they were eating lunch, another family traipsed through the other side of the meadow. Benjy waved.

"Those peo-ple don't know it's my birth-day," he said.

"But we do," Ellie said, raising her cupful of lemonade to make a toast. "Congratulations, brother."

Just before they were finished eating, a small cloud passed overhead and the bright colors of the meadow momentarily dimmed. "That's an unusually dark cloud," Nicole commented to Ellie. Moments later it was gone and the grasses and flowers were again bathed in sunlight.

"Do you want your pudding now?" Nicole asked Benjy. "Or do you want to wait?"

"Let's play catch first," Benjy replied. He took the baseball equipment out of the picnic bag and handed a glove to Ellie. "Let's go," he said, running out into the meadow.

While her two children were throwing the baseball back and forth, Nicole cleaned up the remains of their lunch. She was about to join Ellie and Benjy when she heard the alarm on her wrist radio. She pressed the receive button and the digital time display was replaced with a television picture. Nicole turned up the volume so that she could hear what Kenji Watanabe had to say.

"I'm sorry to bother you, Nicole," Kenji said, "but we have an emergency. A rape complaint has been filed and the family wants an indictment immediately. It's a sensitive case, in your jurisdiction, and I think it should be handled now. . . . I don't want to say anything else on the line."

"I'll be there in half an hour," Nicole responded.

At first Benjy was crestfallen that his picnic was going to be cut short. However, Ellie convinced her mother that it was all right for her to stay in the forest with Benjy for another couple of hours. Just as she departed from the meadow, Nicole handed the map of Sherwood Forest to Ellie. At that moment another, larger cloud moved in front of the artificial New Eden sun.

*   *   *

There was no sign of any life at Katie's apartment. Patrick was temporarily stymied. Where should he look for her? None of his university friends lived in Vegas, so he really didn't know where to start.

He called Max Puckett from a public phone. Max gave Patrick the names, addresses, and phone numbers of three individuals he knew in Vegas. "None of these people is the kind you would want to invite home to dinner with your parents, if you know what I mean," Max said with a laugh, "but they are all good-hearted and will probably help you find your sister."

The only name Patrick recognized was Samantha Porter, whose apartment was just a few hundred meters from the phone booth. Even though it was the early afternoon, Samantha was still in her robe when she finally answered the door. "I thought that was you, when I looked on the monitor," she said with a sexy smile. "You're Patrick O'Toole, aren't you?"

Patrick nodded and then shifted his feet uncomfortably during a long silence. "Miss Porter," he said at length, "I have a problem—"

"You're much too *young* to have a problem," Samantha interrupted. She laughed heartily. "Why don't you come inside and we'll talk about it?"

Patrick blushed. "No, ma'am," he said, "it's not that kind of a problem. . . . I just can't find my sister Katie and I thought maybe you could help me."

Samantha, who had half turned to lead Patrick into her apartment, turned back to stare at the young man. "*That's* why you've come to see me?" she said. She shook her head and laughed again. "What a disappointment! I thought that you had come to fool around. Then I could tell everybody, once and for all, whether or not you really are an alien."

Patrick continued to fidget in the entryway. After several seconds Samantha shrugged. "I believe that Katie spends most of her time in the palace," she said. "Go to the casino and ask for Sherry. She'll know how to find your sister."

"Yes, yes, Mr. Kobayashi, I understand. *Wakarimasu,*" Nicole was saying to the Japanese gentleman in her office. "I can appreciate what you must be feeling. You can be sure that justice will be done."

She escorted the man into the waiting room, where he joined his wife. Mrs. Kobayashi's eyes were still swollen from her tears. Their sixteen-year-old daughter Mariko was in the New Eden Hospital, undergoing a full medical examination. She had been badly beaten, but was not in critical condition.

Nicole called Dr. Turner after she finished talking to the Kobayashis. "There's fresh semen in the girl's vagina," the doctor said, "and bruises on almost every square centimeter of her body. She's an emotional wreck as well—rape is definitely a possibility."

Nicole sighed. Mariko Kobayashi had named Pedro Martinez, the young man who had starred with Ellie in the school play, as the rapist. Could it be possible? Nicole rolled her chair across the floor of her office and accessed the colony data base through her computer.

MARTINEZ, PEDRO ESCOBAR . . . born 26 May 2228, Managua, Nicaragua . . . mother unwed, Maria Escobar, maid, domestic, often unemployed . . . father probably Ramon Martinez, black dockworker from Haiti . . . six half brothers and sisters, all younger . . . convicted for selling kokomo, 2241, 2242 . . . rape, 2243 . . . eight months Managua Correction Home . . . model prisoner . . . transfer to Covenant House in Mexico City, 2244 . . . IE 1.86, SC 52.

Nicole read the short computer entry twice before calling Pedro into her office. He sat down, as Nicole suggested, and then stared at the floor. A Lincoln biot stood in the corner throughout the interview and carefully recorded the conversation.

"Pedro," Nicole said softly. There was no response. He did not even look up. "Pedro Martinez," she repeated more forcefully, "do you understand that you have been accused of raping Mariko Kobayashi last night? I'm sure I don't need to explain to you that this is a very serious accusation. . . . You are being given a chance now to respond to her charges."

Pedro still did not say anything. "In New Eden," Nicole continued at length, "we have a judicial system that may be different from the one you experienced in Nicaragua. Here criminal cases cannot proceed to indictment unless a judge, after examining the facts, believes that there is sufficient reason for indictment. That is why I am talking to you."

After a long silence the young man, without looking up at all, mumbled something that was inaudible.

"What?" Nicole asked.

"She's lying," Pedro said, much louder. "I don't know why, but Mariko's lying."

"Would you like to tell me your version of what happened?"

"What difference would it make? Nobody is going to believe me anyway."

"Pedro, listen to me. If, on the basis of an initial investigation, my court concludes that there is insufficient reason to proceed with the prosecution, your case can be dismissed. Of course, the seriousness of this charge demands a very thorough investigation, which means you will have to make a complete statement and answer some very tough questions."

Pedro Martinez lifted his head and stared at Nicole with sorrowful eyes. "Judge Wakefield," he said quietly, "Mariko and I *did* have sex last night . . . but it was her idea. She thought it would be fun to go into the forest—" The young man stopped talking and looked back down at the floor.

"Had you had intercourse with Mariko before?" Nicole asked after several seconds.

"Only once—about ten days ago," Pedro answered.

"Pedro, was your lovemaking last night . . . was it extremely physical?"

Tears eased out of Pedro's eyes and rolled onto his cheeks. "I did not beat her," he said passionately. "I would never have hurt her."

As he spoke there was a strange sound in the distance, like the cracking of a long whip, except much deeper in tone.

"What was that?" Nicole wondered out loud.

"Sounded like thunder," Pedro remarked.

The thunder could also be heard in the village of Hakone, where Patrick was sitting in a luxurious suite in Nakamura's palace, talking to his sister Katie. She was dressed in an expensive blue silk lounging outfit.

Patrick ignored the unexplained noise. He was angry. "Are you telling me that you won't even *try* to make it to Benjy's party tonight? What am I supposed to tell Mother?"

"Tell her anything you want," Katie said. She took a cigarette from her case and placed it in her mouth. "Tell her you couldn't find me." She lit the cigarette with a gold lighter and blew the smoke in her brother's direction. He tried to wave it away with his hand.

"Come on, baby brother," Katie said with a laugh. "It won't kill you."

"Not immediately, anyway," he answered.

"Look, Patrick," Katie said, standing up and starting to pace around the suite, "Benjy's an idiot, a moron. We've never been very close. He won't even realize that I'm not there unless someone mentions it to him."

"You're wrong, Katie. He's more intelligent than you think. He asks about you all the time."

"That's crap, baby brother," Katie replied. "You're just saying it to make me feel guilty. . . . Look, I'm not coming. I mean, I might consider it if it were just you and Benjy and Ellie—although she's been a pain in the ass ever since her 'wonderful' speech. But you know what it's like for me around Mother. She's on my case all the time."

"She's worried about you, Katie."

Katie laughed nervously and took a deep drag to finish her cigarette. "Sure she is, Patrick. All she's really worried about is whether I'll embarrass the family."

Patrick stood up to leave. "You don't have to go now," Katie said. "Why don't you stay for a while? I'll put on some clothes and we'll go down to the casino. Remember how much fun we used to have together?"

Katie started toward the bedroom. "Are you using drugs?" Patrick asked suddenly.

She stopped and stared at her brother. "Who wants to know?" Katie said defiantly. "You or Madame Cosmonaut Doctor Governor Judge Nicole des Jardins Wakefield?"

"I want to know," Patrick said quietly.

Katie walked across the room and put her hands on Patrick's cheeks. "I'm your sister and I love you," she said. "Nothing else is important."

The dark clouds had all gathered over the small rolling hills of Sherwood Forest. Wind was sweeping through the trees, blowing Ellie's hair behind her. There was a bolt of lightning and an almost simultaneous crack of thunder.

Benjy recoiled and Ellie pulled him close beside her. "According to the map," she said, "we're only about one kilometer from the edge of the forest."

"How far is that?" Benjy asked.

"If we walk quickly," Ellie shouted above the wind, "then we can make it out in about ten minutes." She grabbed Benjy's hand and pulled him alongside her on the path.

An instant later lightning split one of the trees beside them and a thick branch fell across the path. The branch struck Benjy on the back and knocked him down. He fell mostly on the path, but his head landed in the green plants and ivy at the base of the trees in the forest. The noise from the thunder nearly deafened him.

He lay on the forest floor for several seconds, trying to understand what had happened to him. At length he struggled to his feet.

"Ellie," he said, looking at the prostrate form of his sister on the other side of the path. Her eyes were closed.

"*Ellie!*" Benjy now screamed, half walking, half crawling over to her side. He grabbed her by the shoulders and shook her lightly. Her eyes did not open. The swelling on her forehead, above and to the side of her right eye, was already the size of a large orange.

"What am I go-ing to do?" Benjy said out loud. He smelled smoke and glanced up into the trees at almost the same moment. He saw fire leaping from branch to branch, driven by the wind. There was another bolt of lightning, more thunder. In front of him, down the trail in the direction that Ellie and he had been going, Benjy could see that a larger fire was sweeping through the trees on both sides of the path. He started to panic.

He held his sister in his arms and slapped her lightly on the face. "Ellie," he said, "please, please wake up." She did not stir. The fire around him was spreading rapidly. Soon this entire portion of the forest would be an inferno.

Benjy was terrified. He tried to lift Ellie up, but stumbled and fell in the process. "No, no, no," he shouted, standing again and bending to lift Ellie to his shoulders. The smoke was getting heavy. Benjy moved slowly down the path, away from the fire, with Ellie on his back.

He was exhausted when he reached the meadow. He gently placed Ellie on one of the concrete tables and sat on a bench himself. The fire was raging out of control on the north side of the meadow. *What do I do now?* he thought. His eye fell on the map sticking out of Ellie's shirt pocket. *That can help me.* He grabbed the map and looked at it. At first he could not understand any of it and he began again to panic.

Relax, Benjy, he heard his mother say in a soothing tone. *It's a little hard, but you can do it. Maps are very important. They tell us where to go. . . . Now, the first thing always is to orient the map so that you can read the writing. See. That's right. Most of the time the up direction is called north. Good. This is a map of Sherwood Forest. . . .*

Benjy turned the map over in his hands until the letters were all right side up. The lightning and thunder continued. A sudden change in the wind pushed smoke into his lungs and he coughed. He tried to read the words on the map.

Again he heard his mother's voice. *If you don't recognize the word at first, then take each letter and sound it out very slowly. Next let all the sounds fall together until it makes a word you understand.*

Benjy glanced at Ellie on the table. "Wake up, oh, please wake up, Ellie," he said. "I need your help." Still she did not move.

He bent down over the map and struggled to concentrate. With painstaking deliberation Benjy sounded out all the letters, over and over, until he had convinced himself that the green patch on the map was the meadow where he was sitting. *The white lines are the paths*, he said to himself. *There are three white lines running into the green patch*.

Benjy looked up from the map, counted the three paths leading out of the meadow, and felt a surge of self-confidence. Moments later, however, a gust of wind carried cinders across the meadow and ignited the trees on the southern side. Benjy moved quickly. *I must go*, he said, again lifting Ellie onto his back.

He now knew that the main fire was in the northern portion of the map, toward the village of Hakone. Benjy stared again at the paper in his hands. *So I must stay on white lines in the bottom part*, he thought.

The young man trundled down the path as another tree exploded in fire far above his head. His sister was over his shoulder, and the lifesaving map was in his right hand. Benjy stopped to look at the map every ten steps, each time verifying that he was still headed in the correct direction. When he finally came to a major trail junction, Benjy placed Ellie gingerly on the ground and traced the white lines on the map with his finger. After a minute he smiled broadly, picked up his sister again, and headed down the trail leading to the village of Positano. Lightning flashed one more time, the thunder boomed, and a drenching shower began to fall on Sherwood Forest.

7

Five hours later Benjy was sleeping soundly in his room. Meanwhile, in the center of the colony, the New Eden hospital was a madhouse. Humans and biots were dashing about, gurneys with bodies were standing in the halls, patients were shouting in agony. Nicole was talking on the phone with Kenji Watanabe. "We need every Tiasso in the colony sent here as quickly as possible. Try to replace those that are doing geriatric or infant care with a Garcia, or even an Einstein. Have humans staff the village clinics. The situation is very serious."

She could barely hear what Kenji was saying above the noise in the hospital. "Bad, really bad," she said in response to his question. "Twenty-seven admitted so far, four dead that we know of. The whole Nara area—that enclave of Japanese-style wood houses that is out behind Vegas, surrounded by the forest—is a disaster. The fire happened too fast. The people panicked."

"Dr. Wakefield, Dr. Wakefield. Please come to room two-oh-four immediately." Nicole hung up the phone and raced down the hall. She bounded up the stairs to the second floor. The man dying in room 204 was an old friend, a Korean, Kim Lee, who had been Nicole's liaison with the Hakone community during the time that she was provisional governor.

Mr. Kim had been one of the first to build a new home in Nara. During the fire he had rushed into his burning house to save his seven-year-old son. The son would live, for Mr. Kim had protected him carefully while he had walked through the flames. But Kim Lee himself had suffered third-degree burns over most of his body.

Nicole passed Dr. Turner in the corridor. "I don't think we can do anything for that friend of yours in room two-oh-four," he said. "I'd like your opinion. Call me down in the emergency room. They just brought in another critical who was trapped in her house."

Nicole took a deep breath and slowly opened the door to the room. Mr. Kim's wife, a pretty Korean woman in her mid-thirties, was sitting quietly in the corner. Nicole walked over and embraced her. While Nicole was comforting Mrs. Kim, the Tiasso who was monitoring all of Mr. Kim's data brought over a set of charts. The man's condition was indeed hopeless. When Nicole glanced up from her reading, she was surprised to see her daughter Ellie, a large bandage on the right side of her head, standing beside Mr. Kim's bed. Ellie was holding the dying man's hand.

"Nicole," Mr. Kim said in an agonized whisper as soon as he recognized her. His face was nothing but blackened skin. Even speaking one word was painful. "I want to die," the man said, nodding at his wife in the corner.

Mrs. Kim stood up and approached Nicole. "My husband wants me to sign the euthanasia papers," she said. "But I am unwilling unless you can tell me that there is absolutely no chance he can ever be happy again." She started to cry but stopped herself.

Nicole hesitated for a moment. "I cannot tell you that, Mrs. Kim," Nicole said grimly. She glanced back and forth between the burned man and his wife. "What I can tell you is that he will probably die sometime in the next twenty-four hours and will suffer ceaselessly until his death. If a medical miracle occurs and he survives, he'll be seriously disfigured and debilitated for the rest of his life."

"I want to die now," Mr. Kim repeated with effort.

Nicole sent the Tiasso for the euthanasia documents. The papers required signatures from the attending physician, the spouse, and the individual himself if, in the opinion of the doctor, he was competent to make his own decisions. While the Tiasso was gone, Nicole motioned to Ellie to meet her out in the hall.

"What are you doing here?" Nicole said quietly to Ellie when they were out of earshot. "I told you to stay at home and rest. You had a bad concussion."

"I'm all right, Mother," Ellie said. "Besides, when I heard that

Mr. Kim was badly burned, I wanted to do something to help. He was such a good friend back in the early days."

"He's in terrible shape," Nicole said, shaking her head. "I can't believe he's still alive."

Ellie reached out and touched her mother on the forearm. "He wants his death to-be useful," she said. "Mrs. Kim talked to me about it. I've already sent for Amadou, but I need for you to talk to Dr. Turner."

Nicole stared at her daughter. "What in the world are you talking about?"

"Don't you remember Amadou Diaba? Eponine's friend, the Nigerian pharmacist with the Senoufo grandmother. He's the one who caught RV-41 from a blood transfusion. . . . Anyway, Eponine told me that his heart is rapidly deteriorating."

Nicole was silent for several seconds. She could not believe what she was hearing. "You want me," she said finally, "to ask Dr. Turner to perform a *manual* heart transplant, right now, in the middle of this crisis?"

"If he decides now, it can be done later tonight, can't it? Mr. Kim's heart can be kept healthy at least that long."

"Look, Ellie," Nicole said, "we don't even know—"

"I already checked," Ellie interrupted. "One of the Tiassos verified that Mr. Kim would be an acceptable donor."

Nicole shook her head again. "All right, all right," she said. "I'll think about it. Meanwhile, I want you to lie down and rest. A concussion is not a trivial injury."

"You're asking me to do *what?*" an incredulous Dr. Robert Turner said to Nicole.

"Now, Dr. Turner," Amadou said in his British accent, "it is not Dr. Wakefield who is really making the request. It is I. I beseech you to perform this operation. And please do not consider it risky. You have yourself told me that I will not live more than three months longer. I know full well that I may die on the operating table. But if I survive, according to the statistics you showed me, I have a fifty-fifty chance of living eight more years. I could even marry and have a child."

Dr. Turner spun around and glanced at the clock on his office wall. "Forget for a moment, Mr. Diaba, that it is past midnight and I have been working nine hours straight with burn victims. Consider what you are asking. I have not performed a heart transplant for *five* years. And I have never *ever* done one without being supported by the finest cardiological staff and equipment on the planet Earth. All the surgical work, for example, was always done by robots."

"I understand all that, Dr. Turner. But it is not really germane. I will certainly die without the operation. There will almost certainly not be another donor in the near future. Besides, Ellie told me that you have recently been reviewing all the heart transplant procedures, as part of your work in preparing your budget request for new equipment—"

Dr. Turner flashed a quizzical look at Ellie. "My mother told me about your thorough preparation, Dr. Turner. I hope you're not upset that I said something to Amadou."

"I will be pleased to assist you in any way I can," Nicole added. "Although I have never done any heart surgery myself, I did complete my residency at a cardiological institute."

Dr. Turner looked around the room, first at Ellie, then at Amadou and Nicole. "Then that settles it, I guess. I don't see where you've given me much choice."

"You'll do it?" Ellie exclaimed with youthful excitement.

"I will try," the doctor answered. He walked over to Amadou Diaba and extended both his hands. "You do know, don't you, that there is very little chance you will ever wake up?"

"Yes, sir, Dr. Turner. But very little chance is better than none. . . . I thank you."

Dr. Turner turned to Nicole. "I'll meet you in my office for a procedure review in fifteen minutes. And by the way, Dr. Wakefield, will you please have a Tiasso bring us a fresh pot of coffee?"

Preparing for the transplant operation brought back memories that Dr. Robert Turner had buried in the recesses of his mind. Once or twice he even imagined for several seconds that he had actually returned to the Dallas Medical Center. He remembered mostly how happy he had been in those distant days on another world. He had loved his work; he had loved his family. His life had been almost perfect.

Drs. Turner and Wakefield carefully wrote down the exact sequence of events that they would follow before they began the procedure. Then, during the operation itself, they stopped to check with each other after each major segment was completed. No untoward events occurred at any time during the procedure. When Dr. Turner removed Amadou's old heart, he turned it over so that Nicole and Ellie (she had insisted on staying in case there was anything she could do to help) could see the badly atrophied muscles. The man's heart was a disaster. Amadou would probably have died in less than a month.

An automatic pump kept the patient's blood circulating while the new heart was "hooked up" to all the principal arteries and veins. This was the most difficult and dangerous phase of the operation. In Dr. Turner's experience, this segment had never ever been performed by human hands.

Dr. Turner's surgical skills had been finely tuned by the many manual operations he had conducted during his three years in New Eden. He surprised even himself with the ease with which he connected the new heart to Amadou's critical blood vessels.

Toward the end of the procedure, when all of the dangerous phases had been completed, Nicole offered to perform the few remaining tasks. But Dr. Turner shook his head. Despite the fact that it was almost dawn in the colony, he was determined to finish the operation himself.

Was it the extreme fatigue that caused Dr. Turner's eyes to play tricks on him during the final minutes of the operation? Or could it perhaps have been the surge of adrenaline that accompanied his realization that the procedure was going to be successful? Whatever the cause, during the terminal stages of the operation, Robert Turner periodically witnessed remarkable changes in the face of Amadou Diaba. Several times his patient's face slowly altered before his eyes, the features of Amadou becoming those of Carl Tyson, the young black man that Dr. Turner had murdered in Dallas. Once, after finishing a stitch, Dr. Turner glanced up at Amadou and was frightened by Carl Tyson's cocky grin. The doctor blinked, and looked again, but it was only Amadou Diaba on the operating table.

After this phenomenon had occurred several times, Dr. Turner asked Nicole if she had noticed anything unusual about Amadou's face. "Nothing but his smile," she replied. "I've never seen anyone smile like that under anesthesia."

When the operation was over and the Tiassos reported that all of the patient's vital signs were excellent, Dr. Turner, Nicole, and Ellie were exultant despite their exhaustion. The doctor invited the two women to join him in his office, for one final celebratory cup of coffee. At that moment, he didn't yet realize that he was going to propose to Ellie.

Ellie was stunned. She just stared at the doctor. He glanced at Nicole and then returned his gaze to Ellie. "I know it's sudden," Dr. Turner said. "But there's no doubt in my mind. I have seen enough. I love you. I want to marry you. The sooner the better."

The room was absolutely quiet for almost a minute. During the silence, the doctor walked over to his office door and locked it. He even disconnected his phone. Ellie started to speak. "No," he said to her with passion, "don't say anything yet. There's something else I must do first."

He sat down in his chair and took a deep breath. "Something that I should have done long ago," he said quietly. "Besides, you both deserve to know the whole truth about me."

Tears welled up in Dr. Turner's eyes even before he began to tell the story. His voice broke the first time he spoke, but he then collected himself and eased into the narrative.

"I was thirty-three years old and blindly, outrageously happy. I was already one of the leading cardiac surgeons in America and I had a beautiful, loving wife with two daughters, aged three and two. We lived in a mansion with a swimming pool inside a country club community about forty kilometers north of Dallas, Texas.

"One night when I came home from the hospital—it was very late, for I had supervised an unusually delicate open heart procedure—I was stopped at the gate of our community by the security guards. They acted rattled, as if they didn't know what to do, but after a phone call and some peculiar glances in my direction, they waved me through.

"Two police cars and an ambulance were parked in front of my house. Three mobile television vans were scattered in the cul-de-sac just beyond my home. When I started to turn in to my driveway, a policeman stopped me. With flashbulbs popping all around and klieg lights from the television cameras blinding my eyes, the policeman led me into my house.

"My wife was lying under a sheet on a cot in the main hall beside the stairway to the second floor. Her throat had been slit. I heard some people talking upstairs and raced up to see my daughters. The girls were still lying where they had been killed—Christie on the floor in the bathroom and Amanda in her bed. The bastard had cut their throats as well."

Huge, desolate sobs wrenched out of Dr. Turner. "I will never forget that horrible sight. Amanda must have been killed in her sleep, for there was no mark on her except for the cut. . . . What kind of human being could kill such innocent creatures?"

Dr. Turner's tears were cascading down his cheeks. His chest was heaving uncontrollably. For several seconds he did not speak. Ellie quietly came over beside his chair and sat on the floor, holding his hand.

"The next five months I was totally numb. I could not work,

I could not eat. People tried to help me—friends, psychiatrists, other doctors—but I could not function. I simply could not accept that my wife and children had been murdered.

"The police had a suspect in less than a week. His name was Carl Tyson. He was a young black man, twenty-three years old, who delivered groceries for a nearby supermarket. My wife always used the television for her shopping. Carl Tyson had been to our home several times before—I even remembered having seen him once or twice myself—and certainly knew his way around the house.

"Despite my daze during that period, I was aware of what was happening in the investigation of Linda's murder. At first, everything seemed so simple. Carl Tyson's fresh fingerprints were found all over the house. He had been inside our community that very afternoon on a delivery. Most of Linda's jewelry was missing, so robbery was the obvious motive. I figured the suspect would be summarily convicted and executed.

"The issue quickly became clouded. None of the jewelry was ever found. The security guards had marked Carl Tyson's entry and departure from the community on the master log, but he was only inside Greenbriar for twenty-two minutes, hardly enough time for him to deliver groceries and commit a robbery plus three murders. In addition, after a famous attorney decided to defend Tyson and helped him prepare his sworn statements, Tyson insisted that Linda had asked him to move some furniture that afternoon. This was a perfect explanation for the presence of his fingerprints all over the house. . . ."

Dr. Turner paused, reflecting, the pain obvious in his face. Ellie squeezed his hand gently and he continued.

"By the time of the trial, the prosecution's argument was that Tyson had brought the groceries to the house in the afternoon and had discovered, after talking with Linda, that I would be in surgery until much later that night. Since my wife was a friendly and trusting woman, it was not unlikely that she might have chatted with the delivery boy and mentioned that I would not be home until late. . . . Anyway, according to the prosecutor, Tyson returned after he finished his shift at the supermarket. He climbed the rock wall that surrounded the country club development and walked across the golf course. Then he entered the house, intending to steal Linda's jewelry and expecting everyone in the family to be asleep. Apparently my wife confronted him and Tyson panicked, killing first Linda and then the children to ensure that there were no witnesses.

"Despite the fact that nobody saw Tyson return to our neighborhood, I thought the prosecution's case was extremely persuasive and that the man would be easily convicted. After all, he had no alibi whatsoever for the time period during which the crime was committed. The mud that was found on Tyson's shoes exactly matched the mud in the creek he would have crossed to reach the back side of the house. He did not show up for work for two days after the murders. In addition, when Tyson was arrested, he was carrying a large amount of cash that he said he won in a poker game.

"During the defense portion of the trial, I really began to have my doubts about the American judicial system. His attorney made the case a racial issue, depicting Carl Tyson as a poor, unfortunate black man who was being railroaded on circumstantial evidence. His lawyer argued emphatically that all Tyson had done on that October day was deliver groceries to my house. Someone else, his attorney said, some unknown maniac, had climbed the Greenbriar fence, stolen the jewelry, and then murdered Linda and the children.

"The last two days of the trial I became convinced, more from watching the body language of the jury than anything else, that Tyson was going to be acquitted. I went insane with righteous indignation. There was no doubt in my mind that the young man had committed the crime. The thought that he might be set free was intolerable.

"Every day during the trial—which lasted about six weeks—I showed up at the courthouse with my small medical bag. At first the security guards checked the bag each time I entered, but after a while, especially since most of them were sympathetic with my anguish, they just let me pass.

"The weekend before the trial concluded I flew to California, ostensibly to attend a medical seminar but actually to buy a black market shotgun that would fit in my medical bag. As I expected, on the day the verdict was being announced, the guards did not make me open my bag.

"When the acquittal was announced, there was an uproar in the courtroom. All the black people in the gallery shouted hooray. Carl Tyson and his attorney, a Jewish guy named Irving Bernstein, threw their arms around each other. I was ready to act. I opened my briefcase, quickly assembled the shotgun, jumped over the barrier, and killed them both, one with each barrel."

Dr. Turner took a deep breath and paused. "I have never admitted before, not even to myself, that what I did was wrong. However, sometime during this operation on your friend Mr. Diaba I understood clearly how much my emotional outrage has poisoned my soul for all these years. . . . My violent act of revenge did not return my wife and children to me. Nor did it make me happy, except for that sick animal pleasure I felt at the instant I knew that both Tyson and his attorney were going to die."

There were now tears of contrition in Dr. Turner's eyes. He glanced over at Ellie. "Although I may not be worthy, I do love you, Ellie Wakefield, and very much want to marry you. I hope that you can forgive me for what I did years ago."

Ellie looked up at Dr. Turner and squeezed his hand again. "I know very little of romance," she said slowly, "for I have had no experience with it. But I do know that what I feel when I think about you is wonderful. I admire you, I respect you, I may even love you. I would like to talk to my parents about this, of course . . . but yes, Dr. Robert Turner, if they do not object I would be very happy to marry you."

8

Nicole leaned over the basin and stared at her face in the mirror. She ran her fingers across the wrinkles under her eyes and smoothed her gray bangs. *You're almost an old woman,* she said to herself. Then she smiled. "I grow old, I grow old, I shall wear the bottoms of my trousers rolled," she said out loud.

Nicole laughed and backed up from the mirror, turning herself around so that she could see what she looked like from the back. The kelly green dress that she planned to wear in Ellie's wedding fit snugly against her body, which was still trim and athletic after all the years. *Not too bad,* Nicole thought approvingly. *At least Ellie won't be embarrassed.*

On the end table beside her bed were the two photographs of Genevieve and her French husband that Kenji Watanabe had given her. After Nicole returned to the bedroom, she picked up the photos and stared at them. *I couldn't be at your wedding, Genevieve,* she thought suddenly with a burst of sadness. *I never even met your husband.*

Struggling with her emotions, Nicole crossed quickly over to the other side of the bedroom. She stared for almost a minute at a photograph of Simone and Michael O'Toole, taken the day of their wedding at the Node. *And I left you only a week after your wedding. . . . You were so very young, Simone,* Nicole thought to herself, *but in many ways you were far more mature than Ellie—*

She did not let herself finish the thought. There was too much heartache in remembering either Simone or Genevieve. It was healthier to focus on the present. Nicole purposely reached up and grabbed the individual picture of Ellie that was hanging on the wall beside her brothers and sisters. *So you will be my third daughter to marry,* Nicole thought. *It seems impossible. Sometimes life moves much too fast.*

A montage of images of Ellie flashed through Nicole's mind. She saw again the shy little baby lying beside her in Rama II, Ellie's awestruck little girl face as they approached the Node in the shuttle, her new adolescent features at the moment of awakening from the long sleep, and finally Ellie's mature determination and courage as she spoke in front of the citizens of New Eden in defense of Dr. Turner's program. It was a powerful emotional journey into the past.

Nicole replaced Ellie's picture on the wall and started to undress. She had just hung her dress in the closet when she heard a strange sound, like someone crying, at the very limit of her hearing. *What was that?* she wondered. Nicole sat still for several minutes, but didn't hear any other noises. When she stood up, however, she suddenly had the eerie feeling that both Genevieve and Simone were in the room with her. Nicole glanced around her quickly, but she was still alone.

What is going on with me? she asked herself. *Have I been working too hard? Has the combination of the Martinez case and the wedding pushed me over the brink? Or is this another of my psychic episodes?*

Nicole tried to calm herself by breathing slowly and deeply. She was not, however, able to shake the feeling that Genevieve and Simone were indeed there in the room with her. Their presence beside her was so strong that Nicole had to restrain herself to keep from talking to them.

She remembered clearly the discussions that she had had with Simone prior to her marriage to Michael O'Toole. *Maybe that's why they are here,* Nicole thought. *They've come to remind me that I've been so busy with my work, I haven't had my wedding talk with Ellie.* Nicole laughed out loud nervously, but the goose bumps remained on her arm.

Forgive me, my darlings, Nicole said to both Ellie's photograph and the spirits of Genevieve and Simone in the room. *I promise that tomorrow—*

This time the shriek was unmistakable. Nicole froze in her bedroom, the adrenaline coursing through her system. Within seconds

she was running across the house to the study where Richard was
working.

"Richard," she said, just before reaching the door to the study,
"did you hear—"

Nicole stopped herself in midsentence. The study was a mess.
Richard was on the floor, surrounded by a pair of monitors and a
jumbled pile of electronic equipment. The little robot Prince Hal
was in one hand and Richard's precious portable computer from the
Newton mission was in the other. Three biots—two Garcias and a
partially disassembled Einstein—were bending over him.

"Why, hello, darling," Richard said nonchalantly. "What are
you doing here? I thought you'd be asleep by now."

"Richard, I am certain that I heard an avian shriek. Only about
a minute ago. It was close by." Nicole hesitated, trying to decide
whether or not to tell him about the visit from Genevieve and
Simone.

Richard's brow furrowed. "I didn't hear anything," he replied.
"Did any of you?" he asked the biots. They all shook their heads,
including the Einstein, whose chest was wide open and connected
by four cables to the monitors on the floor.

"I *know* I heard something," Nicole reiterated. She was silent
for a moment. *Is this another sign of terminal stress?* she asked herself.
Nicole now surveyed the chaos on the floor in front of her. "By the
way, darling, what are you doing?"

"This?" Richard said with a vague sweep of his hand. "Oh, it's
nothing special. Just another project of mine."

"Richard Wakefield," she said quickly, "you are not telling me
the truth. This mess all over the floor could not possibly be 'nothing
special'—I know you better than that. Now, what's so secret—"

Richard had changed the displays on all three of his active monitors and was now shaking his head vigorously. "I don't like this,"
he mumbled. "Not at all." He glanced up at Nicole. "Have you by
any chance accessed my recent data files that are stored in the central
supercomputer? Even inadvertently?"

"No, of course not. I don't even know your entry code. . . .
But that's not what I want to talk about—"

"Somebody has." Richard quickly keyed in a diagnostic security
subroutine and studied one of the monitors. "At least five times in
the last three weeks. You're certain that it wasn't you?"

"Yes, Richard," Nicole said emphatically. "But you're still trying to change the subject. I want you to tell me what *this* is all
about."

Richard set Prince Hal down on the floor in front of him and looked up at Nicole. "I'm not quite ready to tell you, darling," he said after a moment's hesitation. "Please give me a couple of days."

Nicole was puzzled. At length, however, her face brightened. "All right, darling. If it's a wedding present for Ellie, then I'll gladly wait."

Richard returned to his work. Nicole plopped down in the only chair in the room that was not cluttered. As she watched her husband, she realized how tired she was. She convinced herself that her fatigue must have caused her to imagine the shriek. And the visits from Simone and Genevieve.

"Darling," Nicole said softly a minute or two later.

"Yes," he answered, glancing up at her from the floor.

"Do you ever wonder what's *really* going on here in New Eden? I mean, why have we been left so utterly alone by the creators of Rama? Most of the colonists go about their lives with hardly a thought about the fact that they're traveling in an interstellar spaceship constructed by extraterrestrials. How can this be possible? Why doesn't the Eagle or some other equally marvelous manifestation of their superior alien technology suddenly appear? Then maybe our petty problems—"

Nicole stopped when Richard started laughing. "What is it?" she said.

"This reminds me of a conversation that I had once with Michael O'Toole. He was frustrated because I would not accept on faith the eyewitness reports of the apostles. He then told me that God should have known that we were a species of doubting Thomases and should have scheduled frequent return visits from the resurrected Christ."

"But that situation was entirely different," Nicole argued.

"Was it?" Richard replied. "What the early Christians reported about Jesus could not have been any harder to accept than our description of the Node and our long, time-dilating journey at relativistic velocities. . . . It's far more comforting for the other colonists to believe that this spaceship was created as an experiment by the ISA. Very few of them understand science well enough to know that Rama is way beyond our technological capability."

Nicole was silent for a moment. "Then is there *nothing* we can do to convince them—"

She was interrupted by the triple buzz that indicated an incoming phone call was urgent. Nicole stumbled across the floor to answer it. Max Puckett's concerned face appeared on the monitor.

"We have a dangerous situation here outside the detention compound," he said. "There's an angry mob, maybe seventy or eighty people, mostly from Hakone. They want access to Martinez. They've already terminated two Garcia biots and attacked three others. Judge Mishkin is trying to reason with them, but they're in a nasty mood. Apparently Mariko Kobayashi committed suicide about two hours ago. Her whole family is here, including her father.''

Nicole was dressed in a sweat suit in less than a minute. Richard tried vainly to argue with her. "It was *my* decision," she said as she climbed on her bicycle. "I should be the one to deal with the consequences."

She eased down the lane to the main bicycle path and then began to pedal furiously. At top speed she would be at the administrative center in four or five minutes, less than half the time it would take her by train at this time of night. *Kenji was wrong*, Nicole thought. *We should have had a press conference this morning. Then I could have explained the decision.*

Almost a hundred colonists were gathered in the main square of Central City. They were milling around in front of the New Eden detention complex where Pedro Martinez had been held since he was first indicted for the rape of Mariko Kobayashi. Judge Mishkin was standing at the top of the steps in front of the detention center. He was speaking to the angry crowd through a megaphone. Twenty biots, mostly Garcias but with a couple of Lincolns and Tiassos in the group, had locked arms in front of Judge Mishkin and were preventing the mob from climbing the stairs to reach the judge.

"Now, folks," the gray-haired Russian was saying, "if Pedro Martinez is indeed guilty, then he will be convicted. But our constitution guarantees him a fair trial—''

''Shut up, old man," someone shouted from the audience.

"We want Martinez," another voice said.

Off to the left, in front of the theater, six young Orientals were finishing a makeshift scaffold. There was a cheer from the crowd as one of them tied a thick rope with a noose over the crossbar. A burly Japanese man in his early twenties pushed to the front of the crowd. "Move out of the way, old man," he said. "And take these mechanical dolts with you. Our quarrel is not with you. We are here to secure justice for the Kobayashi family."

"Remember Mariko," a young woman shouted. There was a crashing sound as a red-haired boy struck one of the Garcias in the face with an aluminum baseball bat. The Garcia, its eyes destroyed and its face disfigured beyond recognition, made no response but did not give up its place in the cordon.

"The biots will not fight back," Judge Mishkin said into the megaphone. "They are programmed to be pacifists. But destroying them serves no purpose. It is senseless, inane violence."

Two runners coming from Hakone arrived in the square and there was a momentary change in the focus of the crowd. Less than a minute later, the unruly mob cheered the appearance of two huge logs, carried by a dozen youths each. "Now we will remove the biots that are protecting that murderer Martinez," the young Japanese spokesman said. "This is your last chance, old man. Move out of the way before you are hurt."

Many individuals in the crowd ran over to take positions on the logs they intended to use as battering rams. At that moment Nicole Wakefield arrived in the square on her bicycle.

She jumped down quickly, walked through the cordon, and raced up the steps to stand beside Judge Mishkin. "Hiro Kobayashi," she shouted into the megaphone before the crowd had recognized her. "I have come to explain to you why there will be no jury trial for Pedro Martinez. Will you come forward so that I can see you?"

The elder Kobayashi, who had been standing off to the side of the square, walked slowly over to the bottom of the steps in front of Nicole.

"Kobayashi-san," Nicole said in Japanese, "I was very sorry to hear about the death of your daughter—"

"Hypocrite," someone shouted in English, and the crowd began to buzz.

". . . As a parent myself," Nicole continued in Japanese, "I can imagine how terrible it must be to experience the death of a child.

"Now," she said, switching to English and addressing the crowd, "let me explain my decision today to all of you. Our New Eden constitution says that each citizen shall have a 'fair trial.' In all other cases since this colony was originally settled, criminal indictments have led to a trial by jury. In the case of Mr. Martinez, however, because of all the publicity, I am convinced that no unbiased jury can be found."

A chorus of whistles and boos briefly interrupted Nicole. "Our constitution does not define," she continued, "what should be done to ensure a 'fair trial' if no jury of peers is to be involved. However, our judges have supposedly been selected to implement the law and are trained to decide cases on the basis of the evidence. That is why I have assigned the Martinez indictment to the jurisdiction of the New Eden Special Court. There all the evidence—some of which has never heretofore been made public—will be carefully weighed."

"But we all know the boy Martinez is guilty," a distraught Mr.

Kobayashi cried in response. "He has even admitted he had sex with my daughter. And we also know he raped a girl in Nicaragua, back on Earth. . . . Why are you protecting him? What about justice for my family?"

"Because the law—" Nicole started to answer, but was drowned out by the crowd.

"We want Martinez. We want Martinez." The chant swelled as the huge logs, which had been laid on the pavement soon after Nicole's appearance, were again hoisted by the people in the square. As the mob struggled to set up a battering ram, one of the logs inadvertently crashed into the monument marking the celestial location of Rama. The sphere shattered and electronic parts that had indicated the nearby stars tumbled out onto the pavement. The small blinking light that had been Rama itself broke into hundreds of pieces.

"Citizens of New Eden," Nicole shouted into the megaphone, "hear me out. There is something about this case that none of you know. If you will just listen—"

"*Kill the nigger bitch*," shouted the red-haired boy who had struck the Garcia biot with the baseball bat.

Nicole glared at the young man with fire in her eyes. "What did you say?" she thundered.

The chanting suddenly ceased. The boy was isolated. He glanced around nervously and grinned. "Kill the nigger bitch," he repeated.

Nicole was down the steps in an instant. The crowd moved aside as she headed straight for the red-haired boy. "Say it one more time," she said, her nostrils flaring, when she was less than a meter away from her antagonist.

"Kill—" he started.

She slapped his cheek hard with her open hand. The smack resounded through the square. Nicole turned around abruptly and started toward the steps, but hands grabbed her from all sides. The shocked boy doubled up his fist—

At that moment two loud booms shook the square. As everyone tried to ascertain what was happening, two more blasts were detonated in the sky over the heads of the crowd. "That's just me and my shotgun," Max Puckett said into the megaphone. "Now, if you folks will just let the lady judge pass . . . there, that's better . . . and then head on home, we'll all be better off."

Nicole broke free from the hands that were holding her, but the crowd did not disperse. Max raised the gun, aimed it at the thick knot of rope above the noose on the makeshift scaffold, and fired again. The rope exploded into pieces, parts of it falling into the crowd.

"Now, folks," Max said. "I'm a lot more ornery than these two judges. And I already know I'm going to spend some time in this here detention center for violating the colony's gun laws. I'd sure as hell hate to have to shoot some of you as well."

Max pointed his gun at the crowd. Everyone instinctively ducked. Max fired blanks over their heads and laughed heartily as the people began to scurry out of the square.

Nicole could not sleep. Over and over again she replayed the same scene. She kept seeing herself walking into the crowd and slapping the red-haired boy. *Which makes me no better than he is*, she thought.

"You're still awake, aren't you?" Richard said.

"Umm-hm."

"Are you all right?"

There was a short silence. "No, Richard," Nicole answered. "I'm not. . . . I'm extremely upset with myself for striking that boy."

"Hey, come on," he said. "Stop beating yourself up. He deserved it. He insulted you in the worst way. People like that don't understand anything but force."

Richard reached over and began rubbing Nicole's back. "My God," he said, "I've never seen you so tense. You're in knots from one end to the other."

"I'm worried," Nicole said. "I have a terrible feeling that the whole fabric of our life here in New Eden is about to come unraveled. . . . And that everything I have done or am doing is absolutely useless."

"You have done your best, darling. I must confess that I am amazed by how hard you have tried." Richard continued to rub Nicole's back very gently. "But you must remember you're dealing with human beings. You can transport them to another world and give them a paradise, but they still come equipped with their fears and insecurities and cultural predilections. A new world could only *really* be new if all the humans involved began with totally empty minds, like new computers with no software and no operating systems, just loads of untapped potential."

Nicole managed a smile. "You're not very optimistic, darling."

"Why should I be? Nothing I have seen here in New Eden or

on Earth suggests to me that humanity is capable of achieving harmony in its relationship with itself, much less with any other living
creatures. Occasionally there is an individual, or even a group, that
is able to transcend the basic genetic and environmental drawbacks
of the species. . . . But these people are miracles, certainly not the
norm."

"I don't agree with you," Nicole said softly. "Your view is too
hopeless. I believe that most people desperately want to achieve
that harmony. We just don't know how to do it. That's why we
need more education. And more good examples."

"Even that red-haired boy? Do you believe he could be edu-
cated out of his intolerance?"

"I have to think so, darling," Nicole said. "Otherwise . . . I
fear I would simply give up."

Richard made a sound somewhere between a cough and a laugh.

"What is it?" Nicole asked.

"I was just wondering," Richard said, "if Sisyphus ever deluded
himself into believing that maybe the next time the boulder would
not roll down the hill again."

Nicole smiled. "He had to believe there was some chance the
boulder would stay at the summit, or he could not have labored so
hard. . . . At least that's what I think."

9

As Kenji Watanabe descended from the train at Hakone, it was impossible for him not to recall another meeting with Toshio Nakamura, years before, on a planet billions of kilometers away. *He had telephoned me that time too*, Kenji thought. *He had insisted that we talk about Keiko.*

Kenji stopped in front of a shop window and straightened his tie. In the distorted reflection he could easily imagine himself as an idealistic Kyoto teenager on his way to a meeting with a rival. *But that was long ago*, Kenji thought to himself, *with nothing at stake except our egos. Now the entire fate of our little world . . .*

His wife Nai had not wanted him to meet with Nakamura at all. She had encouraged Kenji to call Nicole for another opinion. Nicole also had been opposed to any meeting between the governor and Toshio Nakamura. "He's a dishonest, power-crazy megalomaniac," Nicole had said. "Nothing good can come from the meeting. He just wants to find your weaknesses."

"But he has said that he can reduce tension in the colony."

"At what price, Kenji? Watch out for the terms. That man never offers to do something for nothing."

So why did you come? a voice inside Kenji's head asked him as he stared at the huge palace his boyhood associate had built for himself. *I'm not certain exactly*, another voice answered. *Maybe honor. Or self-respect. Something deep in my heritage.*

Nakamura's palace and the surrounding homes were built of wood in the classic Kyoto style. Blue tile roofs, carefully manicured gardens, sheltering trees, immaculately clean walkways—even the smell of the flowers reminded Kenji of his home city on a faraway planet.

He was met at the door by a lovely young girl in sandals and kimono, who bowed and said, *"Ohairi kudasai,"* in the very formal Japanese way. Kenji left his shoes on the rack and put on sandals himself. The girl's eyes were always on the floor as she guided him through the few Western rooms of the palace into the tatami mat area where, it was said, Nakamura spent most of his free time gamboling with his concubines.

After a short walk the girl stopped and pulled aside a paper screen decorated with cranes in flight. *"Dozo,"* she said, gesturing inside. Kenji walked into the six-mat room and sat cross-legged on one of the two cushions in front of a shiny black lacquer table. *He will be late*, Kenji thought. *That's all part of the strategy.*

A different young girl, also pretty, self-effacing, and dressed in a lovely pastel kimono, came noiselessly into the room carrying water and Japanese tea. Kenji sipped the tea slowly while his eyes roamed around the room. In one corner was a wooden screen with four panels. Kenji could tell from his distance of a few meters that it was exquisitely carved. He rose from his cushion to take a closer look.

The side facing toward him featured the beauty of Japan, one panel for each of the four seasons. The winter picture showed a ski resort in the Japanese Alps smothered in meters of snow; the spring panel depicted the cherry trees in blossom along the Kama River in Kyoto. Summer was a pristine clear day with Mount Fuji's snow-capped summit rising above the verdant countryside. The autumn panel presented a riot of color in the trees surrounding the Tokugawa family shrine and mausoleum at Nikko.

All this amazing beauty, Kenji thought, suddenly feeling deeply homesick. *He has tried to recreate the world we have left behind. But why? Why does he spend his sordid money on such magnificent art? He is a strange, inconsistent man.*

The four panels on the backside of the screen told of another Japan. The rich colors displayed the battle of Osaka Castle, in the early seventeenth century, after which Ieyasu Tokugawa was virtually unopposed as shogun of Japan. The screen was covered with human figures—samurai warriors in battle, male and female members of the court scattered throughout the castle grounds, even the Lord Tokugawa himself, larger than the rest and looking supremely content with his victory. Kenji noticed with amusement that the carved shogun bore more than a passing resemblance to Nakamura.

Kenji was about to sit back down on the cushion when the screen opened and his adversary entered. *"Omachido sama deshita,"* Nakamura said, bowing slightly in his direction.

Kenji bowed back, somewhat awkwardly because he could not take his eyes off his countryman. Toshio Nakamura was dressed in a complete samurai outfit, including the sword and dagger! *This is all part of some psychological ploy*, Kenji told himself. *It is designed to confuse or scare me.*

"Ano, hajememashoka," Nakamura said, sitting down on the cushion opposite Kenji. *"Kocha ga, oishii desu, ne?"*

"Totemo oishii desu," Kenji replied, taking another sip. The tea was indeed excellent. *But he is not my shogun*, Kenji thought. *I must change this atmosphere before any serious discussion starts.*

"Nakamura-san, we are both busy men," Governor Watanabe said in English. "It is important to me that we dispense with the formalities and cut straight to the heart of the matter. Your representative told me on the phone this morning that you are 'disturbed' about the events of the last twenty-four hours and have some 'positive suggestions' for reducing the current tension in New Eden. This is why I have come to talk to you."

Nakamura's face showed nothing; however, the slight hiss as he was speaking indicated his displeasure with Kenji's directness. "You have forgotten your Japanese manners, Watanabe-san. It is grievously impolite to start a business discussion before you have complimented your host on the surroundings and inquired about his well-being. Such impropriety almost always leads to unpleasant disagreement, which can be avoided—"

"I'm sorry," Kenji interrupted with a trace of impatience, "but I don't need a lesson from you, of all people, on manners. Besides, we are not in Japan, we are not even on Earth, and our ancient Japanese customs are about as germane now as the outfit you are wearing—"

Kenji had not intended to insult Nakamura, but he could not have had a better strategy for causing his adversary to reveal his true intentions. The tycoon rose to his feet abruptly. For a moment the governor thought Nakamura was going to draw his samurai sword.

"All right," said Nakamura, his eyes implacably hostile, "we will do this your way. . . . Watanabe, you have lost control of the colony. The citizens are very unhappy with your leadership and my people tell me there is widespread talk of impeachment and/or insurrection. You have botched the environmental and RV-41 issues, and now your black woman judge, after innumerable delays, has announced that a nigger rapist will not be subject to a trial by jury. Some of the more thoughtful of the colonists, knowing that you and I have a common background, have asked me to intercede, to try to convince you to step aside before there is widespread bloodshed and chaos."

This is incredible, Kenji thought as he listened to Nakamura. *The man is absolutely out of his mind.* The governor resolved to say very little in the conversation.

"So you believe I should resign?" Kenji asked after a protracted silence.

"Yes," answered Nakamura, his tone growing more imperious. "But not immediately. Not until tomorrow. Today you should exercise your executive privilege to change the jurisdiction for the Martinez case away from Nicole des Jardins Wakefield. She is obviously prejudiced. Judges Iannella or Rodriguez, either one, would be more appropriate. Notice," he said, forcing a smile, "that I am not suggesting the case be transferred to Judge Nishimura's court."

"Is there anything else?" Kenji asked.

"Only one more thing. Tell Ulanov to withdraw from the election. He doesn't have any chance to win and continuing this divisive campaign will only make it more difficult for us to pull together after the Macmillan victory. We need to be united. I foresee a serious threat to the colony from whatever enemy inhabits the other habitat. The leggies, that you seem to believe are 'harmless observers,' are just their advance scouts. . . ."

Kenji was astonished by what he was hearing. How had Nakamura become so warped? Or had he always been this way?

". . . I must stress that time is of the essence," Nakamura was saying, "especially with respect to the Martinez issue and your resignation. I have asked Kobayashi-san and the other members of the Asian community not to act too hastily, but after last night I'm not certain I can restrain them. His daughter was a beautiful, talented young woman. Her suicide note makes it clear that she could not live with the shame implied by the continual delays in the trial of her rapist. There is genuine anger throughout—"

Governor Watanabe temporarily forgot his resolution to remain quiet. "Are you aware," he said, also standing up, "that semen from two different individuals was found in Mariko Kobayashi after the night during which she was allegedly raped? And that both Mariko and Pedro Martinez repeatedly insisted that they were alone together the entire evening? Even when Nicole hinted to Mariko last week that there was evidence of additional intercourse, the young woman stuck to her story."

Nakamura momentarily lost his composure. He stared blankly at Kenji Watanabe.

"We have not been able to identify the other party," Kenji continued. "The semen samples mysteriously disappeared from the hospital laboratory before the full DNA analysis could be completed. All we have is the record of the original examination."

"That record could be wrong," asserted Nakamura, his self-confidence returning.

"Very, very unlikely. But at any rate, now you can understand Judge Wakefield's dilemma. Everyone in this colony has already decided Pedro is guilty. She did not want a jury to convict him wrongly."

There was a long silence. The governor started to depart. "I'm surprised at you, Watanabe," Nakamura said at length. "You've missed the point of this meeting entirely. Whether or not that jiga-boo Martinez raped Mariko Kobayashi is really not that important. I have promised her father that the Nicaraguan boy will be punished. And that's what counts."

Kenji Watanabe stared at his boyhood classmate with disgust. "I'm going to leave now" he said, "before I become really angry."

"You will not be given another chance," Nakamura said, his eyes again full of hostility. "This was my first and final offer."

Kenji shook his head, pulled back the paper screen himself, and walked out into the corridor.

Nicole was walking along a beach in beautiful sunlight. Ahead of her about fifty meters, Ellie was standing beside Dr. Turner. She was wearing her wedding dress, but the groom was dressed in a bathing suit. Nicole's great-grandfather Omeh was performing the ceremony in his long green tribal robe.

Omeh placed Ellie's hands in Dr. Turner's and began a Senoufo chant. He raised his eyes to the sky. A solitary avian soared over-heard, shrieking in rhythm with the wedding chant. As Nicole watched the avian flying above her, the sky darkened. Storm clouds rushed in, displacing the placid sky.

The ocean began to churn and the wind to blow. Nicole's hair, now completely gray, streamed out behind her. The wedding party was in disarray. Everyone ran inland to escape the coming storm. Nicole could not move. Her eyes were fixed on a large object being tossed upon the waves.

The object was a huge green bag, like the plastic bags used for lawn trash back in the twenty-first century. The bag was full and was coming toward the shore. Nicole would have tried to grab it, but she was afraid of the moiling sea. She pointed at the bag. She yelled for help.

In the upper left-hand corner of her dream screen she saw a long canoe. As it drew closer, Nicole realized that the eight occupants of the canoe were extraterrestrials, orange in color, smaller than humans. They looked as if they were made from bread dough. They had eyes and faces but no bodily hair. The aliens steered the canoe over to the large green bag and picked it up.

The orange extraterrestrials deposited the green bag on the beach. Nicole did not approach until they climbed back into their canoe and returned to the ocean. She waved good-bye to them and walked over to the bag. It had a zipper, which she carefully opened. Nicole pulled back the top half and stared at the dead face of Kenji Watanabe.

Nicole shuddered, screamed, and sat up in bed. She reached over for Richard, but the bed was empty. The digital clock on the table read 2:48 A.M. Nicole tried to slow her breathing and clear her mind of the horrible dream.

The vivid image of the dead Kenji Watanabe lingered in her mind. As she walked over to the bathroom, Nicole remembered her premonitory dreams about the death of her mother, back when she was only ten years old. *What if Kenji is really going to die?* she thought, feeling the first wave of panic. She forced herself to think about something else. *Now where is Richard at this time of night?* she wondered. Nicole pulled on her robe and left the bedroom area.

She walked quietly past the children's rooms toward the front of the house. Benjy was snoring, as usual. The light was on in the study, but Richard was not there. Two of the new biots plus Prince Hal were also gone. One of the monitors on Richard's work table still contained a display.

Nicole smiled to herself and remembered their agreement. She touched the keys NICOLE on the keyboard and the display changed.

Dearest Nicole, [the message appeared], If you awaken before I return, do not worry. I plan to be back by dawn, eight o'clock tomorrow morning at the very latest. I have been doing some work with the 300 series biots—

you remember, the ones that are not completely programmed in firmware and therefore can be designed for special tasks—and have reason to believe that someone has been spying on my work. Therefore, I have accelerated the completion of my current project and have gone outside New Eden for a final test. I love you. Richard.

It was dark and cold out on the Central Plain. Richard tried to be patient. He had sent his upgraded Einstein (Richard referred to it as Super-Al) and Garcia #325 over to the second habitat probe site before him. They had explained to the night watchman, a standard Garcia biot, that the published experiment schedule had changed and that a special investigation was presently going to be conducted. With Richard still out of sight, Super-Al had then withdrawn all the equipment from the opening into the other habitat and placed it on the ground. The process had consumed over an hour of precious time. Now that Super-Al was finally finished, he signaled Richard to approach. Garcia #325 cleverly led the watchman biot off to another area around the probe site so it wouldn't be able to see Richard.

He wasted no time. Richard pulled Prince Hal out of his pocket and put him in the opening. "Go quickly," Richard said, setting his small monitor up on the floor of the passage. The opening into the other habitat had been gradually widened over the weeks so that it was now approximately a square, eighty centimeters on a side. There was more than enough room for the tiny robot.

Prince Hal hurried through to the other side. The drop from the passage to the inside floor was about a meter. The robot adroitly attached a small cable to a stanchion he glued to the floor of the passage and then let himself down. Richard watched Hal's every move on his screen and communicated instructions by radio.

Richard had expected that there would be an outer annulus protecting the second habitat. He was correct. *So the basic design of the two habitats is similar,* he thought. Richard had also anticipated that there would be an opening of some kind in the inner wall, some gate or door through which the leggies must come and go, and that Prince Hal would be small enough to enter the inside of the habitat by the same portal.

It did not take long for Hal to locate the entrance into the main part of the habitat. However, what was obviously a door was also more than twenty meters above the floor of the annulus. Having watched the video recordings of the leggies moving up vertical surfaces on the bulldozer biots at the Avalon survey site, Richard had prepared for this possibility as well.

"Climb," he ordered Prince Hal after a nervous glance at his watch. It was almost six o'clock. Dawn would be coming soon in New Eden. Soon thereafter the regular scientists and engineers would be returning to this probe site.

The entrance to the inside of the habitat was one hundred times Prince Hal's height above the floor. The robot's ascent would be the equivalent of a human going straight up a sixty-story building. At home Richard had had the little robot practice by scaling the house, but he had always been there beside him. Were there grooves for hand- and footholds on the wall Hal was climbing? Richard could not tell from the monitor. Were all the correct equations in Prince Hal's mechanical engineering subprocessor? *I'll find out soon enough*, Richard thought as his star pupil began his climb.

Prince Hal slipped and dangled by his hands once, but eventually succeeded in making it to the top. However, the ascent took another thirty minutes. Richard knew he was running out of time. As Hal pulled himself onto the windowsill of a circular porthole, Richard saw that the robot's ingress into the habitat was blocked by a mesh screen. However, a small part of the interior was barely visible in the dim light. Richard carefully positioned Hal's tiny camera so that it could see through the gridwork.

"The watchman insists it must return to its main station," Garcia #325 announced to Richard on the radio. "It is required to make its daily report at 0630."

Shit, thought Richard, *that's only six minutes*. He moved Hal slowly around on the lip of the porthole to see if he could identify any objects in the habitat interior. Richard could see nothing specific. "Shriek," Richard then ordered, switching the robot's audio volume to full. "Shriek until I tell you to stop."

Richard had not tested the new amplifier he had installed in Prince Hal at its maximum output. He was therefore astonished at the amplitude of Hal's avian mimicry. It resounded from the passage and Richard jumped back. *Pretty damn good*, Richard said after collecting himself. *At least if my memory is accurate.*

The watchman biot was soon upon Richard, following its preprogrammed instructions by demanding his personal papers and an explanation of what he was doing. Super-Al and Garcia #325 tried to confuse the watchman, but when it could not obtain Richard's cooperation, the biot insisted it must make an emergency report. On the monitor, Richard saw the entire mesh screen swing open and six leggies swarmed onto Prince Hal. The robot continued to shriek.

The watchman Garcia began to broadcast its emergency. Richard was aware that he had only a few minutes before he would be forced to leave. *"Come, dammit, come,"* he said, watching the monitor in between furtive glances behind him in the Central Plain. There were no lights yet approaching from his home colony in the distance.

At first Richard thought he had imagined it. Then it repeated, the sound of large wings flapping. One of the leggies was partially obscuring his view, but moments later Richard definitely saw a familiar talon reaching out for Prince Hal. The avian shriek that followed confirmed the sighting. The image on the monitor became fuzzy.

"If you have a chance," Richard screamed into the radio, "try to return to the passage. I'll come back for you later."

He turned around, quickly packing his monitor in his bag. "Let's go," Richard said to his two biot associates. They began to run toward New Eden.

Richard was triumphant as he hurried toward home. *My hunch was right*, he said exultantly to himself. *This changes everything. . . . Now I have a daughter to give away.*

10

The wedding was scheduled to take place at seven o'clock in the evening in the theater at Central High School. The reception, for a much larger group, was planned for the gymnasium, an adjacent building no more than twenty meters away. All day long Nicole struggled with last-minute items, rescuing the preparations from one potential disaster after another.

She did not have time to contemplate the significance of Richard's new discovery. He had come home full of excitement, wanting to discuss the avians, and even who might be spying on his research, but Nicole had simply not been able to focus on anything except the wedding. They had both agreed not to tell anyone else about the avians until after they had had a chance for a lengthy discussion.

Nicole had gone for a morning walk in the park with Ellie. They had talked about marriage, love, and sex for over an hour, but Ellie had been so excited about the wedding that she had not been able to concentrate fully on what her mother was saying. Toward the end of their walk, Nicole had stopped under a tree to summarize her message.

"Remember at least this one thing, Ellie," Nicole had said, holding both her daughter's hands in hers. "Sex is an important component of marriage, but it is not the most important. Because of your lack of experience, it is unlikely that sex will be wonderful for you at the beginning. However, if you and Robert love and trust each other, and both of you genuinely want to give and receive pleasure, you will find that your physical compatibility will increase year after year."

Two hours before the ceremony Nicole, Nai, and Ellie arrived together at the school. Eponine was already there waiting for them. "Are you nervous?" the teacher said with a smile. Ellie nodded. "I'm scared to death," Eponine added, "and I'm only one of the bridesmaids."

Ellie had asked her mother to be matron of honor. Nai Watanabe, Eponine, and her sister Katie were the bridesmaids. Dr. Edward Stafford, a man who shared Robert Turner's passion for medical history, was the best man. Because he had no other close associates, except for the biots at the hospital, Robert picked the rest of his attendants from the Wakefield family and friends. Kenji Watanabe, Patrick, and Benjy were his three groomsmen.

"Mother, I feel nauseous," Ellie said soon after they were all gathered in the dressing room. "I'll be so embarrassed if I throw up on my wedding dress. Should I try to eat something?" Nicole had anticipated this situation. She handed Ellie a banana and some yogurt, assuring her daughter that it was completely normal to feel queasy before such a big event.

Nicole's uneasiness about the day increased as time passed and Katie did not show up. With everything in order in the bride's dressing room, she decided to cross the hall to talk to Patrick. The men had finished dressing before Nicole knocked on their door.

"How is the mother of the bride?" Judge Mishkin asked when she entered. The grand old judge was going to perform the wedding ceremony.

"A little spooked," Nicole answered with a wan smile. She found Patrick in the back of the room, adjusting Benjy's clothes.

"How do I look?" Benjy asked his mother as she approached.

"Very, very handsome," Nicole replied to her beaming son. "Have you talked to Katie this morning?" she asked Patrick.

"No," he said. "But I reconfirmed the time with her, as you requested, just last night. . . . Is she not here yet?"

Nicole shook her head. It was already six-fifteen, only forty-five minutes before the cermony was scheduled to start. She walked out in the hall to use the phone, but the smell of cigarette smoke told her that Katie had finally arrived.

"Just think, little sister," Katie was saying in a loud voice as

Nicole crossed back to the bride's dressing room, "tonight you get to have your first sex. Oooeee! I bet the thought just drives that gorgeous body of yours absolutely wild."

"Katie," Eponine said, "I don't think that's entirely appropriate—"

Nicole walked into the room and Eponine fell silent. "Why, Mother," Katie said, "how beautiful you look. I had forgotten that there was a woman lurking behind those judge's robes."

Katie expelled smoke into the air and took a drink from the champagne bottle on the counter beside her. "So here we are," she said with a flourish, "about to witness the marriage of my baby sister—"

"Stop it, Katie, you've had too much to drink." Nicole's voice was cold and hard. She picked up the champagne and Katie's pack of cigarettes. "Just finish dressing and stop the clowning. You can have these back after the ceremony."

"Okay, Judge . . . whatever you say," Katie said, inhaling deeply and blowing out smoke rings. She grinned at the other ladies. Then, as Katie reached for the wastebasket to flick the ash off her cigarette, she lost her balance. Katie fell painfully against the counter, hitting several open bottles of cosmetics before landing on the floor in a mess. Eponine and Ellie both rushed over to help her.

"Are you all right?" Ellie asked.

"Watch out for your dress, Ellie," Nicole said, looking disapprovingly at Katie sprawled on the floor. Nicole grabbed some paper towels and began cleaning up what Katie had spilled.

"Yeah, Ellie," Katie said sarcastically a few seconds later when she was again standing up. "Watch out for that dress. You want to be absolutely spotless when you marry your double murderer."

Nobody breathed in the room. Nicole was livid. She approached Katie and then stood directly in front of her. "Apologize to your sister," she ordered.

"I will *not*," Katie replied defiantly just moments before Nicole's open hand landed on her cheek. Tears burst into Katie's eyes. "Ah-hah," she said, wiping at her face, "it's New Eden's most famous slapper. Only two days after resorting to physical violence in Central City Square, she strikes her own daughter in a replay of her most famous deed—"

"Mother, don't . . . please," Ellie interrupted, fearing that Nicole would slap Katie again.

Nicole turned around and looked at the distraught bride. "I'm sorry," she mumbled.

"That's right," said Katie angrily. "Tell *her* you're sorry. *I'm* the one you hit, Judge. Remember me? Your older, unmarried daughter? The one you called 'disgusting' only three weeks ago yesterday. . . . You told me that my friends were 'sleazy and immoral'—are those the exact words?—yet your precious Ellie, that paragon of virtue, you hand over to a double murderer . . . with another murderer as a bridesmaid to boot."

All of the women realized at roughly the same moment that Katie was not just drunk and truculent. She was deeply disturbed. Her wild eyes condemned them all as she continued her rambling diatribe.

She is drowning, Nicole said to herself, *and crying desperately for help. Not only have I ignored her cries, I have pushed her deeper into the water.*

"Katie," Nicole said quietly, "I'm sorry. I acted foolishly and without thought." She walked toward her daughter with her arms outstretched.

"No," Katie replied, pushing her mother's arms away. "No, no, no . . . I don't want your pity." She moved back toward the door. "In fact, I don't want to be in this goddamn wedding. . . . I don't belong here. Good luck, little sister. Tell me someday how the handsome doctor is in bed."

Katie turned around and stumbled through the door. Both Ellie and Nicole were silently weeping as she left.

Nicole tried to concentrate on the wedding, but her heart was heavy after the untoward scene with Katie. She helped Ellie put on her makeup again, repeatedly chastising herself for having responded angrily to Katie.

Just before the ceremony started, Nicole returned to the men's dressing room and informed them that Katie had decided not to be in the wedding. She then peeked briefly at the gathering crowd, noticing that there were about a dozen biots already seated. *My goodness,* Nicole thought, *we weren't specific enough in the invitations.* It was not abnormal for some of the colonists to bring their Lincolns or Tiassos with them to special functions, especially if they had children. Before she returned to the bride's dressing room, Nicole fretted momentarily about whether or not there would be enough seats for everybody.

Moments later, or so it seemed, the bridal party was gathered on the stage around Judge Mishkin and the music announced the arrival of the bride. Like everyone else, Nicole turned around and looked to the back of the theater. There was her gorgeous youngest daughter, resplendent in her white dress with the red trim, coming down the aisle on Richard's arm. Nicole fought back the tears, but when she saw big drops glistening on the cheeks of the bride, she could control herself no longer. *I love you, my Ellie,* Nicole said to herself. *How I hope that you will be happy.*

Judge Mishkin had prepared an eclectic ceremony at the couple's request. It praised the love of a man and a woman, and talked about how important their bond was in the proper creation of a family. His words counseled tolerance, patience, and selflessness. He offered a nondenominational prayer, invoking God to "call forth" from the bride and groom that "compassion and understanding that ennobles the human species."

The ceremony was short, but elegant. Dr. Turner and Ellie exchanged rings and recited their vows with strong, positive voices. They turned to Judge Mishkin and he placed their hands together. "With the authority granted me by the colony of New Eden, I pronounce Robert Turner and Eleanor Wakefield husband and wife."

As Dr. Turner was gently lifting Ellie's veil for the traditional kiss, a shot rang out, followed an instant later by another. Judge Mishkin pitched forward on the bridal couple, blood spurting from his forehead. Kenji Watanabe collapsed beside him. Eponine dove between the bridal couple and the guests as a third and fourth shots were heard. Everyone was screaming. There was chaos in the theater.

Two more shots followed in rapid succession. In the third row Max Puckett finally disarmed the Lincoln biot that had been the gunman. Max had turned around almost instantly, as soon as he had heard the first shot, and had leapt over the chairs a second later. However, the Lincoln biot, who had risen from its seat at the word *wife,* fired its automatic gun a total of six times before Max subdued it completely.

Blood was all over the stage. Nicole crawled over and examined Governor Watanabe. He was already dead. Dr. Turner cradled Judge Mishkin as the gracious old man closed his eyes for the final time. The third bullet had apparently been intended for Dr. Turner, for Eponine had caught it in her side after her frantic dive to save the bride and groom.

Nicole picked up the microphone that had fallen with Judge Mishkin. "Ladies and gentlemen. This is a terrible, terrible tragedy. Please do not panic. I believe there is no more danger. Please just hold your places until we can tend to the injured."

The final four bullets had not done too much damage. Eponine was bleeding, but her condition was not critical. Max had struck the Lincoln just before it fired the fourth bullet, almost certainly saving Nicole's life, since that particular bullet had missed her by only centimeters. Two of the guests had been grazed by the final shots as the Lincoln was falling.

Richard joined Max and Patrick, who were restraining the killer biot. "He won't answer a single goddamn question," Max said.

Richard looked at the Lincoln's shoulder. The biot was number 333. "Take him into the back," Richard said. "I want to look at him later."

On the stage Nai Watanabe was sitting on her knees, holding the head of her beloved Kenji on her lap. Her body was trembling with deep, desperate sobs. Beside her the twins Galileo and Kepler were wailing with fright. Ellie, blood all over her wedding dress, was trying to comfort the little boys.

Dr. Turner was attending to Eponine. "An ambulance should be here in just a few minutes," he said after dressing her wound. He kissed her on the forehead. "There's no way that Ellie and I can ever thank you for what you did."

Nicole was down with the guests, making certain that neither of the bystanders who had been struck by bullets was seriously injured. She was about to return to the microphone and tell everyone that they could begin to leave when a hysterical colonist burst into the theater.

"An Einstein has gone mad," he shouted before surveying the scene in front of him. "Ulanov and Judge Iannella are both dead."

"We should both leave. And now," Richard said. "But even if you won't, Nicole, I am going to go. I know too much about the three-hundred-series biots—and what Nakamura's people have done to change them. They'll be after me tonight or in the morning."

"All right, darling," Nicole replied. "I understand. But I cannot go. Someone must stay to take care of the family. And to fight Nakamura. Even if it's hopeless. We must not submit to his tyranny."

It was three hours after the aborted end of Ellie's wedding. Panic was sweeping the colony. The television had just reported that five or six biots had simultaneously gone mad and that as many as eleven of New Eden's most prominent citizens had been killed. Luckily the Kawabata biot performing the concert in Vegas had failed in its attack on gubernatorial candidate Ian Macmillan and noted industrialist Toshio Nakamura.

"Bullshit," Richard had said as he had watched. "That was just another part of their plan."

He was certain that the entire assassination activity had been planned and orchestrated by the Nakamura camp. Moreover, Richard had no doubt that he and Nicole had also been intended targets. He was convinced that the day's events would result in a totally different New Eden under the control of Nakamura, with Ian Macmillan as his puppet governor.

"Won't you at least say good-bye to Patrick and Benjy?" Nicole asked.

"I'd better not," Richard answered. "Not because I don't love them, but because I'm afraid I might change my mind . . ."

"Are you going to use the emergency exit?" Nicole said.

Richard nodded. "They'd never let me out the normal way."

While he was checking his diving apparatus Nicole came into the study. "It was just reported on the news that people are smashing their biots all over the colony. One of the colonists interviewed said the entire mass murder was part of an alien plot."

"Great," Richard said grimly. "The propaganda has already begun."

He packed as much food and water as he thought he could comfortably carry. When he was ready, he held Nicole tightly against him for over a minute. There were tears in both their eyes as he departed.

"Do you know where you're going?" Nicole asked softly.

"More or less," Richard answered as he stood in the back door. "I'm not telling you, of course, so you can't be implicated . . . Please tell the children good-bye for me."

"Be careful," she said. They both heard something at the front of the house and Richard dashed out into the backyard.

The train to Lake Shakespeare was not running. The Garcia operating an earlier train on the same track had been terminated by a group of angry colonists and the whole system had shut down. Richard began walking toward the eastern side of Lake Shakespeare.

As he trudged along carrying his heavy diving equipment and backpack, he had the feeling that he was being followed. Twice Richard thought he saw someone out of the corner of his eye, but when he stopped and looked around, he saw nothing. Finally he reached the lake. It was after midnight. He took one final look at the lights of the colony and began to put on his diving apparatus. Richard's blood ran cold as a Garcia came out of the bushes while he was undressing.

He expected to be killed. After several long seconds the Garcia spoke. "Are you Richard Wakefield?" it asked.

Richard did not move or say anything. "If you are," the biot said at length, "I am bringing a message from your wife. She says she loves you and Godspeed."

Richard took a long slow breath. "Tell her I love her also," he said.

THE TRIAL

1

In the deepest part of Lake Shakespeare there was an open entrance to a long submarine channel that ran under both the village of Beauvois and the habitat wall. During the design of New Eden, Richard, who had had considerable practical experience with contingency engineering, had stressed the importance of an emergency exit from the colony.

"But what would you need it for?" the Eagle had asked.

"I don't know," Richard had said. "But unforeseen situations often arise in life. A robust engineering design always has contingency protection."

Richard swam carefully through the tunnel, slowing down every several minutes to check his air supply. When he reached the end he moved through a series of locks that left him eventually in a dry subterranean passage. He walked for about a hundred meters before he removed his diving apparatus and stored it at the side of the tunnel. When he reached the exit, which was at the eastern edge of the enclosed area that included both the habitats in the Northern Hemicylinder of Rama, Richard pulled his thermal jacket out of his waterproof pack.

Even though he realized that nobody could possibly know where he was, Richard opened the round door in the passage ceiling very cautiously. Then he eased out into the Central Plain. *So far, so good,* he thought, breathing a sigh of relief. *Now for Plan B.*

For four days Richard remained on the eastern side of the plain. Using his excellent small binoculars, he could see the lights indicating activities around the control center, the Avalon region, or the second habitat probe site. As Richard had anticipated, there were search parties out in the interhabitat region for a day or two, but only one group came in his direction and they were easy for him to avoid.

His eyes grew accustomed to what he had thought was total darkness in the Central Plain. Actually there was a small amount of background light, due to reflection off the surfaces of Rama. Richard conjectured that the source or sources of the light must be in the Southern Hemicylinder, on the other side of the far wall of the second habitat.

Richard wished that he could fly, so that he would be able to soar over the walls and move freely in the vastness of the cylindrical world. The existence of the very low levels of reflected light piqued his interest in the rest of Rama. Was there still a Cylindrical Sea to the south of the barrier wall? Did New York still exist as an island in that sea? And what, if anything, was in the Southern Hemicylinder, a region even larger than the one that contained the two northern habitats?

On the fifth day after his escape Richard awoke from an especially disturbing dream about his father and started to walk in the direction of what he now called the avian habitat. He had shifted his sleeping pattern to be directly opposite the diurnal cycle in New Eden, so the time inside the colony was about seven in the evening. He assumed that all the humans who were working at the probe site had already finished for the day.

When he was about half a kilometer away from the opening in the avian habitat wall, Richard stopped to verify, using his binoculars, that there were no longer any people in the region. He then sent Falstaff to decoy the site watchman biot.

Richard was not certain how uniform the passage was that led into the second habitat. He had drawn an eighty-centimeter square on the floor of his study, and had convinced himself that he should be able to crawl through it. But what if the size of the passage was irregular? *We'll find out soon enough,* Richard said to himself as he approached the site.

Only one set of cables and instruments had been reinserted into the passage, so it was not difficult for Richard to clear them out.

Falstaff had also been successful—Richard neither heard nor saw the watchman biot. He threw his small pack into the opening and then tried to climb in himself. It was impossible. He took off his jacket first, then his shirt, pants, and shoes. Wearing only his underwear and socks, Richard could barely fit into the passage. He tied his clothes together in a bundle, affixed them to the side of his pack, and squeezed into the opening.

It was a very slow crawl. Richard inched forward on his stomach using his hands and elbows, pushing his pack in front of him. He brushed his body against the walls and the ceiling with every movement. He stopped, his muscles already beginning to tire, after he was fifteen meters into the tunnel. The other side was still almost forty meters away.

As he rested Richard realized that his elbows, knees, and even the top of his balding head were already scraped and bleeding. Retrieving bandages from his pack was out of the question—just rolling over on his back and looking behind him was a monumental effort in the cramped quarters.

He also realized that he was very cold. While he had been crawling, the energy required to make forward progress had kept him warm. Once he had stopped, however, his exposed body had chilled rapidly. Having so much of his body resting against cold, metallic surfaces did not help either. His teeth began to chatter.

Richard pressed on slowly, painfully, for another fifteen minutes. Then his right hip cramped and in his body's involuntary response he smashed his head against the top of the passage. A little woozy from the blow, he became alarmed when he felt blood running down the side of his head.

There was no light in front of him. The dim illumination that had allowed him to monitor Prince Hal's progress had vanished. He struggled to roll over and see behind him. It was dark everywhere and he was becoming cold again. Richard felt his head and tried to determine how severely he had been cut. His panic started when he realized that he was still hemorrhaging.

Until that moment he had not felt claustrophobic. Now, all of a sudden, wedged into a dark passage that Richard could feel pressing against him from all sides, he felt as if he could not breathe. The walls seemed to be crushing him. He could not control himself. He screamed.

In less than half a minute some kind of light was being shone into the passage from his rear. He heard the funny English accent of the Garcia biot but could not understand what it was saying.

Almost certainly, he thought, *it is filing an emergency report. I'd better move quickly.*

He began to crawl again, ignoring his fatigue, his bleeding head, and his skinless knees and elbows. Richard estimated that he had only ten more meters to go, fifteen at the most, when the passage seemed to shrink. He couldn't get through! He strained every muscle, but it was useless. He was definitely stymied. While he was trying to find a different crawling position that might be more geometrically favorable, he heard a soft pitter-patter approaching him from the direction of the avian habitat.

Moments later they were all over him. Richard spent five seconds of absolute terror before his mind informed him that the tickling sensations he was feeling all over his skin were caused by the leggies. He remembered seeing them on television—little spherical creatures about two centimeters in diameter attached to six radially symmetrical, multijointed legs almost ten centimeters long if fully extended.

One had stopped and was directly on his face, its legs straddling his nose and mouth. He tried to brush it off but bumped his head again. Richard began squirming around to shake off the leggies and somehow managed to make forward progress. With the leggies still all over him, he crawled the final meters to the exit.

He reached the outer avian annulus just as he heard a human voice behind him. "Hello, is there somebody in there?" it said. "Whoever you are, please identify yourself. We're here to help you." A strong searchlight illuminated the passage.

Richard now discovered he had another problem. His exit was one meter above the floor of the annulus. *I should have crawled backward*, he thought, *and dragged my pack and clothes. It would have been much easier.*

It was too late for hindsight. With his pack and clothes on the floor below him and a second human voice now asking questions from behind, Richard continued to crawl forward until his body was halfway out of the passage. When he felt himself falling, Richard put his hands behind his head, tucked his chin against his chest, and tried to make himself into a ball. He then bounced and rolled into the avian annulus. As he was falling the leggies jumped off and disappeared in the darkness.

The lights the humans were shining into the passage reflected off the inner wall of the annulus. After first ascertaining that he was not injured, and that his head was no longer seriously bleeding, Richard picked up his belongings and hobbled two hundred meters to the left. He stopped just under the porthole where Prince Hal had been captured by the avian.

Despite his fatigue, Richard wasted no time scaling the wall. As soon as he had finished dressing and tending to his wounds, he started the ascent. He was certain that a deployable camera would soon be pushed into the annulus to look for him.

Fortunately, there was a small ledge in front of the porthole that was large enough to accommodate Richard. He sat there while he cut through the metal mesh screen and then pushed it aside. He expected the leggies to show up at any minute, but he remained alone. Richard didn't see or hear anything from the habitat interior. Although he twice tried to summon Prince Hal on his radio, there was no response to his call.

Richard stared into the complete darkness of the avian habitat. *What is in there?* he wondered. The atmosphere in the interior, he reasoned, must be the same as that in the annulus, because air was allowed to circulate freely back and forth. Richard had just decided to pull out his flashlight for a look into the habitat interior when he heard sounds below and behind him. Seconds later he saw a light beam coming in his direction down on the floor of the annulus.

He scrunched himself over toward the interior of the habitat as far as he dared, to avoid the light, and listened carefully to the sounds. *It's the deployable camera,* he thought. *But it has limited range. It cannot operate without the tether.*

Richard sat very still. *What do I do now?* he said to himself, when it became apparent that the light attached to the camera was continuing to sweep the same area below the porthole. *They must have seen something. If I turn on my flashlight and there's any reflection, they'll know where I am.*

He dropped a small object from his pack into the habitat to ensure that its floor level was the same as the annulus. He heard nothing. Richard tried another, slightly larger object, but still there was no sound of it striking the floor.

His heart rate surged as his mind told him that the floor of the habitat interior was far below the floor of the annulus. He recalled the basic structure of Rama, with its thick external shell, and realized that the habitat bottom could be several hundred meters below where he was sitting. Richard leaned over and stared again into the void.

The deployable camera suddenly stopped moving and its light remained focused on a specific spot in the annulus. Richard guessed that something must have fallen out of his pack while he was hurriedly hobbling from the passage to the area underneath the porthole. He knew that other lights and cameras would be coming soon. In his mind's eye Richard envisioned being captured and taken back to New Eden. He did not know specifically which colony laws he had broken, but he knew that he had committed many violations. A deep resentment coursed through him as he contemplated spending months or even years in detention. *Under no circumstances*, he told himself, *will I let that happen*.

He reached down the inside wall of the habitat to ascertain if there were enough irregularities to find places to put his feet and hands. Satisfied that it was not an impossible descent, he fumbled in his pack for his climbing line and anchored one end of it to the hinges supporting the mesh door. *Just in case I should slip*, he told himself.

A second light was now in the annulus behind him. Richard eased himself into the habitat with the line wrapped securely around his waist. He did not rappel, but he did use the line for occasional support while he was groping for footholds in the dark. The climb was not technically difficult; there were many small ledges on which Richard could place his feet.

Down and down he went. When he estimated that he had descended sixty or seventy meters, Richard decided to stop and take his flashlight out of his pack. He was not comforted when he shone the light down the wall. He still could not see the bottom. What he could see, maybe fifty more meters below him, was very diffuse, like a cloud, or even fog. *Great*, thought Richard sarcastically, *that's just great*.

Another thirty meters and he had reached the end of his climbing line. Richard could already feel the moisture from the fog. By now he was extremely tired. Since he was not willing to give up the security of the line, he backtracked up the wall a few meters, wrapped the line around himself several times, and went to sleep with his body pressed against the wall.

2

His dreams were very strange. Often he was falling, head over heels, down, down, and never hitting a bottom. In the last dream before Richard awakened, Toshio Nakamura and two Oriental toughs were interrogating him in a small room with white walls.

When he woke up Richard did not know where he was for several seconds. His first movement was to pull his right cheek away from the metallic surface of the wall. A few moments later, after Richard recalled that he had gone to sleep in a vertical position on the wall in the interior of the avian habitat, he switched on his flashlight and looked down. His heart skipped a beat when he saw that the fog was no longer there. Instead he could see the wall extending far, far below, and what appeared to be water where the wall finally terminated.

He leaned his head back and gazed above him. Since he knew he was about ninety meters below the porthole (the climbing line was a hundred meters long), he estimated that the distance down to the water was about two hundred and fifty more meters. His knees became weak as his brain began to comprehend fully his predicament. When Richard started to untangle himself from the extra loops he had made in the line before going to sleep, he noticed that his arms and hands were trembling.

He had a tremendous desire to flee, to ascend again to the porthole, and then leave this alien world altogether. *No*, Richard told himself, fighting his instinctive reaction. *Not yet. Only if there are no other viable options.*

He decided he would first have something to eat. Very gingerly Richard freed himself from part of the line and pulled some food and water out of his pack. Then he turned partially around and pointed his light into the interior of the habitat. Richard thought he could see shapes and forms off in the distance, but he couldn't be certain. *It could be just my imagination*, he thought.

When he was finished eating, he checked his food and water supplies and then made a mental list of his options. *It's all very simple*, Richard said to himself with a nervous laugh. *I can return to New Eden and become a convict. Maybe even a corpse. Or I can give up the security of my line and continue on down the wall.* He paused a moment, glancing up and down. *Or I can stay here and hope for a miracle.*

Remembering that an avian had come quickly when Prince Hal had shrieked, Richard began to shout. After two or three minutes, he stopped shouting and started to sing. He sang intermittently for most of an hour. He began with tunes from his days at Cambridge University and then switched to songs that had been popular during his lonely teenage years. Richard was astonished by how well he remembered the lyrics. *The memory is an amazing device*, he mused to himself. *What accounts for its selective reliability? Why can I remember almost all the words of these dumb songs from my adolescence and virtually nothing from my odyssey in Rama?*

Richard was reaching into his pack for another drink of water when there was suddenly light in the habitat. He was so startled that his feet slipped off the wall and all his weight was on the climbing line for a few seconds. The light was not blinding, as it had been when dawn had arrived in Rama II while he was riding the chairlift, but it was light nevertheless. As soon as Richard was again secure, he surveyed the world that was now unveiled in front of him.

The source of the illumination was a great, hooded ball hanging from the ceiling of the habitat. Richard estimated that the ball was about four kilometers away from him and roughly one kilometer directly above the top of the most prominent structure in sight, a large brown cylinder in the geometrical center of the habitat. An opaque hood covered the top three fourths of the glowing ball, so most of its light was directed downward.

The basic design principle of the habitat interior was radial symmetry. At its center was the upright brown cylinder, looking as if it was made from soil, that probably measured fifteen hundred meters from top to bottom. Richard of course could only see one side of the structure, but from its curvature he estimated that its diameter was between two and three kilometers.

There were no windows or doors on the outside of the cylinder. No light escaped anywhere from its interior. The only pattern on the side of the structure was a set of widely spaced curved lines, each one of which started at the top and ran entirely around the cylinder before reaching the bottom directly underneath its point of origination. The bottom of the cylinder was sitting on an elevated plateau at approximately the same altitude as the porthole through which Richard had entered.

Circumscribing the cylinder was an array of small white structures that formed a ring about three hundred meters in diameter. The two northern quadrants (Richard had entered the avian habitat through the north porthole) of this ring were identical; each quadrant had fifty or sixty buildings that were laid out in the same pattern. Richard assumed from the symmetry that the other two quadrants would conform to the same design.

A thin circular canal, maybe seventy or eighty meters wide, surrounded the ring of structures. Both the canal and the white buildings were located on the plateau at the same altitude as the bottom of the brown cylinder. Outside the canal, however, a large region of what appeared to be growing things, primarily green in color, occupied most of the rest of the habitat. The ground in this green region sloped monotonically down from the canal to the shores of the four-hundred-meter-wide moat that was just inside the interior wall. The four apparently identical quadrants in the green region were further subdivided into four sectors each, which Richard, basing his designations on Earth analogues, called jungle, forest, grassland, and desert.

For about ten minutes Richard stared quietly at the vast panorama. Because the level of illumination dropped in direct proportion to the distance from the cylinder, he could not see the closer regions any more clearly than those in the distance. Nevertheless, the details were still impressive. The more he looked, the more new things he noticed. There were small lakes and rivers in the green region, an occasional tiny island in the moat, and what looked like roads between the white buildings. *Of course,* he found himself thinking. *Why would I have expected otherwise? We have reproduced a small Earth in New Eden. This must represent, in some way, the home planet of the avians.*

His last thought reminded him that both Nicole and he had been convinced from the beginning that the avians were no longer (if they had ever been) a high-technology, spacefaring species. Richard pulled out his binoculars and studied the brown cylinder in the distance. *What secrets do you hold?* he wondered, thrilled momentarily by the possibilities for adventure and discovery.

Richard next searched the skies for some sign of the avians. He was disappointed. He thought he saw flying creatures once or twice at the top of the brown cylinder, but the flecks flitted in and out of his binocular vision so quickly that he couldn't be absolutely certain. Everywhere else he looked—in all parts of the green region, in the neighborhood of the white buildings, even in the moat—he saw no evidence of movement. There was no positive indication that anything was alive in the avian habitat.

The light disappeared after four hours and Richard was again left in the dark in the middle of the vertical wall. He checked his thermometer, including its historical data base. The temperature had not varied more than half a degree from twenty-six degrees Celsius since he had entered the habitat. *Impressive thermal control,* Richard said to himself. *But why so stringent? Why use so much of the power resource to keep a fixed temperature?*

As the darkness stretched into hours, Richard became impatient. Even though he regularly rested each set of muscles by temporarily supporting himself in different ways with his line, his body was slowly wearing out. It was time for him to consider taking some action. Reluctantly he decided that it would be foolhardy for him to abandon the line and descend to the moat. *What would I do when I reached there anyway?* he thought. *Swim across? And then what? I'd still have to turn around if I didn't find food immediately.*

He began to climb slowly toward the porthole. While he was resting about halfway to the exit he thought he heard something very faint off to his right. Richard stopped and quietly reached into his pack for his receiver set. With a minimum of motion he turned the gain up to its highest level and put on the earphones. At first he heard nothing. But after several minutes he picked up a sound below him, coming from the moat. It was impossible to identify exactly what he was hearing—it could have been several boats moving through the water—but there was no doubt that some kind of activity was occurring down there.

Was that a faint flapping of wings as well, again somewhere off to his right? With no warning Richard suddenly screamed at the top of his lungs, and then truncated the scream abruptly. The flurry of wing sounds died out quickly, but for a second or two they were unmistakable.

Richard was exultant. "I know you're there," he shouted gleefully. "I know you're watching me."

He had a plan. It was certainly a long shot, but it was definitely better than nothing. Richard checked his food and water, assured himself that they were both marginally adequate, and took a deep breath. *It's now or never,* he thought.

He practiced descending without relying on the line for support. It made progress more difficult, but he could do it. When he reached the end of the line, Richard unharnessed himself and shone his light down the wall. At least as far as the top of the fog, which by now had returned, there were plenty of ledges available. He continued down very carefully, admitting to himself that he was frightened. Several times he thought he could hear his own heart beating in his earphones.

Now, if I'm right, Richard thought when he descended into the fog, *I'm going to have company down here.* The moisture made the descent doubly difficult. Once he slipped and almost fell, but he managed to recover. Richard stopped at a spot where his hand- and footholds were unusually solid. He estimated that he was about fifty meters above the moat. *I'll wait now until I hear something. They'll have to come closer in the fog.*

In a short while he heard the wings again. This time it sounded as if it was a pair of avians. Richard stood where he was for over an hour, until the fog began to thin. Several more times he heard the wings of his observers.

He had planned to wait until it was light again to descend all the way to the water. But when the fog lifted and the lights still did not return, Richard began to worry about the time. He started down the wall in the dark. About ten meters above the moat he heard his observers fly away. Two minutes later the interior of the avian habitat was again illuminated.

Richard wasted no time. His plan was simple. Based on the boatlike noises that he had heard in the dark, Richard assumed that there was something happening in the moat that was critical to the avians or whoever it was that lived in the brown cylinder. If not, he reasoned, why had they proceeded with the activity, knowing that he might hear it? If they had postponed it for even a few hours, he would almost certainly have been gone from the habitat.

Richard intended to enter the moat. *If the avians feel threatened in any way*, he reasoned, *they will take some action. If not, I will immediately begin my ascent and take my chances in New Eden.*

Just before he eased into the water, Richard took off his shoes and with some difficulty put them into his waterproof pack. At least they wouldn't be wet if he had to climb out. Seconds later, as soon as he was completely in the water, a pair of avians flew at him from where they had been hiding in the green region directly across the moat.

They were frantic. They jabbered and shrieked and acted as if they were going to tear Richard apart with their talons. He was so ecstatic that his plan had worked that he virtually ignored their displays. The avians hovered over him and tried to herd him back to the wall. He treaded water and studied them closely.

These two were slightly different from the ones that he and Nicole had encountered in Rama II. These avians had the velvet body coverings, just like the others, but the velvet was purple. The single ring around each of their necks was black. They were also smaller (*Perhaps they're younger*, Richard thought) than the earlier avians, and much more frenetic. One of the creatures actually touched Richard's cheek with its talon when he didn't move swiftly enough to the wall.

At length Richard did climb up onto the wall, barely out of the water, but that did not seem to appease the avians. Almost immediately the two large birds began taking turns flying narrow patterns up the wall, showing Richard that they wanted him to ascend. When he didn't move they became more and more frantic.

"I want to go with you," Richard said, pointing at the brown cylinder in the distance. Each time he repeated his hand signal the huge creatures shrieked and jabbered and flew up in the direction of the porthole.

The avians were becoming frustrated and Richard started to worry that perhaps they might attack him. Suddenly he had a brilliant idea. *But can I remember the entry code?* he asked himself excitedly. *It's been so many years.*

When he reached in his pack the avians flew away immediately. "That proves," Richard said out loud as he switched on his beloved portable computer, "that the leggies *are* your electronic observers. How else could you have possibly known that human beings may keep weapons in packs like these?"

He punched five letters on the keyboard and then smiled broadly when the display activated. "Come here," Richard said, waving at the pair of avians who had retreated almost to the other side of the moat. "Come here," he repeated, "I have something to show you."

He held up the monitor and displayed the complex computer graphic that he had used many years before in Rama II to convince the creatures to carry Nicole and him across the Cylindrical Sea. It was an elegant graphic showing three avians carrying two human figures across a body of water in a harness. The two giant birds approached tentatively. *That's it*, Richard said to himself excitedly. *Come over here and take a good look.*

3

Richard did not know exactly how long he had been living in the dim room. He had lost track of time soon after they had taken his pack away from him. His routine had been the same, day after day. He slept in the corner of the room. Whenever he awakened, whether from a nap or a long sleep, two avians would enter his room from the corridor and hand him a manna melon to eat. He knew they came through the locked door at the end of the corridor, but if he tried to sleep near the door they simply denied him his food. It had been an easy lesson for Richard to learn.

Every other day or so a different pair of avians would enter his prison and clean up his wastes. His clothes were rank, and Richard knew that he was unbearably filthy, but he had not been able to communicate to his captors that he wanted a bath.

He had been exultant in the beginning. When the two juvenile avians had finally approached close enough to watch the graphic, and then had made their first attempt to take the computer from him several minutes later, Richard had decided to program the display to repeat indefinitely.

In less than an hour the largest avian he had ever seen, one with a gray velvet body and three brilliant cherry red rings around its neck, had returned with the two juveniles, and the three of them had picked Richard up in their talons. They had carried him across the moat, put him down temporarily in a desert area, and then, after a series of jabbers among the three of them that must have been a discussion about the optimal way of carrying him, they had lifted him high into the air.

It had been a breathtaking flight. The view that Richard had had of the landscape in the habitat had reminded him of a ride he had once taken in a hot air balloon in southern France. He had flown in the clutches of the avians all the way to the top of the brown cylinder, directly underneath the bright hooded ball. They had been met by a half dozen additional avians, one holding Richard's computer, which was still repeating its graphics. Later they had been escorted down a wide vertical corridor into the interior of the cylinder.

That first fifteen hours or so Richard had been taken from one large group of avians to another. He had thought that his hosts were just introducing him to all the citizens of avianland. Assuming that there were not too many avians who attended more than one of the short jabber and shriek sessions, Richard estimated that there were about seven hundred individual birds.

After his parade through the conference halls of the avian realm, Richard had been taken to a small room where the three-ringed avian and two of its associates, each large creatures as well with three red neck rings, watched him day and night for about a week. During that time Richard was allowed access to his computer and all the items in the pack. At the end of that observation period, however, they had taken away all his belongings and moved him to his prison.

That must have been three months ago, give or take a week, Richard said to himself one day as he began his twice-daily walk that was his primary regular exercise. The corridor outside his room was approximately two hundred meters long. He usually made eight complete laps, back and forth from the door at the end of the corridor to the rock wall just outside his room.

And during this entire period there has not been one single visit from the leaders. So the observation period must have been my trial—at least the avian equivalent. . . . And was I found guilty of something? Is that why I have been restricted to this dingy cell?

Richard's shoes were wearing out and his clothes were already tattered. Since the temperature was comfortable (he conjectured that it must be twenty-six degrees Celsius everywhere in the avian habitat), he wasn't worried about being cold. But for many reasons he wasn't looking forward to being naked all the time after his clothes eventually disintegrated. He smiled to himself, remembering his modesty during the observation period. *Taking a crap when three giant birds are watching your every move is certainly not an easy task.*

He had grown tired of eating manna melon for every meal, but at least it was nourishing. The liquid at the center was refreshing and the moist meat had a pleasant taste. But Richard longed for something different to eat. *Even that synthetic stuff from Rama II would be a welcome change,* he had told himself several times.

In his solitude Richard's greatest challenge had been to retain his mental acumen. He had begun by doing mathematical problems in his head. More recently, worried that the sharpness of his memory had already decayed measurably because of his age, he had started to pass the time by reconstructing events and even entire major chronological segments of his life.

Of particular interest to him during these memory exercises were the huge gaps associated with his odyssey in Rama II during the voyage from the Earth to the Node. Although it was difficult for Richard to recall many specific events from the odyssey, eating the manna melon always evoked memory fragments from his long stay with the avians during that journey.

Once, after a meal, he had suddenly recalled a large ceremony with many avians. He had remembered a fire in a domelike structure and all the avians wailing in unison after the fire was over. Richard had been puzzled. He had not been able to remember anything about the context of the memory. *Where did that take place? Was that just before I was captured by the octospiders?* he had wondered. But as usual, when he had tried to remember something about what he had experienced with the octospiders, he had ended up with a whopping headache.

Richard was thinking about his earlier odyssey again when, on the last lap of his daily walk, he passed underneath the solitary light in the corridor. He looked in front of him and saw that the door to his prison was open. *That's it,* he said to himself, *I've finally gone crazy. Now I'm seeing things.*

But the door remained open as he approached it. Richard walked on through, stopping to touch the open door and to verify that he had not lost his sanity. He passed two more lights before he came to a small open storage room on the right. Eight or nine manna melons were neatly stacked on the shelves. *Ah-ha,* Richard thought. *I get it. They've expanded my prison. From now on I'm allowed to obtain my own food. Now, if there's just a bathroom somewhere. . . .*

Farther down the hallway there was indeed running water in

another small room on the left. Richard drank heartily, washed his face, and was sorely tempted to bathe. However, his curiosity was too strong. He wanted to know the extent of his new domain.

The corridor that ran just outside his cell ended at a perpendicular intersection. Richard could go either way. Thinking perhaps that he was in some kind of maze to test his mental capabilities, he dropped his outer shirt at the intersection and proceeded to the right. There were definitely more lights in that direction.

After he had walked for twenty meters or so, he saw a pair of avians approaching in the distance. Actually he heard their jabber first, for they were involved in an animated discussion. When they were only five meters away Richard stopped. The two avians glanced at him, acknowledged him with a short shriek at a different pitch, and then continued on down the corridor.

He next encountered a trio of avians with roughly the same interaction. *What is going on here?* Richard wondered as he continued to walk. *Am I no longer in prison?*

In the first large room that he passed, four avians were sitting together in a circle, passing a set of polished sticks back and forth and jabbering constantly. Later, just before the hallway widened into a major meeting room, Richard stood in the doorway of another chamber and watched with fascination as a pair of leggies did what appeared to be push-ups on the top of a square table. Half a dozen quiet avians studied the leggies intently.

There were twenty of the birdlike creatures in the meeting room. They were all gathered around a table, staring at a paperlike document that had been spread out in front of them. One of the avians had a pointer in its talon and was using it to indicate specific items on the document. There were strange squiggles on the paper that were totally incomprehensible, but Richard convinced himself that the avians were looking at a map.

When Richard tried to move closer to the table so that he could see better, the avians in front of him graciously moved aside. Once in the ensuing conversation, Richard even thought from the body language around the table that one of the questions had been directed at him. *I really am losing my mind,* he told himself, shaking his head.

But I still don't know why I have been given all this freedom, Richard thought as he sat in his room and ate his manna melon. Six weeks had passed since he had found the door to his prison opened. Many changes had been made in his cell. Two of the lanternlike lights had been installed on his walls and Richard was now sleeping on a pile of material that reminded him of hay. There was even a constantly filled container of fresh water in the corner of his room.

Richard had felt certain, when his restrictions were initially lifted, that it was only a matter of hours or at most a day or two before something really significant happened. In a sense he had been correct, for the next morning two juvenile aliens had awakened him from his sleep and begun his avian language lessons. They had started with simple items, like the manna melon, water, and Richard himself, at which they would first point and then slowly repeat a sound, clearly the jabberword for that particular item. With some effort Richard had learned a great deal of vocabulary, although his ability to differentiate between closely related shrieks and jabbers was not too sharp. He was absolutely hopeless when it came to making the sounds on his own. He simply didn't have the physical equipment to speak in the avian language.

But Richard had expected that somehow his knowledge of the bigger picture would become clearer, and that had not happened. Certainly the avians were trying to educate him, and they had given him freedom to roam anywhere he wanted in their cylinder—he even ate with them occasionally when he was in their midst and the manna melons showed up—but what was it all for? The way they looked at him, especially the leaders, suggested to Richard that they were expecting some kind of response. *But what response?* Richard asked himself for the hundredth time as he finished his manna melon.

As far as Richard could tell, the avians did not have a written language. He had seen no books and none of the creatures ever wrote anything. There were those strange maplike documents that they occasionally studied, or at least that was Richard's interpretation of their activity, but they never created any of them . . . or *marked* on any of them. It was a puzzle.

And what about the leggies? Richard encountered the creatures two or three times a week and once had a pair in his room for several hours, but they would never sit still and let him analyze one of them. One time, when he had tried to grasp a leggie in his hand, Richard had received a rude shock, an electric current almost certainly, that had caused him to release the leggie immediately.

Richard's mind jumped from image to image as he tried to ascertain some sensible pattern to his life in avianland. He was extremely frustrated. Yet he would not accept for a minute that there was *no* plan behind his capture and then subsequent increased freedom. He continued to search for an answer by reviewing all his experiences in their domain.

There was only one major area of the avian living quarters that was off limits to Richard, and he probably could not have reached it anyway since he was unable to fly. Occasionally he would see one or two avians descend in the great vertical corridor and go below the levels that he normally frequented. Once Richard even saw a pair of hatchlings, no larger than a human hand, being carried up from the dark regions below. On another occasion Richard had pointed down at the darkness and his accompanying avian had shaken its head. Most of the creatures had learned the simple head motions of yes and no in Richard's language.

But somewhere, Richard thought, *there must be additional information. I must be missing some clues.* He vowed to conduct an exhaustive survey of the entire avian living area, including not only the dense apartments on the opposite side of the vertical corridor, where he usually felt unwanted, but also the large manna melon storehouses on the bottom level. *I will make a thorough map,* he said to himself, *to make certain that I haven't neglected something critical.*

As soon as Richard had rendered the avian living area in his three-dimensional graphics, he knew what he had been overlooking. The often disorganized passageways in the cylinder, including horizontal and vertical corridors for both walking and flight, had never been synthesized by Richard into one coherent picture. *Of course,* he said to himself as he projected different views of his complex map onto his computer monitor. *How could I have been so stupid? More than seventy percent of the cylinder is still unaccounted for.*

Richard resolved to take his computer pictures to one of the avian leaders and request, somehow, to see the rest of the cylinder. It was not an easy task. Some kind of crisis was disturbing the avians that particular day, as the corridors were full of jabbers, shrieks, and avians rushing to and fro. Out in the great vertical corridor Richard watched thirty or forty of the largest creatures fly up and out of the cylinder in some kind of organized formation.

Finally Richard managed to obtain the attention of one of the three-ringed giants. It was fascinated by the detail it saw on the computer monitor and by all the different geometrical representations of its home. But Richard was unable to convey his primary message— that he wanted to see the rest of the cylinder.

The leader called in some colleagues to watch the demonstration and Richard was treated to appreciative avian jabber. He was dismissed, however, when another bird broke into their meeting with what must have been important news about their ongoing crisis.

Richard returned to his cell. He was dejected. He lay on his hay mat and thought of the family that he had left behind in New Eden. *Maybe it's time for me to leave,* he thought, wondering what the protocol was in avianland for obtaining permission to depart. While he was lying down a visitor came into his room.

Richard had never seen this particular avian before. It had four cobalt blue rings around its neck and the velvet covering of its body was a deep black with occasional white tufts. Its eyes were astonishingly clear and—or so Richard surmised—very sad. The avian waited for Richard to stand and then started speaking, very slowly. Richard understood some of the words, most importantly the oft-repeated combination "follow me."

Outside his cell three other avians were respectfully standing. They walked behind Richard and his important visitor. The group left Richard's cell area, crossed the single bridge that spanned the great vertical corridor, and entered the section of the cylinder where the manna melons were stored.

At the back of one of the manna melon storehouses were indentations in the wall that Richard had not noticed when he had conducted his survey. When Richard and the avians approached within a few meters of the indentations, the wall slid to the side and revealed what appeared to be an enormous elevator. The avian superleader gestured for him to enter.

Once he was inside, the four avians each jabbered good-bye and formed into a circle to formalize their parting with a turn and a bow. Richard tried his best to imitate their jabber for good-bye before he also bowed and backed into the elevator. The wall closed seconds later.

4

The elevator ride was painfully slow. The immense car had a square floor approximately twenty meters on a side, with a ceiling that was another eight to ten meters above Richard's head. The floor of the car was flat everywhere except for two pairs of parallel grooves, one pair on either side of Richard, that ran from the door to the back of the elevator. *They can certainly transport huge loads in this,* Richard thought, staring at the ceiling far above him.

He tried to estimate the rate of descent of the elevator, but it was impossible. He had no frame of reference. According to Richard's map of the cylinder, the manna melon storehouses should have been about eleven hundred meters above the base. *So if we're going all the way to the bottom, at what would be a normal elevator speed on Earth, then this trip may take several minutes.*

It was the longest three minutes of his life. Richard had absolutely no idea what he would find when the elevator doors opened. *Maybe I'll be outside,* he thought suddenly. *Maybe I'll be on the edge of that region with the white structures. . . . Could they be sending me home?*

He had just begun to wonder how life might have changed in New Eden when the elevator came to a stop. The large doors opened and for several seconds Richard was certain that his heart had jumped out of his body. Standing directly in front of him, and obviously staring at him with all their eyes, were two creatures far stranger than any he had ever imagined.

Richard could not move. What he was seeing was so unbelievable that he was physically paralyzed while his mind struggled with the bizarre inputs it was receiving from his senses. Each of the beings in front of him had four eyes on its "head." In addition to the two large, milky ovals on either side of an invisible line of symmetry that bisected the head, each creature had two additional eyes attached to stalks raised ten to twelve centimeters above the top of its forehead. Behind the large head, their bodies had three segments, with a pair of appendages for each segment, giving them six legs altogether. The aliens were standing upright on their two back legs, their front four appendages neatly tucked against their smooth, cream-colored underbellies.

They moved toward him in the elevator and Richard backed away, frightened. The two creatures turned to each other and communicated in a high-frequency noise that originated from a small circular orifice below the oval eyes. Richard blinked, felt dizzy, and dropped down on one knee to steady himself. His heart was still pumping furiously.

The aliens also changed position, putting their middle legs on the floor. In that posture they resembled giant ants with their front two legs off the ground and their heads raised high. The entire time the black spheres at the end of the eye stalks continued to pivot, scanning the full three hundred and sixty degrees, and the milky material in the dark brown ovals moved from side to side.

For several minutes they sat more or less stationary, as if they were encouraging Richard to examine them. Fighting against his fear, he tried to study them in an objective, scientific fashion. The creatures were roughly the size of medium-sized dogs, but they certainly weighed much less. Their bodies were thin and quite trim. The front and back segments were larger than the middle one, and all three body divisions displayed a polished carapace on top that was made of some kind of hard material.

Richard would have classified them as very large insects except for their extraordinary appendages, which were thick, perhaps even muscled, and covered with a short, very dense, black-and-white-striped "hair" that made it appear as if the creatures were wearing panty hose. Their hands, if that was the proper appellation, were free of the hairy covering and had four fingers each, including an opposing thumb on the front pair.

Richard had just summoned enough courage to look again at

their incredible heads when there was a high-pitched, sirenlike noise behind the two aliens. They turned around. Richard stood up and saw a third creature approaching at a rapid clip. Its motion was marvelous to watch. It ran like a cat with six legs, stretching out parallel to the ground and pushing off with a different pair of legs at each point in its stride.

The three engaged in a quick conversation and the newcomer, lifting up its head and front legs, motioned unambiguously for Richard to leave the elevator. He walked out behind the trio and entered a very large chamber.

This room was a manna melon storehouse also, but that was its only similarity to the one in the avian portion of the cylinder. High technology and automated equipment were everywhere. In the ceiling ten meters above them, a mechanical cherry picker was moving on a rail system. It would grasp individual melons and load them in freight cars on grooves at one end of the room. While Richard and his hosts watched, a freight car moved down the groove and came to a stop in the elevator.

The creatures bounced off down one of the aisles in the room and Richard hastened to follow. They waited for him at the door, then raced to their left, looking backward to see if he was still in sight. Richard ran after them for most of the next two minutes, until they reached a wide open atrium, many meters high, with a transportation device in its center.

The device was a remote cousin of the escalator. Actually there were two of them, one going up and another down, that spiraled around the two thick poles in the center of the atrium. The escalators moved very quickly at quite a steep angle. Every five meters or so they reached the next level, or floor, and the passengers then walked a meter to the spiral escalator around the other pole. What passed for a railing on the side of the escalator was a barrier only thirty centimeters high. The alien creatures rode in the horizontal position, with all six legs on the moving ramp. Richard, who was standing originally, quickly dropped down to all fours to keep from falling out.

During the ride a dozen or so other aliens, riding on the down half of the escalator, passed Richard and gawked at him with their amazing faces. *But how do they eat?* Richard wondered, noting that the circular hole they used for communication was certainly not large enough for much food. There were no other orifices on their heads, although there were some small knobs and wrinkles whose purposes were unknown.

Where they were taking Richard was on the eighth or ninth level. All three of the creatures waited for him until he reached the appointed platform. Richard followed them into a hexagonal building with bright red markings on the front. *That's funny*, Richard thought, staring at the strange squiggles. *I've seen that writing before. . . . Of course, on the map or whatever document it was the avians were reading.*

Richard was placed in a room that was well lit and tastefully decorated in black and white with geometric patterns. There were objects around him of all shapes and sizes, but Richard had no idea what any of them were. The aliens used sign language to inform Richard that this was where he was going to stay. Then they departed. A weary Richard studied the furniture, trying to figure out which thing might be the bed, and then stretched out on the floor to sleep.

Myrmicats. That's what I'll call them. Richard had awakened after sleeping for four hours and could not stop thinking about the alien creatures. He wanted to give them a good name. After dismissing both cat-ant and catsect, he remembered that someone who studies ants is called a myrmecologist. He chose myrmicat because it looked better in his mind when spelled with an *i* instead of an *e*.

Richard looked around him. Every place he had been in the myrmicat habitat had had good illumination, which was in marked contrast to the dark, catacomblike corridors of the upper portions of the brown cylinder. *I have not seen any of the avians since the elevator ride*, Richard was thinking. *So apparently these two species do not live together. At least not completely. But they both use manna melons. . . . What exactly is their connection?*

A pair of myrmicats bounded through the entry, placed a neatly sectioned melon and a cup of water in front of him, and then disappeared. Richard was both hungry and thirsty. Several seconds after he had finished with his breakfast, the pair of creatures returned. Using the hands on their front legs, the myrmicats gestured for him to stand up. Richard stared at them. *Are these the same creatures as yesterday?* he wondered. *And are they the same pair that brought the melon and the water?* He thought back over all the myrmicats he had seen, including those who had passed him going down the escalator. He could not recall a single distinguishing or identifying characteristic in any individual. *So they all look the same?* he thought. *Then how do they tell each other apart?*

The myrmicats led him out into the corridor and bolted away to the right. *This is great*, Richard said to himself, starting to jog after spending a few seconds admiring the beauty of their gait. *They must think humans are all athletes.* One of the myrmicats stopped about forty meters in front of him. It did not turn around, but Richard could tell it was watching him because both of its stalk eyes were bent back in his direction. "I'm coming," Richard shouted. "But I can't run that fast."

It wasn't long before Richard figured out that the pair of aliens was giving him a guided tour of the myrmicat domain. The tour was very logically planned. The first stop, a very brief one, was at a manna melon storehouse. Richard watched two freight cars filled with melons slide down grooves into an elevator similar to (or identical with) the one in which he had descended the day before.

After another five-minute jog, Richard entered an entirely different section of the myrmicat den. Whereas the walls in the other section had been mostly metallic gray or white, except in his room, here the rooms and corridors were all decorated profusely, either with colors or geometric patterns or both. One vast chamber was about the size of a theater and had three liquid pools in its floor. About a hundred myrmicats were in this room, half apparently swimming in the pools (with only their stalk eyes and the top half of their carapaces above the water line), and the other half either sitting on the ridges dividing the three pools from each other, or milling around in a weird building on the far side of the room.

But were they actually swimming? On closer inspection Richard noticed that the creatures did not move around in the pool—they just submerged in a given spot and stayed under the water for several minutes. Two of the pools were quite thick, roughly the consistency of a rich, creamy soup on Earth, and the third, clear pool was almost certainly water. Richard followed a single myrmicat as it moved from one of the thick pools to the water, then over to the other thick pool. *What are they doing?* Richard wondered. *And why have they brought me here?*

As if on cue he was tapped on the back by one of the myrmicats. It pointed to Richard, then to the pools, and then to Richard's mouth. He had no idea what it was telling him. The guide myrmicat next walked down the slope toward the pools and submerged itself in one of the thicker pools. When it returned it stood on its back pair of legs and pointed to the grooves between the segments of its soft, cream-colored underbelly.

It was clearly important to the myrmicats that Richard understand what was going on at the pools. At the next stop he watched a combination of myrmicats and some high-technology machines grinding up fibrous material and then mixing it with water and other liquids to create a thin slurry that looked like what was in one of the pools. At length one of the aliens put its finger into the slurry and then touched the material to Richard's lips. *They must be telling me that the pools are for feeding,* Richard thought. *So they don't eat manna melon after all? Or at least they have a more varied diet? This is all fascinating.*

Soon they were off on another jog to another distant corner of the den. Here Richard saw thirty or forty smaller creatures, obviously juvenile myrmicats, engaged in activities with supervisory adults. In physical appearance the little ones resembled their elders except for one major difference—they had no carapace. Richard concluded that the hard top covering was probably not exuded by the creature until its growth was complete. Although Richard imagined that what he saw occurring with the juveniles was a rough approximation of school, or perhaps a nursery, he of course had no way of knowing for certain. But at one point he was sure that he heard the juveniles repeating in unison a sequence of sounds made by an adult myrmicat.

Richard next rode the escalator with his pair of tour guides. On about the twentieth level the creatures left the escalator and the open atrium, racing quickly down a corridor that ended in a vast factory filled with myrmicats and machines engaged in an impressive array of tasks. His guides always seemed to be in a hurry, so it was difficult for Richard to study any particular process. The factory was like a machine shop on Earth. There were noises of all kinds, smells of chemicals and metals, and the whine of myrmicat communication throughout the room. At one position Richard watched a pair of myrmicats repair a cherry picker similar to the machine that he had seen operating in the manna melon storehouse the day before.

In one corner of the factory was a special area that was sealed off from the rest of the work. Although his guides did not lead him in that direction, Richard's curiosity was piqued. Nobody stopped him when he crossed the threshold of the special area. Inside the large cubicle a myrmicat operator was presiding over an automated manufacturing process.

Long, skinny, jointed pieces of light metal or plastic came into the room on a conveyor belt from one direction. Small spheres about two centimeters in diameter entered from an adjacent cubicle on another conveyor. Where the two belts merged, a large, rectangular machine, mounted in housing that was hanging from the high ceiling, descended onto the parts with a peculiar sucking sound. Thirty seconds later the myrmicat operator caused the machine to withdraw and a pair of leggies scrambled off the belt, folded their long legs around them, and jumped into positions in a box that looked like a gigantic egg carton.

Richard watched the process repeat several times. He was fascinated. He was also slightly bewildered. *So the myrmicats make the leggies. And the maps. And probably the spacecraft too, wherever they and the avians come from. So what is this? Some advanced kind of symbiosis?*

He shook his head as the leggie assembly process in front of him continued. Moments later Richard heard a myrmicat noise behind him. He turned around. One of his guides extended a slice of manna melon in his direction.

Richard was becoming exhausted. He had no idea how long he had been touring, but he felt as if it had been many, many hours.

There was no way he could possibly synthesize everything he had seen. After the ride in the small elevator to the upper reaches of the myrmicat region, where Richard not only had visited the avian hospital staffed and run by the myrmicats, but also had watched the avians hatching out of brown, leathery eggs under the watchful eyes of myrmicat doctors, Richard knew for certain that there was indeed a complex symbiotic relationship between the two species. *But why?* he wondered as his guides allowed him to rest temporarily near the top of the escalator. *The avians clearly benefit from the myrmicats. But what do these giant ant-cats get from the avians?*

His guides led him down a broad corridor toward a large door several hundred meters in the distance. For once they were not running. As they neared the door, three other myrmicats entered the hallway from smaller side corridors and the creatures began to talk in their high-frequency language. At one point all five of them stopped and Richard imagined that an argument was under way. He studied them carefully while they talked, especially their faces. Even the wrinkles and folds around the noisemaking orifice and oval eyes were identical from creature to creature. There was absolutely no way of distinguishing one myrmicat from another.

At length the entire group began again to walk toward the door. From the distance Richard had underestimated its size. As he drew near, he could see that it was twelve to fifteen meters tall, and more than three meters wide. Its surface was intricately and magnificently carved, the central focus of the artwork being a square, four-panel decoration with a flying avian in the upper left quadrant, a manna melon in the upper right, a running myrmicat in the lower left partition, and something that looked like cotton candy with scattered thick, clustered lumps in the lower right.

Richard stopped to admire the artwork. At first he had a vague feeling that he had seen this door, or at least the design, before, but he told himself that it couldn't be possible. However, as he was running his fingers across the sculpted figure of the myrmicat, his memory suddenly awoke. *Yes,* Richard thought excitedly to himself, *of course. At the back of the avian lair in Rama II. That was where the fire was.*

Moments later the door swung open and Richard was ushered into what resembled a large underground cathedral. The room in which he found himself was over fifty meters tall. Its basic floor shape was a circle, about thirty meters in diameter, and there were six separate naves off to the side, around the circle. The walls were dazzling. Virtually every square inch contained sculptures or supporting frescoes meticulously created with great attention to detail. It was overwhelmingly beautiful.

At the center of the cathedral was an elevated platform on which a myrmicat was standing and speaking. Below him were a dozen others, all sitting on their back four legs and watching the speaker with rapt attention.

As Richard wandered around in the room he realized that the decorations on the wall, in a meter-wide strip about eighty centimeters above the floor, were telling an orderly story. Richard quietly followed the artwork until he reached what he thought was the beginning of the story. The first decoration was a sculptured portrait of a manna melon. In the next three panels something could be seen growing inside the melon. Whatever was growing was tiny in the second panel, but by the fourth sculpture it occupied almost the entire interior of the melon.

In the fifth panel a tiny head with two milky, oval eyes, stalk nubs, and a small circular orifice below the eyes could be seen poking its way out of the melon. The sixth sculpture, which showed a juvenile myrmicat very much like the ones Richard had seen earlier in the day, confirmed what he had been surmising as he had been following the decorations. *Holy shit,* Richard said to himself. *So a manna melon is a myrmicat egg!* His thoughts raced ahead. *But that doesn't make sense. The avians eat the melons. . . . In fact, the myrmicats even feed them to me. . . . What's going on here?*

Richard was so astonished by what he had discovered (and so tired from all the running during the tour) that he sat down in front of the sculpture containing the juvenile myrmicats. He tried to figure out the relationship between the myrmicats and the avians. He could cite no parallel symbiosis on Earth, although he was well aware that species often worked together to improve each other's chances for survival. But how could one species remain friendly with another when its eggs were the sole food for the second species? Richard concluded that what he had thought were fundamental biological tenets did not apply to the avians and the myrmicats.

While Richard was pondering the strange new things he had learned, a group of myrmicats gathered around him. They all motioned for him to stand up. A minute later he was following them down a winding ramp on the other side of the room to a special crypt in the basement of their cathedral.

For the first time since Richard had entered the habitat the lighting was dim. The myrmicats beside him moved slowly, almost reverently, as they proceeded down a broad passage with an arched ceiling. At the other end of the passage was a pair of doors that opened into a large room filled with a soft white material. Although the material, which looked like cotton from a distance, was densely arrayed, its individual filaments were mostly very thin, except where they came together in clumps, or ganglia, that were scattered in no definable pattern throughout the large white volume.

Richard and the myrmicats stopped in the entryway, a meter or so away from where the material began. The cottony network extended in all directions for as far as Richard could see. While he was studying its intricate mesh construction, the elements of the material very slowly began to move, pulling apart to form a lane that would continue the path from the passage into the interior of its network. *It's alive,* Richard thought, his pulse racing as he watched in fascination and terror.

Five minutes later, an alley had opened up that was just large enough for Richard to walk ten meters into the material. The myrmicats around him were all pointing toward the cottony web. Richard started shaking his head. *I'm sorry, fellas,* Richard wanted to say, *but there's something about this situation that I don't like. So I'll just skip this part of the tour if it's all right with you.*

The myrmicats kept pointing. Richard had no choice, and he knew it. *What is it going to do to me?* he asked as he took his first step forward. *Eat me? Is that what this has been all about? That would make no sense at all.*

He turned around. The myrmicats had not moved. Richard took a deep breath and walked the full ten meters into the lane, to a spot where he could reach out and touch one of the odd ganglia in the living mesh. As he was examining the ganglion carefully, the material around him began to move again. Richard whirled around and saw that the lane behind him was closing. Momentarily frantic, he tried to run in that direction, back toward the passage, but it was a waste of energy. The net caught him and he resigned himself to accept whatever was going to happen next.

Richard stood perfectly still as the web enveloped him. The tiny elements, like threads, were about a millimeter wide. Slowly, steadily, they began to cover his body. *Wait,* Richard thought, *wait. You're going to suffocate me.* But surprisingly, even though hundreds of filaments were already wrapping around his head and face, he was having no difficulty breathing.

Before his hands were immobilized, Richard tried to pull one of the tiny elements off his arm. It was almost impossible. As they had been wrapping around him, the threads had also been making insertions in his skin. After many tugs, he finally succeeded in freeing the white filaments from one small portion of his forearm, but he was bleeding in the areas that had been freed. Richard surveyed his body and estimated that he probably had a million or so pieces of the living mesh underneath the outer layer of his skin. He shuddered.

Richard was still amazed that he had not suffocated. As his mind began to wonder how air was getting to him through the web, he heard another voice inside his head. *Stop trying to analyze everything,* it said. *You'll never understand it anyway. For once in your life just experience the incredible adventure.*

5

Again Richard had lost track of time. Sometime during the days (or had it been weeks?) that he had been living inside the alien net, he had changed positions. His clothes had also been removed by his hosts during one of his long naps. Richard was now lying on his back, supported by an extremely dense section of the fine mesh network enveloping his body.

His mind no longer actively wondered how he was managing to survive. Somehow, whenever he felt hunger or thirst, his needs were swiftly satisfied. His wastes always disappeared within minutes. Breathing was easy even though he was completely surrounded by the living web.

Richard passed many of his conscious hours studying the creature around him. If he looked carefully, he could see the tiny elements constantly in motion. The patterns in the net around him altered very slowly, but they definitely did change. Richard mentally plotted the trajectories of the ganglia that he could see. At one point three separate ganglia migrated into his vicinity and formed a triangle in front of his head.

The net developed a regular cycle of interacting with Richard. It would keep its millions of filaments attached to him for fifteen to twenty hours at a time, and then release him completely for several hours. Richard slept without dreaming whenever he was not attached to the web. If he happened to awaken still in the unattached mode, he was enervated and listless. But each time the threads began to wind around him again he felt a renewed surge of energy.

His dreams were active and vivid if he slept while attached to the alien net. Richard had never dreamed much before and had often laughed at Nicole's preoccupation with her dreams. But as his sleeping images became more complex, and in some cases quite bizarre, Richard began to appreciate why Nicole paid so much attention to them. One night he dreamed that he was again a teenager and was watching a theatrical performance of *As You Like It* in his hometown of Stratford-on-Avon. The lovely blond girl who was playing Rosalind came down from the stage and whispered in his ear.

"Are you Richard Wakefield?" she asked in the dream.

"Yes," he answered.

The actress began to kiss Richard, first slowly, then more passionately with a lively, tickling tongue darting around inside his mouth. He felt a surge of overpowering desire and then woke up abruptly, strangely embarrassed by both his nakedness and his erection. *Now, what was that all about?* Richard wondered, echoing the phrase he had often heard from Nicole.

At some stage in his captivity his recollections of Nicole became much sharper, more clearly delineated. Richard found to his surprise that in the absence of other stimuli he was able, if he concentrated, to recall entire conversations with Nicole, including such details as the kind of facial expressions she used to punctuate her sentences. In the protracted solitude of his long period inside the web, Richard often ached with loneliness, the vivid memories making him miss his beloved wife even more.

His memories of the children were equally sharp. He missed them all as well, especially Katie. He remembered his last conversation with his special daughter, several days before the wedding, when she had come by the house to pick up some of her clothes. Katie had been depressed, and needed support, but Richard had been unable to help her. *The connection just wasn't there*, Richard thought. The recent image of Katie as a sexy young woman was replaced by a picture of a reckless ten-year-old girl scampering across the plazas of New York. The juxtaposition of the two images provoked a profound feeling of loss in Richard. *I was never comfortable with Katie after she awakened*, he realized with a sigh. *I still wanted my little girl.*

The clarity of his recollections of Nicole and Katie convinced

Richard that something extraordinary was happening to his memory. He discovered that he could also recall the exact scores of every World Cup quarterfinal, semifinal, and final between 2174 and 2190. Richard had known all that useless information as a young man, for he had been an avid soccer fan. However, during the years before the launch of the Newton, when so many new things had crowded into his brain, he had often been unable, even during soccer discussions with his friends, to recall even the participants in a key World Cup match.

As the visual images from his memories continued to sharpen, Richard found that he was also recalling the emotions that had been associated with the pictures. It was almost as if he were completely reliving the experiences. In one long recollection he remembered not only the overpowering feelings of love and adoration that he had felt for Sarah Tydings when he had first seen her perform onstage, but also the thrill and excitement of their courtship, including the unbridled passion of their first night of love. It had left him breathless then; and now, many years later, enveloped by an alien creature resembling a neural net, Richard's response was equally powerful.

Soon it seemed as if Richard no longer had any control over which memories were activated in his brain. In the beginning, or so he believed, he had purposely thought about Nicole or his children or even his courtship with the young Sarah Tydings, just to make himself happy. *Now*, he said one day in an imaginary conversation with the sessile net, *after refreshing my memory—for God knows what purpose—it seems that you are reading it all out.*

For many hours Richard enjoyed the forced memory readout, especially those portions covering his life at Cambridge and the Space Academy, when his days were enlivened by the constant joy of new knowledge. Quantum physics, the Cambrian explosion, probability and statistics, even the long-forgotten vocabulary words from his German lessons reminded him how much of his happiness in life had been due to the excitement of learning. In another particularly satisfying remembrance, his mind jumped swiftly from play to play, covering every live performance of Shakespeare that he had seen between the ages of ten and seventeen. *Everyone needs a hero*, Richard thought after the montage of scenes, *as impetus to bring out the best in himself. My hero was definitely William Shakespeare.*

Some of the memories were painful, especially those from his childhood. In one of them Richard was eight years old again, sitting on a bench at the small table in his family's dining room. The atmosphere at the table was tense. His father, drunk and angry at the world, was glowering at all of them as they ate their dinner in silence. Richard accidentally spilled some of his soup and seconds later the back of his father's hand hit him hard on the cheek, knocking him off his bench and into the corner of the room, where he trembled from fear and shock. He had not thought about that moment for years. Richard was unable to restrain his tears as he recalled how helpless and scared he had been around his neurotic, abusive father.

One day Richard suddenly began to remember details from his long odyssey in Rama II and a powerful headache almost blinded him. He saw himself in a strange room, lying on a floor surrounded by three or four octospiders. Dozens of probes and other instruments had been implanted in him and some kind of test was under way.

"Stop, stop," Richard shouted, destroying the memory picture with his acute agitation. "My head is killing me."

Miraculously his headache began to fade and Richard was again among the octospiders in his memory. He recalled the days and days of testing that he had experienced and the tiny living creatures that had been inserted into his body. He recalled also a peculiar set of sexual experiments in which he had been subjected to all kinds of external stimulation and rewarded when he ejaculated.

Richard was startled by these new memories that he had never accessed before, never once since he had awakened from the coma in which his family had found him in New York. *Now I remember other things about the octospiders too*, he thought excitedly. *They talked to each other in colors that wrapped around their heads. They were basically friendly, but determined to learn everything they could about me. They—*

The mental picture vanished and Richard's headache returned. The threads from the net had just disconnected. Richard was exhausted and quickly fell asleep.

After days and days of one memory after another, the readout abruptly ceased. Richard's mind was no longer driven by an external forcing function. The threads of the net remained unattached for long periods of time.

A week passed without incident. In the second week, however, an unusual spherical ganglion, far larger and more densely wrapped than the normal clumps in the living web, began to develop about twenty centimeters away from Richard's head. The ganglion grew until it was about the size of a basketball. Soon thereafter the immense clump issued hundreds of filaments that inserted themselves into the skin around the circumference of Richard's skull. *At last,* Richard thought, ignoring the pain caused by the invasion of the threads into his brain, *now we will see what this has all been about.*

He began immediately to see some kind of pictures, although they were so fuzzy that he could not identify anything specific. The quality of Richard's mental images improved very quickly, however, for he cleverly devised a rudimentary way of communicating with the web. As soon as the first image appeared in his mind, Richard concluded that the net, which had been reading his memory output for days, was now trying to *write* into his brain. But the web obviously had no way of measuring the quality of the images that Richard was receiving. Remembering his trips to the eye doctor as a boy and the communication pattern that resulted in the final specifications for his eyeglass lenses, Richard pointed his thumb up or down to indicate whether each change the net made in its transmission process made the picture better or worse. In that manner Richard was soon able to "see" what the alien was attempting to show him.

The first pictures were images of a planet taken from a spacecraft. The cloud-covered world with two smallish moons and a distant, solitary yellow star as its heat and light source was almost certainly the home planet of the sessile webs. The suite of pictures that followed showed Richard various landscapes from the planet.

Fog was ubiquitous on the home world of the sessiles. Below the fog in most of the images was a brown, rockless, barren surface. Only in the littorals where the barren ground encountered the waves of the green liquid lakes and oceans was there any suggestion of life. In one of these oases Richard saw not only several avians, but also a fascinating mélange of other living things. Richard could have spent days examining just one or two of these pictures, but he was not in control of the image sequence. The net had some purpose for its communication, he was certain, and the first set of pictures was only an introduction.

All of the remaining images featured either an avian, a manna melon, a myrmicat, a sessile web, or some combination of the quartet. The scenes were all taken from what Richard assumed was "normal life" on their home planet, and expanded on the general theme of symbiosis among the species. In several pictures the aliens were shown defending the subterranean colonies of the myrmicats and sessiles from invasions by what appeared to be small animals and plants. Other images depicted the myrmicats ministering to avian hatchlings or transporting large quantities of manna melons to an avian mound.

Richard was puzzled when he saw several pictures that showed tiny manna melons embedded inside the sessile creatures. *Why would the myrmicats lay their eggs in here?* he wondered. *For protection? Or are these weird webs a kind of thinking placenta?*

One definite impression left upon Richard by the sequence of images was that the sessiles were, in a hierarchical sense, the dominant species of the three. The pictures all suggested that both the myrmicats and the avians paid homage to the web creatures. *Do these nets, then, somehow do all the important thinking for the avians and myrmicats?* Richard asked himself. *What incredible symbiotic relationships. . . . How in the world could they possibly have evolved?*

There were several thousand frames altogether in the sequence. After it repeated twice, the filaments detached themselves from Richard and returned to the giant ganglion. In the days that followed Richard was essentially left alone, the attachments to his host being limited to those necessary for him to survive.

When a lane formed in the web and Richard could see the door through which he had entered many weeks before, he thought that he was going to be released. His momentary excitement, however, was quickly dampened. At his first attempt to move, the sessile net tightened its grip on all parts of his body.

So what is the purpose of the lane? As Richard watched, a trio of myrmicats entered from the hallway. The creature in the middle had two broken legs, and its back segment was crushed, as if it had been run over by a heavy car or truck. Its two companions carried the disabled myrmicat into the web and then departed. Within seconds the sessile began to wrap itself around the new arrival.

Richard was about two meters away from the crippled myrmicat. The region between him and the injured creature emptied of all filaments and clumps. Richard had never before seen such a gap inside the sessile. *So my education continues,* he mused. *What is it that I am supposed to learn now? That sessiles are doctors to the myrmicats, just as the myrmicats are doctors to the avians?*

The web did not limit its attention to the injured portions of the myrmicat. In fact, during one long waking period Richard watched the net completely enclose the creature in a tight cocoon. At the same time, the large ganglion in Richard's immediate vicinity migrated over to the cocoon.

Later, after a nap, Richard noticed that the ganglion had returned to his side. The cocoon across the gap had almost finished unraveling. Richard's pulse rate doubled as the cocoon completely disappeared and there was no trace of the myrmicat.

Richard didn't have much time to wonder what had happened

to the myrmicat. Within minutes the filaments from the large ganglion were again attached to his skull and another picture show was playing inside his brain. In the very first image Richard saw five human soldiers camping on the shore of the moat inside the avian habitat. They were eating a meal. Beside them were an impressive array of weapons, including two machine guns.

The pictures that followed showed humans on the attack throughout the second habitat. Two of the early scenes were especially gruesome. In the first a juvenile avian had been decapitated in midair and was falling to the ground. A pair of satisfied humans congratulated each other in the lower left portion of the same frame. The second image depicted a large square hole in one of the grassland sectors of the green region. Inside the hole could be seen the remains of several dead avians. A human with a wheelbarrow containing another pair of avian corpses was approaching the mass grave from the left.

Richard was staggered by what he was seeing. *What are these pictures anyway?* he wondered. *And why am I seeing them now?* He quickly reviewed all the recent events in his sessile world and concluded, with considerable shock, that the disabled myrmicat must have actually *seen* everything Richard was being shown, and that the web creature had somehow removed the images from the mind of the myrmicat and transferred them into Richard's brain.

Once he understood what he was seeing, Richard paid more attention to the pictures themselves. He was completely outraged by the invasion and slaughter that he saw. In one of the later images three human soldiers were shown raiding an avian apartment complex inside the brown cylinder. There were no survivors.

These poor creatures are doomed, Richard said to himself, *and they must know it. . . .*

Tears suddenly formed in Richard's eyes and a profound sadness, deeper than any he had ever known, accompanied his realization that members of his own species were systematically exterminating the avians. *No, no*, he shouted silently. *Stop, oh, please stop. Can't you see what you are doing? These avians, too, proclaim the miracle of chemicals raised to consciousness. They are like us. They are our brothers*.

In the next several seconds Richard's many interactions with the birdlike creatures flooded his memory and chased away the implanted images. *They saved my life*, he thought, his mind focusing on the flight long ago across the Cylindrical Sea. *With absolutely no benefit to themselves. What human*, he said to himself bitterly, *would have done such a good deed for an avian?*

Richard had rarely sobbed in his life. But his sorrow for the avians overpowered him. As he wept, all his experiences since entering the avian habitat filed through his mind. Richard recalled especially the sudden change in their treatment of him and his subsequent transfer to the realm of the myrmicats. *Then came the guided tour and my eventual placement here. . . . It's obvious they have been trying to communicate with me. But why?*

At that instant Richard had an epiphany of such power that tears rushed into his eyes again. *Because they are desperate,* he answered himself. *They are begging me to help.*

6

Again a large void was created in the interior of the sessile. Richard watched carefully as thirty small ganglia formed into a sphere with a diameter of about fifty centimeters on the other side of the gap. An unusually thick filament connected each of the ganglia with the center of the sphere. At first, Richard could detect nothing inside the sphere. After the ganglia had moved to another location, however, he saw, where the sphere had been, a tiny green object with hundreds of infinitesimal threads anchoring it to the rest of the web.

It grew very slowly. The ganglia had already finished migrating to three new positions, repeating the same spherical configuration each time, before Richard recognized that what was growing in the sessile was a manna melon. He was thunderstruck. Richard could not imagine how the vanished myrmicat could possibly have left behind eggs that had taken so long to germinate. *And they must have been only a few cells then. Tiny, tiny embryos somehow nurtured here. . . .*

His own thoughts were interrupted by his realization that these new manna melons were developing in a region of the sessile that was almost twenty meters away from where the myrmicat had been cocooned. *So this web creature transported the eggs from one place to another? And then retained them for weeks?*

Richard's logical mind began to reject the hypothesis that the vanished myrmicat had laid any eggs at all. Slowly but surely, he developed an alternative explanation for what he had observed that suggested a biology more complex than any he had ever encountered on Earth. *What if*, he asked himself, *the manna melons, myrmicats, and this sessile web are all manifestations of what we would call the same species?*

Staggered by the ramifications of this simple thought, Richard spent two long waking periods reviewing everything he had seen inside the second habitat. As he stared at the four manna melons growing across the gap from him, Richard envisioned a cycle of metamorphosis in which the manna melons gave birth to the myrmicats, who in turn came to die and add new matter to the sessile net, which then laid the manna melon eggs that began the process again. There was nothing he had observed that was inconsistent with this explanation. But Richard's brain was exploding with thousands of questions, not only about *how* this intricate set of metamorphoses took place, but also about *why* this species had evolved into such a complex being in the first place.

Most of Richard's academic study had been in fields that he had always proudly called "hard science." Mathematics and physics had been the primary elements of his education. As he struggled to understand the possible life cycle of the creature in which he had been living for many weeks, Richard was bewildered by his ignorance. He wished that he had learned much more about biology. *For how can I help them?* he asked himself. *I have no idea even where to start.*

Much later, Richard would wonder if by this time in his stay inside the sessile, the creature had learned not only how to read his memory, but also how to interpret his thoughts. His visitors arrived a few days afterward. Again a lane formed in the sessile between Richard's position and the original entryway. Four identical myrmicats walked down the lane and gestured for Richard to join them. They were carrying his clothes. When Richard made an effort to move, his alien host did not try to restrain him. His legs were wobbly, but after dressing, Richard managed to follow the myrmicats back into the corridor deep within the brown cylinder.

The large chamber had obviously been recently modified. The vast mural on its walls was not yet completed. In fact, at the same time that Richard's myrmicat teacher was pointing to specific items in the painting that had already been finished, myrmicat artists were still at work on the remainder of the mural. During Richard's early lessons in the room, as many as a dozen of the creatures were engaged in sketching or painting the other sections.

Only one visit to the mural chamber was necessary for Richard to ascertain its purpose. The entire room was being created to give him information on how he could help the alien species survive. It was clear these extraterrestrials knew that they were about to be overrun and destroyed by the humans. The paintings in this room were their attempt to provide Richard with the data he might need to save them. But could he learn enough simply from the pictures?

The artwork was brilliant. From time to time Richard would suspend the activity in his left brain that was trying to interpret the messages in the paintings so that his right brain could appreciate the talent of the myrmicat artists. The creatures worked in the upright position, their back two legs on the floor and their four front legs operating together to implement the sketch or painting. They talked among themselves, apparently asking questions, but did not make so much noise that Richard was disturbed across the chamber.

The entire first half of the mural was a textbook in alien biology. It proved that Richard's fundamental understanding of the strange creature was correct. There were over a hundred individual paintings in the main sequence, of which two dozen showed different stages in the development of the myrmicat embryo, expanding considerably the knowledge that Richard had gleaned from the sculptures inside the myrmicat cathedral. The primary panels explaining the embryological progression followed a straight line around the walls of the chamber. Above and below these main sequence pictures were supporting or supplementary frames, most of which were beyond Richard's comprehension.

For example, a quartet of supporting paintings had been arranged around a picture of a manna melon that had recently been removed from a sessile web, but had not yet begun any myrmicat development activity in its interior. Richard was certain that these four additional pictures were trying to give him specific information about the ambient conditions required for the germination process to begin. However, the myrmicat artists had used scenes from their home planet, illustrating the desired conditions with landscapes of fogs and lakes and their native flora and fauna, to communicate the data. Richard just shook his head when the myrmicat teacher pointed at these paintings.

A diagram across the top of the main sequence used suns and moons to specify time scales. Richard understood from the arrangement that the lifetime of the myrmicat manifestation of the species was very short when compared with the lifetime of the sessiles. He was unable, however, to figure out anything else the diagram was trying to convey.

Richard was also somewhat confused about the numerical relationships among the different manifestations of the species. It was clear that each manna melon resulted in a single myrmicat (there were no examples of twins shown), and that a sessile could produce many manna melons. But what was the ratio of sessiles to myrmicats? In one frame a large sessile was presented with a dozen different myrmicats in its interior, each in a different phase of cocooning. What was that supposed to indicate?

Richard slept in a small room not far from the mural chamber. His lessons lasted three to four hours each, after which he would be fed or allowed to sleep. Sometimes, when he entered the chamber, Richard would glance over at the paintings, some still incomplete, in the second half of the mural. If that happened, the lights in the chamber would immediately be extinguished. The myrmicats wanted to be certain that Richard learned his biology first.

After about ten days the second half of the mural was finished. Richard was stunned when he was finally allowed to study it. The renderings of the many human beings and avians were exceptionally accurate. Richard himself appeared half a dozen times in the paintings. With his long hair and beard, both of them more than half white, he almost didn't recognize himself. *I could pass for Christ in these pictures*, he joked as he wandered around the chamber.

Part of the remaining mural was a historical summary of the invasion of the alien habitat by the humans. There was more detail than Richard had seen in his mental picture show while he was inside the sessile, but he did not learn anything substantively new. He was, however, again disturbed emotionally by the horrible details of the continuing massacre.

The pictures also triggered an interesting question in his mind. Why had the contents of this mural not been transferred *directly* to him by the sessile, thereby obviating the entire effort by the myrmicat artists? *Perhaps*, Richard mused, *the sessile is a recording device only, and is incapable of imagination. Maybe it can only show me what has already been seen by one of the myrmicats.*

What was left of the mural explicitly defined what the myrmicat/sessile creatures were asking Richard to do. In each of his portraits he was wearing a large blue pack over his shoulders. The pack had two large pockets in the front, and two more in the back, each containing a manna melon. There were two additional, smaller pockets on the sides of the pack. One was stuffed with a silver cylindrical tube about fifteen centimeters long and the other contained two small, leathery avian eggs.

The mural showed Richard's suggested activity in an orderly sequence. He would leave the brown cylinder through an exit below the ground level, and come out in the green region on the other side of both the ring of white buildings and the thin canal. There, guided by a pair of avians, he would descend to the shore of the moat, where he would be picked up by a small submarine. The submarine would dive under the module wall, enter a large body of water, and then surface on the shore of an island with many skyscrapers.

Richard smiled as he studied the mural. *So both the Cylindrical Sea and New York are still here,* he thought. He remembered what the Eagle had said about not making unnecessary changes to Rama. *That means our lair may be there as well.*

There were many additional pictures surrounding Richard's escape sequence, some giving more details about the alien plants and animals in the green region, and others providing explicit instructions on how to operate the submarine. When Richard tried to copy what he thought was the most important of this information into his portable computer from the Newton, the myrmicat teacher suddenly seemed impatient. Richard wondered if the crisis situation had worsened.

The next day, after a long nap, Richard was outfitted with his pack and ushered into the sessile chamber by his hosts. There the four manna melons he had watched growing two weeks previous were removed from the web by the myrmicats and placed in his pack. They were quite heavy. Richard estimated that they weighed twenty kilograms altogether. Another myrmicat then used an instrument similar to a large scissors to remove from the sessile a cylindrical volume containing four ganglia and their associated filaments. This sessile material was placed in a silver tube and inserted in one of Richard's smaller side pockets. The avian eggs were the last elements to be loaded.

Richard took a deep breath. *This must be good-bye,* he thought as the myrmicats pointed down the corridor. For some reason he remembered Nai Watanabe's insistence that the Thai greeting called the *wai*, a small bow with hands clasped together in front of the upper chest, was a universal sign of respect. Smiling to himself, Richard performed a *wai* to the half dozen myrmicats surrounding him. To his astonishment, each of them placed its four forward legs together in pairs in front of its underbelly and made a slight bow in his direction.

The deep basement of the brown cylinder was obviously uninhabited. After leaving the sessile chamber, Richard and his guide had first passed many other myrmicats, especially in the vicinity of the atrium. But once they had entered the ramp that descended to the basement, they had never encountered even a single myrmicat.

Richard's guide dispatched a leggie in front of them. It raced along the final narrow tunnel and through the vaultlike emergency exit into the green region. When the leggie returned, it stood on the back of the myrmicat's head for several seconds and then scampered down to the floor. The guide motioned for Richard to proceed into the tunnel.

Outside, in the green region, Richard was met by two large avians who immediately became airborne. One of them had an ugly scar on its wing, as if it had been hit by a spray of bullets. Richard was in a moderately dense forest, with growth around him up to three or four meters off the ground. Even though the light was dim, it was not difficult for Richard to find a pathway or to follow the avians above him. Occasionally he heard sporadic gunfire off in the distance.

The first fifteen minutes passed without incident. The forest thickness lessened. Richard had just estimated that he should be at the moat for the rendezvous with the submarine in another ten minutes when, without any warning, a machine gun began to fire no more than a hundred meters away. One of the guide avians crashed to the ground. The other avian disappeared. Richard hid himself in a dark thicket when he heard the soldiers coming in his direction.

"Two rings for certain," one of them said. "Maybe even three. That would give me twenty rings this week alone."

"Shit, man, that was no contest. It shouldn't even count. The damn bird didn't even know you were there."

"That's his problem, not mine. I still get to count his rings. Ah, here he is. . . . Crap, he only has two."

The men were only about fifteen meters away from Richard. He stood absolutely still, not daring to move, for more than five minutes. The soldiers, meanwhile, stayed in the vicinity of the avian corpse, smoking and talking about the war.

Richard began to feel pain in his right foot. He shifted his weight ever so slightly, thinking he would relieve whatever muscle was being strained, but the pain only increased. At length he glanced down and discovered to his horror that one of the rodentlike creatures he had seen in the mural chamber had eaten through what was left of his shoe and was now chomping on his foot. Richard tried to shake his leg vigorously but noiselessly. He was not completely successful. Although the rodent released his foot, the soldiers heard the sound and started moving toward him.

Richard could not run. Even if there had been an escape route, the extra weight he was carrying would have made him easy prey for the soldiers. Within a minute one of the men yelled, "Over here, Bruce, I think there's something in this thicket."

The man was pointing his gun in Richard's direction. "Don't shoot," Richard said. "I'm a human."

The second soldier had just joined his comrade. "What the fuck are you doing out here alone?"

"I'm taking a hike," Richard answered.

"Are you crazy?" the first soldier said. "Come on out of there. Let us take a look at you."

Richard slowly walked out of the underbrush. Even in the dim light he must have been an astonishing sight with his long hair and beard plus the bulging blue jacket.

"Jesus Christ. Who the hell are you? Where's your outfit positioned?"

"This ain't no goddamn soldier," the other man said, still staring at Richard. "This here's a loony tune. He must have escaped from the facility in Avalon and wandered over here by mistake. . . . Hey, asshole, don't you know this is dangerous territory? You could be killed—"

"Look at his pockets," the first soldier interrupted. "He's carrying four *huge* goddamn melons—"

Suddenly they struck from the sky. There must have been a dozen of the avians altogether, consumed by fury and shrieking as they attacked. The two human soldiers were knocked to the ground. Richard started to run. One of the avians landed on the face of the first soldier and began to tear it apart with its talons. Gunfire erupted as other soldiers in the vicinity, hearing the fracas, hurried into the area to help the patrol.

Richard did not know how he was going to find the submarine. He raced downhill as fast as his feet and his load would allow him. The gunfire behind him increased. He heard the screams of pain of the soldiers and the death shrieks of the avians.

He found the moat but there was no sign of the submarine.

Richard could hear human voices coming down the slope behind him. Just when he was about to panic, he heard a short shriek from a large bush on his right. The leader avian with the four cobalt rings flew past his head, not far off the ground, and continued down the shore of the moat to the left.

They located the small submarine in three more minutes. The ship had already submerged before the pursuing humans broke into the clear in the green region. Inside, Richard took off his pack and placed it behind him in the small control compartment. He looked at his avian companion and tried a couple of simple jabber phrases. The avian leader replied, very slowly and very clearly, with the jabber equivalent of "We all thank you very much."

The journey took slightly more than an hour. Richard and the avian said very little to each other. During the early part of the voyage, Richard carefully watched the avian leader operating the submarine. He made notes in his computer and, during the second half of the trip, even took over the controls himself for a short period of time. When he was not too busy, Richard's mind was asking questions about everything he had experienced in the second habitat. Above all, he wanted to know why it was *he* in the submarine with the melons, the avian eggs, and the sessile slice, and *not* one of the myrmicats. *I must be missing something,* he mused to himself.

Soon thereafter the submarine surfaced and Richard was in familiar territory. The skyscrapers of New York loomed above him. "Hallelujah," Richard said out loud, carrying his full pack onto the island.

The avian leader anchored the submarine just offshore and quickly prepared to leave. He turned around in a circle, bowed slightly to Richard, and then took off toward the north. As he was watching the birdlike creature fly away, Richard realized that he was standing in the exact spot where he and Nicole had waited, many many years before in Rama II, for the three avians who would carry them across the Cylindrical Sea to freedom.

7

During the first second that Richard stood on the surface in New York, a hundred billion billion bits of data were acquired by the infinitesimal Raman sensors scattered throughout the giant cylindrical spacecraft. These data were transmitted in realtime to local data-handling centers, still microscopic in size, where they were stored until the allocated time for them to be relayed to the central telecommunications processor buried beneath the Southern Hemicylinder.

Every second of every hour of every day the Raman sensors acquire these hundred quintillion data bits. At the telecommunications processor, the data are labeled, sifted, analyzed, compressed, and stored in recording devices whose individual components are smaller than an atom. After storage, the data are accessed by the dozens of distributed processors, each managing a separate function, that together control the Rama spacecraft. Thousands of algorithms spread among the processors then operate on the data, extracting trend and synthesis information in preparation for the regularly scheduled data bursts that transmit the mission status to the Nodal Intelligence.

The data bursts contain a mixture of raw, compressed, and synthesized data, depending on the exact formats selected by the different processors. The most important part of each burst is the narrative report, in which the unified but distributed intelligence of Rama presents its prioritized summary of the progress of the mission. The rest of the burst is essentially supporting information, images or measurements or sensor outputs that either provide additional background data or directly support the conclusions contained in the summary.

The language used for the narrative summary is mathematical in structure, precise in definition, and highly coded. It is also rich in footnotes, each equivalent phrase or sentence containing, as part of its transmission structure, the pointers to the actual data buttressing the particular statement being made. The report could not, in the truest sense, be translated into any language as primitive as the ones used by human beings. Nevertheless, what follows is a crude approximation of the summary report received by the Nodal Intelligence from Rama soon after Richard's arrival in New York.

REPORT #298
Time of Transmission: 156 307 872 491.5116
Time Since First-Stage Alert: 29.2873
References: Node 23-419
                Spacecraft 947
                Spacefarers 47 249 (A & B)
                         32 806
                          2 666

During the last interval the humans (Spacefarer #32 806) have continued to wage a successful war against the avian/sessile symbiotic pair (#47 249—A & B). The humans now control almost all the interior of the avian/sessile habitat, including the upper portion of the brown cylinder where the avians formerly lived. The avians have fought courageously but vainly against the human invasion. They have been killed unmercifully, and less than a hundred of them now remain.

Thus far the humans have not breached the integrity of the sessile domain. They have, however, found the elevator shafts leading to the lower parts of the brown cylinder. The humans are currently developing plans for an attack on the sessile lair.

The sessiles are a defenseless species. There are no weapons of any kind in their domain. Even their mobile form, which has the physical dexterity to use weapons, is essentially nonviolent. To protect themselves from what they fear will be an inevitable invasion by the humans, the sessiles have directed the mobile myrmicats to build fortresses surrounding the four oldest and most developed of their species. Meanwhile, no more manna melons are being allowed to germinate and those myrmicats not involved in the construction process are cocooning early.

If the humans delay their attack several more intervals, as seems likely, it is possible they will encounter only a few myrmicats during their invasion.

The human habitat continues to be dominated by individuals with characteristics decidedly different from the human contingent observed inside Rama II and at the Node. The focus of the current human leaders is the retention of personal power, without serious consideration of the welfare of the colony. Despite both the video message and the presence of messenger humans in their group, these leaders must not believe they are actually being watched, for their behavior in no way reflects the possible existence of a set of values or ethical laws that supersedes their own dominion.

The humans have continued to prosecute the war against the avian/sessiles primarily because it distracts attention from the other problems in their colony, including the human-initiated environmental degradation and the recent precipitous decline in living standards. The human leaders, and indeed most of the colonists, have shown no remorse whatsoever over the destruction and possible extermination of the avians.

The human family that remained for over a year at the Node no longer has any significant impact on the affairs of the colony. The woman who was the primary messenger is still imprisoned, essentially because she opposes the actions of the existing leaders, and is in danger of being executed. Her husband has been living with the avians and sessiles and is now a critical component in their attempt to survive the human onslaught. The children are not yet mature enough to be a major factor in the human colony.

Very recently, the husband escaped from the sessile domain to the island in the middle of the spacecraft. He carried both avian and sessile embryos with him. He is currently located in a familiar environment, and therefore should be able both to survive and to nurture the young of the other species. His successful escape may have been at least partly due to the noninvasive intercession that began at the time of the first-stage alert. The intercession signals almost certainly played a role in the decision by the sessiles to trust their embryos to a human being.

There is no evidence, however, that the intercession transmissions have affected the behavior of any of the humans. For the sessiles, information processing is a primary activity and, therefore, it is not surprising that they would be susceptible to intercessionary suggestions. The humans, however, especially the leaders, have their lives so filled with activity that there is very little, if any, time for cogitation.

There is an additional problem with humans and noninvasive intercession. As a species they are so varied, from individual to individual, that a transmission package cannot be designed with broad applicability. A set of signals that might result in a positive behavior modification for one human will almost certainly have no impact on anyone else. Experiments with different types of intercession processes are currently being conducted, but it may well be that humans belong to that small group of spacefarers who are immune to noninvasive intercession.

In the south of the spacecraft, the octospiders (#2 666) continue to thrive in a colony almost indistinguishable from any of their other isolated colonies in space. The full range of possible biological expression remains latent, primarily because of restricted territorial resources and no true competition. However, they are carrying with them the significant potential for expansion that has characterized their several successful transfers from one star system to another.

Until the humans probed through the wall of their own habitat and broke the seal on their enclosure, the octospiders paid very little attention to the other two species in the spacecraft. Since the humans began to explore, however, the octospiders have watched the events in the north with increasing interest. Their existence is still unknown to the humans, but the octospiders have already started formulating a contingency plan to cover a possible interaction with their aggressive neighbors.

The potential loss of the entire avian/sessile community greatly reduces the value of the mission. It is possible that the only sessile and avian survivors of the voyage will be those in the small octospider zoo and, perhaps, those raised by the human on the island. Even irrevocable loss of a single species does not call for a stage two alert; nevertheless, the continued unpredictable and life-negative behavior of the current human leaders provides an unmitigated worry that the mission may suffer additional serious losses. Intercessionary activity in the near future will be focused on those humans who both oppose the present leaders and have indicated, by their behavior, growth beyond territoriality and aggression.

8

"My country was called Thailand. It had a king, whose name was also Rama, like our spaceship. Your grandmother and grandfather—my mother and father—probably still live there, in a town called Lamphun. . . . Here it is."

Nai pointed at a spot on the faded map. The boys' attention had started to wander. *They're still too young,* she thought. *Even for bright children it's too much to expect at four.*

"All right, now," she said, folding up the map, "you can go outside and play."

Galileo and Kepler put on their heavy jackets, picked up a ball, and raced out the door into the street. Within seconds they were engaged in a one-on-one soccer match. *Oh, Kenji,* Nai thought, watching the boys from the entryway. *How they have missed you. There's just no way one parent can be both mother and father.*

She had begun the geography lesson, as she always did, by reminding the boys that all of the colonists in New Eden had come originally from a planet called Earth. Nai had then shown the boys a world map for their home planet, first discussing the basic concept of continents and oceans, and then identifying Japan, their father's native country. The activity had made Nai both homesick and lonely.

Maybe these lessons aren't for you at all, she thought, still watching the soccer game under the dim streetlights of Avalon. Galileo dribbled around Kepler and fired at an imaginary goal. *Maybe they're really for me.*

Eponine was coming down the street in their direction. She picked up the ball and threw it back to the boys. Nai smiled at her friend. "What a delight to see you," she said. "I can definitely use a happy face today."

"What's the matter, Nai?" Eponine asked. "Life in Avalon getting you down? . . . At least it's a Sunday. You're not working in the gun factory and the boys aren't over at the center."

The two women walked inside. "And certainly your living conditions cannot be the cause of your despair." Eponine waved her arm at the room. "After all, you have a *large* room for the three of you, half a toilet, and a bath you share with five other families. What more could you want?"

Nai laughed and hugged Eponine. "You're a big help," she said.

"Mommy, Mommy." Kepler was standing in the doorway a moment later. "Come quickly," the little boy said. "He's back . . . and he's talking to Galileo."

Nai and Eponine returned to the door. A man with a severely disfigured face was kneeling down in the dirt next to Galileo. The boy was obviously frightened. The man was holding a sheet of paper in his gloved hand. On it a large human face with long hair and a full beard had been carefully drawn.

"You know this face, don't you?" the man said insistently. "It's Mr. Richard Wakefield, isn't it?"

Nai and Eponine approached the man cautiously. "We told you last time," Nai said firmly, "not to bother the boys anymore. Now go back to the ward or we will call the police."

The man's eyes were wild. "I saw him again last night," he said. "He looked like Jesus, but he was Richard Wakefield all right. I started to shoot him and they attacked me. Five of them. They tore my face apart. . . ." The man started to weep.

An orderly came running down the street. He grabbed the man. "I saw him," the wild man shouted as he was led away. "I know I did. Please believe me."

Galileo was crying. Nai bent down to comfort her son. "Mama," the boy said, "do you think that man really saw Mr. Wakefield?"

"I don't know," she answered. Nai glanced at Eponine. "But some of us would like to believe it."

*   *   *

The boys had finally fallen asleep in their beds in the corner. Nai and Eponine sat next to each other in the two chairs. "The rumor is she's very ill," Eponine said quietly. "They hardly feed her at all. They make her suffer in every possible way."

"Nicole will never give up," Nai said proudly. "I wish I had her strength and courage."

"Neither Ellie nor Robert has been allowed to see her for over six months. . . . Nicole doesn't even know she has a granddaughter."

"Ellie told me last week that she has filed another petition with Nakamura to visit her mother," Nai said. "I worry about Ellie. She continues to push very, very hard."

Eponine smiled. "Ellie is so wonderful, even if she is incredibly naive. She insists that if she obeys all the colony laws, Nakamura will leave her alone."

"That's not surprising . . . especially when you consider that Ellie still thinks her father is alive," Nai said. "She has talked with every one of the people who claim to have seen Richard since he disappeared."

"All the stories about Richard give her hope," Eponine said. "We can still use a dosage of hope from time to time. . . ."

There was a momentary lull in the conversation. "What about you, Eponine?" Nai asked. "Do you allow yourself—"

"No," Eponine interrupted. "I am always honest with myself. . . . I am going to die soon; I just don't know when. Besides, why should I fight to keep living? Conditions here in Avalon are far worse than they were even in the detention camp at Bourges. If it weren't for the few children in the school—"

They both heard the noise outside the door at the same time. Nai and Eponine sat completely still. If their conversation had been recorded by one of Nakamura's roving biots, then—

The door suddenly swung open. The two women nearly jumped out of their skins. Max Puckett stumbled in, grinning. "You're under arrest," he said, "for engaging in seditious conversation."

Max was carrying a large wooden box. The two women helped him place it in the corner. Max took off his heavy jacket. "Sorry to show up so late, ladies, but I couldn't help it."

"Another food run to the troops?" Nai asked in a soft voice. She pointed at the sleeping twins.

Max nodded. "The king Jap," he said in a lower voice, "always reminds me that an army travels on its stomach."

"That was one of Napoléon's maxims." Eponine looked at Max with a sarcastic smile. "I don't suppose you ever heard of him out there in Arkansas."

"Uh-oh," Max replied. "The lovely lady teacher is in a smartass mood tonight." He pulled an unopened pack of cigarettes out of his shirt pocket. "Maybe I should just keep her gift for myself."

Eponine laughed and jumped up to grab the cigarettes. After a short mock struggle, Max surrendered them to her. "Thanks, Max," Eponine said in a genuine manner. "There aren't many pleasures allowed to those of us—"

"Now, look here," Max said, still grinning. "I didn't come all the way out here to listen to you feeling sorry for yourself. I stopped in Avalon to be inspired by your beautiful face. If you're going to be depressed, I'll just take my corn and tomatoes—"

"Corn and tomatoes!" Nai and Eponine exclaimed in unison. The women ran over to the box. "The children haven't had any fresh produce in weeks," Nai said excitedly as Max opened the box with a steel bar.

"Be very, very careful with these," Max said seriously. "You know that what I am doing is absolutely illegal. There's barely enough fresh food for the army and the government leaders. But I decided you deserved something better than leftover rice."

Eponine gave Max a hug. "Thank you," she said.

"The boys and I are very grateful, Max," Nai said. "I don't know how we'll ever repay you."

"I'll find some way," Max said.

The two women returned to their chairs and Max sat down on the floor between them. "Incidentally," he said, "I ran into Patrick O'Toole over in the second habitat. He asked me to say hello to both of you."

"How is he?" Eponine asked.

"Troubled, I would say," Max replied. "When he was drafted, he let Katie talk him into reporting to the army—which I'm certain he would never have done if either Nicole or Richard could have spoken to him even once—and I think he realizes now what a mistake he made. He didn't say anything, but I could sense his distress. Nakamura keeps him in the front line because of Nicole."

"Is this war almost over?" Eponine asked.

"I think so," Max said. "But it's not clear the king Jap wants it to be over. From what the soldiers told me, there's very little resistance left. They're mostly mopping up inside the brown cylinder."

Nai leaned forward. "We heard a rumor that another intelligent species was also living in the cylinder—something altogether different from the avians."

Max laughed. "Who knows what to believe? The television and newspaper say whatever Nakamura tells them, and everyone knows it. There are always hundreds of rumors. I myself have encountered some bizarre alien plants and animals inside that habitat, so nothing would surprise me."

Nai stifled a yawn. "I best be leaving," Max said, standing up, "and let our hostess go to bed." He glanced at Eponine. "Would you like someone to walk you home?"

"Depends on who the someone is," Eponine said with a smile.

A few minutes later, Max and Eponine reached her tiny hut on one of the side streets of Avalon. Max dropped the cigarette they had been sharing and ground it into the dirt. "Would you like someone . . ." he started.

"Yes, Max, of course I would," Eponine replied with a sigh. "And if that someone were anyone, it would definitely be you." She looked directly in his eyes. "But if you shared my bed, even one time, then I would want more. And if, by some awful chance, no matter how careful we were, you were ever, *ever* to test positive for RV-41, I would never forgive myself."

Eponine pressed herself against him to hide her tears. "Thanks for everything," she said. "You're a good man, Max Puckett, maybe the only one left in this crazy universe."

Eponine was in a museum in Paris surrounded by hundreds of masterpieces. A large group of tourists passed through the museum. They spent a total of forty-five seconds looking at five magnificent paintings by Renoir and Monet. "Stop," Eponine shouted in her dream. "You can't possibly have *seen* them."

The knocking on her door chased the dream away. "It's us, Eponine," she heard Ellie say. "If it's too early, we can try to come back later, before you go to school. Robert was worried that we might get tied up in the psychiatric ward."

Eponine leaned over and grabbed the robe hanging on the room's solitary chair. "Just a minute," she said, "I'm coming."

She opened the door for her friends. Ellie was in her nurse's uniform, with little Nicole in a makeshift carrier on her back. The sleeping baby was wrapped cleverly in cotton to protect her from the cold.

"May we come in?"

"Of course," replied Eponine. "I'm sorry," she said, "I must not have heard you."

"It's a ridiculous time for us to visit," Ellie said. "But with all our work at the hospital, if we didn't come out here early in the morning, we'd never make it."

"How have you been feeling?" Dr. Turner asked a few seconds later. He was holding a scanner in front of Eponine and data was already being displayed on the portable computer monitor.

"A little tired," Eponine said. "But it could be just psychological. Since you told me two months ago that my heart was beginning to show some signs of degradation, I have imagined myself having a heart attack at least once a day."

During the examination Ellie operated the keyboard that was attached to the monitor. She made certain that the most important information from the checkup was recorded in the computer. Eponine craned around to see the screen. "How's the new system working, Robert?"

"We've had several failures with the probes," he replied. "Ed Stafford says that's to be expected because of our inadequate testing. And we don't yet have a good data management scheme, but on the whole we're very pleased."

"It's been a savior, Eponine," Ellie said without glancing up from the keyboard. "With our limited funds, and all the wounded from the war, there would have been no way we could have kept the RV-41 files current without this kind of automation."

"I only wish we had been able to use more of Nicole's expertise in the original design," Robert Turner said. "I hadn't realized she was such an expert on internal monitoring systems." The doctor saw something unusual in a graph that appeared on the screen. "Print a copy of that, will you, darling? I want to show it to Ed."

"Have you heard anything new about your mother?" Eponine asked Ellie as the examination neared its completion.

"We saw Katie two nights ago," Ellie replied very slowly. "It was a difficult evening. She had another 'deal' from Nakamura and Macmillan she wanted to discuss. . . ." Her voice trailed off. "Anyway, Katie says that there will definitely be a trial before Settlement Day."

"Has she seen Nicole?"

"No," Ellie answered. "As far as we know, nobody has. Her food is brought in by a Garcia and her monthly checkups are done by a Tiasso."

Baby Nicole stirred and whimpered on her mother's back. Eponine reached down and touched the portion of the child's cheek that was exposed to the air. "They are so unbelievably soft," she said. At that moment the little girl's eyes opened and she began to cry.

"Do I have time to nurse her, Robert?" Ellie asked.

Dr. Turner glanced at his watch. "All right," he said. "We're basically finished here. Since both Wilma Margolin and Bill Tucker are in the next block, why don't I call on them by myself and then come back?"

"You can handle them without me?"

"With difficulty," he said grimly. "Especially poor Tucker."

"Bill Tucker is dying very slowly," Ellie said to Eponine in explanation. "He's alone and in great pain. But since the government has now outlawed euthanasia, there's nothing we can do."

"There's no indication of additional atrophy in your data," Dr. Turner said to Eponine a few moments later. "I guess we should be thankful."

She didn't hear him. In her mind's eye, Eponine was imagining her own slow and painful death. *I will not let it happen that way*, she told herself. *Never. As soon as I am no longer useful . . . Max will bring me a gun.*

"I'm sorry, Robert," she said. "I must be sleepier than I thought. What did you say?"

"You're no worse." Robert gave Eponine a kiss on the cheek and started for the door. "I'll be back in about twenty minutes," he said to Ellie.

"Robert looks very tired," Eponine said when he departed.

"He is," Ellie replied. "He still works all the time . . . and worries when he's not working." Ellie was sitting on the dirt floor with her back against the wall of the hut. Nicole was cradled in her arms, suckling at a breast and cooing intermittently.

"That looks like fun," Eponine said.

"Nothing I have ever experienced is even remotely similar. The pleasure is indescribable."

It's not for me, Eponine's inner voice said. *Not now. Not ever.* In a fleeting moment Eponine recalled a night of passion when she almost hadn't said no to Max Puckett. A deep feeling of bitterness welled up inside her. She struggled to fight it.

"I had a nice walk with Benjy yesterday," she said, changing the subject.

"I'm sure he'll tell me all about it this morning," Ellie said. "He loves his Sunday walks with you. It's all he has left, except for my occasional visits. . . . You know that I am very grateful."

"Forget it. I like Benjy. I also need to feel needed, if you know what I mean. . . . Benjy actually has adjusted surprisingly well. He doesn't complain as much as the forty-ones, and certainly not as much as the people assigned here to work at the gun factory."

"He hides his pain," Ellie replied. "Benjy's much smarter than anyone thinks. He really dislikes the ward but knows that he can't take care of himself. And he doesn't want to be a burden to anybody—"

Tears suddenly formed in Ellie's eyes and her body trembled slightly. Baby Nicole stopped nursing and stared at her mother. "Are you all right?" Eponine asked.

Ellie shook her head affirmatively and wiped her eyes with the small cotton cloth that she was holding next to her breasts to catch any leakage. Nicole resumed nursing. "Suffering is difficult enough to watch," Ellie said. "Unnecessary suffering tears your heart out."

The guard looked carefully at their identification papers and handed them to another uniformed man sitting behind him at a computer console. The second man made an entry into the computer and returned the documents to the guard.

"Why," Ellie said, when they were out of earshot, "does that man stare at our photographs every single day? He must have passed us through this checkpoint personally a dozen times in the last month."

They were walking along the lane that led from the module exit to Positano. "It's his job," Robert replied, "and he likes to feel important. If he doesn't make a ceremony out of it each time, then we might forget the power he has over us."

"The process was much smoother when the biots were handling the entrance."

"The ones that are still functioning are too critical to the war effort. Besides, Nakamura is afraid that the ghost of Richard Wakefield will appear and somehow confound the biots."

They walked in silence for several seconds. "You don't think my father is still alive, do you, darling?"

"No, dear," Robert answered after a short hesitation. He was surprised by the directness of the question. "But even though I don't *think* he's alive, I still *hope* that he is."

Robert and Ellie finally reached the outskirts of Positano. A few new houses, European in style, lined the lane that sloped gently down into the heart of the village. "By the way, Ellie," Robert said, "talking about your father reminded me of something I wanted to discuss with you. . . . Do you remember that project I was telling you about, the one that Ed Stafford is doing?"

Ellie shook her head.

"He's trying to classify and categorize the entire colony in terms of general genetic groupings. He thinks that such classifications, even though they are completely arbitrary, may offer clues about which individuals are likely to have which diseases. I don't completely agree with his approach—it seems too forced and numerical, rather than medical—but parallel studies have been done on Earth and they showed that people with similar genes do indeed have similar disease tendencies."

Ellie stopped walking and looked at her husband quizzically. "Why did you want to discuss this with me?"

Robert laughed. "Yes, yes," he said. "I'm coming to that. . . . Anyway, Ed defined a difference metric—a numerical method of measuring how different any two individuals are, using the way in which the four basic amino acids are chained in the genome—and then, as a test, divided all the citizens of New Eden into groups. Now, the metric didn't really mean anything—"

"Robert Turner," Ellie interrupted. She was laughing. "Will you please get to the point? What are you trying to tell me?"

"Well, it's weird," he said. "We don't quite know what to make of it. When Ed made his first classification structure, two of the people tested did not belong to any group. By fiddling with the definitions of the categories, he was eventually able to define a quantitative spread that covered one of them. But the amino acid chaining structure of the final person was so different from every other person in New Eden that she couldn't be placed into any of the groups. . . ."

Ellie was staring at Robert as if he had lost his mind.

"The two individuals were your brother Benjy and you," Robert concluded awkwardly. "You were the one outside all the groupings."

"Should I be worried about this?" Ellie said after they had walked another thirty meters in silence.

"I don't think so," Robert said casually. "It's probably just an artifice of the particular metric that Ed chose. Or perhaps a mistake was made. . . . But it would be fascinating if somehow cosmic radiation might have altered your genetic structure during your embryological development."

By this time they had arrived at the main square of Positano. Ellie leaned over and kissed her husband. "That was very interesting, dear," she said, teasing him a little, "but I must admit that I'm still not sure what it was all about."

A large bicycle rack occupied most of the square. Two dozen rows and as many columns of parking positions were spread out over the area in front of what had been the train station. All the colonists, with the exception of the government leaders, who had electric cars, now used bicycles for transportation.

The train service in New Eden had been discontinued soon after the war began. The trains had originally been constructed by the extraterrestrials from very light and exceptionally strong materials that the human factories in the colony had never been able to duplicate. These alloys were extremely valuable in many different military functions. By the middle stages of the war, therefore, the defense agency had requisitioned all the cars in the train system.

Ellie and Robert rode their bicycles, side by side along the banks of Lake Shakespeare. Little Nicole had awakened and was quietly watching the landscape around her. They passed the park, where the Settlement Day picnic was always held, and turned toward the north.

"Robert," Ellie said very seriously, "have you thought any more about our long discussion last night?"

"About Nakamura and politics?"

"Yes," she answered. "I still think we should *both* oppose his edict suspending elections until after the war is over. . . . You have a lot of stature in the colony. Most of the health professionals will follow your lead. Nai even thinks that the factory workers in Avalon might strike."

"I can't do it," Robert said after a long silence.

"Why not, darling?" Ellie asked.

"Because I don't think it will work. In your idealistic view of the world, Ellie, people act out of commitment to principles or values. In reality, they don't behave that way at all. If we were to oppose Nakamura, the most likely result is that we would both be imprisoned. What would happen then to our daughter? In addition, all the support for the RV-41 work would be withdrawn, leaving those poor people in even worse shape than they are. The hospital would be more shorthanded. . . . Many people would suffer because of our idealism. As a doctor, I find these possible consequences unacceptable."

Ellie drove off the bicycle path into a small park about five hundred meters from the first buildings of Central City. "Why are we stopping here?" Robert asked. "They're expecting us at the hospital."

"I want to take five minutes to see the trees, smell the flowers, and hug Nicole."

After Ellie dismounted, Robert helped her disengage the baby carrier from her back. Ellie then sat on the grass with Nicole in her lap. Neither of the adults said anything while they watched Nicole study the three blades of grass that she had grabbed with her chubby hands.

At length Ellie spread out a blanket and laid her daughter gently upon it. She approached her husband and put her arms around his neck. "I love you, Robert, very, very much," she said. "But I must say that sometimes I do not agree with you at all."

9

The light from the solitary window in the cell made a pattern on the dirt wall opposite Nicole's bed. The bars on the window created a reflected square with a tic-tac-toe design, a near perfect three-by-three matrix. The light in her cell signaled to Nicole that it was time to rise. She crossed the room from the wooden bunk on which she had been sleeping and washed her face in the basin. She then took a deep breath and tried to summon her strength for another day.

Nicole was fairly certain that her latest prison, where she had been for about five months, was somewhere in the New Eden farming strip between Hakone and San Miguel. She had been blindfolded when they had moved her the last time. Nicole had quickly concluded, however, that she was in a rural location. Occasionally a strong smell of animals drifted into her cell through the forty-centimeter-square window just below the ceiling. In addition, Nicole could see no reflected light of any kind outside the window when it was night in New Eden.

These last months have been the worst, Nicole thought as she stood on tiptoe to push a few grams of flavored rice through the windows. *No conversation, no reading, no exercise. Two meals a day of rice and water.* The little red squirrel who visited her each morning appeared outside. Nicole could hear him. She backed across the cell so she could see him eating the rice.

"You are my only company, my handsome friend," Nicole said out loud. The squirrel stopped eating and listened, always alert for any possible danger. "And you have never understood a single word that I have said."

The squirrel didn't stay long. When he had finished eating his ration of rice, he departed, leaving Nicole alone. For several minutes she stared out the window where the squirrel had been, wondering what was happening with her family.

Until six months earlier, when her trial for sedition had been "indefinitely postponed" at the last minute, Nicole had been allowed one visitor each week for one hour. Even though the conversation had been chaperoned by a guard, and any discussion of politics or current events had been strictly prohibited, she had eagerly awaited those weekly sessions with Ellie or Patrick. Usually it had been Ellie who had come. From some very carefully worded statements by both her children, Nicole had deduced that Patrick was involved in some kind of government work and was only available at limited times.

Nicole had been first angry, and then depressed, when she had learned that Benjy had been institutionalized and would not be permitted to see her. Ellie had tried to assure her mother that Benjy was all right, considering the circumstances. There had been very little discussion of Katie. Neither Patrick nor Ellie had known how to explain to Nicole that their older sister had really shown no interest in visiting her mother.

Ellie's pregnancy was always a safe topic of conversation during those earlier visits. Nicole was thrilled to touch her daughter's stomach, or to talk about the special feelings of a mother-to-be. If Ellie would mention how active the baby was, Nicole would share and compare her own experiences ("When I was pregnant with Patrick," Nicole said one time, "I was never tired. You, on the other hand, were a mother's nightmare—always thrashing around in the middle of the night when I wanted to sleep"); if Ellie was not feeling well, Nicole would prescribe foods or physical activities that had helped her deal with the same conditions.

Ellie's last visit had been two months before the due date for the baby. Nicole had been moved to her new cell the following week, and had not talked to a human being since then. The mute biots who attended Nicole never gave any indication that they even heard her questions. Once, in a pique of frustration, she had shouted at the Tiasso giving her the weekly bath. "Don't you understand?" she had said. "My daughter was supposed to have a baby, my grandchild, sometime last week. I need to know if they are all right."

In her previous cells Nicole had always been allowed to read. New bookdiscs had been brought to her from the library whenever she had asked, so the days between visits had passed fairly quickly. She had reread almost all her father's historical novels, as well as some poetry, history, and a few of her more interesting medical books. Nicole had been especially fascinated by the parallels between her life and the lives of her two childhood heroines, Joan of Arc and Eleanor of Aquitaine. Nicole buttressed her own strength by noting that neither of the two other women allowed her basic attitudes to change despite long and difficult periods in prison.

Right after she was moved, when the Garcia who attended her in the new cell did not return her electronic reader with her personal effects, Nicole thought that a simple mistake had been made. However, after she asked for the reader several times and it still never appeared, she realized that she was now being denied the privilege of reading.

The time passed very slowly for Nicole in her new cell. For several hours each day she deliberately paced about, trying to keep her body and mind active. She attempted to organize these pacing sessions, steering them away from thoughts about her family, which inevitably caused her feelings of loneliness and depression to intensify, and toward more general philosophic concepts or ideas. Often at the conclusion of these sessions she would focus on some past event in her life and try to derive some new or meaningful insight from it.

During one such session Nicole remembered sharply a sequence of events that had taken place when she was fifteen years old. By that time she and her father were already comfortably ensconced at Beauvois and Nicole was performing brilliantly at school. She decided to enter the national competition to select three girls to play Joan of Arc in the set of pageants that would commemorate the 750th anniversary of the maid's martyrdom at Rouen. Nicole threw herself into the contest with a passion and single-mindedness that both thrilled and worried her father. After Nicole won the regional contest at Tours, Pierre even stopped working on his novels for six weeks to help his beloved daughter prepare for the national finals at Rouen.

Nicole placed first in both the athletic and intellectual components of the contest. She even scored very high in the acting evaluations. She and her father had been certain that she was going to be selected. But when the winners were announced, Nicole had been a second runner-up.

For years, Nicole thought as she walked around her cell in New Eden, *I thought that I had failed. What my father said about France not being ready for a copper-skinned Joan of Arc did not matter. In my mind I was a failure. I was devastated. My self-esteem did not really recover until the Olympics, and then it was only a few days before Henry knocked me down again.*

The price was terrible, Nicole continued. *I was completely self-absorbed for years because of my lack of self-esteem. It was much later before I was finally happy with myself. And only then was I able to give to others.* She paused for a moment in her thoughts. *Why is it that so many of us go through the same experience? Why is youth so selfish, and why must we first find ourselves to realize how much more there is to life?*

When the Garcia who always brought her meals included some fresh bread and a few raw carrots with her dinner, Nicole suspected that there was about to be a change in her regimen. Two days later the Tiasso came into her cell with a portable bathtub, a hairbrush, some makeup, a mirror, and even a small bottle of perfume. Nicole took a long, luxurious bath and freshened herself for the first time in months. As the biot picked up the wooden tub and prepared to leave, it handed her a note. "You will have a visitor tomorrow morning," the note said.

Nicole could not sleep. In the morning she chattered like a little girl to her friend the squirrel, discussing both her hopes and her anxieties about the coming rendezvous. She fussed with her face and hair several times before declaring both of them to be hopeless. The time went by very slowly.

At long last, just before lunch, she heard human footsteps coming down the corridor toward her cell. Nicole rushed forward expectantly. "Katie," she yelled when she saw her daughter walking around the final corridor.

"Hello, Mother," Katie said, unlocking the door and entering the cell. The two women hugged for many seconds. Nicole did not try to restrain the tears that were pouring from her eyes.

They sat on Nicole's bed, the only furniture in the cell, and talked amiably for several minutes about the family. Katie informed Nicole that she had a new granddaughter ("Nicole des Jardins Turner," she said. "You should be very proud"), and then pulled out about twenty photographs. The pictures included recent snapshots of the baby with her parents, Ellie and Benjy together in a park somewhere, Patrick in a uniform, and even a couple of Katie in an evening dress. Nicole studied them, one by one, her eyes brimming repeatedly. "Oh, Katie," she exclaimed several times.

When she was finished, Nicole thanked her daughter profusely for having brought the photographs. "You can have them, Mother," Katie said, standing up and walking over to the window. She opened her purse and pulled out cigarettes and a lighter.

"Darling," Nicole said hesitantly, "would you please not smoke in here? The ventilation is terrible. I would smell it for weeks."

Katie stared at her mother for a few seconds and then placed her cigarettes and lighter back in her purse. At that moment a pair of Garcias arrived outside the cell with a table and two chairs.

"What's this?" Nicole asked.

Katie smiled. "We're going to have lunch together," she said. "I've had something special prepared for the occasion—chicken in a mushroom and wine sauce."

The food, which smelled divine, was soon carried into the cell by a third Garcia and placed on the covered table beside the fine china and silver. There was even a bottle of wine and two crystal glasses.

It was difficult for Nicole to remember her manners. The chicken was so delicious, the mushrooms so tender, that she ate her meal without talking. Every so often, when she took a swallow of the wine, Nicole would murmur "Umm" or "This is fantastic," but she basically said nothing until her plate was completely clean.

Katie, who had become a very light eater, nibbled at her food and watched her mother. When Nicole was finished, Katie called in a Garcia to take away the dishes and bring some coffee. Nicole had not had a good cup of coffee for almost two years.

"So, Katie," Nicole said with a warm smile after thanking her for the meal, "how about you? What are you doing with yourself?"

Katie laughed coarsely. "Same old shit," she said. "I'm now director of entertainment for the whole Vegas resort. . . . I book all the acts into the clubs. . . . Business is great even though—" Katie caught herself, remembering that her mother knew nothing of the war in the second habitat.

"Have you found a man who can appreciate all your attributes?" Nicole asked tactfully.

"Not one who will stay around." Katie was self-conscious about her answer and suddenly became agitated. "Look, Mother," she said, leaning across the table. "I didn't come here to discuss my love life. . . . I have a proposition for you—or rather, the family has a proposition for you that we all support."

Nicole looked at her daughter with a puzzled frown. She noticed for the first time that Katie had aged considerably in the two years since she had last seen her. "I don't understand," Nicole said. "What kind of a proposition?"

"Well, as you may know, the government has been preparing its case against you for some time. They are now ready to go to trial. The charge of course is sedition, which carries a mandatory death penalty. The prosecutor has told us that the evidence against you is overwhelming, and that you are certain to be convicted. However, because of your past services to the colony, if you will plead guilty to the lesser charge of involuntary sedition, he will drop—"

"But I am not guilty of anything," Nicole said firmly.

"I know that, Mother," Katie replied with a trace of impatience. "But we—Ellie, Patrick, and I—all agree that there is a high likelihood that you will be convicted. The prosecutor has promised us that if you will simply plead guilty to the reduced charge, you will be moved immediately to nicer surroundings and allowed to visit with your family, including your new granddaughter. . . . He even hinted that he might intercede with the authorities to allow Benjy to live with Robert and Ellie. . . ."

Nicole was in turmoil. "And all of you think that I should accept this plea bargain and acknowledge my guilt, even though I have steadfastly proclaimed my innocence since the moment I was arrested?"

Katie nodded. "We don't want you to die," she said. "Especially for no reason."

"For no *reason*." Nicole's eyes suddenly flashed. "You think I would be dying for no *reason*!" She pushed away from the table, stood up, and paced around the cell. "I would be dying for *justice*," Nicole said, more to herself than to Katie, "in my mind at least, even if there is not a single soul anywhere else in the universe who can understand it."

"But Mother," Katie now interjected, "what purpose would it serve? Your children and granddaughter would be deprived forever of your company, Benjy would remain in that foul institution—"

"So now here's the deal," Nicole interrupted, her voice rising, "a more insidious version of Faust's pact with the devil. . . . Abandon your principles, Nicole, and acknowledge your guilt, even though you have not transgressed at all. And do not sell your soul for mere personal Earthly reward. No, that would be too easy to reject. . . . You are asked to take the deal because your family will benefit. Can there be any possible appeal to a mother that is more likely to sway her?"

Nicole's eyes were on fire. Katie reached into her purse, pulled out a cigarette, and lit it with a trembling hand.

"And who is it that comes to me with such a proposition?" Nicole continued. She was now shouting. "Who brings me delicious food and wine and pictures of my family to soften me up for the self-inflicted knife that will surely kill me with much more pain than any electric chair? Why, it is my own daughter, the beloved issue of my womb."

Nicole suddenly moved forward and grabbed Katie. "Do not play Judas for them, Katie," Nicole said, shaking her frightened daughter. "You are so much better than that. In time, if they convict and execute me on these specious charges, you will appreciate what I am doing."

Katie freed herself from her mother's grasp and staggered backward. She took a drag from her cigarette. "This is bullshit, Mother," she said a moment later. "Total bullshit. You're just being your usual self-righteous . . . Look, I came here to help you, to offer you a chance to go on living. Why can't you listen to someone else just one time in your goddamn life?"

Nicole stared at Katie for several seconds. Her voice was softer when she spoke again. "I have been listening to you, Katie, and I do not like what I have heard. I have also been watching you. . . . I don't think for a moment that you came here today to help *me*. That would be completely inconsistent with what I have seen of your character these last few years. There must be something in all this for you.

"Nor do I believe that you in any way represent Ellie and Patrick. If that were the case, they would have come with you. I must confess that for a while earlier I was confused and feeling that perhaps I was causing too much pain for all my children. But in these last few minutes I have seen what is going on here very clearly. . . . Katie, my dear Katie—"

"Don't you touch me again," Katie shouted as Nicole approached her. Katie's eyes were full of tears. "And spare me your self-righteous pity."

The cell was momentarily quiet. Katie finished her cigarette and tried to compose herself. "Look," she said at length, "I don't give a shit what you feel about me—that's not important—but why, Mother, why can't you think about Patrick and Ellie and even little

Nicole? Is being a saint so important to you that they should suffer because of it?"

"In time," Nicole replied, "they will understand."

"In time," Katie said angrily, "you'll be dead. In a very short time. . . . Do you realize that the moment I walk out of here and tell Nakamura that there's no deal, the date for your trial will be set? And that you have no chance at all, absolutely no fucking chance?"

"You cannot scare me, Katie."

"I cannot scare you, I cannot touch you, I cannot even appeal to your judgment. Like all good saints, you listen to your own voices."

Katie took a deep breath. "Then I guess this is it. . . . Good-bye, Mother." Despite herself, fresh tears appeared in Katie's eyes.

Nicole wept openly. "Good-bye, Katie," she said. "I love you."

10

"The defense may now make its closing statement."

Nicole rose from her chair and walked around the table. She was surprised that she was so tired. The two years in prison had definitely diminished her legendary stamina.

She slowly approached the jury of four men and two women. The woman in the front row, Karen Stolz, had been originally from Switzerland. Nicole had known the woman fairly well when Mrs. Stolz and her husband had owned and operated the bakery around the corner from the Wakefield home in Beauvois.

"Hello again, Karen," Nicole said quietly, stopping directly in front of the jurors. They were sitting in two rows of three seats each. "How are John and Marie? They must be teenagers by now."

Mrs. Stolz squirmed in her seat. "They're fine, Nicole," she replied very softly.

Nicole smiled. "And do you still make those wonderful cinnamon rolls every Sunday morning?"

The crack of the gavel resounded through the courtroom. "Mrs. Wakefield," Judge Nakamura said, "this is hardly the time for small talk. Your closing statement is limited to five minutes and the clock has already started."

Nicole ignored the judge. She leaned across the barrier between her and the jury, her eyes focusing on a magnificent necklace around Karen Stolz's neck. "The jewels are beautiful," she said in a whisper. "But they would have paid much, much more."

Again the gavel cracked. Two guards quickly approached Nicole, but she had already backed away from Mrs. Stolz. "Ladies and gentlemen of the jury," Nicole said, "all this week you have listened as the prosecution has repeatedly insisted that I have incited resistance to the legitimate government of New Eden. For my putative actions I have been charged with sedition. You must now decide, on the basis of the evidence presented at this trial, if I am guilty. Please remember as you deliberate that sedition is a capital offense—a guilty verdict carries with it a mandatory death penalty.

"In my closing statement, I would like to examine carefully the structure of the prosecution's case. The testimony on the first day, all of which was totally irrelevant to the charges against me and, I believe, was permitted by Judge Nakamura in clear violation of the colony codicils covering testimony in capital offense trials—"

"Mrs. Wakefield," Judge Nakamura angrily interrupted, "as I have told you before this week, I cannot tolerate such disrespectful comments in my courtroom. One more similar remark and I will not only cite you for contempt, I will also terminate your closing statement altogether."

"That entire day, the prosecution attempted to show that my sexual morality was questionable, and that therefore I was somehow a likely candidate to engage in political conspiracy," Nicole continued, without so much as glancing at the judge. "Ladies and gentlemen, I would be happy to discuss privately with you the unusual circumstances associated with the conception of each of my six children. However, my sex life—past, present, or even future—has no bearing whatsoever on this trial. Except for its possible value as entertainment, that first day of testimony was absolutely meaningless."

There were a few titters in the packed gallery, but the guards quickly quieted the crowd. "The prosecution's next set of witnesses," Nicole continued, "spent many hours implicating my husband for seditious activities. I freely admit that I am married to Richard Wakefield. But his guilt—or lack of it, for that matter—is not of any importance at this trial either. Only evidence that purports to show *me* guilty of sedition is germane to your verdict here.

"The prosecution has suggested that my seditious acts originated with my involvement in the video that eventually resulted in the establishment of this colony. I acknowledge that I did help prepare the video that was transmitted from Rama to the Earth, but I categorically deny that I either conspired from the beginning with the aliens or in any way schemed with the extraterrestrials who built this spaceship against my fellow humans.

"I participated in the making of that video, as I indicated yesterday when I allowed the prosecutor to cross-examine me, because I felt I had no choice. My family and I were at the mercy of an intelligence and power far beyond anything any of us had ever imagined. There was a significant concern that failure to accede to their request for help with the video would have resulted in reprisals against us."

Nicole returned to the defense table briefly and drank some water. She then turned around to face the jury again. "That leaves only two possible sources for any real evidence to convict me of sedition—my daughter Katie's testimony and that strange audio recording, a disjointed collection of comments that I made to other members of my family after I was imprisoned, that you heard yesterday morning.

"You are all well aware how easily recordings like that can be twisted and manipulated. The two key audio technicians both admitted yesterday on the witness stand that they had listened to hundreds of hours of conversation between my children and me before coming up with that thirty minutes of 'damaging evidence,' no more than *eighteen seconds* of which were taken from any single conversation. To say that my comments on that recording were presented out of context would be an understatement.

"With respect to the testimony of my daughter Katie Wakefield, I can only say, with great sorrow, that she lied repeatedly in her original remarks. I have not *ever* had any knowledge of my husband Richard's supposedly illegal activities and I have certainly never supported him in them.

"You recall that under cross-examination by me, Katie became confused about the facts and ultimately repudiated her earlier testimony before collapsing on the witness stand. The judge has advised you that my daughter has recently been in fragile mental health, and that you should ignore the comments she made under emotional duress during my questioning. I beseech you to remember every word that Katie said, not only when the prosecutor was asking her questions, but also during the time that I was trying to obtain the specific dates and places for the seditious actions that she had ascribed to me."

Nicole approached the jurors one final time, carefully making eye contact with each of them. "Ultimately, you must judge where the truth lies in this case. I face you now with a heavy heart, disbelieving even as I stand here the events that have led to my being accused of these serious crimes. I have served both the colony and the human species well. I am not guilty of any of the charges against me. Whatever power or intelligence exists in this amazing universe will recognize that fact, regardless of the outcome of this trial.''

The outside light was fading quickly. A contemplative Nicole leaned against the wall in her cell, wondering if this would be the last night of her life. She shuddered involuntarily. Since the verdict had been announced, Nicole had gone to sleep each night expecting to die the next day.

The Garcia brought her dinner soon after it was dark. The food had been much better the last few days. As she slowly ate her grilled fish Nicole reflected on the five years since she and her family had met that first scouting party from the Pinta. *What went wrong here?* Nicole asked herself. *What were our fundamental mistakes?*

She could hear Richard's voice in her head. Always cynical and distrustful of human behavior, he had suggested at the end of the first year that New Eden was too good for humanity. "We'll eventually ruin it as we have the Earth," he had said. "Our genetic baggage—the whole bit, you know, territoriality and aggression and reptilian behavior—is too strong for education and enlightenment to overcome. Look at O'Toole's heroes, both of them, Jesus and that young Italian, St. Michael of Siena. They were destroyed because they suggested that humans should try to be more than clever chimpanzees.''

But here, in New Eden, Nicole thought, *there was so much opportunity for a better world. The basics of life were provided. We were surrounded by unambiguous evidence that there was intelligence in the universe far beyond ours. That should have produced an environment in which . . .*

She finished her fish and pulled the small chocolate pudding over in front of her. Nicole smiled to herself, remembering how much Richard had loved chocolate. *I have missed him very much,* she thought. *Especially his conversation and his insight.*

Nicole was startled to hear footsteps coming toward her cell. A deep chill of fear coursed through her body. Her visitors were two young men, each of them carrying lanterns. They were wearing the uniforms of Nakamura's special police.

The men came into the cell in a very businesslike manner. They did not introduce themselves. The older one, probably in his mid-thirties, quickly pulled out a document and began to read.

"Nicole des Jardins Wakefield," he said, "you have been convicted of the crime of sedition and will be executed at 0800 tomorrow morning. Your breakfast will be served at 0630, ten minutes after first light, and we will come to take you to the execution chamber at 0730. You will be strapped into the electric chair at 0758 and current will be applied exactly two minutes later. . . . Do you have any questions?"

Nicole's heart was beating so rapidly she could hardly breathe. She struggled to calm herself. "Do you have any questions?" the policeman repeated.

"What is your name, young man?" Nicole asked, her voice breaking.

"Franz," the man answered after a puzzled hesitation.

"Franz what?" Nicole said.

"Franz Bauer," he replied.

"Well, Franz Bauer," Nicole said, trying to force a smile. "Can you please tell me how long it will take me to die? After you apply the current, of course."

"I don't really know," he said, somewhat flustered. "You'll lose consciousness almost instantly, in just a couple of seconds. But I don't know how long—"

"Thank you," Nicole said, starting to feel faint. "Could you go now, please? I would like to be alone." The two men opened the door to the cell. "Oh, by the way," Nicole added, "could you possibly leave the lantern? And maybe a pen and paper, or even an electronic notebook?"

Franz Bauer shook his head. "I'm sorry," he said. "We cannot."

Nicole waved him away and crossed to the far side of her cell. *Two letters*, she said to herself, breathing slowly to gather strength. *I only wanted to write two letters. One to Katie and one to Richard. I've made my final peace with everyone else.*

After the policemen had departed Nicole recalled the long hours that she had spent in the pit in Rama II many years before, when she had expected to die from starvation. She had passed what she had then thought were her last days reliving the happy moments of her life. *That's not necessary now*, she thought. *There is no event from my past that has not been thoroughly scrutinized already. That's the benefit of two years in prison.*

Nicole was surprised to discover that she was angry about not being able to write the final two letters. *I'll bring the subject up again in the morning. They'll let me write the letters if I make enough noise.* Despite herself, Nicole smiled. "Do not go gently. . ." she quoted out loud.

Suddenly she felt her pulse rate increase again. In her mind's eye Nicole saw an electric chair in a dark room. She was sitting in it; a strange helmet was wrapped around her head. The helmet began to glow and Nicole saw herself slump forward.

Dear God, she thought, *wherever and whatever you are. Please give me some courage now. I am very frightened.*

Nicole sat down on her bed in the darkness of her room. In a few minutes she felt better, almost calm. She found herself wondering what the instant of death would be like. *Is it just like going to sleep, and then there's nothing? Or does something special happen at that very last moment, something that no living person can ever know?*

There was a voice calling her from far away. Nicole stirred but did not wake up completely. "Mrs. Wakefield," the voice called again.

Nicole sat up quickly in her bed, thinking it was morning. She felt a surge of fear as her mind told her that she had only two more hours to live. "Mrs. Wakefield," the voice said, "over here, outside your cell. . . . It's Amadou Diaba."

Nicole rubbed her eyes and strained to see the figure in the dark by the door. "Who?" she said, slowly walking across the room.

"Amadou Diaba. Two years ago you helped Dr. Turner do my heart transplant."

"What are you doing here, Amadou? And how did you get inside?"

"I came to bring you something. I bribed everybody necessary. I had to see you."

Even though the man was only five meters away from her, Nicole could see only his vague outline in the darkness. Her tired eyes were playing tricks on her as well. Once, when she tried especially hard to focus, she momentarily thought her visitor was her great-grandfather Omeh. A sharp chill raced through her body.

"All right, Amadou," Nicole said at length. "What is it that you have brought me?"

"I must explain it first," he said. "And even then it may not make any sense. . . . I don't understand it fully myself. I just know that I had to bring it to you tonight."

He paused a moment. When Nicole did not say anything, Amadou told his story very rapidly. "The day after I was selected for Lowell Colony, while I was still in Lagos, I received this strange message from my Senoufo grandmother, telling me that it was very urgent that I come to see her. I went at my first opportunity, which was two weeks later, after I had received still another message from my grandmother insisting that my visit was a matter of life and death.

"When I arrived at her village in the Ivory Coast, it was the middle of the night. My grandmother awakened and dressed immediately. Accompanied by our village medicine man, we took a long trek across the savanna that very night. I was exhausted by the time we reached our destination, a little village named Nidougou."

"Nidougou?" Nicole interrupted.

"That's right," Amadou replied. "Anyway, there was a strange, wizened man there who must have been some kind of super shaman. My grandmother and our medicine man stayed in Nidougou while this man and I made the strenuous climb up a nearby barren mountain to the side of a small lake. We arrived just before sunrise. 'Look,' the old man said when the first rays of the sun hit the lake. 'Look into the Lake of Wisdom. What do you see?'

"I told him I saw thirty or forty melonlike objects resting on the bottom of one side of the lake. 'Good,' he said with a smile. 'You are indeed the one.'

" 'I am the one what?' " I asked.

"He never answered. We walked around the lake, nearer to where the melons had been submerged—we couldn't see them any longer as the sun rose higher in the sky—and the super shaman pulled out a small vial. He dipped it into the water, put a cap on it, and handed it to me. He also gave me a small stone, which looked and was shaped like the melonlike objects on the bottom of the lake.

" 'These are the most important gifts you will ever receive,' he said.

" 'Why?' " I said.

"A few seconds later his eyes became completely white and he fell into a trance, chanting in rhythmic Senoufo. He danced for several minutes and then suddenly jumped into the cold lake for a swim.

" 'Wait a minute,' I shouted. 'What shall I do with your gifts?'

" 'Take them with you everywhere,' he said. 'You will know the time to use them.' "

Nicole thought that the beating of her heart was so loud that even Amadou could hear it. She extended her arm through the bars of her cell and touched his shoulder. "And last night," she said, "a voice in a dream, or maybe it wasn't a dream after all, told you to bring the vial and the stone to me tonight."

"Exactly," Amadou said. He paused. "How did you know?"

Nicole did not answer. She could not speak. Her entire body was trembling. Moments later, when Nicole felt the two objects in her hand, her knees were so weak that she thought she was going to fall. She thanked Amadou twice and urged him to leave before he was discovered.

She walked slowly across the cell to her bed. *Can it be? And how can it be? All this somehow known from the beginning? Manna melons on the Earth?* Nicole's system was overloaded. *I have lost control,* she thought, *and I have not even drunk from the vial yet.*

Just holding the vial and the stone reminded Nicole vividly of the incredible vision she had experienced at the bottom of the pit in Rama II. Nicole opened the vial. She took two deep breaths and swallowed its contents hurriedly.

At first she thought nothing was happening. The blackness all around her did not seem to change. Then suddenly a great orange ball formed in the middle of the cell. It exploded, spreading color all across the darkness. A red ball followed, then a purple one. While Nicole was recoiling from the brilliance of the purple explosion, she heard a loud laugh outside her window. She glanced in that direction. The cell disappeared. Nicole was outside in a field.

It was dark, but she could still see outlines of objects. Off in the distance Nicole heard the laugh again. *Amadou,* she called in her mind. Nicole raced across the field at blinding speed. She was catching the man. As she drew closer, his face changed. It was not Amadou at all. It was Omeh.

He laughed again and Nicole stopped. *Ronata,* he called. His face was growing. Larger, ever larger, it was as big as a car, then as big as a house. His laughter was deafening. Omeh's face was a huge balloon, rising high, ever higher into the dark night. He laughed once more and his balloon face exploded, showering Nicole with water.

She was drenched. She was submerged, swimming underneath the water. When Nicole surfaced she was in the oasis pond in the Ivory Coast, where as a seven-year-old girl she had confronted the lioness during the Poro. The same lioness was prowling the perimeter of the pond. Nicole was a little girl again. She was very frightened.

I want my mother, Nicole thought. *Lay thee down / Now and rest / May thy slumber be blessed,* she sang. Nicole started to walk out of the water. The lioness did not bother her. Nicole glanced at the animal once more and the face of the lioness had changed into the face of her mother. Nicole ran over to embrace her mother. Instead, Nicole became the lioness herself, prowling on the shore of the oasis pond in the middle of the African savanna.

There were now six swimmers altogether in the pond, all children. As lioness Nicole continued to sing the Brahms Lullaby, one by one the children emerged from the water. Genevieve was first, then Simone, Katie, Benjy, Patrick, and Ellie. Each of them walked past her, heading into the savanna. Nicole raced after them.

She was running on an infield in a packed stadium. Nicole was a human again, young and athletic. Her final jump was announced. As she headed for the top of the triple jump runway, a Japanese judge approached her. It was Toshio Nakamura. *You are going to foul,* he said with a scowl.

Nicole thought she was flying as she sped down the approach. She hit the board perfectly, soared into the air on her hop, executed a balanced skip, and powered far out into the pit with her jump. She knew it had been a good one. Nicole bounded over to where she had left her warm-ups. Her father and Henry both came over to give her a hug. *Well done,* they said in unison. *Very well done.*

Joan of Arc brought the gold medal to the victory stand and hung it around Nicole's neck. Eleanor of Aquitaine handed her a dozen roses. Kenji Watanabe and Judge Mishkin stood beside her and offered their congratulations. The announcer said that her jump was a new world record. The crowd was giving her a standing ovation. Nicole looked out at the sea of faces and noticed that there weren't just humans in the crowd. The Eagle was there, in a special box, sitting beside an entire section of octospiders. Everyone was saluting her, even the avians and the spherical creatures with the gossamer tentacles and the dozen caped eels pressed against the window of a gigantic enclosed bowl. Nicole waved to them all.

Her arms changed to wings and she began to fly. Nicole was a hawk soaring high above the farming strip in New Eden. She looked down on the building where she had been imprisoned. Nicole turned west and found Max Puckett's farm. Even though it was the middle of the night, Max was outside, working on what appeared to be an addition to one of his barns.

Nicole continued to fly west, heading toward the bright lights of Vegas. She descended when she reached the complex, flying behind the big nightclubs, one by one. Katie was sitting outside on some back steps, all by herself. She had her face buried in her hands and her body was shaking. Nicole tried to comfort her but the only sound was a hawk's cry in the night. Katie looked up at the sky, puzzled.

Nicole flew over to Positano, near the habitat exit, and waited for the outside door to open. Startling the guard, hawk Nicole departed from New Eden. She reached Avalon in less than a minute. Robert, Ellie, little Nicole, and even an orderly were all in the lounge with Benjy in the ward. Nicole had no idea why they were all awake in the middle of the night. She cried to them. Benjy came over to the window and gazed out into the darkness.

Nicole heard a voice calling her. It was faint, far to the south. She flew rapidly to the second habitat, entering through the gaping hole that the humans had cut into the exterior wall. After speeding through the annulus and finding a portal, she soared over the green region in the interior. She could no longer hear the voice. But Nicole could see her son Patrick camped with other soldiers near the base of the brown cylinder.

An avian with four cobalt rings met her in midair. *He's not here anymore*, it said. *Try New York.* Nicole exited quickly from the second habitat and returned to the Central Plain. She heard the voice again. Up, up she went. Hawk Nicole could barely breathe.

She flew south over the perimeter wall enclosing the Northern Hemicylinder. The Cylindrical Sea was below her. The voice was now more distinct. It was Richard. Her hawk heart was pounding furiously.

He was standing on the shore, in front of the skyscrapers, waving at her. *Come to me, Nicole*, his voice said. She could see his eyes even in the dark. Nicole flew down and landed on Richard's shoulder.

There was blackness around her. Nicole was back in her cell. Was that a bird she heard flying just outside her window? Her heart was still fluttering.

She walked across the small room. *Thank you, Amadou*, she said. *Or Omeh*. She smiled. *Or God*.

Nicole stretched out on her bed. A few seconds later she was asleep.